THE DUKE'S RELUCTANT BRIDE

LAUREN ROYAL
DEVON ROYAL

June 2021 Edition
SWEET CHASE BRIDES

THE DUKE'S RELUCTANT BRIDE by Lauren Royal & Devon Royal

Published by Novelty Books, a division of Novelty Publishers, LLC, 205 Avenida Del Mar #275, San Clemente, CA 92674

June 2021 Edition

Cover by Kimberly Killion

Learn more about the authors and their books at www.LaurenandDevonRoyal.com.

ISBN: 978-1-63469-178-9

For Emma, Ashley, Elizabeth,
Kailee, Lauren, and Meggie,
the best bridesmaids a girl could ask for!

ONE

Sussex, England
June 1668

KENDRA CHASE adored her brothers, except when she wanted to kill them.

"Jason is right," Ford told her as they rattled down the road in a shabby public coach. "You're eighteen years old, and it's high time you take a husband."

"You're eighteen as well," she retorted, glaring at her twin, "but I don't see *you* being dangled before every eligible lady in the county."

Ford rolled his eyes. "It's different for men, Kendra, and you know it."

She did know it. But she didn't have to like it.

"We only wish to see you live a life of comfort," Jason put in. Crammed onto the bench seat between Kendra and his wife, Caithren, he tried unsuccessfully to stretch his long legs. "Or would you prefer to travel this way all the time?"

As if to drive home his point, the springless vehicle lurched in and out of a rut, rattling Kendra's teeth. She gritted them. Though Jason was careful with money, he was, after all, the

Marquess of Cainewood, and they did own a much more luxurious carriage. But one of its wheels had broken on their way out of London, and they'd been forced to take public transport—or else risk missing an urgent appointment back home at Cainewood Castle.

An appointment to introduce Kendra to the latest "suitable" man her brothers planned to foist upon her.

"Better the public coach than the Duke of Lechmere's," she said stubbornly. "I vow and swear, I'll not become a duchess and be 'your graced' for the rest of my life."

"And what, pray tell, would be wrong with that?" Jason shook his head. "I've never understood what you have against dukes."

Kendra turned her glare on her eldest brother. "You may not understand my feelings, but plainly you were aware of them—and yet you approached Lechmere anyhow." She noticed the other passenger, a stranger dressed in simple clothing, was observing their argument with frank interest. She glared at him, too.

A noise of agreement rose from Caithren's corner of the coach. "I told you, Jase, that his grace wouldn't suit Kendra," she said in her Scottish brogue.

"And *I* told *you*, Cait, that she's got no good reason to refuse him."

Kendra huffed. "But he's a—"

"Yes, he's a duke," Jason snapped, "that most abominable of creatures." He began gathering the cards from the hand of piquet they'd just played. "You've dithered long enough. This is your last chance to make your own choice. If you won't marry Lechmere, you'll have to select one of the other gentlemen who have offered for you. Or *I* will do the selecting."

"The other gentlemen?" Scoffing, Kendra tossed her head of dark red curls. "Old but well-off, or widowed and settled with children, or young but just plain *boring*. Stable, wealthy gentlemen in the good graces of King Charles, every last one of them."

Jason's green eyes flashed. "Yes, perfectly acceptable, every last one of them."

"As it should be," Ford put in, earning a kick from his twin sister. She would have kicked Jason, too, if she thought for an instant he meant to enforce his ultimatum. The wretched day had put him in a bad mood, that was all. He'd never marry her to someone she disliked.

Would he?

In any case, Caithren wouldn't let him.

Kendra leaned forward to give her sister-in-law an imploring look. "They'll never understand, will they?"

Cait's eyes filled with sympathy and a bit of shared exasperation. She laid a hand on her husband's arm. "I've told you before, Kendra wishes to marry for love, not—"

"Stand and deliver!" a deep voice interrupted from outside.

With an unnerving suddenness, the coach ground to a halt. Stopped in mid-sentence, Cait's mouth gaped, and Kendra's stomach clenched in fear.

Ford leaned forward and pushed open the door. A man on horseback—a highwayman!—poked his head inside.

The most gorgeous head Kendra had ever seen.

"*You?*" Jason and Ford said together.

They knew this villain?

Since Kendra hadn't heard that either of her brothers had been hurt—or even robbed, come to think of it—most of her fear dissipated, and her heart lifted with excitement instead.

Nothing like this had ever happened to her!

Looking slightly disconcerted, the highwayman dismounted. "Aye, it's me," he said slowly. Beneath the mask that concealed the upper half of his face, a grin emerged, a slash of perfect white.

Well, not precisely perfect. One of his front teeth had a small chip, but she found that tiny imperfection charming. And he was dashing, not to mention dangerous. Why, if any of her hopeful suitors had been like this highwayman, she'd have married him in a trice!

She wanted to say something to make him notice her. But for the first time in her memory, her mouth refused to work.

His gaze swept the coach's dim interior as though she weren't even there. "You," he said succinctly, motioning to the ashen-faced stranger seated beside Ford. "Get out."

"There be five of us in here, three of them men, likely with pistols," the man said stiffly. From his haircut, plain clothes, and the short, boxy jacket beneath his cloak, Kendra knew he was a Puritan. "Perhaps thee had better think again."

"Oh, it's violence you threaten, aye?" The highwayman's voice was deep and a little husky, with, curiously, the barest hint of an accent. "Perhaps *you* had better think again. My friends," he drawled, gesturing toward the hill behind him, "would make certain you cease to exist within the minute. Get out. Now."

Kendra looked out the door and up. Sure enough, there were a dozen or so men at the top of the hill, their guns trained on the coach.

The Puritan must have recognized the threat, for he reluctantly climbed down. Kendra shifted within the coach, the better to see out.

The victim was a good foot shorter than the robber, who looked impossibly tall and elegant in a jet-black velvet surcoat. Close-faced and resigned, the Puritan emptied his pockets and handed over his money, then turned to reenter the coach.

The highwayman reached to grab the victim's sleeve. "Not so fast."

Visibly shaken, the smaller, older man stilled but said nothing.

The highwayman hesitated. "Surely a...man of business, such as yourself, will be carrying more gold on his person than this. Where is it? Sewn into your cloak? Hidden in your luggage?"

Though Kendra could see the rise and fall of his agitated breathing, the Puritan turned back boldly. "Surely *thee* has no need of gold," he spat out, tugging his sleeve from the bigger man's grasp while eyeing his groomed appearance and expensive, tailored suit. "A…*gentleman* such as thyself."

The highwayman's eyes were amber, edged in a deeper hue —bronze, Kendra decided—that now spread in toward the center as his expression hardened. "Your luggage *and* your cloak, then—seeing as you won't cooperate."

He swung his pistol in the coachman's direction. The driver scrambled down and fumbled with the ropes securing the passengers' belongings. A shove sent the Puritan's trunk to the rutted road with a decisive *thunk*.

"Your cloak." The highwayman held out his free hand, almost as though he were bored, while his victim struggled out of his plain mantle.

"What about *them*?" he sputtered, handing it over. His gaze swung toward the Chases.

The highwayman glanced inside and flashed Kendra's brothers a conspiratorial smile before answering. "They're friends. Good day."

"Good day? *Good day?*" The poor man looked as red as a squalling newborn, and Kendra almost felt sorry for him—until she reminded herself that it was his ilk who had killed her parents during the Civil War.

Her brothers indeed carried pistols—and swords and knives and heaven knew what else—and had the man not been a Roundhead, she was sure one or both of them would have jumped to his defense. But because of men like this one, Jason had been left to raise his orphaned siblings, all of them forced to spend the Commonwealth years in poverty and exile.

She turned to watch the amber man remount and make his way down the road and up the hill toward his cohorts. He'd been superb. Magnificent.

Romantic, she thought on a sigh.

Amber. His clean-shaven, suntanned complexion. His eyes, a deep gold the color of the finest liquor. The black plume on his cavalier's hat fluttered as he rode, and beneath it he wore a crimped brown periwig that rather reminded her of Ford's hair. But she was certain the highwayman's real hair wasn't brown. Though many men had shaven heads under their periwigs, he wouldn't. His own hair would be cut short, but not *off*, certainly —she shuddered at the thought—and it would be golden. Amber.

"Are thee going to let him get away with this?" the Puritan demanded, clambering up and glaring at her brothers with their rapiers at their sides.

One of Jason's black brows rose, and he spoke for them both. "I expect so."

The coach lurched and they continued on, but the atmosphere was decidedly strained, and the Roundhead got off at the next stop.

Kendra moved to sit in the now-vacant spot beside Ford. "A highwayman," she breathed as soon as the carriage resumed moving.

"Why didn't he rob us?" Caithren asked. "How is it you know him? He called you friends."

"He uses the term lightly." Jason's smile was enigmatic. "We've run into him before. But he's never robbed us."

"He didn't look like he needed to rob anybody," Kendra pointed out. "His suit was nicer than yours."

He'd looked nicer than Jason all around, she mused. Not that Jason was hideous, but he had the general look of her family, a look she was inured to, to say the least. The highwayman, on the other hand, had looked...exotic. All golden and dressed in black—black suit, black shirt, black boots, black mask—not the look of your typical scruffy outlaw, that was for sure.

Jason shrugged, absently running a hand through his wife's straight, dark-blond hair. "Almost anyone can afford one nice suit of clothes, if he makes it his priority. You cannot judge a man by his looks, Kendra."

But she had, of course. Judged him, and liked what she saw.

Jason raised Cait's hand and brushed a kiss over her knuckles, earning a smile in return. "Perhaps we should turn him in," he suggested playfully. "This is getting to be somewhat of a nuisance."

"You wouldn't dare!" Kendra burst out. "He's so…well…um, he's obviously a Royalist. He robbed only the Roundhead."

"There could be a reward for him. And Lakefield House is in sad shape," Viscount Lakefield, otherwise known as Ford, lamented half-seriously. "I cannot live with Jason forever."

"Oh, yes, you can," Kendra said heatedly.

Jason turned to her. "Is it that important to you, then? I didn't realize your Royalist loyalty ran so deep."

"Well…it does," she declared, thinking about the highwayman's broad shoulders.

"Well, then." Ford's deep-blue eyes gleamed with mischief. "I suppose we'll have to leave him be. At least it provides him with a stake for the card games."

Jason glared at their brother.

"What?" Kendra asked. "What card games?"

"All highwaymen play cards," Jason said firmly. He picked up their own deck and shuffled it expertly, then dealt out new hands.

Kendra arranged her cards slowly, her mind not on the game.

She remembered the highwayman's voice. He'd spoken cautiously, as though he were considering each word. Not like her family. The Chases, as a rule, blurted everything that came into their heads, generally at the tops of their lungs.

"What was his accent?" she asked. "Did you hear it?"

"Scots, aye?" Cait said, exaggerating her own burr. "Though I'd guess he hasn't been home for many a year. I'm surprised you even noticed."

When Jason looked up sharply, Kendra pretended to study

her fan of cards. He frowned back down at his own hand. "Why do you want to know?"

Why? She could scarcely comprehend such a stupid question. She wanted to know everything about the mysterious highwayman.

"Just curious," she said lightly, leading with a jack of hearts. "Your turn."

TWO

*T*HE DUKE OF Lechmere turned out to be everything Kendra had feared and then some. He was the epitome of what she did *not* want in a husband.

His skin appeared to have never seen the sun. She had no idea what color his hair was, since it was hidden beneath a periwig dusted with enough powder to choke a horse. She suspected he was bald underneath, anyway. His eyes were a pale, lifeless gray.

Not that looks were paramount, but his suit was peacock satin, adorned with so much dangling ribbon and lace that it seemed to quiver when he breathed. No matter the current fashion, Kendra had an aversion to men who wore prettier clothes than she did. A simple, dark velvet suit—like those her brothers favored—was far more to her taste.

Not to mention the expense of Lechmere's apparel could probably fund an orphanage for a month. Having been orphaned herself at the age of one, she would much rather have seen the money spent there.

And he was a *duke*.

"Kendra plays the harpsichord like an angel," Jason said, patting her arm from the coral-colored velvet armchair beside hers. She darted him a look. While it was true she played well, never in her life had she heard her name and the word *angel* in the same sentence. Especially not from her oldest brother, who had seen her through more than a few rebellious stages.

"An admirable accomplishment." The duke waved a ring-encrusted hand. "I should like to hear Lady Kendra perform this eve."

"And she's a brilliant conversationalist," Ford added, sending her into a coughing fit. Od's fish, her twin hardly drew breath but to tell her she talked too much! Oh, she'd give him an earful of *brilliant conversation* later.

Just as soon as she figured out how to get rid of this mullipuff.

"Though she seems rather tongue-tied now," Jason drawled. "First time in my memory."

Kendra would have thrown a cushion at him were they not in polite company.

Actually, that was an idea. Men of Lechmere's age and station were exceedingly dignified and stuffy, weren't they? Perhaps exhibiting poor manners would put him off.

She was startled from her thoughts by a sound like a trumpet, which proved to be the duke blowing his nose, loudly and long, into a frilly handkerchief.

Perhaps not.

"As I was saying," Lechmere sniffed, stuffing the handkerchief into his sleeve, "speechlessness in a lady is no sin." Kendra disliked the way his unsmiling gray gaze swept her from head to toe. "I assure you, my dear, I'm not looking for conversation. I prefer a quiet, docile woman."

Heavens above. She'd better think of something, and quick.

When Jason asked her to pour the wine, she rose from her armchair and let herself trip on the edge of the drawing room's patterned black-and-coral carpet.

"Oh, I'm so clumsy," Kendra said.

She wasn't.

"Take care," Jason warned under his breath, then smiled at Lechmere. Kendra giggled.

She never giggled.

"That's quite all right," the duke said, calmly offering his goblet. He didn't seem put off in the least.

Hang it. She'd have to do worse.

With exaggerated force, she pulled the stopper from the decanter and let it fly across the room to hit a portrait of one of her ancestors square on his painted forehead. Her great-great grandfather, the second Marquess of Cainewood.

"Kendra!" Ford and Jason cried.

She turned to see the duke's reaction: he had his face buried in his handkerchief again. He'd missed the whole thing.

Hang it! She looked back to the second marquess for help. He seemed rather less forbidding than many of her other ancestors. Still, no advice was forthcoming.

"Quite all right, my dear." Lechmere repeated, clearing his throat. "It's natural for a young girl to be nervous when meeting a man of my stature. When you're a duchess—"

"When I'm a duchess, I shall open lots of orphanages!" she said, changing tactics. "There are so many disadvantaged children who would blossom with a proper education in a caring environment. And speaking of blossoms, have you extensive gardens, your grace? Because I've theories on crossbreeding flowers—"

"I told you she's a good conversationalist," Ford interrupted.

"She certainly has, hmm, creative ideas," said the duke, not unindulgently.

Hang it, hang it, hang it!

"Here, your grace, let me just take this goblet." She reached to snatch it from his hand, cringing when her fingers met his cold, clammy ones. "My, what a lovely ruby." The ring she was speaking of sported a stone wider than the thumb it was lodged on. "Amy would adore seeing it, I'm sure."

"Amy?"

"My sister-in-law. My brother Colin's wife. She's a jeweler." Kendra set the goblet on the table with a *bang* that made everyone jump.

"Your brother's wife is a *jeweler*?" The duke looked positively scandalized.

Aha!

She had him now.

"Oh, yes." Kendra couldn't quite keep a triumphant grin off her face. "Colin found Amy on the streets of London." Which was true, in a sense—since he'd rescued her from the Great Fire two years earlier—but more than a tad misleading. Though her family had been commoners, Amy was educated and wealthy in her own right. "Of course, she's a countess now as well, but a jeweler all the same."

"Hmmph," the duke sniffed.

"Yes, your grace. It's an admirable thing for a woman to be more than just a lady, don't you think? Well, let me just pour, then."

And she did—right into his lap.

He jumped up, watching in horror as a red stain spread on the turquoise satin in a very embarrassing place. "I think I've had enough, my lady, of both the wine and yourself. If you'll excuse me." With his pointy nose in the air, he strode stiffly from the room.

"Crossbreeding flowers?" When her twin's eyes met her own, they both burst out laughing.

But Jason wasn't amused. "Very charming, Kendra." Elbows on the arms of his chair, fingers steepled, he pinned her with stern green eyes. "That's one prospect off your list. Need I remind you who is left? I'll expect a decision after the weekend, and you'll be wed by the end of the summer."

THREE

*K*ENDRA AWOKE the next morning with a massive headache.

Jason couldn't be serious.

He and Ford and Colin were off to a monthly house party they attended—no females allowed—and, as usual, she and Caithren would be joined by their sister-in-law, Amy, and her baby daughter, Jewel, for the weekend. Usually they had something of a house party of their own, playing with the babe and gossiping until the men returned.

But when the men returned this time, they'd be expecting to hear whom she'd decided to marry.

She stared up at the underside of the mint-green canopy she'd begged for in her girlhood. Although their parents had depleted the family fortune financing the king in the Civil War, Jason had always seen to it that she'd never wanted for anything. To the best of his abilities, he'd indulged her every whim. Would he really force her to marry now?

He had *seemed* rather serious…

With a huff, she rose and pulled on her new hunter-green riding habit. She ran a comb through her hair, not bothering to call her maid in to curl and pin it. Amy would be here within the hour, but she needed to think. Alone.

In no time at all, she was mounted on Pandora, her mare, galloping across the Sussex Downs. Her brothers would be mightily vexed if they knew she was riding unescorted, but the three of them could go hang for all she cared right now.

Besides, they were away all weekend and would never know.

The fresh country air eased her aching head, but just thinking about that weasel Lechmere made her shiver. And the rest of her prospects weren't much better.

The Earl of Shrewsbury came complete with a meddling mother—the "shrew" in her title was all too fitting. The Marquess of Rochford was a widower and kind enough, but his hair was completely gray—doubtless from dealing with his seven unruly children. Viscount Davenport didn't talk, he whined. The Duke of Lancashire lived in, well, Lancashire— which was entirely too far from her family. The Earl of Morely was wealthy and kind, but nearing fifty. Lord Rosslyn was young, handsome, and fun loving, but lacking somewhat in brains. She wondered if he could read.

Jason couldn't be serious.

Coming out of her thoughts, she slowed to a stop. She hadn't realized how far she'd ridden. In fact, she noticed with a start, she was at the same spot where they'd seen the highwayman yesterday.

His friends had been atop that hill, lying on their stomachs, their hats pulled down to conceal their faces, training an impressive assortment of pistols on the hapless Puritan.

This morning, the hill was deserted and the highwayman nowhere in sight. In an attempt to judge the time, Kendra glanced at the sky, but it was all clouded over. The day was turning beastly. Not cold, but muggy, with a definite threat of rain. With no sun to confirm it, she guessed the time to be about ten o'clock. Perhaps highwaymen slept in.

Plainly, highway robbery wasn't a full-time occupation. Not

that she had any idea of what she'd have done if the highwayman *had* been here. Run for her life, in all probability. But she drifted into a vague reverie, seeing herself riding down the road at breakneck speed, her long, dark red hair floating on the breeze, impressing him with her horsemanship and her grace. In her fantasy he stared after her, openmouthed with surprise and appreciation, struck temporarily dumb by a bolt of…love at first sight.

Well, second sight, actually—but he hadn't paid any attention to her the first time, so surely that didn't count.

Then she would turn around, ride back, stop in the middle of the road, right in front of him, and slide off Pandora slowly…so slowly. Still gazing at her, he'd come forward, reaching her in two or three of his long strides, his large, strong hands spanning her waist as he eased her to the ground. And then…

She had no idea. Inexperience didn't make for detailed fantasies. And she certainly wouldn't have anything to do with a highwayman, anyway. Her reverie wasn't only boring, it was absurd.

But instead of turning back, she rode along the crest of the hill a spell, then turned away from the lane. And there, perhaps a hundred feet distant, was a very mysterious mound.

It wasn't sculpted by nature, Kendra realized immediately. Its shape was angular, its surface dirt, not grass.

A grave. A fresh grave.

Her hands tightened on the reins as she approached the tomb. Who could be buried there? The highwayman? A victim of his? Either one was unthinkable. She bit the inside of her cheek, worrying the soft flesh with her teeth.

A single raindrop fell on one of her clenched fists, and a gust of wind whooshed as she reached the mound. From her perch atop Pandora, she saw the loose dirt blow across it, revealing a sheet of canvas underneath. Her heart hammered at the sight. Was the body not buried properly, then—just covered with a spot of fabric?

She slid off Pandora and led her forward to investigate. Leaning down, she took a corner of the canvas, just a corner, in two shaking fingers and lifted it...

If her brothers had been here, they'd have told her, as usual, not to jump to conclusions. And this time, they'd have been right. Her shout of laughter rang across the Downs as she threw back the canvas.

Twelve blocks of wood. Twelve narrow pipes of various gauges. Twelve hats with different colored plumes and a variety of hatbands.

She tethered Pandora to a tree. Atop a nearby hill, she set a hat on a block of wood with a pipe sticking out from under it. When she ran back down and glanced up, it looked for all the world like a man lying on his stomach, pointing a gun at her.

He was clever, this highwayman. Very clever.

"What do you think you're doing?"

She froze. She hadn't heard anyone approach, and for the barest second she thought the voice was in her head. But he was standing behind her. She could feel his presence, maybe three feet away.

"I'm..." Words failed her. "I'm..."

"You're letting my hat get wet."

"Oh." Kendra put a hand to her head, feeling the mass of her hair curling with dampness. She hadn't noticed the increasing drizzle. "It's raining."

"Very observant of you."

She turned then and gazed up at him, and he looked exactly the way she'd known he would. His hair *was* golden—thick, silky, and straight. It was cut short, not chin-length like a Puritan's, nor cropped like a wig-wearing Royalist's, but somewhere in between, and the front was hanging in his eyes. She wanted to reach out and sweep it off his forehead, but she seemed rooted in place, and she wouldn't have dared to touch him anyway.

His snug black breeches were wool, not velvet, and his shirt was white, not black. He wasn't here for business, then.

"I've come to save my props from the rain. Will you help me, seeing as you're here?"

Help him? She ought to be bolting for Pandora at this very moment. "Of course."

Had she said that? She knew she shouldn't have. He ran up the hill and snatched up the three props, then turned and strode back to the rest of them. Windblown, his golden hair bounced in time with his steps as she followed.

She concentrated on his broad back, watching the play of muscles beneath his thin shirt as he flipped over the canvas and piled the hats on top, bundling them up and tying the four corners in a neat knot to make a parcel. He hefted it, testing its weight, then turned to her. "You can carry this, aye? Before you, on your horse?"

He didn't sound angry at her, more like he was simply resolved to complete his task in the most efficient manner possible. Kendra was somewhat relieved, but she moved in a haze of unreality.

She managed to find her voice, however. "If you'll hand it up to me, yes, I'm sure I can carry it. Where are we taking it?"

"A cottage over the next hill, not too far." He gathered the pipes under one arm and lifted the bundle by its knot. "Let's be off, before it starts raining in earnest."

His horse was tied by hers—amber, of course, his glossy coat a tawny tan color. Pandora's hide was a deep chestnut, and Kendra thought they made a handsome pair.

It was difficult to see over the bundle in front of her, but it was a short ride.

The cottage was unlocked, and the highwayman made short work of tethering their horses before depositing the pipes inside and returning for the bundle. After handing it to him, Kendra slid off Pandora slowly...so slowly...and a second later he was back, and his large, strong hands were spanning her waist as he eased her to the ground.

His fingers lingered on her waist a little longer than necessary, and she felt their warmth through her habit. She looked up at him. He looked older than her, but not as old as most of her suitors. He had a wide mouth, the full lower lip perfectly straight across the center bottom edge. She wanted to touch him, just there.

Her eyes locked on his, and her breath caught in her throat.

A crash of thunder rent the air, and big raindrops began pelting to the earth. He jumped back, motioning her to follow him inside.

She should leave. Now. But it was pouring…

The cottage looked more like a well-appointed hunting lodge, warm and cozy and very masculine. He shut the door behind them and wandered to a leather-upholstered couch, throwing his long form onto it with a surprising grace. "Close, aye? Five more minutes, and my hats would have been ruined. I thank you for your help."

"You're welcome," Kendra said from just inside the door where she still stood in a daze. She couldn't believe she was in a hunting lodge with this dangerous man. It was incredible—and, all of a sudden, incredibly scary. She couldn't remember ever having been alone with a man, save her brothers. And she didn't know the first thing about this one—except that he was an outlaw.

The fear must have shown on her face, because he sat straight and waved at the cushion beside him. "You can sit—I don't bite. You'll stay till it stops raining, aye?"

"Aye—I mean, yes." Outlaw or not, she loved the way he talked, the words slow and melodic. Though her heart was pounding, she screwed up her courage and moved to sit gingerly beside him. "I'm Kendra. Kendra Chase."

"Trick Caldwell."

"Trick?" she echoed, startled. She turned to him, forgetting for a moment that he was supposed to be frightening. "What kind of a name is Trick?"

"Ah, and that's a story." He smiled at her, a wide white smile that seemed to light up the cottage and belie the dreary day. Leaning forward, he reached out a hand and placed it on her wrist, just lightly, but a tingle raced up her arm and throughout her, warming her in the strangest way. Something snapped inside her, and the sense of unreality was gone.

She was here, really here, with the amber highwayman—no, Trick, she corrected herself—alone, and he wasn't scary at all.

Well, not very.

FOUR

"**ARE YOU** hungry?" Trick asked suddenly.

She shook her head, wondering if he actually had food here. Surely he didn't own this cottage. Well, maybe he knew where the owner kept stores, and she shouldn't be surprised he would use them.

He was a thief, after all.

"Thirsty, then? Aye, I'm guessing a spot of wine would do you. You look tense."

Tense didn't begin to describe how Kendra felt. She glanced down at his long fingers ringed lightly around her wrist. "A… spot of wine would be nice, if you have it. Thank you."

Releasing her, he rose with a leonine grace and made straight for one of the cabinets, as though he knew every nook and cranny of the place. Crystal goblets and a matching decanter were hidden behind the doors. He filled two glasses, and she took one, hoping he didn't see her hand shake.

"I'll just settle the horses and return, aye?"

"Where…?"

"There's a small stable in the back." He set his goblet on the mantel. Taking a heavy cloak that dangled from a peg on the wall, he shrugged into it and was out the door with a whoosh of wind.

She sat on the couch, listening to the rain on the roof and sipping the sweetish Madeira. Though she wasn't cold, she shivered. Looking around, she wondered how he could describe this as a cottage.

The cottages in the village of Cainewood were generally tiny and dark, single-room buildings with rough plastered walls and trodden earth floors. This cottage was impeccably clean and boasted large glass windows. The wooden walls and floors were polished to a gleam, and her feet rested on a lovely Oriental carpet. Besides the couch, there were two chairs and several small tables, two marquetry cabinets, and a desk in one corner.

She walked over to it and ran a hand along the smooth, rich wood. Everything on top was neatly arranged. Setting down her goblet, she slid open the top drawer to find a stack of paper and bottles of ink. Her hand went to the bottom drawer and tugged, but it was stuck closed or locked. She frowned at it, then turned to survey the rest of the large room.

A beautiful carved dining table and chairs sat on another patterned carpet, obviously imported from lands far away. A peek through an archway revealed a spotless, quite modern kitchen, the shelves heavily stocked with victuals. Another archway opened onto a corridor, which apparently led to several more rooms.

Some cottage, Kendra thought. All furnished, food and drink… Trick seemed quite at home. Maybe he lived here, after all. She'd never thought about where a highwayman might live, but she hadn't expected it would be a hunting lodge, or a cottage, or whatever he wanted to call it. She'd assumed they slept in inns or the like.

When the door opened and Trick walked in and swept off his cloak, she rushed back to the desk and reclaimed her goblet.

"It's not letting up," he announced, stomping the rain off his boots.

She was relieved that he didn't seem to care she'd been nosing around. "Is this…yours?" she blurted, making her way to sit on the couch. "I mean, do you live here?"

"Um…close enough."

Kendra felt her face heat. She really shouldn't be so curious. It was none of her business whom the cottage belonged to, and now she'd put Trick on the spot.

Of course he didn't own it. Many highwaymen had a reputation for being gentlemanly, but that didn't mean they were actual *gentlemen*. Men of property didn't turn to the roads for sustenance.

Thankfully, he looked amused rather than annoyed or embarrassed. He swiped his wine off the mantel and sat beside her.

The room was quiet except for the soft pit-pat of rain. She sipped from her own goblet, peeking at him over the rim. He gazed at her through the ends of his damp golden hair, and she saw his eyes darken. But surely he had no reason to be angry.

No, it was something else.

Her heart sped up, and of its own accord her hand rose to sweep clear his forehead. Horrified at herself, she snatched it back just in time.

With a sudden grin, he gave a toss of his head that flung the hair from his eyes. "We were speaking of my name," he reminded her—or himself.

She gulped more wine. "What did your parents name you, really?"

"Patrick Iain Caldwell." He settled back slowly. "But my father was away when I was born—Father was always away—so my mother named me. Scots–Irish, she was. In any case, he was appalled when he finally ventured home to meet me. Said she'd tricked him good, giving his English son two barbarian names."

Kendra grinned. "Trick…since she'd tricked him?"

"And short for Patrick, though he'd never admit it. They hated each other, they did. It was an arranged marriage."

"That sounds rather old-fashioned. Why?"

"The deuce knows." He drained his goblet and stared at it pensively, twirling it by its stubby stem. "Neither of them would talk of the other long enough for me to find out."

"How sad," she murmured, the sincere tone of her voice drawing his gaze.

FIVE

*T*RICK LOOKED up to see Lady Kendra shaking her pretty head. Her hair bounced, releasing a scent of sunshine and flowers that belied the dreary, rainy day. He felt the strangest urge to lean close and bury his nose in her deep red curls.

He knew he shouldn't have asked her to the cottage. Her brothers would have his head if they knew she was here with him, unescorted. But it had been merely a gentlemanly impulse; it would have been unkind to abandon a lady in all this rain. So he'd taken pity on the Chase girl.

Still, the last thing he wanted was *her* pity.

"Not so sad," he said, and moved his gaze from her face—only to have it land on her figure, evident beneath her riding habit's collarless jacket. His eyes drifted down to her waist, and he remembered the feel of his hands spanning it. He shifted to look out the window. Raindrops trailed down in slow, crooked lines. "Arranged marriages are common enough."

"For some, perhaps. The peerage is often required to wed for alliance."

She thought he was a commoner. She really had no idea who he was. Trick smiled to himself, then sobered.

If she'd been told nothing of him despite yesterday's encounter, her brothers were even more protective than he'd thought.

He rose to set his empty goblet on the mantel, then turned and leaned back against it, crossing his arms. "Your folks were different, then?"

"Oh, yes. They had a perfect, romantic marriage and loved each other very much. Too much, according to my brother Colin. He says they loved each other and the monarchy, and there was nothing left for us."

"But you don't agree."

A statement, not a question. He watched her eyes as she considered it, noting the bright intelligence. "No," she said at last. "I never knew them, really, as they died in the war when I was yet a babe. But I always felt they loved me."

"You felt their love from beyond the grave, aye?" Once he would have laughed outright at such a statement, but now, twenty-three years old and wiser, he knew better than to mock another's foibles. He was far from perfect himself.

Still, she must have caught something of his skepticism, because her brow furrowed. "You don't believe the departed can love?"

He shrugged. "I don't believe in love at all."

"You don't love anyone? No one loves you?" Her light green eyes looked incredulous. "Not anyone, in any form?" She colored suddenly and stood up. "I'm sorry," she mumbled. "I'm…we don't know each other. I shouldn't ask such questions."

He watched her stride to the window, her steps sure, not the mincing progress that passed for walking among the tittering ladies at court. He couldn't picture her whispering behind a fan, either, though surely she attended balls and the like, and probably had a wonderful time.

Not a social animal himself, he shuddered at the thought. His gaze followed her graceful hand as she traced the path of a rain-drop with one finger.

"Ask away," he assured her. "I've nothing to hide." It wasn't the truth—it wasn't even close to the truth—but it sounded nice. "No, I don't love anyone."

He saw her watching his reflection in the windowpane. "Your parents…?"

"Made my life miserable."

She turned to face him. "Brothers or sisters?"

"I have none. I reckon my folks only tolerated each other's presence long enough to make me."

At his frank words, her cheeks flushed a becoming pink. "And what of God?"

He considered his answer. "Well, of course I love God, but that's different. It's love between people that's an illusion."

Her mouth dropped open, then closed. It was a pretty mouth, he noticed, not over-plump, but perfectly shaped. "It's no illu-sion," she stated in a tone that brooked no argument.

"You love someone, then?"

"Oh, yes." The sunshiny smile was back. "My brothers, all three of them. And my new sisters—my sisters-in-law, actually—and my niece. When I first held her tiny body in my arms and she looked into my eyes, it was love at first sight." Her gaze focused on him and darkened. "I guess you don't believe in love at first sight, either?"

He grinned at her exasperation. "For a babe in arms… perhaps. Between two full-grown adults…not a chance."

She shook her head, her eyes once more full of pity. "You've no plans to marry, then? Not ever?"

"Of course I do," he said lightly. Avoiding her eyes, he lifted his goblet and crossed to the cabinet to pour himself more wine. "Perhaps a decade from now. But love won't have anything to do with it."

"Someday," she said, "someone will change your mind. Someday you'll fall in love."

"You make it sound like a promise," he said, amused.

"Then you can take it that way. And a Chase promise is never given lightly."

He seemed to remember hearing one of her brothers use those words. "I hope you're right. But I'm not going to lay money on it."

She smiled. "I'm not much for gambling anyhow. Is there something on my face?"

"Beg pardon?"

Frowning, she rubbed her chin. "You're staring at my face."

Actually, he'd been staring at her lips.

Flustered, he dropped his gaze to the empty goblet in his hand. "Was I?" he said vaguely, and cleared his throat. "Would you care for more wine?"

With a glance out the window at the pounding rain, she nodded and came forward to hand him her goblet. He poured, then handed it back. Their fingers met, his warm, hers cool.

Between them the goblet slipped to the floor.

She gasped, staring as a dark stain spread on the cream background color of the patterned carpet, then dropped to her knees to collect the broken crystal and dab at the blot with the hem of her riding habit.

Trick gazed down at her bright, panicked head. "Stop," he pleaded through stifled laughter. "You'll ruin your skirt."

"I'll ruin my *skirt*?" Worried green eyes looked up. "Then will the stain not come out of the carpet, either?"

"I haven't the slightest idea," he mused. Surely one of the servants would know how to remove it. If not, he could always bring another rug from his London warehouse.

"But...I'm not usually clumsy." She scrutinized the stain, then sat back and wrapped her arms around her bent knees. "And I've got you in trouble, then."

"In trouble?" he repeated stupidly.

"The crystal and the carpet..." She bit her lip, then her eyes cleared. "Tell the owner I'll pay for it all. Or rather, my brother will. It won't be a problem."

Tell the owner. Oh, she was precious. She thought he was a criminal, yet she worried about his carpet and angering his presumed landlord.

She'd be more on target worrying about his self-control, he thought wryly, reaching down a hand to help her rise. Then he stood blinking down at her, wondering where that odd thought had come from, and realizing it was true.

At her full height, the top of her head came just to his chin. She tilted her face to meet his gaze. Her hand was still in his, and seemed likely to remain that way for the immediate future. He could hear her breath coming rather fast over the patter of rain on the roof.

Slowly, her free hand came up to sweep the hair from his eyes. "I'm sorry," she whispered, then she touched a fingertip to his lower lip, exactly in the center, so lightly he wondered if he imagined it.

Real or imagined, he felt it. He stared at her pretty mouth. "Don't be sorry."

She blinked and pulled her hand from his.

He nearly made a grab for her before remembering who she was. He gave himself a little shake, thinking it had better stop raining soon.

"Come, there's water in the bedchamber." He turned on his heel and headed for the corridor, knowing she would follow. "We'll rinse the stain from your skirt before it can set."

He poured water into the washbowl and set it on the low table by the bed, then beckoned her near and handed her a towel.

She wetted it and leaned down to dab daintily at her hem. Frowning, she dipped again and dabbed harder. Finally, she sat on the bed, rucking her skirts up about her knees so she could plunge the offending stain into the bowl. She stared into space, holding the fabric in place with one hand.

Thinking she had well-shaped calves—had he ever noticed a girl's calves before?—Trick settled himself on the bed a safe distance from her. "You're going to sit there till it comes out?"

She turned to look at him. "It won't take long this way."

He watched the water soaking her skirt. A dark circle grew to encompass much more than the stain, but she didn't seem to notice. She was too busy watching him.

She swallowed and licked her lips.

The distance suddenly didn't seem so safe anymore. He meant to move away—really, he did—but somehow found himself scooting closer instead, then closer still when he caught a whiff of her sun-fresh skin and lavender-scented hair. Then he couldn't recall why he was supposed to be moving the other way. Couldn't recall much of anything beyond a pair of wide green eyes and a rosebud mouth.

From the main room of the cottage, he heard the door fly open and slam against the wall. He thought it must be the wind. Though he meant get up and close it—really, truly meant to— instead he found his arms curving around Lady Kendra's waist, his head sinking toward hers, toward that perfect, soft-looking mouth.

"Hey, are you here? We need your help to find our…"

Jason Chase arrived in the doorway, his brothers Colin and Ford close on his heels.

"…sister," he finished weakly.

Kendra and Trick sprang apart, taking the porcelain bowl with them. It fell to the polished floor with a loud crash.

"Not again," Lady Kendra groaned. "I *never* drop things, honestly."

"This isn't what it looks like," Trick hurried to say.

"No?" A muscle in Cainewood's jaw twitched. "You mean to say I didn't see you on a bed with your arms around my sister and her gown pulled up around her waist?"

"My knees," she corrected.

Jason just glared at her.

"What were you doing, then?" Colin asked.

Trick wondered why he felt so uneasy. "Rinsing a stain from her skirt."

Ford rolled his eyes. "You expect us to believe that?" He turned on his sister. "What the deuce are you doing here?"

"I was…riding. And it started raining, and Trick came along—"

"Trick, is it?" Colin's eyes bore into hers, and Trick saw her flinch. "Exactly how well do you know this fellow?"

"For heaven's sake, Colin—we just met."

"And you let him put his hands beneath your skirt."

Trick leapt to her defense. "I did no such thing, Greystone—I told you, we were rinsing out a stain."

"A bloodstain, would that be?"

Lady Kendra's eyes narrowed with puzzlement. "No," she said. "Why would you ask—"

"How can you think such a thing?" Trick interrupted.

"How could we not?"

"I'm disappointed," Jason said, stepping closer to Trick. "Very disappointed. Kendra has never acted particularly wisely, but she's been very sheltered and you ought to know better." He gazed at Trick with doleful eyes. "At least tell me you didn't know who she was."

"Of course I knew who she was!" Trick exploded. "I saw her with you yesterday."

Beside him, Lady Kendra gave a surprised gasp.

"Ah, yes," Jason responded, looking resigned. "That will have to stop, you know."

"What on earth are you talking about?"

"The highway robbery. You don't need the money, and Kendra doesn't need to see her husband strung up at Tyburn."

"Her husband?" Trick's heart pounded. Her brothers didn't know the truth. Or rather, they knew he wasn't posing as a highwayman for the money, but they weren't likely to learn the real reason anytime soon. King Charles had sworn him to secrecy.

And now they thought… "You think I bedded your sister? You must be mad!"

"They *are* mad!" Lady Kendra railed. She turned to Jason. "You have to listen." And to Colin. "It was only a stain. A *wine* stain." And to Ford. "You're always telling me *I* jump to conclusions—"

Ford's hand shot out to grasp his sister's arm. "Come along, Kendra." With a murderous look at Trick, he pulled her from the room.

"We'll call on you when the banns have been posted," Jason ground out.

"No," Colin said. "It will have to be by special license."

"Confound it, you're right." Jason rubbed the back of his neck. "She could be with child."

With child? Trick couldn't believe what he was hearing. One minute he was washing out a wine stain, the next he was accused of fathering a child. With a girl he'd never even kissed.

Never mind that he'd wanted to.

SIX

KENDRA WAS soaked to the skin. Water streamed from her hair into her tear-blurred eyes. She was shivering. But she'd rip her own tongue out before asking her abominable brothers for one of their cloaks.

Riding behind them, she heard the murmurs of a deeply involved conversation. She took slow, fortifying breaths, wishing she could make out their words. She couldn't let them make her go through with this. But they wouldn't, would they? Surely they didn't intend for her to actually wed a highwayman. A highwayman she hadn't so much as kissed!

Which was a shame. Because she'd wanted to kiss Trick more than she'd wanted to do most anything else, ever.

She knew full well he'd been about to kiss her, and she'd been ready—no, not just ready, *thrilled*—to cooperate. But it hadn't happened. Not even a little.

Besides which, a mere kiss hardly warranted a forced marriage!

Still, heavens above, the real amber highwayman had turned out to be even better than her fantasy version. She'd nearly melted just looking at him, and when his arms came around her, her whole body had seemed on fire. What would it have felt like if he'd actually kissed her—something hotter than fire? The center of a volcano?

It would have been the first time she'd kissed anyone.

Oh, she'd been kissed, of course—she was eighteen, after all, and not shy—but she'd never kissed anyone back. She blamed those exasperating brothers of hers. Every time a gentleman managed to smuggle her into an alcove or onto a balcony, one of her brothers would materialize right at the crucial moment, staring daggers into the unfortunate swain's eyes. And until now, she hadn't been enamored enough of anyone to make an issue of it.

Why did her brothers always have to turn up and ruin it all? Didn't they have anything better to do?

At long last, Jason sent the others ahead, then halted until she drew even with him. "I cannot believe you did that," he said.

"It was raining." She was seething inside, but somehow she managed to sound calm. "All I did was come in from the rain."

"That's not the way it looked," he said as though that were the end of the discussion.

She stared at his determined profile. A highwayman...her brother was letting—no, *making*—her wed a highwayman. Even if Jason was convinced the man had ruined her, the fact that he'd as good as pledged her to an outlaw was beyond belief.

Her stare turned to a glare that drew his gaze. He blinked. "What were you thinking, riding out alone?"

Ignoring that, she drew breath. "I cannot believe you expect me to marry a highwayman. You, who wouldn't let Lord Harrison near me because he was only a baron!"

For a moment, Jason just looked at her. Then his lips quirked into a smile before he threw back his head and laughed.

Incredulous, Kendra watched, wishing the rain pouring into his mouth would drown him.

"You—you—you don't know who he is, do you?" he choked out.

"Trick Caldwell. Patrick Iain Caldwell," Kendra returned

through clenched teeth. "Do you think you would have found me in a man's bedchamber—never mind that nothing happened there—if I didn't so much as know his name?"

Jason only laughed harder. "Patrick Iain Caldwell What?"

"What? What do you mean, what? That's not his name?" Kendra bit the inside of her cheek. "I should have guessed he'd lie to me," she muttered, more to herself than her brother. "He's a cursed highwayman, after all."

"You don't know who he is." Apparently failing to notice her unladylike language, Jason actually snorted. "You really don't know who he is." With another shout of laughter, he dug in his heels and raced up to meet their brothers.

Kendra could hear their loud guffaws through the distance and the driving rain.

She rode behind them for another few minutes, listening to their whoops of laughter, hoping they'd expire from lack of air. A buzzard circled lazily overhead. Not exactly Ares's bird, the vulture, but close enough. A fury was rising in her that would do Ares, the God of War, proud.

At last she couldn't stand it. She raced up to meet her brothers, nosing Pandora between Jason's and Ford's mounts.

"He's titled, isn't he?" she demanded. "Or you wouldn't even be jesting about this marriage. Who is he?"

Ford looked at her, his blue eyes all innocence. "Who?"

"The man you just betrothed me to! What's his name, blast it?"

"Oh, you mean Trick? Trick Caldwell?"

"All right. Enough is enough." She glared at them one by one. "I did nothing wrong. No matter what you think it looked like, we were washing a wine stain from my skirt. There's no reason for me to marry him."

Her brothers stared at her and then at one another over her head. Individually they nodded.

Then Jason spoke for them all. "Did you choose another of your suitors to marry, then?"

"That again? I don't believe this. None of my *suitors* are at all suitable, and I won't marry any of them. You're finished ordering me around."

"You're right about that," he said. "I'm finished. It's time you wed, and Trick's as good a man as any."

"But he's a highwayman," she wailed.

"Not anymore," Jason snapped. The brothers closed ranks, and nothing else was said for the rest of the ride home.

SEVEN

*T*RICK PACED around the cottage for a good fifteen minutes, huffing in disbelief, wondering how a simple errand to save his props from the rain had ended in such disaster.

When pacing failed to resolve anything, he rode home to Amberley House to dismiss the rest of his houseguests.

Compton, his butler, met him at the door. "Good afternoon, your grace."

"Is it?" Trick handed him his drenched cloak. "What happened while I was gone?"

Compton frowned, one of his habitual expressions. "Lords Cainewood, Greystone, and Lakefield have taken their leave. A messenger arrived with word that their sister had disappeared. They went off to find you, to enlist your help—"

"They succeeded."

And turned his life upside down in the process.

Leaving the butler mid-sentence, Trick stalked into his card room. "My apologies, gentlemen, but the party's over."

Peevishly, he waved a hand in a hopeless attempt to clear the smoky air. The four remaining guests, all aristocrats from neighboring estates, had apparently passed the time by smoking

Trick's small hoard of expensive Virginia cheroots, which were literally worth their weight in silver.

He coughed and waved some more. "It seems I'm soon to be wed, and I'm in no mood for cards. Besides which, the Chase brothers won't be returning, so we haven't enough for two tables—"

"Wed? As in married?" David Fielding interrupted in a puff of tobacco, blinking his brown eyes, which always looked a little crossed. "You cannot be serious."

"Aye, as in married." Trick smiled mournfully. "And I assure you, I've never been more serious in my life."

The only one without a cheroot between his teeth, John Garrick heaved his paunchy form from his chair. "Amberley, I...I don't know what to say."

Garrick, speechless. Imagine that. The pompous fellow usually never shut up, especially once he got started on one of his tirades against gambling, drinking, smoking, or whatever vice he'd decided to condemn this month (shockingly, he never chose overeating). Trick was all in favor of purging men's failings, but he'd as soon leave sermonizing in the hands of the clergy and judgment in the hands of God, for neither sat well in the greasy hands of a smug hypocrite.

Garrick showed no signs of his usual smugness now. "I...I just don't know what to say."

"Then don't say anything," Trick suggested.

Being the youngest member of the group but for Ford, Trick was usually respectful toward these men, but today distress made him bold. Striding across the room, he plucked a half-smoked cheroot from Fielding's lips, then did the same with Robert Faraday and Thomas Milner. They sat there, their mouths in little Os where the brown cheroots used to be, while he stubbed out the burning tobacco in one of the crystal dishes he kept on the card tables for that purpose.

"I'll send servants to help you pack," he informed them.

"And someone else will have to host next month, as a lady will be living here."

"But…Amberley." Robert Faraday finally found his voice. He skimmed the long brown hair from his face and rubbed his stubbled chin. "No surcoats, no shaving, no periwigs, no women. You laid down the rules when you set up the card club. And you said then that you'd marry the day the devil settled in heaven."

"He's arrived, gentlemen."

At Trick's grim pronouncement, Garrick narrowed his eyes. The other men rose, and they all drifted toward the door, presumably to collect their things.

"Who will host?" Trick pressed. "Faraday, Milner? Blast it, you both have wives. Garrick?"

"I'm…remodeling. No space at present."

Trick frowned; the man lived in a fifty-room manor house. Old, yes, and in dire need of renovations, but surely there was an area they could use to play cards and enough bedrooms in sufficient shape to accommodate seven guests.

"We'll ask Cainewood," Milner suggested. "Lady Cainewood can go stay with his brother's wife. I'll drop by there later this—"

"Cainewood has that sister," Fielding interrupted. "Er…Lady Kendra, that's it."

"Oh, yes. You're right. He'd have to send her to Greystone, too."

"Nay, gentlemen. Lady Kendra will be here. Though you'll address her as Her Grace the Duchess of Amberley." When the men's mouths dropped open again, Trick shot them a wry smile. "Aye, the Chases will host—it's the least they can do. Till next month, then?"

Before they could ask any questions he'd rather not answer, Trick grabbed a fresh cheroot and left to closet himself in his study, where he went straight to the carved walnut cabinet and poured himself a shot of strong Scotch whisky.

Kendra. He couldn't decide which he wanted more: to kiss her or throttle her brothers. Though it probably wouldn't be wise to threaten the Chases. Greystone, especially. From what he'd heard, Colin was deadly with a sword.

Trick sighed and dropped into his favorite worn leather chair. In the six months since King Charles had insisted he take up residence in his father's absurdly ostentatious house, this was the only room he'd redecorated to his own taste—classic, familiar, and comfortable. Lifting a heavy silver candlestick, he lit the cheroot and stuck it between his teeth, then sat back and carefully inhaled as Fielding had taught him.

Rolling the glass between his palms, he watched the candlelight glint off the faceted crystal. What was he going to do? What *could* he do? What did he *want* to do?

The answer came to him, as clear as the flawless crystal cupped between his hands.

He wanted to marry Kendra.

He'd wanted to kiss her the moment he'd glimpsed her in the shadows of that carriage. At first, his mind had refused to recognize the strong, strange impulse—he'd never felt anything quite like it before. Why should Cainewood's sister, of all people, affect him so?

Part of it, perhaps, was a consequence of Cainewood's status as the last bastion of respectability in a society where morals were meaningless. No one at King Charles II's court was virtuous; no one, that was, except Lady Kendra Chase. The Chase brothers had sheltered her for all of her eighteen years. Even Trick knew enough of her reputation at court—although he made it a point to keep as far from court as humanly possible—to realize Kendra was the quintessential forbidden fruit. Was that the basis of her singular appeal? Had Trick merely been afflicted with a childish instinct to want what he couldn't have?

Well, he could have her now. In fact, he couldn't avoid her.

And yet she'd lost none of that appeal.

Of course, the wedding would be a bit of a bother, but he may as well marry now as later—he had to sire an heir at some point. And Kendra would make as fine a wife as any. She was lovely, intelligent, and of suitable aristocratic birth. While she probably had no dowry to speak of—Cainewood was as cash-strapped as most of the Royalist nobility—the fact was, Trick didn't need anyone else's money. He had more of his own than he knew what to do with.

He blew out a wobbly smoke ring and watched it rise to the Amberley crests carved into the oak ceiling. His vision blurred until he could almost see Kendra's expressive face, with its unexpected, refreshing beauty. He didn't love her, of course, but he did like her. He supposed he was lucky to find that in a wife.

Aye, he would marry her. Smiling to himself, he sipped his whisky. The warmth of the liquor curled in his stomach. The more he thought about his impending marriage, the better he felt about it.

But that didn't mean he'd appreciated being bullied by his future brothers-in-law.

"Pardon the interruption, your grace."

Trick jerked around, choking on a mouthful of smoke. He hastily stubbed out the cheroot and downed the whisky to soothe his throat—which made it feel worse. "Aye, Compton?" he forced out between coughs.

"The Earl of Greystone is here to see you, your grace."

Trick was still uneasy with the formal address—*your grace*—despite having held the title for two years already. He'd never wanted it; heaven knew he'd never wanted anything that came from his father. But the old man had died, and now people—most especially Father's former retainers, like stuffy Compton—insisted on addressing Trick formally.

Swallowing and rubbing his throat, he blinked up at the middle-aged butler. Trick often wondered if the man had been born with a pike for a spine. Compton's receding gray hair was combed straight back from his forehead, and his jowls sometimes shook when he spoke, making Trick want to laugh.

But he wasn't laughing now.

Colin was here? Already? Could this family not leave him in

peace for one evening? Trick half-feared his visitor meant to challenge him to a duel—which Greystone would surely win.

Trick sighed expansively, causing Compton's nostrils to flare in disapproval of such a show of emotion. "Bring him in," Trick muttered, rising to pour himself another drink.

"Congratulations, Amberley," Colin Chase said from behind him. "Shall we toast your wedding tomorrow afternoon?"

Trick paused, then selected another glass from the cabinet. "Tomorrow, is it?" Turning to proffer the drink, he met Colin's eyes, which were a deeper green than Kendra's. "Can you not give a man time to get used to the idea?"

Colin sipped before answering, watching Trick over the rim. "Jason can pull strings if he wants to. And time is of the essence…your heir may be on his way already."

"We didn't—"

"I'm not judging you, Amberley."

Trick's gaze went to the hilt of Colin's ever-present sword. His reply was slow and measured. "I've told you, nothing untoward happened between Lady Kendra and me."

"You know, Kendra is claiming much the same thing. Doing her fighting best to convince us of it, too."

He'd bet she was. "You don't believe her?"

"Jason doesn't know what to believe. Frankly, I suspect he doesn't care. She's absolutely refused to consider anyone suitable, so as far as he's concerned, this circumstance is a dream come true. You know, she would never have looked at you twice if she'd realized you're a duke. A stubborn one, Kendra is."

"And now that she's realized?"

"She hasn't." Colin laughed. "Thinks you're an impoverished minor aristocrat forced to highway robbery, and she's cursing us for condoning the match. To our faces, that is. I suspect that, privately, she's walking on air. The girl's clearly in love."

"Love?" Trick rolled his eyes. He'd forgotten about her naïve ideas on that particular topic. "Don't tell me you're another believer in love at first sight?"

"It seems to be the Chase way," Colin mused. "My wife, Amethyst, had me with a single glance across a jeweler's counter."

"It's insane," Trick declared, and threw back the rest of his whisky. It burned his raw throat. "You're all insane. This is utterly outrageous."

"You're angry, then?"

Trick considered that for a moment. "Yes," he said slowly. "And no. I think your strong-arm tactics are obnoxious, but as to the outcome…I suppose I must wed, and your sister's as good a choice as any."

Before long, he hoped—just as soon as he'd satisfied the king's demand—he'd be back at the London docks where he belonged. Having Kendra here in the countryside, awaiting his visits and, eventually, raising his children, was not an unhappy prospect.

"I haven't the temperament for courtship," he added, "so a business arrangement suits my purposes just fine."

"Business arrangement?" Colin raised a single eyebrow. "I know what a fellow looks like when he wants someone, and I saw that look in your eyes. You'd better not hurt my sister."

"Hurt her? *I'm* not the one forcing her into this marriage."

Colin looked astonished at that accusation. "There's no way she'd be forced into any marriage—this one included—if we weren't one hundred percent certain this is right for her. If her happiness weren't our primary concern, she'd have been off our hands already—you'd need only see her list of rejected suitors to be convinced of that." He met Trick's gaze. "She wants this."

Trick realized his mouth was open, and closed it. "You think you know what she wants better than she does?"

Colin sighed. "Pride will keep her from admitting it, even to herself. But you're the first suitor she hasn't outright refused, whether she realizes it or not. And maybe it's true nothing happened today, but there's something between you two, Amberley—you cannot deny it."

While Trick attempted to digest that, Colin drew breath and smiled. "I'm sure it will work out all around." He raised his glass. "To the groom."

Trick looked at his own empty glass, then shrugged and went to refill it. He might as well get foxed on his last night as a free man, aye? "To the groom," he echoed wryly before tossing the whisky down in one gulp.

Colin drained his own drink and set it on a table. "Well, I'd best get home. Big day tomorrow for all of us, isn't it?"

Trick nodded.

Nodding in return, Colin stuck out his hand. "Till tomorrow, then. Let me just send the messenger back to Cainewood. Jason will be relieved to hear you've agreed."

"Agreed?" Incredulous, Trick pulled his hand from Colin's grasp. "I thought I had no choice."

"Of course you had a choice. What kind of people do you take us for?"

"But—"

"Did you think I came here to run you through if you failed to cooperate?"

"The thought crossed my mind," Trick said dryly.

"You said yourself it was a sound decision. Coercion was the last thing in our heads. We're not looking to gain an enemy for an in-law. We want Kendra to be happy." He pivoted on a heel, heading for the door. "And you, of course."

"But you made it sound—"

"Good evening, Amberley. Sleep well," he said and left.

For the second time that day, Trick found himself wondering what had happened. He was embarking on a new life, his ship about to sail for ports unknown.

For someone accustomed to being in charge, this was not an auspicious start.

EIGHT

"THANK YOU, Jane." Kendra smiled at her kindly, round-faced maid and put a hand to her carefully coiffed hair. "You did a lovely job."

Even if it was for nothing, she added silently.

As Jane left, Kendra crossed her bedchamber with a sigh. Pushing the drapes aside, she gazed out the diamond-paned window. In Cainewood's quadrangle below, her "betrothed" chatted with her three brothers and a clergyman—or someone dressed like one, anyway.

"No, poppet." Her sister-in-law, Amy, disentangled her eleven-month-old's hands from her ebony tresses and set the baby on her unsteady feet. Jewel had just started walking last week. "Kendra. They're waiting."

"I can see that." Letting the curtain drop, she focused on Amy. "But what they're waiting *for*, I can only imagine. To laugh their heads off at me, I'm thinking."

"Laugh?" In a rustle of dusky rose satin, Caithren came close and tweaked one of Kendra's long curls into place. "Why would they laugh?"

"This has to be a jest. Very well done, I must admit, but there isn't a chance they'll make me go through with it."

"No, Jewel, don't eat that." Amy took an ivory comb from her daughter's mouth and set it back on the dressing table. "I'm not too sure they'd joke about this."

Kendra brushed at the silver tissue underskirt that gleamed from beneath the split front of the blue silk gown she had dressed in for her "wedding." "It's so like them to make me get all ready, isn't it? Their idea of justice, having found me in a seemingly compromising position. But they won't actually make me wed a highwayman."

"I don't think he's just a highwayman, Kendra." Cait's hazel eyes looked concerned. "He must be suitable. Jason seemed dead serious to me."

"He's serious about scaring me, making me come to a decision. This will be called off at the last minute, at which point Jason will expect me to happily choose one of the other men who has offered. As for Trick being *just* a highwayman, I couldn't say. I don't know the first thing about him."

"But you like him, aye?"

"He's…interesting." A vast understatement. Kendra only hoped her sisters-in-law wouldn't ask for elaboration.

"I like the way you say *interesting*." Amy's grin was too knowing for Kendra's comfort. "Sometimes we find love in unexpected places." Her fine features softened as she doubtless considered her own unconventional marriage, that of a shopgirl and a nobleman.

"Aye, she's right." Cait nodded her agreement. "If you'd told me I'd ever be in love with a man and living in *England*"—despite her love for both Jason and their home, she pronounced the word with a mild distaste—"I'd have said you were sodieheid for certain." Her gaze narrowed at the puzzled look on Amy's face. "Featherbrained," she added in translation.

Inwardly, Kendra sighed. While it was true she dreamt of the kind of happiness both her sisters-in-law had found, she didn't think she would find it in a sham wedding to a highwayman. There had to be more to marriage than kissing, after all.

"Up," Jewel demanded, providing a welcome distraction as she toddled over to her mother.

Amy lifted her to perch on one violet-taffeta-clad hip. "Did you know Colin called on Trick last night? He offered him a chance to back out of this arrangement, but he turned it down."

"Or so Colin told you." Could the amber highwayman possibly care for her? Kendra wondered. She didn't think so, and she knew for sure that the little leap of excitement she felt at that thought was all wrong. "If Colin did call on him, I'm sure it was to plot this absurd, elaborate ruse. Colin is nothing if not the ultimate prankster."

"Maybe you're right, and this wedding is naught but a jest. But just in case"—Cait held out a silver coin—"you'll want to put this in your shoe."

"There she goes with her superstitions." An indulgent smile curving her lips, Kendra took the coin and tucked it into one high-heeled satin slipper. "What other old wives' tales might you be worrying about?"

"I've never said I believe it, mind you, but you know what they say. Something old, something new, something borrowed, something blue…"

"This gown fills three of those requirements. Old, borrowed, and blue." There'd been no time to have a wedding dress made, so Kendra was wearing Cait's. She brushed again at the shimmering silk skirts. "I always wanted to wear green for my wedding."

"I've told you, you wouldn't want to do that," Cait admonished. "Green is the choice of the fairies."

As though that explained anything.

"And as for something new…" Amy moved closer, trying to maneuver an object out of her pocket.

"I'll take her," Caithren offered, reaching for Jewel. Kendra thought she cuddled her niece rather wistfully. Cait and Jason had been married for nearly a year, yet there was still no sign of a babe.

Amy finally extricated a bracelet from her pocket—smooth-polished ovals of amber set in heavy gold links. Studded with sparkling diamonds, the circlet glittered in her hand. "A wedding gift," she said, "from your future husband. Colin asked me to pass it on to you."

"This isn't a real wedding. And as for new, it doesn't look it."

"It isn't," Amy said in confident tones. "By the cut of the diamonds, it's actually very old. But new to you. And it cannot hurt to wear it." The golden stones seemed to glow from within, secrets of past centuries locked inside their translucent depths. "When Colin gave it to me, he said it would be quite fitting."

Amy looked curious, but Kendra wasn't about to admit she thought of Trick as the amber highwayman. How had Colin known? Had she said something inadvertently? She wasn't usually indiscreet.

"I cannot believe the lengths your husband will go to in planning his practical jokes." She reluctantly held out her arm. "It *is* beautiful."

After Amy fastened the clasp, Kendra turned her wrist, watching the diamonds catch the light. Surely the bracelet wasn't really Trick's, which meant she could make her brothers let her keep it after this farce of a wedding was called off. For putting her through this, they owed her that much.

It would remind her of Trick, of the exhilaration she'd felt when he'd nearly kissed her. It would remind her not to settle for less—not to let her brothers pressure her into a loveless marriage, no matter how hard they tried.

She touched the amber pensively—warm, it somehow seemed—and drifted over to her dressing table. Watching herself in the mirror, she settled a gossamer lace veil over her hair and drew it down, tucking the ends into the sides of her neckline to secure it.

Her brothers wanted her to play the part of a blushing bride, and a blushing bride they'd get. She leaned closer. Pale, too. Which was ridiculous—this was but a game.

"No, poppet," Amy said, reattaching one of the tabs on Caithren's stomacher where Jewel's pudgy fingers had managed to unfasten it.

Handing the baby to Amy, Cait moved closer and touched Kendra's arm. "Did Jason talk to you about what will happen on your wedding night?"

"Or Colin?" Amy added.

"No," Kendra said. "Because this isn't a real wedding. Besides, I know what happens. I've lived in the countryside most of my life. I've seen animals in the fields—"

She was cut short by Cait's snort. Her sisters-in-law exchanged an amused glance, then sobered. "It's not like the animals, not really," Cait said gently. "You should know it will hurt, but only—"

A knock interrupted before the door opened to reveal Jason and Colin. "Are you ready?" Jason asked. "It's time."

It would hurt? *That* was unwelcome news. Telling herself she had no reason to be alarmed, because this wasn't a real wedding, Kendra nodded. "Shall we get this little drama over with?"

NINE

"**N**ERVOUS, MAN?"

"Of course not." Trick shot Lady Kendra's twin, Ford, a smile—a confident one, he hoped. The shakiness in his legs must be a symptom of last night's overindulgence. He clenched his fists to keep his hands from giving him away, then shoved them into the pockets of his midnight blue velvet surcoat.

He'd last worn the suit a few years ago in Paris, for one of those intolerable social occasions Father insisted he attend to further the "business." It was more fitted than the current style, but Trick had only one other formal suit at his home in the countryside, and he wasn't about to wed in his highwayman clothes.

His gaze swept over the groomed lawn of Cainewood Castle's quadrangle, then darted away when he spotted the parson, hands clasped behind his back. He seemed a kind enough sort, but the sight of him made Trick's stomach lurch. He looked back to Ford...but, nay, he'd as soon not look at Ford, either. His bride's twin and most certainly the person who knew her best.

His eyes strayed to the ancient keep, the worn stone an imposing reminder of the strength of Lady Kendra's line. Four hundred years the Chases had lived here, as Jason told it, save during the Commonwealth. Kendra knew who she was and what she had come from, unlike Trick. He'd always thought of himself as a mongrel.

A mangy one.

Distracted by the bang of a thick oak door, he turned to see his bride descending Cainewood's front steps.

Stunning in a sky-blue gown, she glided his way. The shimmering silk overskirt opened down the front to reveal an underskirt of costly silver tissue—he knew the expense, having bolts of the very fabric stacked in his London warehouse. The sleeves were double-puffed with a spill of silver lace at the wrists, which had made its way from Italy, if he didn't miss his guess.

Swathed within the lace, her hands looked small. In fact, everything about her looked small. He hadn't noticed that before.

He hadn't had time to notice much of anything, he told himself, watching a faint blush creep up from her scooped neckline. His gaze wanted to linger on her lips, but he forced himself to meet her eyes instead. A crisp shade of light green, they looked alert and wary, but as they locked with his, a hint of something else seemed to kindle in their depths. Something that made his own cheeks grow warm.

Deliberately looking away, Lady Kendra walked toward the family's small private chapel, Jason and Colin at her sides. Their wives trailed behind, a tiny, pink-dressed lass holding their hands, tripping along and giggling between them.

In no time at all, Trick found himself mounting the chapel's stone steps. Inside, sunshine streamed through brilliant-colored windows to cast the sanctuary in rainbow hues. Squaring his shoulders, he went to face the parson. Jason and Colin kissed their sister before Ford walked her to join Trick at the altar, delivering her into his care with a kiss and a hug and something whispered into her ear that Trick wished he could hear.

Lady Kendra shook her head and rolled her eyes as she pulled away.

Every inch of Trick was aware of her standing beside him. Her fiery hair was covered by a fine lace veil that framed her face, the ends tucked into her neckline. Trick reached for her hand, feeling it cold and clammy in his.

"Wait," he said, and pulled her to the side of the sanctuary, ignoring the questioning looks on her siblings' faces.

"You don't have to go through with this," he told her in a whisper.

She looked even more at a loss than before. "I...I don't think—"

"I'll be asked to take my vows first. When the time comes, if you wish to call this off, just shake your head *no* and I won't say 'I will.'"

Lifting her hand, he ran his fingers over the bracelet's amber stones, feeling slightly disoriented at the sight of the family heirloom on her wrist. It made this all seem so real, yet unreal at the same time.

He looked up. "I don't expect they can actually force us to marry," he added, thinking of Colin's sword and hoping he was right.

She peeked around at her brothers, then lifted her chin. "If you're willing, then I am, too."

He had his reasons to be willing...he just wondered what hers were. What was wrong with her, then, that she thought she couldn't do better than a thief for a husband? He wasn't really one, of course, but he was aware she didn't know that—doubly aware, since her brothers had made a point of keeping his identity from her, to the extent of asking this afternoon if it would be acceptable for his title to be left out of the proceedings.

She had a problem with dukes, they'd said, and since he didn't care for the title either, he hardly thought it mattered. Married was married.

"Very well, then." He nodded, and they returned to the altar.

The clergyman began the ceremony, and Lady Kendra kept looking around, as though she expected something unforeseen to happen. Not that Trick could blame her. He found the circumstances more than a little unnerving himself.

The preliminaries went entirely too quickly. Nobody showed just cause why they could not be lawfully joined together, and before Trick knew it, the parson was reciting the vows.

"Patrick Iain Caldwell, wilt thou have this woman to thy wedded wife, to live together after God's ordinance in the holy estate of matrimony? Wilt thou love her, comfort her, honor, and keep her in sickness and in health; and, forsaking all others, keep thee only unto her, so long as ye both shall live?"

Trick slanted Kendra a glance, but she didn't shake her head. "I will," he said, and his stomach flip-flopped with the enormity of the step he was taking, but also with a sudden realization.

Kendra had no idea he was a duke.

Well, he'd known that already, of course—but she really had *no idea*. Whatever her reasons for agreeing to marry him, they had nothing to do with his title or his money. She didn't know he had either. She wasn't marrying the Duke of Amberley. She was marrying Trick Caldwell.

Despite the bizarre circumstances, the thought brought a smile to his face. Looking surprised, Kendra returned it with a tiny smile of her own.

A few more words, a simple gold band slid onto her finger, and Trick's arms slipped around her waist, just as they had yesterday. He bent his head toward hers, toward the perfect mouth he'd spent the entire ceremony trying not to stare at.

As their lips touched, she melted against him, her lavender scent surrounding him like a cloud. She let out a tiny gasp— surely not even the nearby parson could have heard it—and then she was kissing him back with such sincere and wholehearted enthusiasm that he quite forgot where they were and who was watching.

And so far as *she* knew, she was kissing plain Trick Caldwell.

When her brothers cleared their throats, he reluctantly pulled away, rather stunned and out of breath. He thought with dismay of the hours and hours between now and when they could be alone, when he brought her back to the cottage tonight. He could scarcely wait.

She wouldn't discover until tomorrow that she was a duchess.

TEN

*A*N IMPROMPTU wedding feast was set out on the mahogany table in Cainewood's dining room. Kendra sat beside her new husband, her head still spinning with disbelief.

She'd been shocked speechless when the priest concluded the ceremony, shook hands all around, and walked through the front door of the chapel, all without her brothers bursting into laughter. Just yesterday she'd been an innocent girl having a silly fantasy, and now it appeared that fantasy had somehow become the rest of her life.

But this couldn't be what it appeared.

Apparently the script called for the farce to go on a little longer. But were she a gambler, she'd wager that before night fell, her brothers would be sending her up to her old bedchamber a husbandless maiden still, congratulating themselves on the success of their practical joke.

"Aren't you going to cut the cake, Kendra?"

Startled, she looked to Amy. Her sister-in-law was grinning widely and holding out a knife. Dominating the center of the table, the bride cake was double frosted, sugar over almond icing. Despite her churning stomach, Kendra's mouth watered; she loved sweets.

Very well, then. If her brothers wished to continue the charade, she'd play her part.

Rising and taking the knife, she reached to cut the confection and felt Trick's hand envelop hers. She turned her head, raising astonished eyes to find him leaning over her, bracing himself with one hand on the table. "We've yet to feast." He nodded toward the servants still carrying in platters.

"Ah, Trick," Jason said, a trace of laughter in his voice. "It's obvious you have much to learn about your new wife. She always eats dessert first."

Colin nodded. "And she's taught Amy her unfortunate habit."

"Cake!" baby Jewel crowed gleefully, banging her spoon on the table.

"Second word she learned," Colin informed them dryly. "Right after Mama and before Papa."

"We've other unfortunate habits as well," Ford chimed in, clapping Trick on the back. "Perhaps you moved too quickly in aligning yourself with the Chases, my friend."

Kendra felt Trick's hand tighten on hers. Beneath his tousled hair, his eyes narrowed. "*I* moved too quickly?"

She stiffened at his words. He seemed to be taking this seriously. Could it be he wasn't in on the joke? Or…

Could it be this was no joke?

Suddenly unsure, she looked around the table at her brothers' faces. Their expressions told her nothing.

When she saw Colin with Amy and Jewel, and Jason together with Cait, she couldn't help but wish to have a family of her own someday, like those her brothers were creating. A whole family, like the one she'd been cheated of growing up displaced and parentless during the Civil War and Commonwealth years. And she knew Colin and Jason wanted no less for her.

But finding love with any of the suitors they had presented?

That was about as likely as seeing Zeus descend from the sky.

This was her *life* they were toying with. She bit the inside of her cheek. Caithren caught her troubled gaze and returned it with heart-wrenching sympathy.

Trick moved again to pull back the knife, but Kendra held steady. When he grinned— approvingly, she thought—her eyes went to the tiny chip in his front tooth. For the hundredth time in the past hour she remembered what it had felt like to kiss him. Like being outside her own body…and yet exquisitely aware of every place it came into contact with Trick's. His hands warm on her waist, hers resting on his wide shoulders, her elbows pressing into his chest as she moved closer. And of course, the gentle pressure of his lips on hers, not hot like a volcano, but sweet like a double-frosted cake—

She stopped breathing, shocked at her thoughts.

Did she *want* this to not be a joke?

Catching her staring, Trick slipped her a wink. "Come, we'll cut it together, *leannan*."

He was an enigma, but at least he was a nice one. Kendra drew a calming breath as they sliced the cake, his hand guiding hers. She placed a piece on Amy's plate, then one on her own.

All the while, Trick remained standing beside her. She could feel his gaze, feel him suddenly shifting, but before she had time to react, he'd reached and plucked the veil from her head.

"What!" She turned and snatched it from his hands.

"I wanted to see your…hair," he finished lamely, blinking at her in seeming bemusement. "What on earth did you do to it?"

"Do to it?"

"The…" He waved a finger, drawing spirals in the air. "The…"

"Curls?" Kendra supplied helpfully. She couldn't help but laugh at his expression. "Jane worked on it for more than an hour. Do you like it?"

"No," he said flatly. "I liked it before."

"Oh." She felt a blush heat her face. Perhaps he wasn't so nice after all. "After this, I'll take it down."

He stepped close and spoke in a low tone that made her spine tingle. "After this, *I'll* take it down."

The wispy lace fluttered from her fingers to the soft blue Oriental carpet. Feeling more confused by the moment, she plopped back onto her chair.

"Mmm...porcupine," Trick said, reseating himself with a satisfied smile. "At least I've married into a family that appreciates good food."

The "porcupine" was actually a stuffed breast of veal, larded all over and studded with small strips of ham, bacon, and pickled cucumber. Trick added a healthy portion to his already-loaded plate.

"Leave room—we've surprise as well," Colin warned. Spearing a bite of cake, Kendra looked up as a servant set the dish called surprise on the table. A stuffed calf's head served up in its original shape, it had bunches of myrtle stuck into its eyes and looked very surprised indeed.

The steam rose off it in tantalizing swirls...and it bellowed.

Kendra screamed. A piece of cake went flying off Amy's fork, splattering on one of the diamond-paned leaded windows. Ford jumped up, his lattice-backed chair clunking to the floor behind him. Trick's and Jason's mouths dropped open.

When the calf bellowed again, Kendra rushed from her chair to take shelter in the door frame with Cait, both poised for flight. Stopping only to snatch up baby Jewel, Amy joined them. The ladies all clung together, staring. Squished between their bodies, Jewel let out a wail.

The calf's head bellowed once more...

No, it croaked.

With a half-amused, half-disgusted groan, Trick dropped his fork, reached to pry the calf's mouth open wider, and lifted its heavy pink tongue. A toad hopped out and looked around, blinking its bulbous eyes before it leapt off the table and headed toward the door.

The ladies broke apart to let it pass between them. Amongst gales of laughter from the gentlemen, Kendra thwacked Colin on the head as she returned to her seat. "For goodness' sake! Have you no sense of propriety?"

"A question of propriety from *your* lips, little sister?" Colin rubbed his head good-naturedly. "Was it not just yesterday we found you—"

"Hush, Colin." Amy dumped their sobbing daughter on her husband's lap. "Here. You made her cry, she's yours." She seated herself and raised her fork, but not before sending him a tolerant smile.

Jewel quieted when Colin bounced her on his knee. "Well, you've seen us at our worst now," he said to Trick around a mouthful of dressed artichoke bottoms. "Welcome to the family."

Trick shrugged noncommittally. Watching him scan the group around the table, Kendra tried to imagine what he was thinking.

It couldn't be good.

It was time to bring this charade to an end. She turned to Jason. She'd been the female head of his household since their parents died seventeen years ago—or at least since she grew old enough to accept the responsibility. "How will you get along without me here to direct the household?"

"We'll manage," her brother said blithely, wrapping an arm around his competent wife. His fingertips played idly in her dark-blond hair. "I set Jane to packing your things."

Trick touched Kendra's hand. "Jane is your maid, I presume? She can follow tomorrow. You'll send her along, Cainewood?"

"Certainly."

"But—" Kendra started.

"Tomorrow," Trick said firmly "You won't be needing her tonight."

Kendra's spoon hung in the air, its bite of cake forgotten. Trick was acting as though they were really married, talking of maids and spending the night together.

Did highwaymen even have servants? She certainly hadn't seen any at the cottage. Was she really married to this man? Toying with the bracelet around her wrist, she recalled what little she knew of him.

It wasn't much, and it wasn't good.

"But you're—" Something in his golden eyes made her falter. "—a highwayman," she finished weakly.

Jason reached for the bread. "Yes, we need to talk about that."

Trick tore his gaze from Kendra. "Aye?"

"It has got to stop."

Trick chewed thoughtfully, then sipped some wine. The silence stretched between him and Jason, almost as though it were a palpable barrier.

"I mean it, Trick. You don't need the money."

"Aye? You think not?" A corner of Trick's wide mouth turned up, and Kendra would swear he was about to start laughing.

Did he really not need the money? Had he enough put aside, then? Could highway robbery be *that* lucrative?

There was something missing here. But she couldn't seem to think straight in his presence; it had been that way since she'd first laid eyes on him. She felt all hot and bothered, and her brain refused to work.

"Why do you do it?" Ford asked.

Trick favored her twin with a mild look. "Maybe it's a pleasant amusement."

"You're finished, Trick." Jason's voice brooked no nonsense. He set down his fork. "Find your amusement somewhere else."

The golden gaze flicked to Kendra. "Aye," he said, the other corner of his mouth turning up. "That I will."

ELEVEN

*T*HE SUN WAS setting, painting the sky in muted tones as they made their way to Trick's home in the impressive two-seater caleche he'd driven to Cainewood. Borrowed, most likely, Kendra thought, along with the matched bay horses...at least she fervently hoped he hadn't stolen them.

A furtive glance to the rear convinced her they weren't being followed—she wasn't being rescued—by any of her brothers. "I cannot believe it," she said.

Trick gave her a long, considered look before responding in that characteristic unhurried way of his. "You cannot believe what?"

"I cannot believe I'm married. It happened so fast."

He raked a hand through his shining hair. "Why did you go through with it?"

"I didn't think it was real. Even now, I'm half-expecting one of my brothers to ride up laughing at their masterful joke."

"They're not coming," Trick said.

"I know." And she knew as well that some tiny part of her had wondered if the wedding might be real all along, and even —maybe—hoped that it was. Of all the men she'd encountered in her life, Trick was the only one with whom she'd ever felt a sort of magic.

But that didn't stop her from wanting to sink her claws into her too-clever brothers. How dare they cook up a scheme like this behind her back?

And what on earth could they mean by marrying her to a known outlaw? He could be a murderer, for all she knew! His rapier rode in the sword belt on his right. Her brothers carried weapons as well, of course, but they didn't draw and use them on a daily basis.

Her teeth ached from clenching them. Consciously relaxing her jaw, she took a deep breath. "I know they're not coming. I'm so furious with them, I swear I won't speak to them for weeks. But I still cannot believe it. All along, I was certain this was a prank." That desperate conviction had helped her cope all the day, and it was frightening to let go of it. "I thought they were trying to teach me a lesson."

Trick turned to her, a hint of a smile on his wide mouth. "Are you due to be taught a lesson?"

"No!" Why did his tone make her so flustered? "They refused to tell me whether you're titled. Are you? *Who* are you?"

"I'm your husband," he said carefully. "And I agree with your brothers that that's all you need to know for now."

Kendra glared at him through the growing dark. He was as bad as they were—worse, in fact. She was accustomed to her family meddling in her life, but what right had this virtual stranger to do the same? It was beginning to dawn on her that "magic" might not be near enough to sustain a marriage. "I can vow not to talk to you as well."

"Who said I was interested in talking tonight?"

His tone sent more tingles down her spine, but, realizing his game, she held on to her anger. Perhaps with other girls he'd been able to seduce his way out of trouble, but that wouldn't work on her! "Who said I'm interested in what you're interested in?" she snapped.

"Oooh, clever riposte."

With a noise of disgust, she crossed her arms and turned her back on him—for a moment. In truth, she was too old for such petulance. They both were. She sighed. "My brothers manipulated you, too, you know. Aren't you angry?"

"Aye, a bit perhaps." He guided the caleche off the main road, onto a less-traveled path. "But not overmuch. And not at you. I know this isn't your fault." When Kendra faced him, his gaze softened, and his words took on the lilt of his homeland. "It's not such a bad bargain I've made, aye?"

Kendra blushed wildly, thankful for the cover of darkness. A fair bargain, was she? She couldn't think of anything to say in return to such a statement, so she remained silent, hugging herself.

Perhaps thinking she was cold, Trick wrapped an arm around her shoulders. She should be terrified, she thought vaguely. She knew little of men in an intimate way, and even less about Trick…besides that he was dangerous.

But his warmth was oddly comforting. She scooted closer, and when his long fingers rubbed up and down her arm, she leaned against him, thinking about when she first saw him and how she'd wanted him to notice her. Remembering yesterday in the cottage, and the thrilling moment when they'd nearly kissed. Today they finally had, and kissing him had been even better than she'd imagined. But now it was their wedding night, and she could only wonder: what came next?

She'd barely grown comfortable against him when the caleche bumped off the path and over a grassy knoll, following a faint trail that led to the cottage. Windows glowed in the distance, the lamps inside already lit.

The cottage looked warm and welcoming, but as they rolled to a stop, she tensed. Tonight she'd become his wife in more than just name, and, despite her curiosity, she wasn't sure she could go through with it. Caithren's words kept rumbling around in her head.

You should know it will hurt…

He helped her down and guided her inside with a hand at the small of her back, touching her where she wasn't used to being touched. The door shut behind them, but he didn't remove his hand.

He was close. Much too close. His gaze locked on hers, his heat penetrating the small space between them. She could smell a soap-fresh masculine scent—sandalwood, if she wasn't mistaken. She wouldn't expect a highwayman to use imported soap, but then, little about any of this had matched her expectations.

Just when she thought she might panic, he turned away. "I'm going to settle the horses, aye?" Before she could react, he was out the door.

How could this be happening to her?

Her fashionable high Louis-heeled shoes made a loud, unnerving sound as she walked around the main room, picking things up and putting them down at random. She tried the bottom drawer of the desk again, but it was still stuck tight.

What had she expected? She'd first tried it only yesterday.

This was incredible.

Too soon, Trick blew through the doorway with a wolfish smile that made her breath catch in her throat. He strolled straight to the cabinet and poured them each a goblet of wine. Yesterday's cups were gone, the broken shards of glass picked up, the stain nonexistent, as though the spill had never happened.

But it *had* happened, and because of it, she was married to Trick Caldwell.

"Here," he said, handing her a goblet. He tapped his against it, the tinkle of expensive crystal sounding pure and loud in the silence that stretched between them. "*Slàinte mhór.*"

Kendra watched his throat muscles work as he drank deeply. Perhaps he wasn't as cavalier about this as he made himself out to be. Her head spinning even without the wine, she took a cautious sip. "*Sl*...what?"

He set down his glass and moved to her, slipping his arms about her—quickly, as if he might lose his nerve. "It's a toast. Good health," he translated quietly. "And don't be too impressed. It's all the Gaelic I can remember."

"I...I'm..." Feeling dizzy, her heart pounding, her face flushed, Kendra placed one hand on his chest and leaned into him, knowing she was giving him the wrong idea but unable to help herself. She felt abandoned and confused, and he was her only anchor. "I'm not impressed."

"Oh, aren't you now?" he drawled, taking the goblet from her other hand. He set it beside his on the table, and then his head dipped, and his mouth covered hers.

Warm. Warm and soft. That was all she could think. His lips moved against hers, sparking a searing heat that spread throughout her body. She tasted wine and Trick, sweet and tart and so delicious she almost forgot how nervous she was. Her arms clasped around him, lest she drop to her knees.

When he broke the kiss, he saw her teetering, and his hands moved to her waist to keep her upright.

A smug smile on his face, he let her catch her breath. "Still not impressed?"

Impressed, she was. And terrified.

He drew a steadying breath of his own and ran a hand back through his hair, and she watched, transfixed, as the front flopped back down into place. "Why don't you cut it?" she asked, casting about for a safe topic of conversation.

"Hmm?" His darkened gaze held hers.

"Your hair, where it hangs down in your eyes."

"Maybe I'm just lazy," he suggested.

"You're hiding," she countered.

"Not tonight." He moved close again and ran his hands over her shoulders, down her arms. "Shall we repair to the bedchamber?"

Kendra hadn't thought her face could get any hotter, but it did as he took her by the hand and led her down the corridor. The bedchamber had been cleaned up, too; no trace remained of the broken washbowl or its spilled contents. A new one stood in its place.

And, of course, there was the bed. Her gaze locked on it, anticipation and apprehension warring somewhere in her stomach. *You should know it will hurt…*

"Are you all right?" Trick asked.

She nodded, swallowing hard.

He shrugged out of his surcoat and draped it over the back of the room's only chair. "Sit," he said, dropping onto it.

There was no other place to sit but the bed. A big bed, very big for a "cottage," and especially big for this small chamber. Somehow yesterday that had failed to register. It was a plush feather bed, too, not straw or wool. The bed-hangings, of palest ice-blue silk, were free of fussy frills and looked very costly and eminently tasteful.

The counterpane had already been folded back. She gingerly pushed aside an embroidered coverlet and lowered herself to sit on smooth, luxurious sheets.

"Second thoughts?" Perched on the chair in only shirt-sleeves, Trick watched her avidly, a pained half-smile on his face. "I offered you a way out of the wedding," he said on a sigh. "I suppose I can also offer you a way out of the wedding night."

Sincere though it might be, she couldn't help but notice the "offer" was uttered in a voice laced with hope.

"I hope to sire an heir," he added, "but it doesn't have to be tonight. I know this has happened quickly. We can wait until you feel ready."

A tempting offer, indeed. But his eyes seemed to plead with her. And her own body was pleading as well, her heart still racing, her hands clenching in her lap.

She remained caught in that imploring gaze while he came

forward and knelt before her. Silently lifting her hand, he began working the clasp on the amber bracelet.

"It's lovely." She sighed, feeling tingles as his fingers brushed her wrist. "Was it really from you, then?"

"Aye." Slowly he drew it off, hefting the weight in one hand. "It belonged to my grandmother, and her mother before her."

"Then why doesn't your mother have it now?"

"My father never considered her worthy."

Worthy. Trick barely knew her, yet he considered *her* worthy. She tried to wrap her mind around the significance of that, but found herself distracted when he raised her now-bare wrist and placed a warm kiss to the inside, where her blood ran near the surface.

The gesture seemed more intimate than a kiss on the mouth.

She shivered as he moved to set the amber bracelet on the night table. The little metallic *click* made her jump.

"Relax," he said, returning to the chair. "I'm not going to pounce."

Watching him remove his cravat and loosen the laces on his shirt, she felt anything but relaxed.

He pulled off his boots and stockings. "So…do you want out?"

She shook her head infinitesimally.

"I'll play your maid, since she's not here," he said, moving to her with an easy smile. He knelt again and drew off her shoes. "Jane, isn't it?"

"Yes, Jane."

He reached beneath her skirts, feeling for the ribbons that tied her garters. No man had ever touched her legs. "Trick, I—"

She broke off, because she didn't know what to say. She had no cause to protest—he was her husband. And he'd offered her an out.

Twice.

"Does your maid not do this?"

"Well, yes." She felt a garter come loose, and his fingers

traced down her calf, rolling the stocking off in a way that sent ripples of sensation over her skin. "But…with Jane it doesn't feel like this," she managed.

"I would hope not." He raised a brow, making short work of the second garter, then held it up, all lace and satin ribbon. "A lovely little French confection, aye?"

"Madame Beaumont imports them. How did you know it came from France?"

He shrugged. "Lucky guess."

She wondered if he'd removed other French garters. He certainly seemed rather good at it.

Her second stocking came off in a whisper of silk, and he stood, bringing her up with him. He pressed his lips to her forehead, and she melted a little inside.

He gathered her close, resting his chin on her crown. "Your hair smells like lavender fields, *leannan*."

His low, throaty voice went right through her. She'd wondered what the marriage bed was all about, and now she had a husband of her own. Very soon she would find out.

You should know it will hurt…

Determined to calm her quivering nerves, to project an inner confidence she didn't feel, she looked up at him. "I thought that toast was the only Gaelic you knew."

"Pardon?"

"What does it mean, that word *leannan*?"

"I…I'm not sure." His brow creased. "It just slipped out. My mother used to call me that, I think."

"Maybe it means 'misbehaving young man.'"

His laughter filled the small chamber. "I think not." Still smiling, he moved to detach her stomacher. "Does your maid do this?"

"Yes," she whispered, watching as he worked the tabs. The silver embroidery on her borrowed gown glistened in the firelight. When…how had it been lit? she wondered vaguely. But

Trick's lips were on her neck, doing strange things to the pit of her stomach, and she couldn't seem to think straight.

He set the stomacher on a chest at the foot of the bed. "Does your maid do this?" His hands moved to pull the pins from her hair. "I think—what is this?" He jerked back, holding up a long red curl, his face registering utter disbelief.

"It's a false curl. To make my hair plumper."

"Plumper? Who needs plump hair?"

He raked his fingers through her tresses, coming out with two more curls and…

"Wires? Why wires?"

"To make the curls stand out." Kendra shifted on her feet, suddenly feeling like Medusa. She tugged her own hands through her hair, plucking out several more wires and three additional curls. "That's six? I think that's all."

"Where do you get these? Wait—I'd rather not know." He tossed the curls away in disgust and combed the tangles from her hair with his fingers. "Have you any more surprises for me, then? Are your pretty lips your own? Maybe some false hips are hiding beneath that lovely gown?"

"No." Her hands went to her hips. "These are mine. You don't…they're too wide, you think?"

"Nothing about you is wide." He settled her hair over her shoulders, a curtain down her back. "Except perhaps your smile, and that hair, but we won't be seeing that again now, will we? Or should I have thrown those curls into the fireplace?" He laughed as his hands covered hers, his thumbs tracing her hipbones. "Ah, the better to bear my children, aye?"

She shook her head. "Trick, the things you say…"

"Ah…" He leaned over her. "The things I say are nothing compared to the things I do." His hands moved to cup her face, and he caught her up in a long, deep kiss.

Her knees buckled. Trick grabbed her, laughing, and swung her into his arms to deposit her on the bed. She felt dwarfed in its middle, the bedposts and ice-blue damask towering around her, but when Trick came down next to her, the bed was the last thing on her mind.

Coming up on an elbow, he leaned over her. "Does your maid do this?" he asked, slowly untying the bow at the top of her laces.

"N-no. At least, not like that," she breathed, feeling his fingers part the front of her dress. Her chemise was under it, but still… "I never—"

She broke off, suddenly more than terrified.

Paralyzed.

He froze as well, watching her. "You never what?"

You should know it will hurt…

"I can't do this," she blurted out. "I'm sorry. It's too soon. I didn't expect to be married. I didn't expect *any* of this. I'm—"

"All right," he said, pulling his hands away.

"I'm not ready—"

"Kendra." He blew out a breath. "I said it's all right. We can wait."

She blinked. "Do you mean it?"

"I wouldn't say it if I didn't mean it." Sitting up on the edge of the bed, he rubbed his face with his hands. "I won't ever force you."

She looked away, feeling so far out of the realm of anything familiar, she had no idea how she should appear, act, or respond. "Thank you," she said finally.

"You're welcome." With a sigh, he rose. "I'll give you time to ready yourself for sleep."

Without another word, he walked over and drew a dressing gown from the wardrobe, then left the room.

It sounded like he was planning to come back. She had no idea what to do. It was night, and she had no nightclothes. Feeling shaky, she rose and removed her gown, then climbed back into the big bed in her long white chemise. There she lay waiting. There was nothing else she could do. For better or worse, she was wed to Trick Caldwell.

She wondered if things could get worse.

A while later, he came back into the room and stood over her. His golden hair gleamed in the firelight. "I tried to take it slow, tried to make this night easy for you. Why did you get scared?"

"I don't know," she hedged, fearing he'd think her a coward. But he was being kind. He was being patient with her. He deserved the truth. "I'm…Caithren told me it will hurt," she found herself confessing in a rush.

"It might." He dropped to sit on the mattress. "But not much, from what I understand, and more importantly, it will hurt only the first time."

"Are you sure?"

"I'm sure." Angling toward her, he smoothed her hair back from her forehead. "Did you come to this marriage a complete innocent? Did your brothers not tell you anything? Anything at all?"

"My brothers always stuttered when I brought up anything of the sort. I believe they each think one of the others took care of this matter."

He shook his head good-naturedly, clearly sympathizing with her brothers' predicament. Then he took a deep breath and blew it out before leaning close. One of his fingers trailed, achingly slowly, from her forehead along the bridge of her nose. He tossed the hair from his eyes and captured her gaze with his, his finger trailing lower, tracing her lips.

"We'll wait," he said, his voice low, his accent so thick she had to strain to catch the words. "We'll wait until you beg me to end the waiting. And you will."

He paused for so long, so still, that Kendra wondered if he'd ceased breathing. Then he moved to the other side of the bed and wormed his way in beside her, leaving her staring at his back and wondering if he was right.

TWELVE

THE NEXT morning, Kendra was more than relieved when Trick awakened her with a breakfast tray and told her he had "things to take care of" and would return late in the afternoon. She guessed he'd gone out to play the highwayman again and didn't quite know how she felt about that.

Or him.

Never mind that he knew how to make a decent cup of chocolate with plenty of sugar to satisfy her sweet tooth, she hadn't any idea what to say to her husband.

It felt a mite ridiculous to put on the wedding dress again, but she had nothing else to wear until her maid arrived with her luggage. She washed up and used Trick's comb to neaten her hair, then clasped on the amber bracelet, pausing for a moment to appreciate how the diamonds caught the light. Though she wondered if Trick still considered her "worthy," the bracelet was beautiful, and she intended to enjoy it.

She munched on bread spread with orange butter as she wandered about the cottage. There were three more rooms off the corridor, but Trick had apparently found no use for them. The few pieces of furniture were covered in sheets, the floors and walls clean but unadorned.

Her work was cut out for her, but at least it would give her something to occupy her time. She was used to caring for an entire estate and found it hard to imagine what she would do with herself here. Looking forward to Jane showing up with her things, she anticipated the two of them spending a pleasant couple of days rearranging furniture and unpacking before she went stark raving mad with inactivity.

She chose a room for Jane and another she thought would suffice for herself, since she didn't plan to share with Trick anymore. The fourth and last room would make a nice nursery, except she had no idea when she'd get brave enough to do what it would take to fill it.

If ever.

Finished with her survey in a depressingly short time, she briefly considered going home to yell at her brothers, but remembered she wasn't speaking to them. She wandered to the bookshelves that lined the corridor. Noticing an abundance of poetry, she chose a book of Shakespeare's sonnets and the first two volumes of Milton's *Paradise Lost*, then sat herself in the main room to await her maid's arrival.

She was bored silly by the time Trick showed up, instead.

~

*H*E'D SAID HE wanted to give her a "tour of the countryside," as though she hadn't lived in the countryside half her life. He'd brought an elaborate supper for them to share in the caleche on the way, though she couldn't imagine where he'd obtained it.

They'd driven through miles of rich farmland and a country village called Amberley that bustled with prosperity. All the while, he'd kept up an entertaining travelogue but raised no personal subjects. Nor had he responded to her discreet probing, skillfully turning the topic back to the scenery instead.

Three hours later she knew nothing more about him than she

had when she said her vows. And after all that had happened between them last night, he hadn't even touched her.

Not that she wasn't relieved, but nothing about him seemed to add up, and that in itself was disquieting.

The sun was low in the sky when she dropped her napkin into the picnic basket and licked roast chicken off her fingers. "What if Jane and my trunks arrive and we're not home to meet her?"

"Don't worry yourself. We'll be there soon." He put his hand on her knee, then looked down and snatched it back, flexing it before gripping the caleche's reins.

Her knee tingled where his fingers had lain. "But—"

"Don't worry," he repeated. "We're nearly home now."

"No, we're not." She had an excellent sense of direction. Though their meandering journey had brought them back near the cottage, he was now driving the opposite way. "It's—"

"There." He inclined his head as he guided the caleche off the road and onto a well-groomed drive. A very long drive. Tall trees lined the way, and an enormous mansion stood at the end.

Built of russet brick with more windows and chimneys than she could count, the mansion had to be at least the size of Cainewood Castle. Except Cainewood was mostly ancient, damaged, and closed-up, while this home sparkled with newness.

"There?" She frowned at an ostentatious clock tower atop the building. Eight o'clock. Little more than a day since she'd been wed, and she'd never felt so lost in her life. "Whatever do you mean? What is this?"

"Your new home." His wide mouth quirked in a half-smile. "Do you like it?"

"L-like it?" she sputtered. "I don't understand." Her hands twisted together in her lap, her fingers finding the amber bracelet and worrying the smooth, polished stones. "Do you work here?"

He blinked, then smiled wider. "Why, yes, I do."

"What of the cottage?"

"No, I don't work there. Not usually, in any case. It's more a place to escape, get off by myself for a while—ah, here we are."

Puzzled, Kendra turned from Trick to the house, where the double doors were flung open and a steady stream of crimson-liveried servants poured out and down the wide marble steps.

"Welcome home, your grace."

"Our congratulations!"

"Such a lovely bride!"

"Your grace." A straight-backed, gray-haired man extended one white-gloved hand to Kendra, presumably to help her down.

She paused before putting her fingers in his, looking about in utter confusion. "Your grace?" she repeated under her breath.

"Your grace," Trick confirmed, helping her to the gravel. Two grooms appeared from nowhere and took the caleche while more servants scurried to join the double line that flanked the tall, carved front doors.

Trick grasped Kendra by the elbow and guided her toward the steps. "May I present my wife, the Duchess of Amberley. I trust you will all do your best to see she's happy here."

Happy? She nodded and smiled stiffly, all the while planning Trick's murder.

Which would come right after her brothers'.

THIRTEEN

"YOU'RE A DUKE! The Duke of *Amberley*, no less!" It was unbelievable. No wonder Colin had said the amber bracelet was fitting. She hooked two fingers through it, barely resisting an urge to rip it off.

"Such venom. Losh, you say it as though a duke is the worst sort of knave."

"In this case, he is." Kendra paced the red-velvet-hung bedchamber. "How dare you keep such a secret from me!"

"I don't hold with lying, Kendra. But your brothers asked me not to tell you, and I reckoned it was harmless enough, in the scheme of things."

"Harmless? You tricked me! I would never have married you had I known—"

"Even though you were in love with me?"

Kendra wanted to slap the smug look off his handsome face. "Love, hah! Why, I don't even know you. Wherever did you get such an absurd idea?"

"Your brothers told me."

"They knew nothing about it." Feeling color creep into her cheeks, she hastened to add, "It wouldn't matter, anyway. Whatever I may or may not have felt for you was destroyed by your lie."

"Heart's wounds." Trick sighed and dropped onto a tufted brocade chair. "It wasn't a lie, and most certainly not an important one."

She only glared at him, her jaw set.

"And what, pray tell, is so bad about being a duchess? Every other girl in England would be thrilled beyond words to find herself wed to a duke."

"I'm not like other girls, and I am never beyond words."

"Why does that not surprise me?" Trick returned dryly. He crossed his long legs at the ankles. "I really don't understand this, Kendra. How can marrying a duke be such a disastrous occurrence?"

"It's too hard to explain."

"Try." He crossed his arms. "I'm listening."

With a huff of impatience, she sat on the red velvet bed. She parked her hands behind her and looked up, trying to think. Above her loomed the underside of a gathered silk canopy fit for a king.

Or a duke, ranked above everyone but royalty.

"Your grace, it isn't the title itself that sets my teeth on edge, but what it symbolizes. To me. To the world in general. All the good people who weren't lucky enough to…"

This wasn't working. Feeling beyond words after all, she sat straight. But the expectant look in Trick's eyes only frustrated her further.

"Just look at this!" She leapt up and gestured wildly at the room: the padded, satin-lined walls, the carved and gilded ceiling, the four-poster bed crowned with garish poufs of red-dyed ostrich feathers. "See what I mean? Who wants to live in a place like this? I swear, it puts Whitehall to shame!"

He gave a short bark of a laugh at what she knew must be a look of utter disgust on her face. "I know women who would kill for—"

"Kill for this? That's the first thing you've said all day that makes any sense."

"I don't care for this decor, either," he said calmly. "But why do you hate it so much? I want to understand."

"Oh, I knew this would be impossible to explain! It's long, and it's convoluted, and it doesn't seem to make sense to anyone but me. It's certainly never made sense to any of my brothers."

"I'm not your brothers. Tell me, however long it takes."

With a sigh, she sat back down and thought for a long minute, then clasped her hands in her lap before beginning.

"I won't pretend I don't enjoy balls and pretty clothes and the other things money can buy as much as the next girl. But I think I know what's important beneath all the trappings. I told my brothers again and again that I don't care about titles. I wanted to marry a man I was wildly in love with, but even more, a man I could admire. For who he was inside, not a false honor that society had settled upon him."

"I didn't ask to be a duke—" Trick began.

Waving him off, she jumped up again, not at all ready to listen yet. "During the Commonwealth," she said as she resumed pacing, "my family's title was a liability, not an asset. We hadn't the choice to stay home and go about our business like normal people. Instead we were exiled paupers, dragged from Paris, to Cologne, to Brussels, Bruges, Antwerp—wherever King Charles and his court wandered. It was then I learned it's what's inside a person that counts. Some people were kind to us, and some were not. And their rank had nothing to do with it." Her voice dropping, she stopped and turned to him. "And…"

"And what?" he asked softly.

She knew this would sound ridiculous, but she couldn't help it—it was how she felt. "As a little girl, I decided the dukes were the worst. The most pompous, the least caring, the most annoyed with orphaned children underfoot. Because of that, to me, they represent the worst of humanity. The worst of everything."

He swept the hair from his face, his expression clearing. "That's why your brothers asked me to marry you under my given name only," he murmured. "Because you would have refused."

"Probably," she conceded. "And now I'm stuck in this gaudy museum."

He looked heavenward—or rather, gilded-ceilingward. "Come now, it's not that bad."

"I would rather live in the cottage."

"Come to think of it, so would I." Evidently it was his turn to pace now, because he rose and did so before the carved stone mantel. "My father built this deuced palace, not I," he said contemplatively. "Let's move to the cottage. I'll alert Cavanaugh to pack my things, and Jane needn't even unpack yours. We'll make haste for the cottage immediately."

She swallowed hard. "Are you sure?"

He turned to her and raised a brow. "Are *you* sure?"

A long silence stretched between them before Kendra sighed. "No," she said, unsure of anything at the moment. "I don't want to live in that little cottage. Well, actually, it's a big cottage, but you know what I mean."

She dropped to sit on the bed. "I'm accustomed to directing a large household, and I'll do you proud. It's only…when I think of all the money it takes to run a place like this—all the servants and goods—for just the two of us…can't we close up some of it? Close up most of it? Most of Cainewood is closed up. We could take the money and put it to good use, helping orphans or the like."

Trick sat beside her, smelling of sandalwood soap. He must have come here and bathed, the wretch, while she'd yawned her way through the day, reading poetry.

He took her hand. "If we close up most of the house, think of the people who will lose their jobs. My father hired them, not I, but I cannot find it in my heart to put them them out on the streets."

"Oh…I hadn't thought of that."

His smile, crooked but genuine, did much to thaw her icy anger. "But I've something to show you tomorrow. Something I think will please you."

"What?" She leaned closer.

But then she caught herself and pulled her hand from his grasp. He'd still lied to her, tricked her, and that was hard to forgive. Especially now, with all the years together that loomed ahead…years and years.

"What do you want to show me?" she asked.

"Patience, lass. Let's get you settled first. Tomorrow will be soon enough." His smile faded when she yawned. "Sleepy, are you?"

"I didn't sleep much last night. So much has happened so fast." She sighed, then fell back to the pillows. "I know it's early still, but I'd like to just go to bed."

"Excellent idea. Yesterday was a long and difficult day." Trick rose, shrugged out of his surcoat, and began unlacing his shirt. "I believe I'll join you."

She leapt from the bed. "Oh! I thought this was *my* chamber."

"It is." The shirt came off over his head, and her eyes widened.

His bare chest looked sculpted, with a light sprinkling of blond hair that glimmered in the firelight. She swallowed hard. "Then where is your chamber?"

"It's mine, too." He sat to pull off his boots. "We're married. We're allowed to share a chamber. I've a piece of paper to prove it."

"But…" She glanced around wildly. "This is a suite, isn't it? What's on the other side of that door?"

"A dressing chamber. Feel free to use it. Your clothes are inside." At her look of astonishment, he added, "Jane has been here all day, arranging your things. I gave her the evening off."

"I thought you said she hadn't unpacked yet. And she's *my* maid."

"I believe she's in my employ, now." His second boot hit the floor with a thud.

"You're a duke, for heaven's sake. Don't you have a valet?"

"Cavanaugh. But I prefer to undress myself, much to the poor man's constant chagrin." His hands on the waistband of his breeches, he looked up. "Actually, I'd prefer to have you undress me, but…" A wry grin revealed that irresistible chipped tooth, and the twinkle in his eye was unsettling. "No, I thought not. But I can play your maid again tonight, if you wish."

"No, thank you." She stalked over to the dressing room and shut the door behind her, then had to duck back into the bedchamber for a candle. Gritting her teeth against his laugh, she closeted herself again and began hunting for a night rail.

Every bit as fancy as the bedchamber, the dressing room had a delicate wood table and two upholstered, fringed stools in the center. One wall was covered with an enormous gilt-framed mirror, another wall was lined with wardrobe cabinets, and there were two walls of those newfangled chests of drawers.

The first drawer she opened was filled with Trick's folded things, and she slammed it shut. She found her own clothes in the third chest she tried. Quickly she stripped out of the wedding dress, diving into the thickest, most voluminous night rail she owned. Her fingers fumbled with the clasp of the amber bracelet, but she finally managed to remove it and set it on the little inlaid table.

The bracelet sat there, taunting her. Amber. The Duchess of Amberley…

Od's fish, however had she ended up in this predicament? Exactly where she'd sworn she'd never be.

When she reopened the door, Trick was in the bed, and—from all she could tell—stark naked. She paced beside the carved gilt monstrosity, hoping he was already asleep.

His hand shot out to grab hers, stopping her in her tracks. "I gave you my word; I won't ever try to coerce you. You needn't worry."

She bit her lip, eyeing his bare arm and shoulders. "Is that so?"

"Aye. You're safe, I assure you."

"Can…can I not have another room?"

"Is something wrong with this one?"

"It's…too masculine."

"Too masculine?"

"Yes." Her tone dared him to disagree, since nothing could be farther from the truth. The red chamber was satin and velvet, feathers and lace—altogether too fussy for her tastes. It looked like a brothel. Or what she imagined a brothel might look like, in any case. "This was your father's chamber, wasn't it? I believe I'd be more comfortable in your mother's chamber. Where is it?"

"In Scotland," he said shortly, patting the mattress beside him. "Come, Kendra, enough of this. I'm sleepy, and you look ready to drop."

With a sigh, she walked around the bed and gingerly lay on top of the covers.

Sounding exasperated, his voice drifted over his shoulder. "Get under the blanket. It's drafty in this gargantuan house."

Her toes *were* going rather numb. Giving in, she scooted beneath the coverlet. The feather bed was soft and comfortable. Lying flat on her back, she could feel the rise and fall of Trick's breathing next to her, the warmth of his body even across the space that divided them.

When he rolled close and laid an arm loosely across her middle, she flinched.

"Shh, it's all right. Rest." He raised himself to kiss the tip of her nose, his lips soft and teasing. His amber eyes held hers, making her stomach flutter. Her arms itched to wrap themselves around his neck and draw him down for one of those heart-stopping kisses.

But she knew what that would lead to.

"Aye, *leannan*, you're right," he whispered, his eyes full of meaning.

Had he read her mind?

She felt his body pressing her into the mattress, and his mouth brushed hers. Despite her reservations, she couldn't stop her pulse speeding up, or the tiny whimper that escaped her throat.

He smiled against her lips. "Aye, you'll be begging soon enough," he said, then turned away to blow out the candle.

Shaking—from vexation and embarrassment and an unwelcome sensation she could only call, well, lust—Kendra stared into the darkness and wondered if she'd ever get any sleep while she was married to Trick Caldwell.

FOURTEEN

"WAKE UP, milady. I mean, your grace."

Kendra forced open her eyes to see Jane standing over her.

"I've brought you some breakfast, or should I say dinner?" The maid set a tray on the bed. "It's late, and his grace is waiting to take you somewhere. A surprise, he said."

"A surprise?" Struggling into a sitting position, Kendra reached for a cup of chocolate. "He said he had something to show me today, but—"

"A surprise, yes." Jane's tall, thin figure disappeared into the dressing room. "He suggested you wear your simplest gown."

The sound of wardrobes opening and closing came through the open door. "Why would that be?" Kendra asked.

"Well, if you're not knowing, then how could I?" The maid came in with a plain peach-velvet gown, unadorned but for a narrow lace edging around the neckline and spills of matching lace at the wrists. No overskirt, no jewels or embroidery on the stomacher. "Do you suppose this will do?"

Kendra swallowed a mouthful of bread and cheese. "I'm sure it's fine," she said without enthusiasm.

Jane ducked into the dressing room again, her chirpy voice drifting back out. "Brown shoes rather than gold, I'm thinking."

Kendra took another bite and chewed, not thinking at all. Her brain was now fuzzy from too much sleep.

"And a chemise, and…lud, would you look at this lovely bracelet? Where'd this come from, milady? I mean, your grace?"

"Milady will more than do," Kendra grumbled. "And leave the bracelet there."

Jane appeared in the open doorway, her round face marred by a puzzled frown. Winking in the noon sun that streamed through the window, the amber bracelet dangled from her fingers. "Was this a gift from your husband?"

"A wedding gift, yes."

"Then for certain he'd want you to wear it."

Setting down the bread, Kendra caught a glimpse of the gold ringing her finger. Enough of a reminder that she was married to a lying duke. "I don't care for it, Jane."

Her maid's mouth hung open. "But it's so beautiful. And his grace is so handsome and kind—do you not want to please him?"

Of course Jane would think Trick was kind—he'd given her half a day off. And he hadn't lied to her, either. "I really don't care for it," Kendra repeated. "Put it away for me, will you? I expect his grace will forget all about it—you know how men are."

"Very well." A doubtful look in her gray eyes, Jane disappeared back into the dressing room. She came out carrying the shoes and chemise and set them on the foot of the bed. "Are you happy here, milady?"

"Of course I'm happy." Gesturing at the rich, garish chamber, Kendra forced a smile. "Look at this place. How could one not be happy here?"

FIFTEEN

"**M**R. CALDWELL!" A dozen children bounded down the steps of the sprawling Tudor manor house and clustered around Trick. Laughing, he reached to squeeze shoulders and pat heads, leaving no child unacknowledged.

Kendra stared in utter disbelief. "Mr. Caldwell?"

"Part of your surprise." He shot her a sheepish grin before turning back to the young ones. They'd focused their attention on Kendra, gaping at her with frank curiosity. Trick waved a hand in her direction. "This is my new wife. Er…Mrs. Caldwell."

"Please, just call me Kendra," she rushed to say, smoothing the skirt of the peach gown. Goodness, a new name was a hard thing to get used to. It felt downright strange.

As a duchess, she had no proper surname anymore—she'd be signing letters with her husband's title, as Kendra Amberley. She didn't feel like a duchess, but neither did she feel like Mrs. Caldwell.

"I'm glad of your acquaintance, Mrs. Kendra." A tall, skinny lad held his hand out to her, looking toward Trick for approval. At her husband's nod, the boy reached to grasp Kendra's hand and kissed the back of it fervently.

"Ahem. Andrew." When the boy looked chagrined, Trick mussed his dark, stick-straight hair. "A lad cannot help but admire a pretty lass, aye?"

"Oh, yes," Andrew said reverently, and Kendra watched Trick bite his lip to keep from laughing.

"Mrs. Jackson, there you are." Trick waded through the sea of children, making his way toward a plump, matronly woman with gray curls and a pleasant face. He fished a black pouch from his surcoat pocket and handed it over. "Here you go. I apologize for being late. I've been…busy."

"I can see that." The woman smiled at Kendra.

"Mrs. Jackson, may I present my wife—"

"Mrs. Kendra," Andrew supplied in a worshipful tone.

Kendra didn't have the heart to correct him. "I'm glad of your acquaintance, Mrs. Jackson." She executed a tiny bow, for all the world as though they were at Whitehall Palace.

Mrs. Jackson beamed. "Likewise, your gr—Mrs. Kendra." Kendra heard the metallic clink of coins as the woman sifted through the pouch. "So generous, Mr. Caldwell! The children are grateful—as ever," she added, with a wink for Kendra.

He waved that away, looking embarrassed. "It's my pleasure. I'll not let the poor things starve so long as I have the means to help."

"Starve?" Mrs. Jackson's belly jiggled beneath her apron as her laughter rang through the heavy summer air. "They're better fed than half the parish. Why, I daresay some villagers pray nightly to be orphaned so they may find themselves at Caldwell Manor."

Caldwell Manor? Did Trick finance this entire operation, then? Kendra looked toward her husband, his golden hair glinting in the late afternoon sun, and her heart softened a little.

He laughed. "Let's hope not. A hearty meal is a sad substitute for parents. How is little Susanna?"

"Much better. Her fever is down and she's sitting and taking milk. I trust she'll be up and about in a day or two."

"I'm pleased to hear it. Maybe I should pay her a visit."

"By all means. She'll be cheered to see you."

"Kendra? If you'll excuse me?"

Without waiting for her agreement, Trick climbed the six front steps in three strides and disappeared into the house. Wearing only breeches and a shirt, no cravat and no coat, he looked decidedly unduke-ish. Through that battered oak door passed someone who had accomplished Kendra's own dream, opening an orphanage.

Stunned, she stared after him while the children scattered through the garden, picking up balls and hoops.

A little boy wandered over with an armful of black and white fur. "Do you want to pet our kitty?"

"Cats make me sneeze," she told him regretfully. "But she's adorable."

"He," the boy corrected. "Our cat is a boy. But our dog is a girl," he added, gesturing across the lawn to where a brown, floppy-eared pup was bounding after a tossed stick.

Did other orphanages have pets? She had no notion. But watching another boy giggle as he played fetch with the enthusiastic dog made her think it was a brilliant idea.

Two girls tugged shyly on her skirts. "Will you play with us, Mrs. Kendra?"

She smiled down at them. "What would you care to play?"

They settled on blindman's buff, and the game went on for a while, other children joining in. When an impish lad named Thomas stole the blindfold and ran away laughing, the others raced after him. Kendra tried to follow but got halfway around the house and stopped. Thanks to her high Louis heels, the merry chase had far outstripped her ability to keep up.

Trick had been right to suggest a plain gown—next time she'd wear flat shoes, too. Wondering what was taking him so long, she made her way over to where Mrs. Jackson was hanging laundry.

"Have you an idea where my h-husband"—her tongue tripped over the word—"might have got himself off to?"

"Of course," the older woman said, tossing a nightshirt back into the basket. "I'll show you the way to the sickroom."

She led her around the corner of the house and up the front steps. "I bless your husband nightly for saving these children."

"Bless you for caring for them," Kendra returned, glancing around the entry. Though the house and its furnishings were well-worn and far out of date, it was clean and cheerful. "Are the children receiving an education?"

"Mercy, yes. His grace has seen to it that tutors attend to that. All but the youngest can figure and read and write—"

"Girls, too?"

"Yes, indeed. Your husband has some odd ideas."

They skirted a few wooden toys on the floor as Mrs. Jackson led her down a corridor. "Are they instructed in the classics? Latin and—"

"Nay, not as yet. I cannot imagine what children like this would be needing with Latin. But with the duke directing things, you never know what will happen next at Caldwell Manor." The woman's ample bosom quivered with a good-natured if slightly befuddled chuckle. "Here we are."

In the room Mrs. Jackson indicated, a young girl, perhaps five or so, sat propped among pillows in a four-poster bed that looked as though it had rested on the same spot for a century or more. Kendra paused in the doorway.

"They're busy," Mrs. Jackson whispered.

Trick sat in a straight-backed chair by the bed, an open book in his lap. The girl leaned forward, apparently engrossed in whatever he was reading. Feeling like an eavesdropper, Kendra listened as well.

"'Then have I gained a right good man this day,' quoth jolly Robin," came Trick's throaty voice. "'What name goest thou by, good fellow?'"

"And what did he say?" the child asked.

"The stranger answered, 'Men call me John Little whence I came.'"

The girl's blond curls bounced as she shook her head. "No, it's Little John!" she corrected, her brown eyes wide with delight.

Trick glanced up from the leather-bound book. "Aye, but that was Will Stutely's doing. He loved a good jest and said"—he looked back down at the book—"'Nay, fair little stranger. I like not thy name and fain would I have it otherwise. Little art thou, indeed, and small of bone and sinew; therefore shalt thou be christened Little John, and I will be thy godfather.' Then Robin Hood and all his band laughed aloud until the stranger began to grow angry…"

Kendra could only gape. She felt like one of the Graiae, three sisters who had but one eye between them. What was she seeing? A highwayman, telling a story to an ill orphan? Or a duke? Right now, he looked like neither.

She backed away from the doorway. She didn't know this man, not in the least.

SIXTEEN

"**ROBIN HOOD,**" Kendra said on their way home, in that forthright way of hers that never failed to make Trick smile. "It's fitting, I'll credit you that."

"Oh?" The caleche's wheels crunched on the dusty road as he wound the horses through the gentle hills toward Amberley House. "Whatever makes you think so?"

"Don't jest with me. It's obvious!"

"Aye?" He looked over at her, but she was gazing straight ahead, her bright hair glistening in the slanting late-afternoon sunshine.

"I do believe I'm beginning to understand you."

"Pray, enlighten me," he said dryly. "I've been struggling to understand myself since childhood."

She snorted. "*You* are playing Robin Hood," she said with that same cocksure confidence that had drawn him to her the first time they'd spoken.

Heart's wounds, was that but three days ago?

"Only instead of stealing from the rich," she continued, "you're robbing the Roundheads, who are no doubt responsible for making most of those children orphans anyway." She sighed. "I do believe I could love you for this."

It was his turn to snort. "The fellow you think you see isn't me at all. I *wish* I could be that fellow," he added under his breath.

"Balderdash. It's well done of you, Trick."

He shook his head. "My father wanted to build himself a monument, so he spent every shilling he'd ever made on the mansion and abandoned that perfectly good manor house. I wanted to see it put to use, that's all. Filled with children, as it might have been had he ever cared a whit for his family."

She turned to him, her heart in her eyes. "That's why you play the highwayman, then, isn't it? To pay for the children, since your father spent all his money on the mansion and left you without adequate funds."

"Not precisely." He was about to add that he'd turned his father's illicit enterprise into a prosperous legitimate shipping company, but thought better of it. He didn't like hiding things from her—especially after how she'd reacted to learning he was a duke—but blast it, his hands were tied.

It was no fault of his he was stuck in this situation. He'd been wracking his brain for a believable excuse to continue playing the highwayman, and she'd just dropped one in his lap. Never mind that he could support Caldwell Manor ten times over. She didn't have to know that. Not right now, anyway.

"When I tell my brothers—"

"Don't. Don't tell them anything. I promised them I'd stop the highway robbery."

"No, you didn't. You ducked that issue cleverly." How very perceptive she was—and how very inconvenient *that* could prove. "If you stop, the children will suffer, and I couldn't bear to be responsible for such a thing. I was an orphan, myself."

"Aye, well, any feeling human being would be sympathetic to their plight." Trick's mind raced, scrambling for an alternative, a way to avoid these secrets and lies. But he saw no choice. He'd promised King Charles he wouldn't breathe a word of the real purpose behind the highwayman ruse.

He sneaked Kendra a guilty glance. She twisted her hands in her lap, and the imported lace fell back from her wrist, leaving it bare. "Why aren't you wearing the amber bracelet?"

"It doesn't go with this plain gown."

He wondered why he found her flip answer so disturbing. "Are you still angry with me for being a duke?"

"I'm not sure what I feel. I don't like being lied to." Though she directed those words to the sky, she soon looked back to him. "Did you ever feel abandoned as a child?"

"In a sense," he said slowly, wishing he and Kendra could go back in time and start over. He didn't want their relationship ending up like his parents'. "My father took me from my mother when I was five—well, very nearly six, actually. I'd seen him but a few times over the years, and I'd never been more than a dozen miles from our home in Scotland." The caleche bumped over a particularly rocky stretch of the path, and he reached to steady Kendra. "He took me to France. It was… unpleasant. He wanted me only to further his business dealings."

"His business dealings?" She subtly shifted away from his touch. "He was a duke, was he not?"

"An impoverished one. He lost everything, including Amberley, helping finance the war. He regained his title and land after the restoration, but there was little money after the war. Not enough for him, anyway. The greedy old boar. Ruthless, too, he was. Not a man one would be proud to claim as a relation." Trick knew he sounded resentful, but he couldn't seem to check the bitterness in his tone. This was why he usually avoided the topic. It was wrong to speak ill of the dead.

And he certainly had nothing good to say about Father.

Gingerly, Kendra prompted: "So he rebuilt his fortune?"

Trick nodded. "Trading in spirits, among other things. Madeira was his ticket to riches. Every bottle that graced the tables at the courts—French and English alike—passed through his hands." He hesitated, then decided to come clean with it.

Enough secrets stood between the two of them already. "He was a smuggler."

She gasped. "A smuggler?"

"Aye. One doesn't amass a fortune paying import taxes—at least not on the scale that he managed. You can imagine why I chose not to continue his enterprise, though it was highly lucrative." Since that half-truth caused him no small discomfort, he added, "And as he made me an accomplice in his crimes, you can imagine as well why I felt lost—abandoned—as a child."

Some small measure of honesty, at least.

"But your mother—"

"She let me go," he said, the words studiously detached. He would never admit it still hurt inside after all this time. "In eighteen years, she never once tried to reclaim me, or even make contact. In all that time, I haven't seen so much as one letter." Crickets chirped as they drove beneath a canopy of trees silhouetted against the cerulean sky. "And besides which, she's just as bad as he was. I had fond memories of her once, when I was too young to see her for what she is—a wicked woman. A Covenanter, plotting against king and country. And a loose woman as well."

"How would you know all that? You weren't even six when you left."

"My father told me. Blackguard though he was, I don't believe he lied about my mother; he must have had good reasons for leaving her. He never did anything without a good reason."

In Trick's estimation, his parents had frankly deserved one another, each as selfish and uncaring as the other. Perhaps that was human nature, but Trick wanted to do better. Was determined to do better.

He would make this marriage work if it killed him.

"Tomorrow I need to go to London," he said.

Kendra's eyes danced. "I love London. Have you a house in town?"

"Aye. And I'm sure you'll find it every bit as disgustingly

opulent as Amberley House." He smiled on the outside while cringing internally. "I'll be going alone this time, though."

"Oh." The light in her eyes died, and his insides twisted. "Why?"

He had to leave—he'd actually, before this whirlwind of a wedding had come up, been planning to leave today. His shipping company needed his attention. The shipping company that he'd decided to keep secret from her for the time being, lest she figure out he could well afford to support the orphanage without resorting to robbery.

"I had arranged it," he said quickly, "before we met."

As he guided the caleche onto Amberley's long approach, he ran a hand through his hair and cast her an appraising glance. Her expression had turned contemplative. He could almost see the wheels turning in her pretty red head.

"Perhaps we can put aside some money and invest," she said. "In the future, with careful planning, playing the highwayman might become unnecessary. With any luck, before you ever get caught and"—her voice dropped—"strung up at Tyburn." She turned on the bench seat to face him. "I'll help you."

"You will not. I won't have you endangering yourself—"

Her laughter rang through the deepening shadows. "I didn't mean with the robberies, but with the investing. I've a knack with finances—you can ask Jason."

"He lets you invest his money?"

She stiffened beside him. "Not independently, but I've helped him make decisions, yes."

"Whoa, there." He put a hand on her arm, pleased when she didn't pull away. "I wasn't disapproving, just asking."

"All right, then." Her expression softened. "It's only that I don't know you, and—"

"I don't know you, either."

"True enough." After a considered pause, an unmistakable glimmer lit her green eyes. "As for the highway robbery, I have a good aim—"

"Ye won't." Hearing his accent broadening, he winced. What was it about her that got under his skin? Pulling up before Amberley House, he tugged on the reins with more force than was necessary before taking her by the shoulders. "I mean it, Kendra."

"I was jesting," she whispered, her smile sweet. Something inside him seemed to shift. It was such a small space to bring his lips to hers; he did it without thinking. Her mouth was soft and yielding, and he felt her pulse race beneath his fingertips on her neck. Their lips clung for a long, heady moment before he pulled away.

"Oh," she whispered. "I cannot keep my head when you do that."

"Aye?" He couldn't help but grin as he handed the reins to a groom and hopped down from the caleche.

Perhaps this marriage wouldn't kill him after all.

SEVENTEEN

SEATED AT Trick's desk, Kendra frowned at the ledger in front of her. "So you've been living here at Amberley for six months?"

"Aye. And I fired Rankill after two." Trick took a sip of bracing whisky, then set the glass on the table beside his favorite leather armchair.

He'd returned from seeing to his London interests to hear his wife had spent the past week examining his books and inspecting his property. After recovering from the shock, he'd decided he was pleased. With that part of their relationship, at least.

Now that he was back home, he'd work on the other part. He'd made progress before he left—he was sure of it. Though he'd as soon strangle her brothers for being right, he had to admit he and Kendra were a good match. They simply needed to get past these initial difficulties.

"Were my suspicions about Rankill's dishonesty on target, then?" he asked her, feeling more than awkward requesting his wife's opinion of his estate business. But between the king's mission and the demands of his shipping company, he had precious little time to see to Amberley. "Was I right to let him go?"

"You should have done it earlier." She glanced up. "Your father died three years ago. What brought you back now?"

He couldn't tell her he'd moved home at King Charles's request to track down a problem in the region. Or that he'd agreed to do so in exchange for a pardon from old smuggling charges. The threat of losing Amberley and the title had been veiled and, truth be told, unnecessary. Trick cared not a whit for his father's legacy and would have agreed to the mission out of patriotism and friendship alone.

But, nay, he couldn't tell Kendra any of that.

"I decided Amberley was in need of my attention," he said instead.

"Well, you haven't paid it much," she retorted.

Noticing she still wasn't wearing his bracelet, he sighed and sipped again, feigning unconcern. "What evidence is there that Rankill embezzled?"

"Look here." She waved him over. "Amberley's northwest quarter is capable of producing many more bushels than are recorded. And in the east"—she startled when he leaned over her—"this land will support more sheep than are shown in the records." Slowly she shifted, turning to meet his eyes.

He'd missed her lavender scent. Bracing himself with one hand on the desk, he held her gaze steadily. "Is that so?"

"Y-yes." She drew a breath and looked back down. "As a matter of fact, I counted fifty more head than are noted in the ledger. And you should purchase yet more. You're not maximizing your profits in this area."

"*Our* profits." They were in this together. He didn't think he'd quite realized that till now, or how much of a relief it was to find himself "saddled" with a wife who had turned out to be so competent.

If only they could get past her fear of the marriage bed, life would be nearly perfect.

"Thank you." He leaned closer and pressed his lips to the top of her head.

She stilled, and he heard her swallow hard. "You're welcome. You can sit back down now."

Seeing her flustered was heartening. He didn't sit back down. A long silence stretched between them before she continued.

"The point is, Amberley is quite a bit more profitable than Rankill led you to believe. Run properly, with no one siphoning income, it should be self-supporting and then some. I realize you have a standard of living to maintain—"

"*We* have a standard of living." With his free hand, he skimmed his knuckles along her cheek.

A pink flush rose where he'd touched. "Well, yes. But, thankfully, it shouldn't be long at all until this mess is resolved and Amberley can support both you—us—and the orphanage." She paused for a breath. "So you can stop the robberies now, except…"

"Aye?"

"There are some matters that need attending. Depending on whether you think they or the children should come first."

"What sort of matters?"

"Repairs and the like. Rankill took money regardless of whether you could afford it. Your people are working with broken equipment, one of the barns needs roofing—"

"You have a list?" He ran a finger down her nose and stopped with it on her lips.

"Y-yes," she whispered against his fingertip. She pulled back, her elbow knocking a quill to the carpet.

"I'll take care of it all." He leaned down to retrieve the feather and flicked it under her chin, grinning at her tiny yelp. "I think I can survive another few highwayman masquerades."

With any luck, that would be all it would take. He'd amassed much of the king's evidence already.

"Weighing your safety against the children's welfare—"

"I'll be fine."

"I hope so," she said.

She really hoped so.

In less than two weeks of being married to the Duke of Amberley, she'd been surprised to discover she liked her life here. Although she adored Jason's wife, she hadn't realized the tension she'd felt at Cainewood—how difficult it had been for her to cede responsibility when Caithren had arrived. Here, the responsibility was her own. The house, the land, the people. And like the extra layer of marzipan on her bride cake, she had her orphanage, too.

"Speaking of the children…" she began.

"Aye?" At last Trick dropped the quill on the desk and went back to sit and reclaim his drink.

Watching him, she realized this was the one chamber in Amberley House where he truly seemed at ease. Comfortable rather than opulent, it was furnished with the same classic eye to design as the cottage. Polish glinted from the deep grooves in the serviceable walnut desk where she sat, and the shelves behind Trick were stocked with well-read tomes.

"What about the children?" he asked.

"You'll remember, before you left, that I said I wanted to teach them some classical myths." She fiddled with the quill in her hands. "They're excellent learners, all of them."

One sandy brow quirked. "Even Thomas?"

"Well, maybe not Thomas." She smiled, thinking of the mischievous towhead and all the other children, all the fun she'd been having with them. "In any case, we're almost finished with the Greek stories, and before we start in on the Romans, I was thinking I'd like to throw an Olympian party."

Trick looked completely nonplussed. "A what?"

"An Olympian party. I know money is tight, but I've been pondering this, and I really don't think it will be expensive. The children can all dress up as their favorite god or goddess—I came across plenty of unused dress lengths in storage that they can wrap toga style. And decorations needn't be too costly. Phillips has agreed to help me make columns—"

"You've talked to the servants about this?"

"They think it's a fine idea. We'll eat ambrosia and drink nectar, and the children can each retell their favorite myth…it would be such a treat for them, don't you think? And reinforce what they learned, so they'll be even more eager for the next—"

"It sounds brilliant."

"It won't cost much—"

"Kendra." He set down his glass. "Have your party with my blessings."

"Really?"

The Duke of Lechmere would never have allowed it. Neither would he have allowed her a hand in the finances, which Trick had accepted with an easy grace. Hang her brothers' method of pushing them together, but she had to admit that she and Trick did suit.

If only he hadn't refused to tell her why he'd gone to London and declined to take her along. Well, not refused precisely, but dodged the question as skillfully as he did many of her others. Then again, she supposed she could hardly expect him to tell her the truth, since she'd decided he must be hiding a mistress in London.

A man has needs, she'd heard her brothers say, and she knew full well she wasn't fulfilling Trick's. So perhaps it was best if he filled those needs elsewhere, even if the thought did rankle. This way, she could have Amberley and her orphanage and Trick's companionship, without worrying about the other.

Marriage was better all around than she'd anticipated. She couldn't imagine why she'd fought it so long.

Life was nearly perfect.

EIGHTEEN

A WEEK LATER, Kendra waved to the children gathered on the steps of Caldwell Manor. "Good-bye! Take care, Mrs. Jackson!"

"Good-bye, Mrs. Kendra!" they called. "Good-bye, Mr. Caldwell!"

Yawning, Kendra wheeled Pandora around to join Trick, who was mounted on his favorite horse, Chaucer. "They're excited about the party," Trick said as they started down the lane.

"Two days. I can hardly wait. But there's still much to arrange."

"You're very organized. With everything else you find to do, I cannot believe you threw this together so quickly."

She shrugged. Planning the party had been the easiest part of her week. It had been much harder to resist her husband.

His offhand touches and occasional fleeting kisses never failed to set her ablaze, igniting her curiosity and desire for more. Yet she never quite forgot her fear.

She presumed he understood that too, as he did not touch her in bed. Though he insisted on sharing, he left her alone, which, in its own way, she found every bit as frustrating.

She hadn't come by much sleep since he'd been home.

"I think we should check on the barn," he said. "See how the roof is coming along."

She yawned again, then shook herself awake. "I'll race you."

He was off without another word.

She kicked Pandora into a gallop after him. His tawny gelding had a head start, but she slowly gained on him until they were neck and neck. She took gulps of the rushing air, feeling it revive her, enjoying the pace, the wind in her hair, the thrill of competition. When Pandora passed the barn first, ahead of Chaucer by a nose, she laughed triumphantly.

"Good girl, Pandora," she cooed, patting the mare's deep-brown neck.

"You won," Trick conceded with a grin. He slid off his horse, coming close. "Why did you name her Pandora?"

"Simple." Craftily Kendra dismounted on the far side. "Like the Greek goddess opening her box of problems, she leads me into trouble."

She started toward the barn, but he rounded Pandora and easily caught up to her. "Leads you into trouble, does she?"

"All the time. She led me to you, didn't she?" With his hand on her arm, Kendra had little choice but to stop. She turned to meet his eyes. "Trouble."

"That was her fault, aye?"

"Yes, it must have been. I certainly didn't head for Amberley on purpose."

"And are you sorry?"

Trapped in his amber gaze, she shook her head. "No," she whispered.

"Neither am I."

Kendra's heart beat double-time when he took her face between his hands. His fingers were warm, and so was his breath as he leaned in for a kiss.

"Amberley!"

Trick's hands dropped from her cheeks, and they both looked up to see a carriage approaching. A florid man stuck his head out the open window. "We've come to pay our respects," the man called. "To you and your lovely bride."

"Garrick," Trick muttered under his breath. "And Fielding, Faraday, and Milner, I'm guessing." The carriage rolled to a stop, and sure enough, four men climbed out.

Kendra recognized all of them—minor aristocrats who lived in the vicinity. Though they weren't important enough to have been on her brothers' list of potential husbands, country life was insular, and she'd met them at various entertainments over the years. Just last summer she'd danced with Fielding and Milner at Jason and Cait's wedding celebration ball. She'd found Fielding rather charming in a bumbling sort of way, but Milner's breath had smelled like overaged cheese.

"Good day, gentlemen," Trick said. "Welcome."

He didn't sound like he meant it.

Garrick walked over to pump Trick's hand. "Congratulations, congratulations."

He had a big round head and a belly to match. Apparently he needed to fill it, because when he took out his pocket watch and flipped it open, his flabby lips broke into a grin.

"We're just in time for supper, are we not?"

NINETEEN

"**T**RICK?" **KENDRA** murmured, awakened by the soft sounds of her husband moving about the bedchamber. Her eyes fluttered open to glimpse his gold hair haloed by the morning sun that streamed through the window.

Turning, he smiled and came close, leaning down to brush his lips over hers. "You fell asleep on me last night," he accused, straightening and disappearing into the dressing room.

"Did I?" She stretched beneath the covers. "I don't remember a thing past supper."

"You nodded into your chicken cullis." His voice sounded muffled, then stronger as he strode back into the room, carrying a pair of boots and a surcoat. "And I'd thought you were enjoying our impromptu party."

"And the cullis was so good," she recalled.

He grinned. "You only liked it so much because it was sweet."

"I don't expect I made a good impression. Are those men really your friends?"

"Aye, and your brothers' friends, too." He sat on a tufted velvet chair to pull on the boots. "We all play whist once a month."

"The mysterious weekend house parties." More secrets. This man was so evasive, she wondered if she'd ever truly come to know him. "Why do men have to be so secretive?" she said more darkly than she intended.

But he didn't seem to notice. "Harmless games," he answered with a shrug. "Did you not like the fellows?"

"Faraday is a terrible flirt, especially given he's married. Fielding is agreeable enough, but never quite seems to know what he's about. Garrick is rather strange, is he not? He couldn't seem to stay seated, always seemed to be poking around. I wonder what he could have been looking for? And Milner wears entirely too much scent. He should think about taking a bath instead."

His gaze on her, Trick rose. "Very astute. I couldn't have summed them up so succinctly, and I've socialized with them for months. You were with them naught but a couple of hours."

She shrugged. *"L'amitié ferme les yeux."*

"Beg pardon?"

"Friendship closes its eyes," she translated. "It's an old French saying I used to hear on the Continent."

"Ah. Quite so."

She watched him shrug into the surcoat. "What do you see in those men?"

"Money. They always lose." He grinned as he slid his sword into his belt, then took a pistol from atop the dressing table, hefting it before arming himself with it as well. "I'll see you this afternoon." He came to her, bending for one more kiss, soft and lingering, before he straightened once again. "Rest up."

With a muted click, the door closed behind him, and she listened to his footsteps retreat down the corridor. It wasn't until a few minutes later, when she replayed his words—and his kisses—in her mind, that she realized he'd been wearing all black.

*H*E WAS GETTING close. With any luck, this would be the last time.

He'd pulled two robberies this week while Kendra was reading to the children at Caldwell Manor. He wished he'd escaped unseen today, but she'd lain abed late, and it had been necessary to leave.

He'd seen a pattern occurring, every third day mid-morning, and today was day number three. He could only hope his wife had been sleepy enough that she hadn't noticed what he'd been about.

She'd been losing sleep. Over him? The thought made him smile.

He was making subtle progress, in more areas than one.

TWENTY

HER PULSE pounding, Kendra dismounted and tethered Pandora to a tree, then made her way on foot to the hill.

As she neared the crest, she dropped to her knees. One hand snaked out and snatched a hat, a handsome brown one with a bright yellow plume. She perched it on her head and slithered forward on her belly, tossing the wooden block behind her and lying low, hopefully at the same level as the other hats. Maneuvering a pipe before her, she propped her chin on it and focused on the road below.

Dear heavens, Trick had someone already. Mounted on Chaucer, he aimed his pistol into the gaping blackness of an open coach door. Her heart thundered in her chest as a gray-garbed man emerged and climbed reluctantly to the road.

"Oh, aye?" Trick's drawl floated up to her. "You may want to reconsider. My *friends* would think it great sport to put a bullet through your chest. Or a dozen, maybe. Ah, a contest. Target practice on your sorry hide."

The man would have been quaking in his boots, except he was wearing ugly thick shoes with dull silver buckles. His eyes flicked nervously up toward Kendra, and she held her breath when Trick's gaze followed. It took every ounce of her will to keep from flinching or ducking as her husband squinted in her direction.

The victim's eyes narrowed. In seeming slow motion, Kendra watched as the man backed away, one hand deliberately rising. He stared at Trick with a tight expression that made a cold knot form in Kendra's stomach, especially because her husband's concentration remained fixed on the place where she hid.

Why, oh why had she come? Recognition lit Trick's eyes along with clear displeasure, and she knew he would kill her—if he didn't die first. As the stranger's hand inched beneath his coat, her fingers clenched on the pipe, vainly searching for the fake gun's nonexistent trigger.

Why wasn't Trick taking heed?

And why wasn't the Roundhead afraid of Trick's "friends"? In her peripheral vision, she could see the hats and pipes lined up in a soldierlike array. An explicit threat to anyone below. But the stranger's edginess was obvious, his gaze glued to Trick, who in turn was still focused on her.

The victim wasn't thinking clearly, Kendra realized—distracted as he was, he couldn't be counted on to act rationally. Which made him dangerous. As his hand delved even deeper, she found it increasingly hard to hold still, and Trick wasn't paying attention.

Silver flashed—a pistol or a knife? It happened so quickly, Kendra couldn't be sure. Her heart seemed to stop, and her mouth opened to cry out a warning. But before it could pass her lips, her husband burst into action.

A blur of flying arms and legs, Trick leapt from his horse. He landed and twisted the Roundhead's hand up behind him, all in one smooth motion. The next thing Kendra knew, a gun had thudded to the ground, and the man was facedown in the dirt with a knee in the small of his back.

Her heart stuttered and restarted. Where on earth had Trick learned to do that? Most of the men she knew trained with pistols and swords, and quite a few were proficient in boxing, besides. But those were gentlemen's sports—nothing like what Trick had just done. She'd never seen such lightning-fast reactions.

Evidently, neither had the Roundhead. Fear was etched on his face, and she could see his legs shaking when Trick finally allowed him to rise, still holding one arm twisted back and high.

Relief singing through her veins, she collapsed flat on her belly. The hat fell off, rolling a foot before it slipped over the edge and tumbled to the road below with a muted *plop* that made her grimace.

But her husband didn't spare it—or her—a glance. At his bidding, the man managed to empty both pockets with his one free hand, defeat evident as he hurried to comply. When Trick demanded his coat as well, he relinquished it without argument.

After a short glimpse into the cabin and a circuit around the coach seemed to convince Trick no more booty was forthcoming, he released the stranger and shoved him inside. Motionless, he held Chaucer's reins while the coach rumbled off down the road.

Dust puffed in its wake, settling slowly to earth as the carriage disappeared into the distance. Nothing but the calls of blackbirds filled the air when Trick finally turned to the hill.

His voice wafted to Kendra, calm, yet dangerous. "What the deuce do you think you're doing up there?"

He led Chaucer forward, stopping to retrieve the victim's gun and the fallen hat before walking around and up the hill. He removed his mask as he went, then stood gazing down at her.

She dropped her head to the grass. Though her face was mashed into the springy blades, she felt his eyes boring into her back.

"Well?"

"I was spying on you," she squeaked.

His breath huffed out. "Sit up, Kendra. I cannot talk to you like this."

She pushed up and sat, her gaze on her hands clenched in her lap. Her pale yellow gown was damp, the area around the knees stained bright grass-green.

"Look at me," he said, unmistakably exasperated. "It's not like you to hide. Not how I envision you at all." As she glanced up, he flicked the long, crimped brown periwig hair over his shoulders.

"I came because I was afraid you'd get hurt," she said.

"What made you think I'd get hurt?" His eyes narrowed, appearing naked without the mask and their usual veil of blond hair. "Do you…care?" he asked slowly.

"Of course I care!" She couldn't remember ever having been more frightened in her life. "I saw him pull the pistol. He could have had a knife, too."

"He did." He drew a long, lethal blade from the man's coat and dropped both to the grass, moving closer. "But I can handle myself, aye? So long as you don't show up and interfere."

"I didn't—"

"Your very presence broke my concentration. And had he seen you up here…do you imagine he'd be put off by a pack of lasses?"

"Were it lasses with guns, I'd hope so!" she shot back.

Blinking, he reached a hand to help her rise. She was surprised to find her knees trembling.

His gaze searched hers. "Do not ever, ever do that again," he said very quietly. He moved closer, so close his breath whispered over her face. "You could have got me killed."

Tears sprang to her eyes.

"Never." She saw a muscle twitch in his jaw. "You understand, aye? Never."

"I'm sorry!" Her arms came up and wrapped around his neck, of their own volition, it seemed. She buried her face in his shoulder, chagrined at her tears. For what? A husband she barely knew, never mind that they were married? A husband who kept secrets and mistresses? Who lied to her?

None of it made any sense.

"Hush, it's all right." His own arms stole around her and held her tight. "No harm done." He kissed her hair. "You care, aye?"

"I don't want you to do it again, Trick. But the children—they depend on you…"

His grip tightened. "I've yet to be hurt—"

"You've been lucky. And luck can change."

"Not luck." He pulled back and fixed her with a calculated grin. "Talent."

Having seen that talent demonstrated, she had to offer him a shaky smile.

"Maybe just a few more times," he said, "and then—"

"There will be enough to invest. And you can stop?"

"Something like that," he murmured.

His eyes searched hers, their amber depths holding her hostage. Summer sun glinted off the roughness on his unshaven cheeks. Her breath caught as his mouth came down on hers.

Slow and gentle, the kiss was a silent apology for his harsh words. None too solid already, her knees turned to pudding. His patience with her, his kindness—even just his *nearness*—ate away at her resistance day by day. How much longer could she hold out? Did she still want to?

When he broke off, her breath came quick and ragged. "No," she whispered.

"No, what, *leannan*?" His smile caught her off guard.

"No, I mean, yes, I…won't come here again."

"Thank you." He nodded solemnly and kissed her again, a short, teasing graze that left her wanting more. She curled a hand around his neck, and he froze, his extraordinary amber eyes widening.

"Losh, you'll make me go back on my word." He raised a suggestive brow. "Unless you've changed your mind?"

"N-no." She took a step back, nearly tumbling down the hill.

He caught her, laughing. "Let's get you out of here."

"Are you finished?"

"It would seem so," he said wryly, gathering the hats. He tossed them onto the canvas spread nearby. "Come to the cottage, and we'll see what we got."

TWENTY-ONE

"**N**OT VERY much." Kendra frowned at the few coins spread on the cottage's dining table.

Trick laughed. "A greedy thief, are you? It's mostly gold, not silver."

"True." She lifted one. "How about in his coat? Anything there?"

He dug into the pockets, felt the collar, the seams, the hem... "Ah."

"Was he hiding something?"

With a quick flick of his knife, he slit the stitches. One by one, more bright gold coins dropped to the table with satisfying little clunks.

Clunk. Clunk. Clunk. *Clink.*

"There it is." Trick scooped up the latest addition. He walked to the window, held it to the light, bit into it. "Eureka," he said softly, then rushed back to the table and opened the rest of the hem, flicking the coins to the surface.

Clunk. Clunk. *Clink.* Clunk. *Clink. Clink. Clink. Clink.* Clunk. *Clink.*

"They're larger denominations," Kendra pointed out.

"Aye."

Clink. Clunk. *Clink. Clink.* Clunk.

"Good?"

"Nay." He pulled the last one from the ragged hem, then sorted them swiftly on the tabletop. "They're counterfeit."

"Counterfeit?" she said with a huff. "Why, that's criminal!"

He pinned her with a pointed look.

"Oh…" Heat rushed to her cheeks.

He moved to her and took her chin. "You're not guilty," he said.

"You're not, either," she countered loyally. "They're Round-head scum. They deserve it, and it's for a good cause."

"The end justifies the means?" Trick walked to the stone fireplace. "I think not." He reached up, sank his fingers into a crack in the mortar, and coaxed out a small key. "Now, can you tell me what the man looked like? Whatever you remember."

"What he looked like?" Kendra watched as he opened the desk's top drawer and slipped the key into a hidden lock. The bottom drawer—the one she'd been unable to open—sprang free. "He was shorter than you, by a good six inches, I'd say." She shut her eyes, trying to remember. "Thin, pale, pale eyes I think, too, although I was at a distance." She opened her eyes as Trick pulled a sheet of paper from the top drawer.

"Hair?" A bottle of ink and a quill came out next.

"His hat covered most of it, but his hair was brown, wasn't it? Gray-brown."

"Just as I remember." He scribbled it all down. "His clothing?"

"Gray, all gray. Plain—well, he was a Puritan. Nothing to distinguish him there. Oh, his shoes had very ugly dull buckles. Square. Pewter, I'm guessing." She frowned as he wrote. "Why does this matter?"

"Wait." He held up a hand, still writing. "Any scars?"

"Too far to see."

"I think he had a healing cut on his chin. And a wart alongside his nose." The quill scratched some more. "There," he said, ending with a flourish. "Job well done. You really are quite observant." He shoved the page into the bottom drawer and slammed it closed.

"Trick?"

"Aye?" He returned to the mantel and reached to replace the key.

"Will you stop doing this? For me?"

He whirled to face her. "I cannot promise that, Kendra."

"We'll find another way to support the orphans. I'll ask my brothers—"

"I cannot stop." Coming closer, he put his hands on her shoulders. "Soon, but not yet."

"It frightens me." Her voice came out a whisper.

"You do have a way of wrenching one's heart." He tilted her chin to meet her eyes. "I'll be careful," he said softly.

"Promise?"

"Cross my heart."

She smiled faintly and touched him lightly on the chest. "This one?"

"That one exactly." He placed his hand over hers and bent to meet her lips.

She leaned against him, sighing into the kiss.

When he finally pulled back, it was with a chuckle. Playfully he tugged on her hand, pulling her toward the corridor. "Shall we try the bed again, do you think?"

She stood her ground. "Not on your life. You think your kisses are good enough to tempt me to try *that*?"

"I'm betting on it." He scooped up the coins and stuffed them into his surcoat pocket. "And I'm not a losing man."

TWENTY-TWO

*T*HEY RODE across the downs, taking a leisurely route to enjoy the warm day. Trick felt better than he had in months. Odds were he had enough information now—he would send a message to the contact the king had provided, meet with the man, and hopefully be done.

Premature though it might be, relief flowed through him in powerful waves.

His gaze drifted over to Kendra, her hair bright in the midday sun. A blade of grass stuck to her dress brought a smile to his lips. Though she was a challenge, he found it impossible to stay angry with her. She was the helpmate he'd never thought to have, and he loved that she felt so protective of him. As soon as word came that his mission was complete, they could start anew.

Their marriage was suspended on a fragile web, but without this secret coming between them, they could begin to spin it stronger.

"Trick?"

"Hmm?"

"Why did you want a description of that man?"

He shrugged uncomfortably, suddenly questioning the wisdom of allowing her to have seen him do that. But he'd always made his notes immediately, while the vision was still fresh in his mind.

"To send to the authorities," he said in an offhand manner. "Anonymously, of course, so they can identify the blackguard without my being involved."

"Why do you suppose he's counterfeiting?"

"To get rich, I imagine."

"I imagine there's another reason. Something tied in with his being a Roundhead." Her eyes unfocused, she stared right through him, clearly lost in contemplation. "I don't think he's acting alone," she said.

"What makes you say that?"

"He didn't seem bright enough."

Not as bright as she was, Trick thought, that was for sure.

"I'm thinking he's part of a bigger operation," she continued, "and if the members are Puritans, perhaps in league with some other Parliamentarians, they might be acting against the king's interests. Passing worthless currency in an attempt to undermine the economy and the people's confidence in the monarchy. A plot to regain the power they once had, the power that died along with Cromwell."

She stole his breath. Both the strength of her reasoning and the fact that she'd hit it on the mark—the very suspicions that Charles had put forth and Trick was attempting to prove. He'd never considered that his pretty young wife might understand the intricate linkage of economics and political power.

But it was dangerous, this line of reasoning. Kendra might have a sharp head and aligning interests, but he couldn't risk her spreading this idea around, allowing the perpetrators to discover someone was on to them.

"Maybe," he said lightly, keeping his face and tone nonchalant. "But I expect he's just trying to get rich."

She studied him, her hands tightening on Pandora's reins. "How easily you dismiss my ideas. Are you still angry that I followed you earlier?"

"Nay," he said, relieved to be on a different subject. "No harm was done." They turned up Amberley's drive, the trees on either side throwing cool shadows across the pathway. "You'd have to do much worse to incur my long-term wrath. Infidelity, for instance—though I've nothing to worry about on that account, have I?"

Yet. In the near future, he hoped, she'd overcome her fear of physical intimacy...and then maybe he'd have something to worry about.

"Infidelity?" A challenge in her voice, Kendra jostled Pandora closer to Chaucer's side. "Most gentlemen expect fidelity only from their mistresses."

Most gentlemen hadn't found their betrothed in bed with someone else. Trick sighed, pushing away those old memories. "You will learn that I am not like most gentlemen."

She shot him an arch look. "And what if I'm not like most ladies? What if I expect the same fidelity from you?"

"Turning the tables, are you?" He risked leaning from the saddle to chuck her under the chin. "You surely know how to try a man's patience."

Her green eyes flashed. "That was no sort of answer."

"I wouldn't ask something of you if I weren't willing to offer it myself."

Her expression said louder than words that she didn't believe him. But she dropped the topic, her gaze drifting to Amberley's impressive facade. "My brother Ford will want to go up the tower and see how the clock works."

"He already has."

Her pretty brow creased in a puzzled frown.

"The house parties, remember? He seems much taken with clocks. Stayed up there half an afternoon, while we twiddled our thumbs waiting for him. Here we are." Trick slid to the gravel and handed his reins to a groom. With a gentle hand at her back, he urged Kendra up the steps of Amberley House.

"Dinner," he said as Compton opened the door. "I'm fair starving. And then—"

"A letter, your grace." The butler proffered a silver tray. "It arrived while you were out."

Frowning, Trick snatched it up. Wrinkled and grubby, it looked as though it had traveled quite a distance. "Thank you, Compton. We'll take it to the study. Let us know when dinner is ready."

"Certainly." Compton's jowls wobbled with the nod of his head. He took himself off to the kitchens, and Trick ushered Kendra into the study, tossing the letter on the marquetry table that sat between two leather chairs.

TWENTY-THREE

ENDRA SAT while Trick poured himself a shot of whisky. He dropped onto the other chair and threw back a gulp. Setting the glass on the table between them, he lifted the letter.

Kendra watched him worry the seal with his long fingers. "Open it," she suggested.

"Not just yet." He turned it over and stared at his name written on the back.

"What is it?" Wondering why he seemed so odd, she hitched herself forward and frowned at the parchment. "Do you know who it's from?"

He looked up at her, his face set in unfamiliar lines. Not teasing, not angry, not thoughtful, not seductive—not any emotion she'd seen there before. Not even evasive—another all-too-common mood she was learning to distinguish.

"It's from my mother," he said softly. "I'd barely learned how to write myself when I left her, but all these years later, I still recognize her hand." He blinked, then suddenly thrust the letter at Kendra. "Here. You read it."

She nearly dropped it, but caught it in time. "No," she protested. "It's addressed to you."

"I'll listen. Then I willnae hear her voice, but yours."

Her heart ached at the pain in his tone, at the telltale Scots word that had slipped into his careful English speech.

"Read it, please." He slumped down in the chair and took a long sip of whisky, then leaned his head back and closed his eyes.

She smoothed the parchment against her skirt and slipped a fingernail under the seal. When it lifted off with a little snapping sound, Trick winced.

"Go ahead," he said huskily.

The paper crackled as she opened it and held it to catch the light from the window. "Her handwriting is beautiful," she said.

He said nothing.

She took a deep breath. "'My dear Patrick Iain,'" she read aloud. "'My heart is heavy with sorrow for all the years we've been apart. Now I am dying, and it is my fondest wish to gaze upon your beloved face once more. Though I know you're a man grown, my bonnie lad you'll always be. Come to me, Patrick, come make an old woman smile as she greets the next world. With all the love in my heart, Mam.'"

Silence. Kendra took one long breath, two…three.

Trick opened his eyes and sipped slowly from his glass.

"Can I go with you?" she asked.

"Where?" He shifted to face her. "You don't think I'll go to her, do you?"

"You must!"

"She cannot ignore me for eighteen years and then expect me to jump to her command."

"She's dying, Trick."

He shrugged.

"You must make your peace. It's your only chance."

"I don't care to give her the satisfaction."

"It's your own satisfaction at stake here. If you fail to go now, you'll always wonder. Always. Go to her and find your answers, before it's too late. Close your heart if you must, but go. Say good-bye."

He drained the glass and rolled it between his palms. "You think yourself wise for your years."

"I didn't get to know my parents." The letter crackled as she folded it and set it on the table. "In my dreams, awake and sleeping, I've accused them of leaving me and I've told them I loved them. I've been angry at them, and sad. But I was too young when they died, so face-to-face, I never got to tell them anything."

He took a deep breath, and the crystal stilled between his hands.

"Go, Trick. Now. Tonight." She'd have to postpone the children's party, but so be it. "I'll come with you."

"No," he said slowly. "I'll go alone. Tomorrow."

TWENTY-FOUR

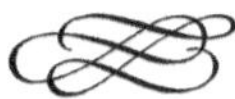

*A*FTER SUPPER, Kendra found herself mounted on Pandora, heading toward the cottage for the second time that day.

She slanted a glance at Trick riding beside her. She'd tried halfheartedly to talk him into taking her along to Scotland, knowing he was absolutely set against it.

Well, perhaps it would be a relief to be free from him for a while. Free to catch up on her sleep. Free from those kisses that made her lose her head. Free to think about whether she wanted to let Trick go past kissing, because she wasn't sure whether to believe what Cait had told her or what he had said.

You should know it will hurt…

But not much, and only the first time…

Still, part of her was reluctant to see him go, so she'd clung to him like a sticky bun all the afternoon, while he completed the tasks that stood in the way of his leaving.

The full moon reflected off the cottage windows as they approached. "I had no idea of the extent of your responsibilities," she said through a yawn.

"I just want to drop off some papers."

Her eyes felt gritty. "And after that?"

Trick slid from Chaucer and reached to help her down. "I still have much to do before I can sleep."

She tethered Pandora and followed him inside. "You're pushing yourself." She closed the door and leaned against it, watching while he lit a single candle. "I know you must be worried for your mother—"

"I'm not particularly worried." Finished, he felt for the key above the fireplace.

"She's dying."

He shot her a look as he unlocked the desk. "You said yourself her writing is beautiful. A woman on her deathbed would have a shaky hand, or dictate to someone else." He pulled a sheaf of papers from his surcoat and slid them into the bottom drawer.

"Perhaps she did dictate it."

"It was her own hand—I'd bet my life on that. Aye, she's up to something." He shut the drawer and relocked it. "I'll play along with her game, just in case I'm wrong, but she's a conniving—"

"You cannot know that, Trick. Not after all these years."

"Time will tell which of us is right. But I won't live in hope that she's changed." He shoved the key back between the stones and began to blow out the flame, then suddenly stopped. "Blast it, I forgot the hats and pipes. I wonder what else I'm forgetting? Wait here—I'll be back." He set the candle on the mantel, and before she knew it, the door had slammed behind him.

She stood still for a moment in guilty indecision before walking slowly to the fireplace. Teetering on her toes, she reached for the key, finding Trick had placed it too high for her reach. She dragged the desk chair close, climbed atop it, and nudged the key from its hiding place.

Jumping down, she rushed to the window. Moonlight illuminated the grounds. Trick was nowhere in sight. Seconds later she had the bottom drawer open and was pawing through its contents.

On top were the notes he'd just dropped off and those he'd concealed there earlier today. Not to keep them from her, obviously—he'd made no secret of the drawer. Surely he wouldn't care if she looked.

Or so she told herself.

She swept the candle off the mantel to examine more pages of descriptions like the one she'd helped Trick make of the Puritan today. She smiled at his writing: very bold, the letters scrawled, clearly written in haste.

Carefully she set the candlestick on the desktop, then put the papers back in the drawer and peeked beneath them. An accounting of some sort. A record of his takings? Quite detailed, including descriptions of individual coins. Today hadn't been the first time he'd run across counterfeits. Underneath that…

She pulled out another stack of papers, some of them older and yellowed. Written by the same hand, but more carefully, the words painstakingly formed, neat and even. They reminded Kendra of the papers she used to write for her tutors, papers written and rewritten before a final, perfect draft was carefully copied.

Choosing one at random, she read.

Pain and sorrow forevermore dwell
Inside the deepest bowels of hell.
Betrayal has yet took from me
What love and trust had once set free.

Poetry. Kendra sat abruptly on the edge of the desk. Trick, a poet? She never would have thought it; in fact, had someone suggested such, she would have laughed herself silly.

She didn't know her husband at all.

He'd been hurt by someone, terribly. Her heart clenched as she suddenly understood his words: *I don't believe in love at all. Love between people is an illusion.*

Who had done what to him to make him feel this way? Was

he never happy? The paper seemed brittle when she set it down —as brittle as the words upon it. But the words on the sheet underneath did nothing to soothe her sympathetic ache.

> *Twixt fathers and tyrants*
> *a difference is known:*
> *Fathers seek their sons' good,*
> *tyrants their own.*

With a sinking heart, she riffled through the pages, pausing to read here and there. The touching verses hinted at events in Trick's life that had shaped him into the young man she saw today. Pain, anger, disillusionment...ah, there it was. Love, happiness. His hand was lighter here; the words fairly leapt off the page in their exuberance.

> *Sweet day, happy, calm and bright*
> *Love has brought me to this light*
> *The sun that sits in yonder sky*
> *Today can shine not more than I*
> *And if tomorrow it should rain*
> *Her smile will make sun shine again*

She bit her lip. Was this written of the same love that had later turned to betrayal? Could this carefree Trick live somewhere inside the cynical man who shared her home? If trust had been shattered by one lady, could another restore it?

Hoofbeats. Oh, heavens, he was on his way back. She stuffed the poems beneath the other papers and locked the drawer, then jumped to the chair to replace the key. She was just pushing the chair back to the desk when the door flew open and Trick sauntered inside with the bundle of hats under one arm, the pipes under the other.

He dropped it all in a corner. "Ready to go?"

His crooked grin made her heart leap; he was so unsuspecting. She flushed, unbearably guilty just looking at him after reading his private compositions.

"I suppose," she said. "Though I was hoping we could talk."

"Now? About what?"

"Life. Yours." She met his gaze, willing him to share some of his past. "And mine, of course. All the years that led to now. The people who loved us—"

"None."

"—and hurt us."

He only shrugged. "None worth talking about."

"And what we like…for instance, do you like to write? I keep a journal, and sometimes I've written poems."

"Poems?" His gaze flickered down to the drawer. "No, I don't like to write." He leaned past her to blow out the candle. "Come along, will you?" he said, going to the door. "I've much to do still before I can leave."

Crushed that he refused to even consider confiding in her, Kendra pushed by him and outside. Before she could mount Pandora, he caught her by the arm.

"I know you mean well," he said softly.

Silent, she searched his eyes, gray in the darkness.

They went darker still. "I'm sorry you're so unhappy," he said.

"I'm not unhappy. Just confused. I'm worried for your life, and I don't like keeping the truth from my brothers about what it is you're doing. There are parts of you I admire—your compassion for the children. And more parts I don't understand—parts I think you've locked away. And now you're leaving."

"I'll be back." The words were a gruff promise. "Maybe you'll miss me while I'm gone." His hand slid down her arm until his fingers were laced with hers, and he leaned to press a soft kiss to her mouth.

When he pulled back, she stared at him helplessly. Her lips tingled. She heard his low chuckle before he turned away to lock the cottage, and it drove her to a decision.

Once, in jest, she had promised he'd find love, and a Chase promise was never given lightly. She would bring back to life what another girl had killed; she would make him believe in love once again.

Accomplishing that while avoiding his bed was not going to be easy.

But then, worthwhile things rarely were.

TWENTY-FIVE

RICK EASED through the bedchamber door and closed it quietly behind him. He carried the candle to the bedside and set it on the table by Kendra's head, where it would illuminate her face.

She looked angelic in sleep, her long, dark lashes feathery against her sun-pinked cheeks, her bright hair tumbled on the pillow, glistening in the candlelight. When he bent and kissed her on the forehead, a faint smile curved her lips, then faded away.

He felt an odd squeezing sensation in his chest. She was more compassionate and forthright than he'd expected, this new wife of his. And distressed. Responsibility for that fell squarely on his shoulders, sparking guilt along with a flash of the sort of senti-mental feelings experience had taught him to disregard. Those feelings would fade. But the guilt…

He had good reasons for hiding so much, he reminded himself. And it wasn't forever—only until his mission for King Charles was completed.

He felt so close to uncovering the truth. Were it not for this summons from his mother, he would soon have this behind him.

Maybe, without secrets between them, he and Kendra could begin to establish something like trust.

But first things first. He undressed swiftly, checking off the list in his head to make sure he'd taken care of everything before he left for Scotland, a journey that might take a month or more, up and back with time spent there.

Letters of instruction to the various people who ran the estate —done.

A purse of gold for Compton to see delivered to Mrs. Jackson at Caldwell Manor—done.

A note to King Charles explaining the delay of his mission —done.

While his staff had been scurrying about, readying to leave— because a duke, no matter his personal preferences, didn't travel unattended—he'd checked a dozen tasks or more off his private list.

Everything, in fact, but the task he'd been most looking forward to…the culmination of his campaign to seduce Kendra.

From all evidence, she had been busy as well. Trick had seen goods for tomorrow's party stacked neatly in the library. A pile of colorful folded fabrics would make unique togas and doubt-less thrill the wee wearers. Small baskets overflowed with sweets and treats that would make the recipients think they had died and gone to heaven. Or Olympia, in this case.

How clever his Kendra was.

He blew out the candle and crawled into bed, nestling against her sleep-heavy form. Slipping an arm about her waist, he pulled her closer, breathing in the faint lavender scent of her freshly scrubbed skin. Flickering light from the fireplace danced over her face and brought out golden glints in her dark-red hair. Brushing soft curls from her face, he leaned up to kiss her cheek.

She shifted, emitting a tiny sigh that brought a smile to his lips.

He kissed her ear.

She stretched beside him like a contented cat, with a purr to match.

What time was it? Three in the morning? Four? No matter, he wouldn't waste these last hours with her by sleeping. He turned her over and kissed her full on the lips.

"Mmm," she murmured low in her throat, her arms twining around his neck. Feeling her truly awaken, he smiled against her lips. Her breathing changed, and that perfect mouth moved with his, making his pulse speed, the blood rush faster through his veins. Never had anyone affected him so, not even…

Nay, he wouldn't think about her. After all these years, whatever had brought her to mind? She was long out of his life, and Kendra was here instead.

Sweet Kendra, warm beneath him now. She was the only girl he wanted. He moved to touch her through the night rail she wore—then stopped cold, his gaze glued to the garment. Yards of pristine white linen enfolded her, covering her up to her neck. She looked small and innocent, like a doll.

What was he doing?

He was man enough to be patient, and he'd been patient so far. He'd ruin everything by moving too soon.

Her eyes fluttered open, a question in their darkened green depths. She reached a hesitant finger to touch his bottom lip, the sensation as light as a whisper.

Sweet heaven…

But no, he wouldn't go back on his word. He wouldn't risk what little trust they'd built between them. They had a lifetime ahead to be together, truly together as man and wife—when she was ready. And he had no doubt she'd be ready eventually, maybe even soon…

But blast it, it was hard to wait.

Especially when the thought of weeks apart made him ache. Odd, that. He couldn't remember the last time he'd missed someone in particular.

For long minutes, he just kissed her. His own hands remained still while hers wandered over his skin. His nerves rippled in response, but still he only kissed her. Forever, it seemed, until he felt her pressing closer, her fingers digging into his shoulders, and a little mewling sound escaped her throat.

"Trick?" she asked breathlessly, the name warm against his mouth.

"Hmm?"

"Can you not…touch me?"

He pulled back and gazed into her glassy eyes. "Nay, I cannot," he said, though he had to force the words past his lips. "Should I touch you, I may not be able to help doing more. And I promised I wouldn't seduce you in bed." He teased her lips with his. "But you like the kissing, aye?"

Her hands tightened in the hair at his nape. "Oh, heavens, yes. I like it. I just want—"

"Hmm?" Let her ask for it. "What do you want?"

"I…I don't know," she whispered, burying her face against his neck.

"You know," he said softly. "We both know. If only you'll say it."

Instead of saying it, she took a ragged breath and released it with a shudder.

"It won't hurt, *leannan*. Not after the first time, and not much even then. I promise."

Kendra felt the words, the promise, vibrate in his throat. She wanted him—truly she did. But what good were promises from a man she couldn't trust? It wasn't fear that held her back now. Or not *only* fear, anyway. Even if he were right—even if it wouldn't hurt—how could she share her body with a man who refused to share his life?

She was touching him now, but she wasn't really. Her hands were upon him, but she had yet to reach him where it counted. A barrier stood between them, and she couldn't bring herself to risk the crossing.

He had built it. He would have to be the one to bring it down.

"What do you want?" he asked again.

"I want—" She turned her head away, staring up at the underside of Trick's red silk canopy. Not hers. No matter how many times he insisted that what was his was hers as well, she didn't feel that way in her heart. Not while he kept the most important thing of all from her.

Himself.

"I want to go to sleep," she whispered.

He trailed his fingers lightly across her cheek. "One more kiss?"

"I think…no," she said on a sigh. Another kiss would only make her more sad, and the lump in her throat was hard to bear already. She rolled away from him, turning her back. "Good night," she whispered.

The words seemed to hover in the heavy air of the still room.

After a moment he settled against her, snug and solid. "Do you think you might miss me?"

The shiver that went through her body was its own answer, and he went to sleep with a smile on his face.

She knew because after his breathing evened out in the pattern of slumber, she turned and gazed upon him, filling herself with the sight of him to hold her through the weeks ahead.

It took her longer than ever to drift off that night, and when she awakened, he was gone.

TWENTY-SIX

"**M**RS. KENDRA?"

"Yes, Thomas?" Kneeling in the grass by little Susanna, Kendra squinted up at the impish towhead.

"We're athletes in the Olympic games, am I right?"

"That's the idea."

"Well, then…" A gleam came into his sparkling blue eyes as his hands went to the fabric draped over his shoulder. "Shouldn't we be naked?"

"Leave that on, you rapscallion!" She was hard put not to laugh at his pout. "I never said we were strictly authentic."

"Aw, all right." With a mischievous grin, he ran off.

"Stand still, Susanna." Kendra tucked the girl's "toga" more tightly, smiling to herself. Luckily her lessons hadn't covered fashion, so her students were ignorant of the fact that the Greeks had worn solid colors, not brightly flowered calico. "There you go."

"My thanks, Mrs. Kendra."

"You're very welcome." She patted Susanna's blond curls and stood, knowing as she sent her off that the girl would be back in a few minutes to be tucked in again.

She'd learned that togas weren't the ideal clothing for young children.

That was her only miscalculation, though—the rest of the party had gone brilliantly. The children's retelling of their favorite myths had been riotous. Now they were participating in Olympic "games," and the victory wreaths she had woven from laurel leaves might as well have been solid gold crowns considering how much they were cherished. Fortunately, she'd brought enough for everyone, and she was not above fixing the contests to see that each child came out a winner.

The party was a wild success, and they hadn't even feasted yet. Nor had she distributed the favors. Her baskets of goodies were still hiding beneath a blanket in the caleche, and she couldn't wait to see the children's faces when they received them.

Wrapped in stately blue stripes, young Andrew tugged on her toga. "Who are you, Mrs. Kendra?"

"Why, Hera, of course." She looked down into adoring dark eyes—his crush had not abated over the weeks. "Do you remember who she was?"

"Zeus's wife," he said proudly. "And the protector of marriage."

"Very good," she returned, although, for her, the job description seemed an ill fit at best.

Rather than protecting her marriage, she'd sent her husband off alone. She should have argued until he agreed to let her go with him. Surely if she'd put up a fight, he would have relented —her brothers almost always did. But she hadn't really tried.

Andrew shifted on his feet, looking shy. "I memorized one of the poems about her."

"Did you?"

He nodded and began to quote.

> *"Golden-throned Hera, among immortals the queen,*
> *Chief among them in beauty, the glorious lady*

All the blessed in high Olympus revere,
Honor even as Zeus, the lord of the thunder."

He finished with an awkward bow that should have brought a smile to Kendra's lips. But in contrast to the Hera of the poem, she was feeling anything but glorious at the moment.

"Mrs. Kendra? Are you all right?"

"I'm fine, Andrew." Amazed at the young man's perception, she forced a smile. "Mrs. Jackson is organizing a chariot race," she said brightly, glancing over to where the buxom woman was lining up four wheelbarrows. "I imagine a tall, strong boy like you, with little Susanna in his chariot, could come out a winner. Run along now—I'm fine."

But despite how well the party was going, she wasn't fine at all.

Trick should have been here. He was supposed to have been Zeus.

He'd made this happen, repeatedly risking his life to feed and shelter these boys and girls. Her gaze followed Andrew as he joined the other laughing children. None of them, herself included, would be here today without Trick.

Hera had always been zealously covetous of Zeus, and heaven help her, she missed her husband.

~

*W*HEN KENDRA arrived home, she stopped only long enough to switch her toga for a riding habit and grab a key from Trick's desk drawer. Then she ran to the stables, mounted Pandora, and fairly flew over the Downs to the cottage.

Once inside, she could almost smell him. Since this morning when she'd awakened in his home, something—his vibrancy— had been missing. Instead of feeling free, she'd felt bereft.

But here in the cottage, she could feel his presence. Unlike

Amberley House, this clearly wasn't designed by his father. Trick's personality was stamped on the walls, the floors, every piece of furniture.

It was astonishing the loss she felt, given she'd known him only a few weeks. It was a physical pain, roiling in her stomach. Just when she was beginning to form a fragile bond with her husband, he'd left.

She strode straight to unlock the drawer and dig to the bottom.

The poetry was gone.

She riffled through all the papers to make sure. Gone, all of it. Suddenly exhausted, she sank to the floor, her heart sinking along with her. She pressed a hand to her chest, struggling to draw breath. Not only was her one link to him missing, he was clearly intent on keeping her at arm's length.

Rushed to begin a long journey, he'd nonetheless taken the time to stop and remove the pages. Remove any possibility that by reading his words, she might discover who he was on the inside.

She should have gone with him.

She couldn't allow him to isolate himself. Not if they were to live a lifetime together.

And now it might be too late.

TWENTY-SEVEN

"**H**E LEFT," Kendra told Caithren the next afternoon. "He had no choice."

"Of course he didn't." Cait stopped beneath one of Amberley's many arbors and played with the ends of her dark-blond hair. "But why didn't you go along?"

"He didn't want me along." Kendra squinted at her sister-in-law in the shadows. "Isn't this the loveliest garden?" Her gesture encompassed more than the vine-covered walkway. "The head gardener told me it was designed by Salaman de Caux himself."

"Salaman who?"

"De Caux. The celebrated Frenchman. Have you not heard of him?"

"Nay. My garden at Leslie was filled with herbs and vegetables." Cait's lips turned up in a self-deprecating smile. "Nary a posy in sight."

Amberley House's gardens were the most extensive Kendra had ever seen. Geometric configurations of flower beds, knots, and borders surrounded a lake where fishes darted beneath the clear water. Avenues lined with painted and gilded stone lions flanked a massive bowling green. Walls of fruit trees divided the charming wilderness garden from those more formal, like the privy garden they were heading toward.

As they strolled from the arbor into the sunshine, her gaze trailed to the massive mansion that loomed over it all. "I'm afraid Trick's father depleted his entire fortune building this place."

"Has Trick said so?"

"Not in so many words," she said, hesitating to say more. Confiding Trick's financial instability might lead to speculation about his continuing highway robbery.

"Then I wouldn't assume so," Cait said. "The estate is very impressive, but then, Trick *is* a duke. And you're very good at changing the subject."

Kendra flashed her a wry smile. "I was hoping you wouldn't notice." She reached overhead to pluck off a fragrant flower, worrying its soft petals between her fingers. After returning from the cottage last night, she'd gone to sleep early and stayed abed late. But her stomach was still in knots. "Part of me still cannot believe I'm married. Do you know, even as we rode away that day, I was sure Colin would come riding after us to say it was all an elaborate joke. I'd convinced myself the parson was in on it—that somehow the ceremony wasn't valid."

"But it was."

"I was furious. I still am. I don't feel like talking to my brothers—any of them." Her voice dropped. "Then I found myself alone with Trick, and still I didn't quite believe it."

"How did it go? The first night, I mean."

"Not well." She looked away, studying the way the light filtered through the leafy canopy of a yew. "I was scared. You'd told me it would hurt."

"I didn't tell you that to frighten you, Kendra. Just to prepare you, so you wouldn't be surprised. I also told you it wouldn't hurt much, and only the first time, aye?"

Her mouth hanging open, Kendra shook her head. "No, you didn't. You just said it would hurt."

"I'm sure I said more." A frown creased Cait's forehead. "Unless…we were interrupted, weren't we?" Her hazel eyes widened. "I meant to tell you, but we were interrupted. Jason and Colin knocked on the door." She focused on Kendra, shading her eyes with a hand. "I'm sorry to hear you were scared and it didn't go well, but it didn't hurt that much, did it? And it went better for you the second time, I expect. Surely it didn't hurt at all then."

Kendra bit her lip. "There hasn't been a second time. There hasn't even been a first time."

"What?" If possible, Cait's eyes widened even more. "You've been married nearly three weeks!"

"I haven't let him. He's being very patient with me."

"It seems you married a saint." Cait shook her head disapprovingly. "Your brothers should have explained everything. Jason will hear from me about this."

"Please, no." Kendra felt her face heat. "He'd make fun of me all my days. What is it he failed to tell me?"

"It hurts most women at first. But not a lot, and only the once, aye? Only that first time, when your maidenhead—"

"I may have heard that word." Kendra frowned. "But I never knew what it meant."

"It's a membrane, inside every female. Every virgin, that is. You could say it guards your entrance. I read once that it's properly called a hymen."

"Hymen is the Greek god of the wedding feast."

"Really? How fitting." Caithren cleared her throat. "Now, the first time you make love it is torn, and you'll bleed—"

"I will?" Kendra asked in alarm.

"Just a little. It's nothing to be concerned about. And you won't bleed the next time. And it won't hurt, either, because the maidenhead will be gone."

Trick had been telling the truth, then. A wave of relief washed over Kendra, tempered by a stab of regret. She should have believed him.

And now she *really* wished she'd gone with him.

Cait knelt to inspect some bell-shaped flowers. "He must be the most patient fellow on earth," she murmured. "The attraction between you two was clear as day. However did you manage to keep him away?"

Kendra gave an evasive shrug. "We were strangers. We still are."

"You will come to know each other. Just give him another chance." She frowned down at the plant. "You have dwale growing here!"

"Dwale?" In the year since Caithren had arrived, she'd taught Kendra many uses for herbs and plants. But they'd never come across this particular sort.

"Black nightshade. Belladonna. Look." She waited until Kendra knelt beside her, then skimmed a fingertip over a dingy purplish flower with a berry in its base. "Do you see these dark green leaves? They're lethal. It's said that Macbeth poisoned a whole army of Danes by calling a false truce and then offering them liquor mixed with an infusion of dwale."

"Then why is it here in the garden?"

"Used properly, the root makes a good liniment. It's the leaves and berries that are poison." When Kendra reached out, Cait held back her hand. "Don't touch. It's possible to fall ill without even eating it."

"What sort of ill?"

"Shock, fever, slowed breathing, dilated eyes, stomach pain—"

"Enough." Kendra rubbed her stomach. She was perversely reminded of her relationship with Trick, parts of which could be gentle, soothing, beneficial, like a liniment.

But other parts felt an awful lot like poison.

You're being melodramatic, she told herself with a rueful smile. Still, she wasn't about to take a chance on the dwale. "I shall tell the head gardener to remove it."

"Make sure he wears gloves." Cait stood and brushed her

hands on her rose-colored skirts. "Now tell me about you and Trick. Besides the trouble in the bedchamber."

Kendra met her sister-in-law's gaze. "He's just…well, I don't understand him, Cait. We didn't wed under the best of circumstances. For either of us."

"Nay, you didn't. But Jase is convinced you'll be happy. Or so he claims."

"Does he?" Even though Kendra had come to accept her life here at Amberley, the anger rushed back. "What possible excuse could he have for deceiving me the way he did? Not even telling me Trick was a duke, for heaven's sake!"

"I asked him the same thing myself after the whole story came out. He claims you would never have married Trick if you'd known he was a duke."

She gritted her teeth. "I hate it when he's right."

"He also said catching you two in a compromising position was a stroke of luck, because Trick would never have consented to court you even if Jason had suggested it. He claimed not to want a wife."

"Not in the near future," Kendra admitted darkly.

"Jason told me his hand was forced, because he knew you two suited perfectly."

"Well, there's where he was wrong." Trick might be a good kisser and tolerant of her non-traditional interests, but a husband who kept secrets would never suit her perfectly.

For a long moment, Caithren was silent. "You must give Trick a chance in your bed," she finally said. "And I hope you'll forgive Jase. He loves you. He's been watching you. He'd never forgive himself if it turned out you were unhappy."

Kendra's jaw went slack. She didn't know whether to feel outraged or touched. "What do you mean, he's been watching me?"

"Nothing as sinister as you're imagining." Cait laid a hand on her arm. "He asked Jane to let him know if anything seems awry. And every day, he sends a messenger to check with her." She offered a tentative smile. "He cares, Kendra."

That explained why every day, sure as the sun rose and set, Jane had been asking if she was happy here at Amberley House. Kendra released a long, slow breath. "Were you sent here as a peacemaker?"

"Aye," Cait admitted, a faint pink coloring her cheeks. "More or less. But I wanted to see you anyway. I have news, and no one else to share it with."

"News?" Kendra seated herself on a carved stone bench. "What sort of news?"

Cait sat beside her, lacing her fingers protectively over her middle. "I'm with child."

"Oh, that's wonderful!" Kendra grabbed her hands and squeezed tightly. "How are you feeling?"

"Fine." Caithren laughed. "Motherhood agrees with me."

"Jason must be thrilled."

"He doesn't know."

"He—*what*?" Kendra dropped Cait's hands. "You haven't told him?"

"Nay, and you mustn't, either. Not until we've gone and returned from Scotland. I don't want to miss my visit home, and I'm afraid Jase wouldn't want me to travel."

"You're right," Kendra said slowly, staring at Caithren's still-flat abdomen. "But won't he be furious when he finds out?"

"I'll tell him I just then discovered it. I've never been pregnant before, so how should I know the signs?" She flashed a conspiratorial smile. "You won't tell him, will you?"

"Of course not. I'm not speaking to him, remember?" Kendra returned Cait's grin. "When do you leave?"

"Tomorrow. That's another reason I wanted to visit. To say farewell for a while."

"For a month, do you think? Trick said he'd be gone a month, up and back and with time spent there."

Cait nodded. "Aye, for a month." She looked around the

enormous, quiet estate. "Maybe you would like to go stay with Ford? Or with Colin and Amy?"

"I'm not speaking to Ford or Colin, either." Kendra's grin went flat. "Anyway, I've much to learn around here. By the time Trick returns, I expect to have this place running like clockwork. It's been missing a good financial manager, not to mention a female touch. Trick said his father built it, and so far as I can tell, there's never been a mistress here at all." She took Cait's hand and rose. "Come, let's have an early supper together. I gave Mrs. Chauncey some new recipes, and you can help me see how she did with them."

Their footsteps crunched on the gravel as they crossed the privy garden. They went through the back entrance to the house.

"A letter, your grace." Just as he'd done for Trick two days ago, Compton held out a silver tray. "It's addressed to his grace, but since he is gone…"

"Thank you, Compton." She took the letter and turned it in her hands. Trick's name was written on the back, but not in his mother's beautiful handwriting, or anyone else's she recognized.

Well, of course she wouldn't—she still didn't know the first thing about her husband or his acquaintances. Chiding herself, she hurried to the study with Caithren following behind.

"It's probably nothing," Cait said as they dropped onto two chairs. "Open it."

"It isn't addressed to me."

"You said yourself he won't be home for a month. It could be important business."

"I suppose you're right." Feeling more than a little uneasy, Kendra slid a fingernail beneath the black seal. "How odd," she said quietly.

"Aye?"

"It's addressed 'Dear Patrick Iain,' rather than by his title." She read further and released a little gasp.

"What does it say?"

"Listen." She drew a deep breath. "'I don't know if you'll

remember me, since eighteen years have passed since I've set eyes on your face. But as a dear old friend of your mother's, I feel honor bound to warn you of possible danger. When Elspeth —'" Kendra paused. "That's Trick's mother," she clarified.

"Go on."

"'When Elspeth wrote the letter to summon you home, she was in perfect health. In the two days since, she has begun a rapid decline that I find inexplicable and alarming. I beg you, take heed. Yours in friendship, Hamish Munroe.'" She looked up. "What could he mean? Why would she write a letter saying she was dying, if she was in perfect health?"

"Maybe she wanted to reconcile, but she didn't believe he'd come home for that alone."

"Possibly," Kendra conceded. But her heart was pounding unevenly. "Yet this Mr. Munroe clearly believes that something is afoot. Trick could be in danger."

"I imagine he can defend himself, seeing as he used to be a highwayman."

Although she was tempted to tell Cait that Trick still was a highwayman—and share her concerns about that—Kendra knew he wouldn't want it discussed. Surprised to find herself bound to him by some form of loyalty, she suppressed the urge to unburden herself.

"I think I should go to him," she said instead.

"Pardon?"

"I think I should go to Trick. He needs to see this letter."

"I don't think Jason—"

"A pox on Jason! He lost his right to tell me what to do when he married me off to Trick. Now I'm duty bound to warn my husband of possible danger."

And she also felt rather obliged to save their relationship. Perhaps if she allowed Trick the physical intimacies he'd been missing, they would grow more intimate in other ways, and he'd begin to open up to her. She had to try.

Besides, now that she knew she had nothing to fear, the

prospect of giving Trick a chance in their bed was more than a little thrilling.

She rose and began to pace. "I must leave immediately." Her mind raced with possible plans.

"Is tomorrow soon enough?" Cait asked.

"Probably. He didn't seem in much of a hurry, so if I rush—" She turned and looked at Cait. "What are you thinking?"

"We're leaving for Scotland tomorrow. Jason and I. Maybe you can come along. But you'll have to talk to your brother," she added with a small smile. "You'll have to break this vow of silence."

"I suppose I will," Kendra said grimly. "And Mrs. Chauncey's supper will have to wait."

TWENTY-EIGHT

"**HOW DARE YOU** marry me off to a duke!"

Seated at the desk in his study at Cainewood, Jason steepled his fingers atop a leather-bound ledger. "Ah, the return of the formidable Kendra. Leaving your husband already?"

"No, he left me."

Seeing his mouth drop open, Kendra felt a small nudge of satisfaction.

"To go to Scotland," she added. "His mother is ill—dying—and she asked to see him. Except she wasn't dying until after she sent the letter. But Trick doesn't know that. I received another letter—"

"Whoa. Slow down." Jason gave a violent shake of his head, then rose from behind the desk and came around it to embrace his sister. "How are you doing?"

"I've been better," she muttered into his chest. "And I hate you, you know."

"I'm sure you do." He pulled back and kissed her on the forehead. "Now sit down and tell me about these letters."

"**F**ORD?" Kendra called softly.

Surrounded by burning candles and dozens of ticking clocks, her twin looked up from the gears in his hands, his gaze going to the dawn-lit window. "Is it morning already?"

"It is." She walked closer, reaching a finger to set a pendulum swinging as she went. "We're leaving."

As he stood and stretched, a clock began chiming, and another, and another, a cacophony of discordant tones. Laughing, Kendra wrapped her arms around her brother. "I'll miss you and all your experiments," she said, her gaze sweeping over beakers and magnets, chemicals and microscopes, and the long, impressive telescope she and Colin had given him as a birthday gift two years ago.

"I'm going to turn base metal into gold," he said, returning her hug. "And then I'll restore Lakefield House to a glorious standard."

"And fill it with machinery, no doubt."

"Of course." He pulled away, smiling. "Come, I'll walk you down."

Outside, early-morning sun slanted against Cainewood's ancient stones, bathing the quadrangle in a golden glow. Kendra pressed a kiss to her twin's cheek and swung up to Pandora's saddle.

"I'll miss you, too," he said. "Are you sure you'd rather not stay here with me? Jason can take the letter to your husband—"

"We've been over this already. I'm going."

Ford looked up at Jason, mounted on his favorite silver gelding. "Impossible, isn't she?" he asked his oldest brother. "I'll wager you're happier than ever she's another man's responsibility now."

"Not yet, it seems." The glint of amusement in Jason's eyes offset his sarcastic tone. "But the minute we reach Duncraven, I'll be happy enough to turn her over."

Sitting atop a shiny red-brown mare, Caithren shook her

head. "Hush up, you two. You don't mean any of this." She turned to Kendra. "They love you, the both of them."

"I know," Kendra said with both a huff and a smile. No matter that she hadn't yet quite forgiven them, she knew her brothers would always be there for her. Family. That was what mattered.

Would she ever forge one with Trick?

Not if they didn't get going. Toying with the stones on her amber bracelet, she looked over at the three carriages—one for themselves should they tire of riding, one for their servants, and one for everyone's baggage—and knew this journey would be a torturously slow affair. With her husband traveling ahead, blithely unaware of the danger that might lurk at his childhood home.

"Are we not going to leave?" She lifted Pandora's reins, an impatience in her voice she felt helpless to control. "Trick has two whole days on us—let's be off."

TWENTY-NINE

NIGHT WAS falling and Trick was spooning up the last of his soup when his wife blew through the door of the World's End tavern.

It was storming outside, and the room was dark, and for the barest moment, he wondered if he were seeing things. Heaven knew he'd thought of little else besides Kendra these two weeks past. She'd consumed his thoughts both waking and sleeping.

But she wasn't a figment of his imagination. She was actually here. He knew that because, had he conjured up his lovely and exasperating wife, he certainly wouldn't have conjured up her brother and sister-in-law along with her.

He stood, nearly knocking over the small square table. "What on earth are you doing in Edinburgh?"

At the sound of his voice, she turned. Then just stood there, halfway out of her cloak, her mouth hanging open.

"Looking for you," Jason answered for his uncharacteristically speechless sister, striding forward to shake Trick's hand. He removed his dripping wide-brimmed hat. "But we had no expectations of catching you. We were planning to bring her to Duncraven tomorrow."

Aghast, Trick dropped back onto the hard wooden bench.

"When did you leave?"

"Two days after your own departure. We were already planning a visit to Leslie, and Kendra talked us into letting her tag along. I can see we made better time than you did. Was your journey unpleasant?"

"It went well." He just hadn't been in a particular hurry. The closer he got to Duncraven, the less he looked forward to a reunion with his mother. Half of him was afraid to hope for a reconciliation—afraid she'd disappoint him again. The other half was hoping too much.

"Finding you here is a timely stroke of luck," Jason added.

Perching her wet cloak on a rack beside Kendra's, Caithren aimed a coquettish glance over her shoulder. "Does this mean we get our own room at an inn tonight?"

Jason's green eyes sparkled down at her. "Just like old times, sweet," he said, referring to their own madcap courtship, conducted mainly on the road.

His wife went on tiptoe to press a kiss to his lips.

"Mmm," he said, pulling back with a grin. "I'm suddenly starving."

"You're always starving," Cait and Kendra chorused.

"Be that as it may, I'm going to get us something to eat." He took Cait's hand and drew her toward the bar.

Kendra slid onto the bench next to Trick.

"How long have they been married?" he asked, moving close.

She smiled. "Almost a year."

"Newlyweds," he murmured.

"We're newlyweds, too," she reminded him. As though he could have forgotten. He moved closer still.

Unbelievably, she leaned against him.

This wasn't the Kendra he remembered—the one who always shied away from his advances. To convince himself she really was here, he ran a hand through her dark, rain-dampened hair. It felt as real as it looked. "I still like it this way best."

She pulled something from her pocket and glanced up at him. "What?"

"Your hair. Loose and streaming down your back. And wet isn't bad, either."

She blushed, then removed his hand from her head and put a letter into it. "I came all the way to bring you this. Read it."

"What could be so important?" Pushing his soup bowl aside, he spread the paper on the table and dragged a candle near. The letter was wrinkled and the ink a wee bit runny, but still readable.

"Dear Patrick Iain," he said under his breath, then scanned the page and whistled.

"It's a good thing I brought it, no?"

He nodded thoughtfully. "It could mean nothing. My mother might have asked him to write it just in case I'd decided not to come. A last ditch effort, if you will. But it's difficult to tell. I'm left to wonder what I'll be walking into."

"What *we'll* be walking into."

He nodded again, not at all sure he was happy about that.

But he was happy to have her here tonight. Wondering what could have prompted the change in her demeanor, he tentatively laced his fingers with hers, smiling when she didn't pull away.

Conversation buzzed around them, mixed with the sounds of eating and drinking. "Do you remember this Mr. Munroe?" she asked.

"Aye. He was a jolly type, always hanging around, it seemed. A very old friend of my mother's—they grew up together." His other hand gripped his tankard, and beneath the table, he pressed his thigh against hers. "From what I remember seeing through the eyes of a lad, I wouldn't be surprised to learn he was sweet on her."

"Did that not bother your father?"

"He was never home. Still, Father accused my mother of all sorts of things..." Musing, he took a long sip. He didn't like to think of his mother as an adulteress, no matter what his father had said.

Something brushed his boot, and regardless that Edinburgh was teeming with rats, he'd lay odds it wasn't one. It was, incredibly, Kendra's shoe. Looking toward her, he gulped more ale.

A faint smile curved her lips. "Now that your father is dead, what's become of her home, then?"

The question jarred him back to his senses. "Why, it belongs to me," he said, surprised at that sudden realization. The truth was, he'd done his fighting best to banish all thoughts of home from his mind. "The castle was her dowry, so it belonged to my father, which means it's now mine. But I won't be selling it out from under her. She may have been an appalling mother, but I won't put her out on the streets."

He drained the rest of his ale, wondering whether to be annoyed or pleased that his wife had materialized in Scotland. Experimentally, he tried to draw his hand from hers, smiling to himself when she held it tight.

He was pleased, he decided. Time spent apart did much to sway a man's emotions. Not to mention the apparent change of heart in Kendra. Mystifying, to say the least.

"Are you hungry?" he asked.

She shook her head. "Only tired." Her gaze flew over to Jason and Cait, heads leaned close at another table as they talked while Jason shoveled meat pie into his mouth. "We ate but a couple of hours ago." She yawned, meeting Trick's eyes. "We're too far from Duncraven to travel there tonight in the darkness, I presume?"

"Aye. It's a good day's ride."

"Then will we stay here?" she asked. "I hope so. I'm really tired."

"I've already taken a room." Something in her eyes—something in the way she was acting— made him hopeful. He swallowed hard. "Shall we go up?"

THIRTY

HE ROOM TRICK had rented was upstairs. Once inside, he paused a fleeting moment to set down the candle he was carrying, then dragged Kendra into his arms.

This was a different sort of kiss than she was used to—heated, insistent, wild. Exhausted though she was, she couldn't help but respond with equal intensity.

It was amazing how much she'd missed him. How much she'd missed *this*.

She plastered herself against him, thrilling to the feel of his solid muscles against her soft curves, the feel of his arms clasped around her, the feel of him holding her tight, as if she were something precious.

A long time later they came up for air, and she tilted her head back, gazing up into his compelling amber eyes. How could she have put him off for so long? Just breathing his sandalwood scent made her head swim.

She felt the knots in her stomach finally begin to loosen and unwind. Shivery and weak with relief, she swayed in his grasp.

"Evidently you really *are* tired," he said, sounding resigned or maybe disappointed. "When was the last time you slept?"

"Two days ago, it feels like," she admitted. "I was so worried for you."

His sudden smile was blinding. "You care, then, and you missed me, aye?" Her heart flip-flopped at his wolfish tone, and when she nodded, he kissed her all over again, even more fiercely, if that were possible.

Her breath was ragged by the time he stepped back. She felt boneless. He lifted one of her limp hands and ran his fingers over the amber stones that circled her wrist. "You're wearing it," he murmured.

"I—it matched my dress."

He pointedly looked her up and down. "Aye. Purple and amber—they go together so well."

She blushed, but he only laughed, a warm sound that sank into her very skin.

"Come, let's get you out of this damp dress and into bed. We'll have a long day tomorrow, and we'll be needing to leave early."

She only nodded as, with practiced fingers, he detached the tabs on her stomacher and unlaced her bodice, then drew her dress down and off, leaving her standing there in her chemise.

Lightly, tentatively, he rested his hands on her hips. She could feel the heat of his fingers through the fabric. "I've wanted to touch you," he said softly. "I've thought of nothing but you since the moment I rode away."

She froze. A little sound of desperation rose from her throat. She wanted to touch him, too. She'd come here wanting to touch him and more.

But she was so weary. Or maybe she was still a little unsure. What if this was a mistake? What if she gave herself to him, but he never opened his heart to her? Would she come to regret tonight?

"Kendra?"

The anxiety must have shown on her face. He sounded so

concerned. She placed her hands over his where they rested and tried to smile.

"It's nothing to worry about now," he assured her, "since we both need our sleep. But I promise, truly, you have nothing to fear—"

"I know," she interrupted. "Caithren told me it wouldn't hurt. Or at least not much, and only the first time, like you said."

"When?"

"After you left."

"You didn't believe her, though, did you?"

"Yes." She nodded frantically. "Yes, I did. And I came here wanting…"

"But then…" he prompted, waiting expectantly.

She bit her lip. "I'm just too tired," she finally said, knowing it was more than that but not knowing how to put it into words.

"Then get some sleep," he said.

She thought she wouldn't. But when he pulled back the covers and she gratefully crawled into bed, exhaustion overcame her.

THIRTY-ONE

T WAS pitch-black when Kendra awakened sometime in the night, the candle long since guttered out. Trick was in bed beside her. In his sleep he was hugging her, his arms wrapped tightly. When she tried to wiggle free, they tightened more, clamping her to his sleep-warmed chest.

She felt smothered, trapped.

But she couldn't fight him, couldn't get away. She was too tired…she would try again later, after she got some more sleep…

Dawn was breaking when next she opened her eyes, feeling inexplicably lonely. Squinting in the faint gray light, she looked over to where Trick lay on his back, apart from her, snoring softly, his hands lax by his sides.

She scooted close, throwing an arm across his chest, but he snored on, still motionless. A stab of hurt, tiny but deep, took her by surprise. Tamping it down, she rolled to her back and stared at the beamed ceiling overhead, replaying last night in her mind.

After the kisses they'd shared, she couldn't believe she'd simply gone to sleep. When she first walked into the tavern and saw him, she'd wanted him more than she could say. She'd embarked on this journey wanting him.

And she knew he wanted her.

And he was her husband, for heaven's sake! What on earth was she waiting for?

She knew the answer, of course, but she also knew it was the wrong answer. Marriage couldn't be about giving something to get something else. If theirs was to succeed, they would both have to share themselves, body *and* soul. And if he couldn't see that…

Well, she would have to show him.

She would have to stop holding back.

"Trick?" she called softly.

No response.

She poked his shoulder. "Trick?"

"Hmm?" Without opening his eyes, he rolled toward her and flung an arm over her middle.

She snuggled happily into his warmth. "Tomorrow," she said, struggling to keep the tremble from her voice, "tomorrow night, I want to sleep with you."

"Sleeping now," he murmured.

"No. I want…I want…"

His eyes slid open and gazed into hers, so close. "Are you begging, *leannan*?" he whispered, a tentative note of hope in the words.

"I'm begging," she answered simply.

He raised up to give her a sleepy smile and an even sleepier kiss. When his head dropped back to the pillow, his arms tightened around her, holding her fast against his body.

And she drifted off to sleep again, not feeling smothered at all.

THIRTY-TWO

"THERE'S THE castle," Trick said after a long day spent on the road. "In the distance, atop that hill. Just as I remembered."

Kendra squinted through the half-light of dusk. "It looks… forbidding." At the end of a narrow, twisty path, twin square towers rose from the hill, thrusting gray and ugly into the leaden sky. "How old is it? Is there no manor house attached?"

"Thirteenth century. It's just the two connected keeps. They're large, though—the distance is deceiving."

"It must be very cold."

"There are fireplaces."

"I'm not talking about the temperature. It doesn't look like a friendly place."

"It isn't," he said shortly.

While two carriages and a luggage cart rolled slowly behind, attended by Trick's servants, they guided their mounts silently past a somber gray-stone church that stood at the edge of a small village. The simple homes seemed eerily empty, however. Though the rain had stopped, no children had come out to play, no women were hanging out wash, no men were at work.

The clip-clop of their horse's hooves sounded loud in the odd stillness.

"Where is everyone?" Kendra asked.

"I'm wondering myself." He glanced up the hill. "Do you hear laughter?"

"Maybe. Far away."

"Up at the castle." As they rode closer, he could hear it better. "They must be holding an entertainment that includes the whole village. Strange…I cannot remember anything like that from when I lived here. My mother doesn't strike me as the type."

"People change in eighteen years."

"I expect you're right." Lost in memories, Trick remained quiet as they made their way to the hill and started up it. The laughter grew louder. When they crested the rise, they saw athletic events in progress on the lawn that bordered the keeps. Five young men were lining up for a foot race while two other lads executed standing jumps and lassies poked fun at their results.

"Will you test your skills?" Kendra asked as they slid off their horses.

"Maybe later." Trick gave her a shaky smile, handing his reins to an Amberley outrider.

A few curious glances were focused their way, but no one made a move to greet them. Shrugging, Trick instructed his staff to find the stables and settle the horses, then took Kendra's elbow and headed inside. Worn stone steps rose to a landing and a small, arched door that stood open, allowing more laughter to drift out into the cool early-evening air.

Beyond the door, a short tunnel led through the twenty-foot-thick wall. At the far end of the passageway they stepped into the first towering keep.

It was every bit as dark and cold as he'd remembered. Iron chandeliers dripped with candles struggling vainly to brighten the great hall, a vaulted chamber of ancient gray stone.

He stood stock still while memories flooded back: having

lessons at the old oak desk with his tutor; taking meals at the long trestle table with his mother; playing at her feet while she sat with her embroidery at the far end where flames roared in the immense canopied fireplace, his toy soldiers lined up on the scarred wooden floor. The Cavalier soldiers had always won, of course, since Father had been away fighting among them.

The chamber was teeming with people, and two children chased around him, but he barely took notice even when one bumped his knees. "I remembered it larger," he told Kendra. "It's not nearly the size of Cainewood's great hall."

"It's large enough."

"I recall thinking as a child that it was so big and high a man on horseback could turn a spear in it with all the ease imaginable."

"He'd have to get through the door first," she said with a grin.

Indeed, the entrance they'd just ducked through was shorter than Trick by a head or more—precisely to stop raiders on horseback from entering. Even on foot, a grown man couldn't enter without stooping, therefore hampering his ability to attack. He remembered asking about that short doorway as a child, over and over, as children were wont to do.

"You look pale," Kendra said.

"Memories." He shrugged, looking around. "I believe there's a painting of Queen Mary of Scots under there," he said, indicating a rectangle draped in black.

"Why is it covered?"

"To prevent the spirit going in the wrong direction."

Trick blinked, wondering who had answered.

"You look oddly familiar," he heard Kendra say, and turned to see the lad she was addressing.

He could only stare. Several heartbeats passed while all around them people cheered on their favorite of two men playing jump-the-stick.

"I'm Niall," the blond young man introduced himself, bewilderment clouding his golden eyes. "And I thank you for attending my dear mother's wake." He paused expectantly and then added, "Whoever you may be."

"Patrick Caldwell, the Duke of Amberley," Trick replied. "And my wife, the Duchess. And I'm looking for *my* mother."

"Crivvens." Niall visibly paled. "I should have guessed. She always said we looked like twins." And he launched himself at Trick, wrapping his arms around him and letting loose a deep, shuddering sob. "You came," he blubbered. "You're a wee bit late, but you came, after all. I told her you would."

At a loss, Trick let the youth hang on his body, wetting his surcoat with heartfelt tears. Hesitantly he placed a hand on the lad's back and gave him a couple of awkward pats. His mind swimming in confusion, he looked to Kendra, sending her a silent plea for help.

She tapped Niall on the shoulder. "Who are you?" she asked.

The young man stilled and pulled back a bit, a frown creasing the forehead above his red-rimmed eyes. He looked to Kendra and blinked hard, swiping a hand under his nose. "I'm your husband's brother," he said slowly.

Feeling blank-headed, Trick gingerly extricated himself. "I have no brother."

"Aye, you do." Niall's gaze trailed to the center of the chamber. "And our mother is in that coffin."

ROBBED OF breath, Trick woodenly followed Niall to the open coffin. He wanted to protest—in his head, he was screaming this couldn't be his brother, it couldn't be his mother in that box—but words wouldn't come. Words were beyond him just now. Stepping closer, he peered inside.

It was she.

She appeared older than he remembered, though her gown looked as though it would befit a younger woman. Her *deid-claes*, he realized—the first duty of a new Scottish wife was to sew the funeral clothes for herself and her husband. She'd obviously followed the custom. Beneath the gown, her legs were encased in the traditional white woolen stockings, and upon her feet were sturdy shoes, symbolic of the thorny path she was about to journey.

He'd traveled all the way here to make his peace with his mother, but that was never to be. His mother was dead.

It seemed impossible.

Her serene appearance sat at odds with the churning in Trick's stomach. Why had she written to him? What would have been said between them had he arrived in time? Questions raced in his head, and he wished mightily that she would open her eyes and answer them.

But there were coins on her lids to keep them closed—it was feared that if one looked a corpse in the eye, it would take you as a companion. And he knew that, coins or not, she wouldn't be answering him, anyway.

His mother was dead, and he seemed rooted to the floor.

"Touch her," Niall urged, doing so himself, his fingers gentle on their mother's cheek. "They say it will banish the ghosts of her from your mind."

Trick reached out, then pulled back. "I cannot."

It had been too long since he'd touched her in life. Eighteen years of loneliness, eighteen years of resentment. This journey had been a pilgrimage of sorts, his chance to mend old wounds, reconcile his past so he could begin again with his new wife.

But inside him, the wounds seemed to gape open fresh.

His mother had always failed him, and this time was no different.

He turned and gazed into his brother's golden eyes. His own eyes, it seemed. Niall's hair was longer, shoulder-length, but the same shining straight blond as Trick's, and though Niall was younger—seventeen, Trick guessed him at—they were of a height.

His brother. He'd never had a sibling. His heart swelling with sudden emotion, Trick slung an arm around the lad's shoulders, and Niall clapped him on the back. Then they pulled apart and looked each other over.

"I have a brother," Trick said, and a small smile ghosted Niall's grief-ravaged face to match the larger smile on Trick's. "Who is your father?" Trick asked.

"Hamish Munroe. His wife died—shortly after you left, I believe—and he and Mam…well, they'd always…" The younger man drew a shuddering breath. "I'll take you to him."

THIRTY-FOUR

NIALL MOTIONED Trick and Kendra to a turret attached to a corner of the great hall.

They followed him single file up a narrow, twisting stone staircase lit by dangerous, old-fashioned torches set at intervals. The rocks looked ancient, and when Kendra put her hand to the wall for balance, she half-expected it to crumble beneath her fingers. But her hand just came away dirty.

She wiped it on her skirts. "I cannot believe people are playing games down there."

"It's the Scots way," Trick told her.

"Folk were somber early in the week," Niall explained. "But Mam has been gone six days now. All the tears have been shed, all the stories of her have been told and told again. The feasting, the games and riddles—it's all in her honor. The wake is a celebration of her life."

They followed him out into a spacious sitting room that seemed lacking in furniture. Though the windows were small and set back in incredibly thick walls, the stone was white-washed here and reflected the candlelight, making this chamber much lighter than the one downstairs. A large tapestry hung on one side, looking like it could use a good cleaning, and across from it, four faded red chairs were arranged to face a fireplace.

"Still and all," Niall continued, "this is nothing like Calum MacKinnon's wake last year. They propped up the dearly departed and put a pipe in his mouth, then took turns throwing boiled turnips at him to try to knock it from his lips. I didn't think Mam would appreciate that."

"I'd expect not!" Kendra exclaimed.

"Da is in here." Niall pushed open a door. "Come along."

The room was sizable as bedchambers went, with substantial oak furnishings lining the walls and a large four-poster bed in the center. A tall, gaunt man lay beneath the coverlet, snoring softly, and a middle-aged couple sat nearby on two chairs. They began to rise, but Niall waved at them to stay seated.

"Da." He reached to jiggle the man's shoulder. "Someone's here to see you."

Hamish Munroe started and opened his eyes, then blinked and looked again. "Patrick? Is that you?"

"Aye, sir, it is."

To Trick's apparent dismay, the older man's eyes flooded with tears. He held out a hand. "Come here, lad. Let me touch you." With seeming reluctance, Trick gripped his fingers. "Elspeth said you would come. I didn't believe her."

"I received your letter," Trick said, slowly reclaiming his hand. "Or rather, my wife did, and came after me to deliver it." He drew Kendra forward. "My wife, the Duchess of Amberley."

"I'm glad of your acquaintance," she said, reaching for the man's outstretched hand. It trembled in her grasp. "Please, just call me Kendra."

The man's fingers weakly squeezed hers, feeling hot and dry. "Then you must call me Hamish. It's pleased I am to meet you." Dropping her hand, he rolled his head on the pillow, indicating the other couple. "These are my oldest friends, Rhona and Gregor Haig."

"Your grace." Rhona rose and curtseyed, first to Trick and then to Kendra. "Your grace."

Kendra hated the formal address as much as she'd always thought she would. She smiled at the pale woman, wishing she could set her at ease. "I'm glad of your acquaintance," she said.

"Pleased to meet you," Rhona returned softly, not quite meeting Kendra's eyes with her shy blue ones.

Gregor bowed. "Your graces." Blue-eyed and silver-haired as well, he resembled his wife in the way that long-married couples often did. Kendra wondered if she and Trick might end up like that some day, but casting his golden countenance a glance, decided not.

"Sit," Hamish said before turning back to Trick. "They've been keeping me company." He paused and grimaced in pain, then blew out a breath. "I've fallen ill with the same plague that killed Elspeth, you see, and Rhona here is a fine healer."

His friend shook her head. "My possets and infusions don't seem to—"

"Hush, woman. I know you've done your best."

Wiping her hands on the skirts of her cranberry-red gown, Kendra stepped closer. "Your letter said that Elspeth's illness was inexplicable and alarming—"

"I thought so, at first," Hamish said. "But it was only that it was such a coincidence, aye, her sending that letter and then..."

When his voice faded, Niall took over. "It seemed such a coincidence that she should claim she was ill and then suddenly succumb. When Da fell ill as well, the doctor came to visit and" —tears flooded the young man's eyes—"and said they were suffering from a bilious fever. Nothing inexplicable."

"Did he say it was fatal?" Trick asked.

Niall crossed his arms, his familiar eyes radiating a mixture of grief and denial. "That doctor's a bampot if ever I met one. Da is stronger than Mam was. He's not going to die."

Gregor shook his head mournfully. "Last night, a coal in the shape of a coffin jumped from the fire to the hearth. Right there." He indicated the fireplace across from the bed.

"Old beggar-woman tales." Clearly agitated, Niall went to the hearth and grabbed a poker. "I don't believe such nonsense."

As if to contradict his son's opinion, Hamish's face contorted with another pain, and he bent over double in the bed.

Rhona rushed to his side and pressed a cup filled with vile-looking green liquid to his lips. "Drink, Hamish." A tear rolled down her wrinkled cheek. "Have a sip for me, will you?"

He did, and then his eyes closed and he seemed to fall asleep. Niall stabbed angrily at the fire, as though daring another coffin-shaped coal to jump out.

Trick moved closer and took Kendra's hand. "Only at Duncraven," he muttered under his breath, "is it cold enough in the middle of summer to keep a fire burning day and night."

"It's cold within Cainewood's thick stone walls as well," she whispered back.

But that was one of few similarities between the two castles. Though both were centuries old, the parts of Cainewood that had been restored were modern and clean, while this place looked aged and worn out. The white paint was chipping off the walls, and cobwebs lurked in the corners.

As the estate's mistress, she would never stand for such slipshod housekeeping. But Elspeth had been ill these weeks past—perhaps that explained the neglect.

"Come along," Trick said. "Let's leave him to sleep."

"Patrick. Wait. I wish to speak with you." Hamish forced open his eyes. They looked black, until Kendra realized they were light brown but seriously dilated. The older man's voice wheezed through paper-dry lips. "About...about your...your mother's letter."

"You're weary, Da." Niall dropped the poker and crossed to his father. "You're always better in the morning," he said, brushing the straggly gray-blond hair off the man's forehead. "You can speak with Patrick then."

"Elspeth's burial is in the morning," Rhona reminded him in a strangled whisper.

"Oh, aye." The young man closed his eyes for a moment while he recovered his composure. "Then after," he said when he opened them. "Or the next day. You don't have the strength now."

When his father nodded and rolled to his side with a grimace and a groan, Niall ushered Trick and Kendra from the room.

THIRTY-FIVE

*B*ACK **DOWNSTAIRS,** Niall beckoned to his newfound brother. "Come, you should sit. This must be quite a shock to you both."

Trick allowed himself to be led through the crowd of reveling mourners. Servants passed among them, offering plates of oatcakes and shortbread. Goblets filled with spirits sat waiting on a sideboard, and he snatched one as he walked by, drinking deeply.

Beside the great hall's magnificent canopied fireplace, Niall pushed him into a seat niched into the wall. Trick drank again, then looked around him and leapt to his feet.

"Nay, you belong in the sedile now," the younger man said, gently easing him back down to the fur that draped the stone bench.

Kendra sat beside Trick in the niche and silently took his hand. He gave her a grateful half-smile. Just as he felt uncomfortable in his father's English mansion, neither did he feel that he belonged in this sedile—the seat of honor for the master of the house. Against his back, the stone felt too cold, too solemn.

But he did belong here now—that much was the truth. No matter how awkwardly that truth rode on his shoulders.

Heat rolled out of the fireplace beside them, and torchlight glinted off the armor scattered around the perimeter of the chamber, a reminder of days gone by. Curious glances were slanted in Trick's direction, and people seemed to be edging their way closer.

Oblivious to it all, his mother lay in a box in the center of the room.

Sipping again, he looked away, up to Niall. "I cannot believe she's dead."

"I share your disbelief." Niall hesitated, then seemed to come to a decision. "But unlike Da, I'm not entirely sure there's no evil force at work. I intend to get to the bottom of it." His suddenly narrowed gaze hinted at bravery beyond his years. "Will you help me?"

"I wasn't planning to stay here," Trick said. "I came at my mother's request, and now she's dead." He had pressing matters back home. The king's mission still awaited completion.

"Who is this?" a woman asked, stepping close. Her dull chestnut hair was pulled back into a severe bun, and she looked to be a few years older than Trick.

"Ah, Annag." Niall's smile failed to reach his eyes. "May I present the Duke of Amberley, my mother's eldest son. Patrick, my half-sister, Annag."

"Pleased to meet you," Annag said, although she clearly wasn't. Her dark brown eyes flashed with some emotion Trick couldn't put a name to, but it was plain enough she didn't like him. Or didn't like him here.

"And Duncan," Niall continued as a man joined their little gathering. Another of Hamish's grown children, from the looks of him. He and Annag bore a marked resemblance to each other, the most obvious being their matching expressions of distaste.

Raising the tankard in his hand, Duncan took a deep swallow. "When are you going home?" he asked, skipping the preliminaries.

Wondering why he felt surrounded by the enemy, Trick

rolled his shoulders and changed his mind about leaving so quickly. "When I'm good and ready. I've only just met my brother, and—"

"Oh, *him*," Annag interrupted, shooting Niall a look every bit as deadly as the one she'd given Trick. "High and mighty Lord Niall."

Apparently Niall had been passed off as the duke's son, and Hamish's other children resented him for it. But the young man only gave a good-natured shrug. "If you cannot be civil, Annag, I will ask you to leave my home."

Duncan took another gulp of his spirits. "It's *his* home now," he said, indicating Trick with a smarmy, pleased gleam in his eye.

Niall flinched, but recovered swiftly. "And so it is, I suppose."

"I won't be throwing you out," Trick assured him.

"I wouldn't trust him," Annag told Niall, as though Trick weren't even there. "He may have been born here, but he's turned English."

When Niall just glared at her, she continued. "Well, listen to the man speak. English through and through. He's forgotten his Scottish roots, and even you, gowk that you are, ought to know better than to trust a Sassenach."

"Don't the women need help in the kitchen?" Niall asked his sister. "And what are your bairns up to? And Duncan, have you sat some time with Da this day? Rhona and Gregor could use a respite. They're good friends, but you're his son." After that brave speech, he looked down to his scuffed black boots. "Give us some peace, will you? Our Mam just died."

"And good riddance," one of them muttered as they shambled away. Trick wasn't sure which, but it didn't seem to matter. So far as he could tell, they both hated him equally. The fact that they'd hated his mother as well came as no surprise.

From what he knew of her, she, at least, hadn't deserved their love or admiration. His father had made no secret of her many faults, and already one had been proven true this night: His mother had been an adulteress. Perhaps Hamish's wife had been dead when Niall was conceived, but Elspeth's husband had not.

Trick slumped in the stone niche and extricated his hand from Kendra's, belatedly realizing she'd been holding it in an iron grip.

"Welcome to Scotland," he said, flexing it ruefully.

*A*LTHOUGH IT had grown late, the castle was still overrun with people. Apparently, after his years away had made it clear to Elspeth that her husband was never returning, she'd invited Hamish to live with her and Niall. Hamish's older children had been grown by then and had homes of their own, but since Elspeth's death they'd been staying here to keep him company. With his grandchildren, too, of course. One big, happy family, as the saying went.

Somehow, Kendra didn't think it applied in this case.

"Are you sure you don't want the master's chamber?" Niall asked.

Trick shook his head. "I wouldn't dream of moving your father. There must be a spare bed here somewhere."

And that was how Trick and Kendra came to follow Niall up what seemed like miles of winding stone stairs, until at last they stepped into a huge, deserted chamber.

Their footfalls echoed off the wooden floor as they entered. A few torches on the walls did little in the way of brightening the place, and the room gave off a musty scent that spoke of long disuse.

Kendra stared up at the gloomy vaulted stone ceiling. "It's spooky."

Niall gave her a wan smile. "Cromwell garrisoned his soldiers in here when he commandeered the castle near the end of the war. A hundred of them, lying foot-to-head on the floor, with a second hundred on another level that rested on those posts you see protruding from the wall." He pressed a key into Trick's hand. "Your staff has moved your things up here already. Shall I have them sent up to attend you? You've a valet, do you not, and a ladies' maid?"

"Aye, my man goes by Cavanaugh, and Jane sees to her grace." Trick's gaze met Kendra's. "But I think we can fend for ourselves tonight."

Though she didn't know if he'd intended to remind her, Kendra's skin prickled as she recalled what she'd promised would happen this evening. Then he looked away, pensively moving off, and she knew that he was no more thinking of such things than she had been.

After all the upheaval today, last night seemed so very long ago.

"Good night, then," Niall said.

"Good night," she returned softly.

Listening to the young man's footsteps fade, she shivered. The candle in her hand wavered, throwing shadows on the gray stone walls. "I dislike to think of Cromwell visiting this place, let alone using it as a headquarters." Oliver Cromwell had been indirectly responsible for the deaths of her parents and her own exile that followed.

"It was against my father's wishes, to say the least. He was a Royalist, through and through." When Trick wandered to one of the deep-set windows, his voice echoed back out from it. "My mother talked him into leaving."

"Did she, really?" Squeezing into the niche, Kendra joined him at the window. In the small space he felt warm and near, yet cold and distant, too. By moonlight, she could barely make out the village below, surrounded by acres of wild pasture and tended fields. "This was her family's ancestral home, wasn't it? Why would she willingly surrender it?"

"She was a Covenanter," he said shortly, stepping back into the room. "Come, our chamber is this way."

He ducked through an arch in the wall and pushed open a thick oak door. On her way inside, she shot one last look at the empty vaulted chamber. The garrison. She wondered if it was haunted by ghosts of dead soldiers.

Not that she believed in anything like that.

The bedchamber was enormous. A four-poster bed in its center looked dwarfed, and after the din of the wake below, the room seemed deathly quiet.

She moved to set the candle on a bedside table, the dull wooden floor sounding gritty beneath her shoes. A fire burned on the hearth, and she wondered who had built it. Jane or Cavanaugh? One of Duncraven's servants? "Are we the only ones up here?"

"Aye. The towers are mirror images. One great room and one bedchamber on each top level." With a rueful smile, he locked the door behind them. "As a child, I was terrified to come up here alone."

"I'm rather terrified now," Kendra admitted. She sat gingerly on the edge of the bed. "After you left the place to Cromwell, how long was it before you returned?"

"Until now." Trick shrugged out of his surcoat, folding it over the back of a chair that sat before an immense carved oak desk. "My father settled my mother with relations and spirited me away to France. I was five." Abruptly he dropped to the chair. "I never saw my mother again." His voice cracked. "And now I never will."

Kendra rose to wind her arms around his neck from behind. "Surely she knows that you cared, that you came for her."

"Maybe." Sighing, he absently slid open the top desk drawer

and riffled through some papers. Dust flew out, tickling her nose. She felt him stiffen. "Losh, would you look at this."

She straightened. "What is it?"

"A letter. From Oliver Cromwell himself."

A chill ran up her spine. "We were just talking about him. How odd." Irrationally afraid to touch the evil man's writings, she kept her distance while Trick scanned the page. "When was it written?"

"Eighteenth November, 1650."

"So long ago. Nearly eighteen years."

"Other than my father, I rarely remember anyone coming up here." His gaze swept the chamber. "Nothing's changed in the interim. The same bed, the same desk. This letter probably sat here all this time."

"What does it say?"

He looked back down to the yellowed parchment. "'I thought fit to send this trumpet to you, to let you know that, if you please to walk away with your company, and deliver the house to such as I shall send to receive it, you shall have liberty to carry off your arms and goods, and such other necessaries as you have. You have harbored such parties in your house as have basely and inhumanly murdered our men; if you necessitate me to bend my cannon against you, you may expect what I doubt you will not be pleased with. I expect your present answer, and rest your servant, O. Cromwell.'"

"Dear heavens." Kendra released the breath she hadn't realized she'd been holding. "Words from the devil himself. Can you blame your mother for wanting to walk away?"

He shrugged uncomfortably. "Father refused at first. He'd fought well and bravely in support of Charles, but when Cromwell opened fire...well, I was inside." He drew a sharp, shuddering breath, obviously remembering.

Kendra was horrified. "He opened fire with a child inside?"

"Aye. The bombardment destroyed the east parapet and tore

a large cavity in the stonework—did you not see it as we came in?"

"I wasn't looking."

"At my mother's behest, Father sent word to the Lord Protector that he saw the point, and he walked away, taking me with him and never looking back."

She folded the bed's simple white coverlet back and lowered herself to the plain sheets below. "She wanted to save you."

"She wanted to save her family's castle." He turned in the chair to face her. "If she'd cared for me, she would have come along with us."

"Maybe your father wouldn't allow her."

"Maybe," Trick conceded. "He was certainly mum on the subject." He shoved the paper into the desk and slammed the drawer. "And I wouldn't blame him if he did leave her that coldly. She was no mother or wife to be proud of. Besides being a Covenanter, she was an adulteress, and—"

"You judge her harshly."

A momentary look of self-doubt crossed his face, then disappeared so fast, she wondered if she'd imagined it. "I've told you how I feel about infidelity."

She'd told him how she felt about infidelity as well, but she knew better than to bring that up. Living with three brothers had taught her how to deal with male moods. Gingerly. "Do you remember her as being that terrible?"

"Nay, but I was only a child."

Kendra glanced down and smoothed her cranberry-colored skirts, then lifted her head to meet his gaze. "If your father and she were at odds, why do you believe everything he told you about her?"

"For the longest time, I didn't want to," he admitted. "But then so much time passed and she never, ever came for me…"

"There are two sides to every story, Trick."

If his sudden silence wasn't agreement, at least he was man enough to consider she had a point. The only sound in the chamber was that of the flames that danced in the fireplace, until at last he said, "But I'll never hear her side of it, will I?"

Pain radiated off him in waves, but she knew that now was not the time to talk about that. It was too fresh. "What is a Covenanter?" she asked instead. "I know English history by rote, and Greek and Roman, but I'm afraid I was never taught much of Scotland's past."

"I cannot say that I'm surprised," Trick said dryly, but the remark didn't sound at all disparaging, merely resigned. He leaned back in the chair and began untying his cravat. "Many men, including my mother's father, signed a document known as the National Covenant. When the Civil War broke out, the Covenanters sided with the English Parliament against the king, in return for Cromwell's promise of a religious reformation in England and Ireland, based on the Scottish Kirk."

"And Cromwell never followed through."

"Nay, he did not. But it took a long time for the Scots to realize they'd been duped."

"They'd thrown their lot in with the devil."

With a grimace, he nodded and slowly drew off the cravat. "I'm afraid this castle was instrumental in Cromwell's victory. My father never forgave my mother for that."

With a flick of his wrist, the cravat landed on the desk in a flurry of frothy white. She stared at it. He was undressing. Whether or not he'd spent the whole day thinking about it, she was sure he expected her to share his bed—*really* share his bed—tonight.

A little ball of anxiety lodged in her middle.

She tore her gaze from the lace-trimmed linen. "My father fought with King Charles, too. And died, along with my mother. He would have sympathized with your father's stance."

His expression hardened. "Father was no saint, believe me. I liked him no more than I did my mother. I'm well rid of them both."

"Trick—" She bit her tongue, reminding herself his parents

had both hurt him terribly—and both were dead. Perhaps this harshness helped him to cope with the loss.

She forced a gentle smile. "How does it feel having a brother?"

He smiled in return—perhaps the first smile she'd seen from him today that wasn't tainted with cynicism. "He's quite pleasant, isn't he?" His eyes softened as his fingers worked to loosen the laces on his shirt. "I find it hard to believe he came from my mother, and—and that man."

She wasn't surprised to find he didn't care for Hamish, either. "Niall looks just like you."

"I know. It's amazing." Leaning forward, he pulled off a boot. "I wish I could stay longer and get to know him. Maybe he'll come visit us at Amberley."

"That would be nice." The more of Trick's clothes that came off, the more her insides turned to jelly. Too nervous to just sit there and watch, she pulled her own shoes and stockings off, then stood and wandered over to a small arched door. "Where does this lead?"

"To another staircase, if I remember right." In bare feet, he padded over and unlatched the iron bar that secured the door, poking his head into the darkness beyond. His voice echoed back. "Aye, another winding stairwell. To the roof above. Prisoner's Leap."

"Prisoner's what?"

"Prisoner's Leap." He turned to her, the stairwell gaping blackly behind him. "In the old days, prisoners were brought up from the dungeons once a year and allowed a chance to gain their freedom by successfully jumping from one tower to the other. Twelve feet, with their hands tied behind their backs and a hundred-foot drop to the bottom. And no running start."

"My heavens. Did any of them make it?"

"I expect not." His lips turned up in a half-smile. "Maybe that's why the villagers were practicing their long jumps today."

A little shiver ran through her. "I'm not sure I like this place, Trick."

"Why? Because I had barbaric ancestors?" Although reserved, his grin did seem to lighten the room somewhat. "There's no one in the dungeons today, so far as I know."

"So far as—"

"I'm jesting." He shut the door to the stairwell, and she relaxed a little. "Come here."

"Not until you bar that door."

With a strangled laugh, he did so. "There, we're safe. Come here, Kendra. I need you tonight."

No one had ever said anything like that to her before, and they were certainly words to melt a girl's heart. Frightened as she was, she walked to him.

When his mouth met hers, an unfamiliar emotion welled up inside her, one that washed away her doubts, soothed her nerves, relaxed her tense muscles. She was a warm puddle of contentment, wanted and cared for and safe.

That's what it is, she realized. For the first time, she felt completely safe in her husband's arms. Tonight he wasn't some distant, imposing stranger. He was a boy who had been afraid of the dark, a son who missed his mother.

A man who needed *her*, Kendra.

Her body humming in anticipation, she wrapped her arms around his neck and threaded her fingers in his short, silky hair. His kisses were soft and sweet, flavored with the faintest trace of the whisky he'd sipped downstairs. He planted little kisses on her cheeks, her nose, her forehead, and finally the sensitive hollow of her neck. He lingered there while his hands went to work unlacing her gown. Her own hands tugged the bottom of his shirt from his breeches.

He pushed her dress down and off, leaving her in only her chemise. She yanked the shirt over his head, and he gave a frustrated laugh when his arms tangled in the full-blown sleeves.

When he ran his hands down her sides and around to pull

her closer, she felt a jolt of excitement. He smelled of soap and sandalwood, and the sight of his bare, golden torso made her unsteady on her feet. Thank goodness he was holding her up.

Slowly he backed her across the room and eased her down to the bed. Settling beside her, he hesitated, propping himself on an elbow, his head hovering above hers. Beneath the ends of his hair, his eyes caught and held hers. The faint stubble on his chin glistened in the candlelight.

Her heart pounding in her ears, she gazed steadily back. She was ready. Her arms reached to pull him close.

The air was rent by a strangled groan.

"I cannot do this," he gritted out and rolled away. "I cannot do this. I cannot do this with my mother lying in a box downstairs."

She felt an instant of stunned disappointment before her head cleared and her arms went around him anyway. She squeezed tight. "It's all right. I understand."

And though she wouldn't tell him so, almost as strong as her disappointment was her relief.

"I'm sorry," he whispered. "I just cannot—"

"Hush," she said. Slowly she drew air into her lungs, giving herself time to adjust. "You have nothing to be sorry for."

She sat and pulled the coverlet over them both, then lay back down. With a regretful sigh, he turned to face her and gathered her close, his head heavy against her shoulder. "I'm sorry," he whispered once more.

And long minutes later, when her heart had calmed, for the second night in a row she fell asleep in his arms.

STILL WIDE awake an hour later, Trick eased away from Kendra and slid from the bed. Quietly he pulled his shirt back over his head, then lit a candle and slipped from the bedchamber, closing the door softly behind him.

The stone steps felt cold and rough beneath his bare feet as he trod carefully down them. A low murmur of voices drifted up the stairwell. Arriving on the ground floor, he stopped and stared.

Annag and Niall sat before his mother's coffin. Behind it, Duncan hid, manipulating a clever arrangement of twine and twigs. A deep, unearthly "Ooooooooooh" issued from his throat as he twisted his hands. Elspeth's body jumped and twitched, and Annag jumped and screeched. Rising to his feet, Duncan burst into laughter and lifted a glass of whisky in a clearly drunken toast.

Trick couldn't believe his eyes.

Niall caught his gaze and offered a small smile. He rose and came to meet him at the bottom of the stairs. "Couldn't you sleep?"

"I kept thinking of her lying down here. Cold, in a box." Trick ran a shaky hand back through his hair. "It seems so unreal. I thought I could just sneak down here and...convince myself, maybe. Sit here a while."

Niall nodded slowly, then turned to his half-siblings and raised his voice. "Give us peace, will you? Go on to bed. We'll sit with Mam alone."

Still laughing, they staggered out, taking a bottle of spirits and their glasses along with them.

The candles surrounding Elspeth's casket flickered in their wake. "Why were they sitting with her?" Trick asked after they'd stumbled out of earshot. "It's plain as anything they held her in no esteem."

"Da wouldn't like to hear they've been shirking their duty. Mam must never be left alone—they say that a corpse left alone will find the road to hell."

Knowing his mother's history, Trick imagined Hamish and Niall *would* worry about her finding such a road. He went to the coffin and set the candle he was carrying beside the others, averting his gaze from his mother's waxen face. "I feel like I should be able to talk to her. I came all the way from England to talk to her."

"Then talk to her," Niall said.

Trick sighed, wishing he had some of his brother's calm confidence—wishing he knew where to start. Owing to Duncan's prank, Elspeth's hands were no longer neatly crossed on her chest. Wincing at the sight of the twine still attached, he began to reach, then stopped.

"Fix her, will you?" he asked in a voice rough with frustration. "Get that off her."

While Niall gently did as he asked, Trick dropped onto a chair, staring blindly ahead. "I would think you'd rather sit by yourself than with those two. Especially considering they accord her no respect. I cannot believe what I saw when I walked in here."

"I cannot sit alone—there must always be two on guard." Niall took the seat beside him. "And a good prank at a wake is often enjoyed, even encouraged. You don't know our ways here, Patrick. For all you were born within these walls."

"You've the right of it there." Trick sighed. He'd never felt very English, but he didn't feel Scottish, either. He only felt confused.

"What did you want to say to her?" Niall asked. "You can say it, aye? Out loud, or in your head. Either way, she'll hear you."

"Do you think so?" Trick turned to gaze at his brother. "You seem a fine lad."

Niall broke into a grin—straight, white, and as familiar as the one Trick saw in the mirror every morning when he was shaving, except none of his brother's teeth were chipped. "I don't think Annag would agree."

"Nay, I expect she wouldn't. How do you put up with those two?"

The younger man gave a sheepish shrug. "They're not as bad as they seem. I grew up with them, aye? It takes two to fight."

"And you refuse to participate."

"More or less. Of course, once in a while…" The engaging grin reappeared before he sobered. "Annag…well, her husband's dead these two years past. And her with three bairns on her own. She wasn't always so bitter."

Trick hadn't realized she was widowed. "And Duncan?"

"He's never wed—no sane woman would have the smaik." Niall scrubbed his hands hard over his face, then blinked and looked at Trick. "The three days of keening have passed, but if you've no words for Mam, perhaps the traditional ones would help."

Trick knew little of this land's traditions. "I'm listening."

Now that the rowdy mourners had gone home to bed, the great hall seemed larger, yawning huge and dark, much more like Trick had remembered. Niall took a deep breath before his voice rose in song—not the mournful, haunting wail that Trick had imagined a keening would be, but a heartfelt, melodic lament that echoed off the vaulted stone ceiling.

"Oh, Mam, ye have left us! *Ochone!*"

He paused and looked at Trick, his golden eyes expectant.

"*Ochone?* Is that some pagan god?"

"Nay, it's Gaelic. Nothing more than an expression of sorrow or regret."

"*Ochone,*" Trick said softly, expecting to feel silly. But he didn't. Sharing the sitting duty with his brother, keening their mother together, felt right.

"Why did ye leave us? *Ochone!* What did we do to ye? *Ochone!* That ye went away from us?"

"*Ochone!*" Trick sang for him.

"'Tis ye that had plenty!"

"*Ochone!*"

"And why did ye leave us?"

"*Ochone! Ochone! Ochone!*" The ancient syllables slipped through Trick's lips, and a tiny sliver of the pain went along with them.

WHEN DAWN HAD broken, Trick made his way upstairs to find a gray-garbed woman in his room, her back to him as she stoked the fire on the ancient, blackened stone hearth. At the sound of him entering, she slowly straightened and turned.

He gasped. "Mrs. Ross?"

"Aye, it be me," the tiny woman said in a reedy voice, coming closer. She was shorter than he remembered, but of course he'd last seen her through the eyes of a child. Her face was even more wrinkled, if that were possible, her blue eyes faded but glittering the same as they always had. "Why, I'd recognize you anywhere, even after all these years. Patrick, dear, how fare you?"

"I'm well." The door banged louder than he would have liked when he shut it behind him, and in the bed, Kendra stirred. "How are *you*?" he asked Mrs. Ross. Heart's wounds, the woman had to be eighty years old.

"No complaints. But your mam..." The blue eyes flooded with tears. "I don't know what happened. She went so fast..."

"Trick?" Kendra blinked herself awake. At the sight of a

stranger in the room, she clutched the blanket over her chemise-clad form and tucked it beneath her chin.

"My wife, the Duchess of Amberley," Trick introduced her. Smiling to himself, he walked over to smooth her sleep-mussed hair. "Good morning, *leannan*. No need to blush—it's only Mrs. Ross, my old nurse."

"And his mam's before him," the older woman added.

"I haven't thought of her as Mam in eighteen years," he murmured. "She's Mother to me now."

Mrs. Ross's thin, bluish lips straightened into a disapproving line. "She was never Mother to you, and well you know it. She was much warmer than that. And why did you not write her, aye?" Her expression hardening, the bird-like woman came near and whacked him on the shoulder, although not without a modicum of affection. "You'd been taught how to write before you left here. Eighteen years and you never once answered one of that poor woman's letters."

Trick rubbed his shoulder. "What on earth are you talking about? She never sent me a letter."

"Oh yes, she did. She cried for weeks after your father dragged you away. Then she started writing the letters—"

"I never received any letters," Trick insisted.

But Mrs. Ross wasn't listening. "—every week at first, then every month, and then, when she never heard back, once a year. Until finally she gave up. You broke her heart, Patrick Iain. I knew you were a bairn yet, but I thought I'd taught you better—"

"Mrs. Ross!"

The woman jumped and began twittering, and Kendra clapped her hands over her ears, her eyes wide as round portholes.

He waited until his old nurse quieted before continuing. "I never received her letters. Did you hear me, Mrs. Ross? I *never* received her letters. Not one."

She stilled, studying him for a long moment. "Did he keep them from you, then?" she whispered and burst into tears.

He gathered her fragile frame into his arms. "There, Mrs. Ross. I know you miss her." Patting her on the back, he silently cursed his father—the blackguard—for hiding the mail. And himself for never considering the possibility. "Mother wouldn't want you to be sad."

"Your mam was like a daughter to me." She raised her tear-stained face. "A woman isn't supposed to outlive her children."

He pulled back and nodded, and they gazed at each other until Kendra shifted on the bed and cleared her throat. "What was she like, Mrs. Ross?"

The old nurse dashed the tears from her wrinkled cheeks and sat herself down to catch her breath. The bulky oak armchair dwarfed her. "She was good. A good woman, Elspeth. She had no easy life."

Kendra slanted Trick a glance, knowing he didn't want to hear this, but also knowing he should. "How is it she came to marry the duke?"

"*Him.*" The woman looked as though she wanted to spit. "King Charles—the first one—arranged the match. Part of his plan to Anglicize Scotland." She twisted her bony fingers in her lap, her voice going softer, as though it were coming from far away. "And my poor Elspeth was so in love with Hamish Munroe...but her father had never liked the lad. Too common for his tastes. A third son, and a businessman besides, buying flax for the weaving and then selling the cloth. He made a fine living, but Elspeth's father was the laird, and he expected better for his daughter. The Stuarts had made him an earl, but that didn't make him English."

"Of course not," Kendra said gently, noting that Trick seemed to be studying his bare toes. "My husband told me his grandfather signed the Covenant."

"Aye, the old earl was a bit of a rebel. It's in the blood. But still and all, he was happy enough when the king matched his daughter with a duke. He forced poor Elspeth into it."

Thinking of her own forced marriage, Kendra bit the inside of her cheek. "How?"

"You don't want to know." The nurse's lips pressed tight, and Kendra knew that her brothers' matchmaking had been nothing like Trick's grandfather's. Unlike Elspeth, deep down she knew a small part of her had *wanted* to wed Trick. And she also knew her brothers wouldn't have pushed her into the marriage if that hadn't been so.

"She was unhappy all her days," Mrs. Ross continued. "Even after the duke left her alone to reclaim her lost love, she never recovered from the loss of her son." She brushed at her gray skirts and stood. "Well, I'd best be off about my duties," she said, looking to Kendra. "Welcome to Duncraven, your grace."

"My pleasure. I hope we can talk more later."

"Aye, we can. After we bury my Elspeth." With a long, miserable sniff and a swish of her skirts, she sailed from the room.

Kendra waited until the door clicked closed behind her, then released a heartfelt sigh. "Oh, how terribly romantic. Doesn't it give you the shivers?"

"Doesn't what give me the shivers?" Trick opened a cabinet and began pulling out clean clothes.

"Thinking about Elspeth and Hamish, in love all those years. And finally getting to be together." While his back was safely turned, she slid from between the sheets and pulled down her chemise, which had ridden up in the night. Relieved, she made her way over to look for a suitable gown to wear to a burial. She wondered what would be an appropriate way to wear her hair. She would have to send for Jane to come up and style it. "Now that I've heard your mother and Hamish's story, I'm so glad she invited him to live with her here. Maybe they found a bit of happiness, after all."

"Maybe my mother sent me letters. But that didn't make her a good woman." He shook out a shirt, then stripped off the one he was wearing, a long pull of his muscles as he drew it over his head. Kendra watched, enjoying the view more than she'd be willing to admit. "She was still an adulteress, and a Covenanter, and she betrayed—"

"Did you not hear a word your nurse said about what happened between her and Hamish?" Pulling out a forest-green dress, she sighed and held it up. "This is the darkest thing I brought. Do you suppose I'll be scorned for not wearing black?" She turned it around and frowned at the scooped neckline. "What will Hamish think? I noticed yesterday that the women here wear more on top."

He blinked at her. "Your top looks fine to me. Niall knows you didn't come here expecting to attend a funeral. And I cannot imagine why you'd care what anyone else thinks. Hamish, especially." He put on the clean shirt, then began to unlace his breeches. "I feel sorry for the old man, but that doesn't mean I like him. He lived in sin with my mother—"

"I suppose, then, that you've never so much as touched a girl without the benefit of wedlock."

His long fingers fumbled on the laces. "Will you stop interrupting me every time I try to make a point?"

Ignoring that request, she stared at him a long moment, until he lifted his head to meet her gaze. "Well?" she pushed.

Clearly fuming, he remained silent while he hopped on one foot and then the other to remove the breeches. Half annoyed, half amused, her gaze followed the breeches down, but his shirt was very long and covered him nearly down to his knees, revealing nothing of particular novelty.

She blushed when he caught her looking, but he only crossed his arms and leveled her with a glare so fierce that, had he been a Gorgon, she would surely have turned to stone. "I've already told you I don't hold with infidelity. I've never touched a married lass."

"I'm glad to hear it. Besides my brothers, you're probably the only male member of Charles's court who can say so." She dropped the green gown over her head and wiggled it into place. "Hamish and your mother were victims, Trick. They shared a love that lasted decades—a perfect love, like my own parents'." Threading the laces across her bodice, she looked up. "Would you deny them what little happiness they found? Have you no mercy?"

"I haven't the choice to deny or allow it, do I? What's done is done. That doesn't mean I have to like it. Or them."

A knock came at the door, and she yanked her laces tight and reached for her stomacher while he stomped over to answer it.

"What now?"

Dressed in a red kilt, Niall took a startled step back. He turned to leave, taking with him an armful of matching tartan.

Trick reached to grab his elbow. "Forgive me, Niall. I thought you were Mrs. Ross. Not that I should have been barking at her, either." He blew out a breath before turning to face Kendra. "And I'm sorry I was so short-tempered with you."

"I understand," she said softly. The stomacher safely attached, she smoothed her skirts and put a hand to her disheveled hair.

Niall didn't seem to notice it, however. "Patrick didn't get any sleep," he told her.

"Did you not?" She cocked her head at her husband speculatively. "Any at all?"

"Nay. Niall and I stayed up with Mam." Kendra thought she caught a look of surprise when he heard his own use of the name. "We did some keening."

"Did you?" She couldn't imagine.

"*Ochone!*" Trick sang, the word vibrating up to the beamed ceiling, and Niall laughed, breaking the tension.

"Come in," her husband said, closing the door behind his brother.

Niall aimed a glance at Trick's bare legs and then held out the length of red tartan. "I've brought this for you."

Trick made no move to take it.

"I thought you might like to wear it to the burial."

"My father wasn't Scottish."

"Your mother was." Niall pushed the woolen fabric into Trick's arms, along with a wide leather belt. "Wear it in her honor. Just this once. She'd have been proud to see you in it."

A long silence stretched between them while Trick shifted the cloth in his hands, a range of conflicting emotions playing across his face. "I don't know how to wear it," he said at last.

His brother's smile managed to look sad, pleased, and relieved, all at the same time. "That I can help you with." He placed the belt on the floor and crouched beside it, his own kilt skimming the wooden planks as he folded the tartan into pleats and arranged it on top of the leather. "Lie down on this," he instructed.

Trick's lips quirked. "You're jesting."

"Nay. The only way to get it on properly is to lie down."

Kendra squelched a laugh as her husband looked askance at his brother, then sighed and lowered his long frame to the floor.

"Nay, move up," Niall said. "The belt must be at your waist." After Trick scooted higher, his brother went about wrapping the pleated material around him and belting it securely. "Now you can stand," he said, offering him a hand up.

Trick flexed his knees experimentally while Niall took the large expanse of fabric above the belt and tucked it into the front, crisscrossing it to make what was essentially two big pockets. Then he drew up the extra cloth in back and draped it over Trick's shoulders.

Trick took a few steps, watching the kilt sway around his knees.

"Feels odd," he said. "As if I'm wearing a dress. What is worn underneath?"

Niall glanced down at his own kilt. "Nothing is worn. Everything underneath is in good working order." He looked up with an impish grin.

Kendra's gaze drifted over to her husband, who looked

mildly scandalized. He also looked devastatingly handsome. Better even than he had in his black highwayman garb, or maybe it was just the intriguing knowledge that there was nothing underneath.

The very thought of that brought heat to her cheeks.

"Well?" Niall asked, and she glanced up to find both men focused on her. "How does he look?"

She felt her cheeks burn even hotter. "F-fine," she managed.

"I cannot wait to get it off," Trick grumbled.

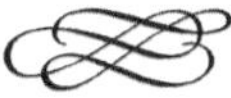

*L*ED BY A PIPER with a black pennant tied to his pipes, Trick and Niall headed the eight bearers carrying their mother's coffin from the castle down to the little kirk. Behind them, family, friends, and castle staff followed along in a rather informal procession.

"Why aren't there more women?" Kendra asked in a low voice from where she walked beside Trick, modestly wrapped in a simple brown shawl she'd borrowed from Mrs. Ross. Her hair was constrained in a plaited bun.

"Most of the women usually remain at the home," Niall explained. "They'll be preparing for the return of the mourners. And keeping my father company. It's not customary for a husband to attend his wife's burial."

"And she was his wife in his heart, I'm sure of it."

Her romantic sigh set Trick's teeth on edge. "Hamish couldn't have come along, anyway. Not in his state of health."

"Well, it's nice to know his illness isn't keeping him from something he'd regret missing later." She leaned close to Trick. "Hardly anyone is wearing black," she observed beneath her breath.

"We don't think it necessary to wear black in order to pay

your respects," Niall said, obviously overhearing her. "Not everyone can afford special clothes for mourning."

After that, she kept quiet. The bagpipe music was loud, the notes sad and lingering. All too soon they were gathered in the small graveyard, and the solemn tune came to an end. The single wreath of heather was removed from atop the oak coffin, and the lid was lifted for one last time.

Stepping closer, Trick peered inside, trying to memorize his mother's features and reconcile them with his faded childhood memories. Had she been the kind, caring woman he sometimes saw in his dreams, or the deceitful one Father had told him about? What had they said, those letters he'd never read? Had they been written out of duty, or had the pages been spattered with her tears?

Knowing this was his last chance, he reached to touch her.

Her body felt cold and unreal, and touching it did nothing to banish the ghosts of her from his mind, as Niall had said it was meant to do. A shiver ran through him. Their painful rift would always stand between him and what should be happy memories.

Others came forward to pay their respects and touch his mother, then two men moved to replace the lid. Trick bent down with it as it was lowered into place, catching a final glimpse of her face.

"Farewell," he whispered, and Kendra squeezed his hand.

He hadn't even realized she'd been holding it.

A short service was read, but he didn't hear what was spoken. His mind was numb, the words filtered through a haze. He shuffled his feet on the soft green grass, his gaze wandering the gentle mounds that marked where bodies lay, many of their headstones rendered smooth and unreadable by the ravages of weather and time.

A bell was rung; then the mourners filed past the tree where it hung, dropping coins into the plate below as they went. Burial silver. For form's sake, he imagined—surely the Dowager

Duchess of Amberley wouldn't need help to defray her funeral expenses.

Or would she? He admittedly knew nothing of his parents' financial arrangements. Upon his father's death, he'd clearly failed in his duty as a son. And now it was too late.

He cursed himself roundly, if silently.

The mournful whine of the bagpipes rose again, and people began drifting out of the little cemetery. As he turned to leave, Kendra came around to face him and took both his hands. "I'm sorry," she whispered.

He shrugged. "It's not that I'll miss her, precisely."

"But you'll miss what could have been."

She was wise, his young wife. Her fingers tightened on his before she dropped his hands and turned to Niall. Without hesitation, Trick's brother walked into her arms and stayed there, his shoulders hitching while she murmured words of comfort.

She was not only wise, but compassionate. She would make a good mother someday, Trick realized, then shook the stray thought from his head.

She would never get to be a mother at the rate they were going.

At long last Niall pulled away and gave Kendra a shaky smile. "Thank you."

"I'm your sister now," she said kindly. "And I'll not leave you to bear it all on your own, Niall. Family should support each other through such grief, but with your father ill, and your sister and brother—" She broke off, flushing pink. "Anyway, I'm here for you."

"I'm here for you, too," Trick put in, surprised by how good it felt to say that. To be needed by someone. He hadn't had that in eighteen years, and he'd never thought he'd have it again.

Despite all his father's tales of his mother's treason and treachery, he looked at the stoic backs of the people walking toward Duncraven and knew that once upon a time he'd felt happy in this place. Even living in that forbidding gray keep at the top of the hill.

And now here was a brother, needing him. And a wife, if only he could overcome the barriers between them.

Clouds were gathering again, and the air held that elusive scent that meant wet weather was on the way. He pulled the wool tartan around his shoulders as they began following the others.

"What happens now back at the castle?" Kendra asked.

"A *draidgie,*" Niall said. "Entertainment, dancing, drinking, eating. Some tears and some merriment."

"More merriment?" She looked incredulous.

"To celebrate the life of the one who passed on. A time to wish the departed spirit a safe landing on the other side."

She nodded, apparently accepting what Trick was coming to realize: Things were different here. Not bad or wrong, just different.

Still, they were both surprised at Niall's next words to Trick.

"Are you ready for a good fight?"

FORTY

*N*IALL STOMPED into the great hall, stuck two fingers in his mouth, and let loose a loud, piercing whistle that had every head snapping in his direction.

The jabbering tapered to an expectant silence.

He drew a deep breath and raised his voice. "It's a sad day when my mother is put into the ground and not even one blow is struck at her funeral!" And without another word, he turned and slapped the nearest man.

Instantly, the chamber erupted in a free-for-all. Colorful tartans whirled in a blur. Food and drink went flying, trestle tables were overturned, and chairs were tossed aside.

Along with the other women, Kendra backed against a wall, not caring that it was rough and probably grungy. She clutched Mrs. Ross's shawl to her chest, unable to believe her eyes. No fists were used, but the sounds of open-handed slaps rang in her ears as family and friends went at each other with enthusiasm.

She watched as Trick delivered a stinging slap to Duncan, who retaliated with a blow across the mouth that had her husband backhanding blood from his lips. But he flashed her a chipped-tooth grin, then pivoted on a heel and slapped a perfect stranger.

He looked to be enjoying himself immensely.

"Men," she muttered under her breath.

The woman beside her shook her head, her gray-brown plaits swishing along with it. "I'll never understand them."

"You want mine?" another woman asked.

A good ten minutes passed before Niall decided enough violence had been done to pay the proper respect to his mother, and finally called for a truce.

Still grinning, Trick made his way over to Kendra. "Could you believe that?"

"No," she said flatly.

"Me, neither. I've never seen anything like it. But it felt good, aye?" He paused for a satisfying breath. "I was angry. I've been angry since I got here. I didn't want to come in the first place, then my mother was dead—"

"But you discovered a brother."

He rolled right over that. "It felt good to whack some people. Cleansing."

With a wry smile, she shook her head, and he smiled back, then winced and put a hand to his mouth.

"Are you hurting?" she asked.

"Not enough to care." As if to prove it, he dragged her close and pressed his lips to hers. She tasted the faint coppery tang of blood, and then the distinctive, slightly sweet flavor she was learning to think of as Trick.

Though she felt conscious of people watching, she couldn't stop her hands from going around him, sliding beneath his plaid to feel the planes of his back through his fine lawn shirt. Her fingers itched to touch his skin, but the shirt was tucked securely into his kilt. His kilt with nothing underneath.

The thought turned her legs to pudding, and she sagged in his arms.

"Is something amiss?" he asked with a grin, setting her away. Her plaited bun was beginning to unravel, and he tucked a rogue strand of hair behind her ear.

Kendra's borrowed shawl had slipped from her shoulders to the floor. "Goodness." She knelt to reclaim it, marveling that his knees looked as firm and golden and appealing as the rest of him. She surprised herself by sneaking a peek beneath the tartan on her way back up, but it was too dark under there to see anything. On this cloudy day, the dozens of candles in the chandeliers overhead were all but useless against Duncraven's gloom.

Trick's lips quirked as he watched her straighten. "I asked Niall what *leannan* means," he said.

"And?"

"Sweetheart." He rubbed a gentle thumb beneath her chin, then bent to brush a soft kiss across her lips. "It means sweetheart."

Something fluttered inside her. "*Leannan*," she whispered.

His expression suddenly sobered, as though he'd just remembered what had happened here today. He dropped his hand and smoothed down the front of his kilt. "Heart's wounds, I'm tired."

"You didn't get any sleep."

Her gaze followed his as he looked around the gathering. A few thoughtful souls were helping tidy the worst of the brawl's aftermath, but most folk were back to eating and downing spirits. Their chatter seemed to grow louder in proportion to the drink they consumed.

"I think maybe I'll lie down a spell," he said.

"Shall I come with you?"

"Nay." He scrubbed his palms over his face, avoiding her gaze. "I'm really tired."

She tried to ignore the rush of disappointment. "Perhaps I'll go sit with Hamish a while."

"That would be kind. It's a difficult day for him."

He began to leave, but she snagged him by the sleeve. "It's a difficult day for you, too, Trick."

When he shrugged and pulled away, she let him go.

FORTY-ONE

"**H**OW IS HE doing, dearie?"

Startling from a doze when Hamish's old friend Rhona came into the room, Kendra bolted upright on her chair. "He slept the whole hour I was here." For the hundredth time since she'd entered the chamber, her gaze darted to the bed and she was relieved to see Hamish still breathing.

Rhona touched a hand to her shoulder. "I thank you for sitting with him. It was a welcome respite."

"I can stay longer."

"Nay, you run along now," she said, settling to her embroidery. "Down at the *draidgie*, all the young people are telling ghost stories."

Kendra slowly rose. "If you're sure, then." At Rhona's nod, she slipped out the door and closed it quietly behind her.

She didn't want to hear ghost stories—this bleak castle gave her shivers as it was. Deciding to check on her husband, she made her way up the dozens of winding stone stairs.

He wasn't in their chamber.

Someone had made their bed after they'd left, and it was clearly undisturbed. He hadn't come up to rest at all. Disappointed that he'd apparently fibbed to get away from her, she wandered to the room's only window, deep in an alcove set into the wall. Resting her palms on the cold stone sill, she leaned out and looked up at the sky.

Gray, to match her mood. The clouds were moving swiftly; rain was on the way. A blackbird fluttered from the heavens and down to the garden below, spreading its wings to make a graceful landing on a stone bench.

Right next to a figure clad in a bright red kilt.

He was hunched over something in his lap. Something white. Paper. The man who'd told her he never wrote anything was outside scribbling up a storm.

She hurried downstairs, huffing and puffing by the time she reached the bottom, and headed for the door.

Niall caught her on her way out. "Why such a rush, lass? Is something amiss?"

"N-no." Of course nothing was amiss—in the midst of catching her breath, Kendra wondered for a moment just exactly what she'd been rushing out to do. Yell at Trick for not taking a nap? Or for pouring his heart out on paper? He was a grown man, entitled to do as he pleased, especially on a disturbing day like this one.

She forced a smile for her brother-in-law. "Nothing is wrong. I thought I'd just go out and take some air."

The bagpiper was warming up discordantly, and a fiddler was busy tuning. "The dancing is about to begin," Niall told her.

She looked around, noticing the tables and chairs had been pushed against the walls. "There's really going to be dancing?"

"Aye, there is. Mam would have expected us to celebrate her life rather than the death that ended it." The musicians launched into a jaunty tune, and Niall made an incongruously solemn bow. "Are you dancin'?"

She could see that he was trying very hard to keep what he considered to be the proper *draidgie* outlook, although she was sure he ached deep inside. Her heart went out to him. No matter that dancing today seemed wrong to her, she dropped a curtsy and gave him the answer he was expecting.

"Are you asking?"

With a laugh that reminded her of Trick's, he twirled her into the center of the room.

The dance was performed by four couples in a circle, and it took all of Kendra's concentration to follow it. Halfway through the complicated pattern, she was already breathless and realized she had little time to think on her troubles, and neither did Niall.

Perhaps dancing on a day like this wasn't such a bad idea, after all.

When the tune ended, he took her by the elbow to draw her from the floor. "My father wants to talk to you and your husband," he said conversationally.

Surprised she hadn't lost it, she resettled the shawl on her shoulders. "He's sleeping."

"Patrick?"

"No, Hamish. Trick is out in the garden."

"Ah, then it was him you were rushing out to see." The music started again, and couples began forming a double line down the middle of the chamber. "Why do you call him Trick?" Niall asked.

"A childhood name. His father called him that."

"But Mam didn't." He sighed. "So much I don't know about my brother."

"He doesn't know you, either. But he'd like to, I'm sure."

He gave her a sad, gentle smile. "He won't be staying long enough to get to know me."

"Not this time. But he'll be back. I'll make certain of it."

"Now, that I don't doubt." The laugh rang out again. "I saw you two kissing earlier, and I'd wager you could make him do anything."

She felt her face heat. She'd never thought of herself as a girl who could persuade with kisses. With words, yes—having been raised a Chase, she could argue with the best of them. But she'd never been much of a flirt, let alone a seductress.

Pleased at the thought, she grinned. "Thank you for the dance, Niall."

"My pleasure." The second dance was ending, but another would start soon. "Will you do me the honor again?"

"Maybe later. I've a man to meet in the garden." And hopefully persuade to open up to her…with kisses, if necessary.

FORTY-TWO

"TRICK."

Her voice was gentle, but he startled anyway, quickly flipping the paper facedown on the bench beside him. He'd been so entrenched in his thoughts, he hadn't heard her approach.

Her soft sigh belied her smile. "You shouldn't chew on your quill."

He swept it from his mouth. "I know," he agreed shortly. Having never let anyone catch him writing, Trick felt sulky at being discovered. He told himself to stop acting childish and took a calming breath. "It's how I chipped my tooth. What are you doing out here?"

"What are *you* doing out here?"

"Nothing." Fiddling with the quill in his hands, he looked up at the sky. "I couldn't sleep."

"Did you try to sleep?"

He was silent a few beats before dropping his gaze to meet hers. "Not really. I…I was writing." Silly that it seemed hard to admit, but there was no point in lying, seeing as she'd found him in the act.

Her expression seemed wary, reserved; then her gaze went to his kilt. He bit back a smile as she met his eyes.

"May I read some of what you wrote?"

His hand moved protectively over the pages. "Why would you want to?"

"What you write is part of you, Trick."

True, but not the best part. What spilled out onto paper was often the parts of himself he didn't like.

"Is it poetry?" she asked.

"Aye. It's just poetry. Pretty words that sound good together. Meaningless."

"It wouldn't be meaningless to me."

Hurt dulled her eyes, and he looked away, wishing he had it in him to give her what she wanted. Rolling the sheets into a narrow tube, he tucked it into the pocketed front of his kilt. "Come, let's walk. The garden is quite whimsical."

He took her down a path where dozens of tiny model castles nestled in the shrubbery on either side. "The castle garden," she said with a smile, brightening with a determination that didn't fool him. "How very clever."

"It was my mother's doing. When I was a lad, she spent hours out here every summer. And when winter kept her inside, she designed and built the little castles. Sometimes she let me help." Their footsteps crunched on the gravel path. "Of course, Father thought it was a waste of time."

"What did he want her to be doing instead?"

"I don't know." He'd never wanted to know; not knowing had felt safer. "I never understood them or the way they were together."

"Was he a difficult man to live with, your father?"

Difficult didn't even begin to describe the late Duke of Amberley. "I cannot say what living with him was like for her, but for me, it was a nightmare."

She slipped her hand into his. "He had high expectations for you, did he?"

"No. At least not in the way you're thinking." He felt as tired as he knew his voice sounded, drained and numb. "I was naught but a means to an end. A pawn in his game. It's safer to send a child to do the dangerous work, you see. Nobody would expect a child to be smuggling goods in his clothing. Nor would they see a child alone on a hill with a lantern, night after long, cold night, and suspect he was there to signal in ships."

"He had you do those things?"

"And worse." His tone closed the subject. He hadn't the energy—or the will—to go into more detail.

"What about when you were older?"

He stopped on the path. "Must we talk about this now?"

There was a long pause while she seemed to come to a decision. "No, of course not," she said with a smile he suspected was forced. "Your mother's castle garden is charming. It's quite secluded back here, isn't it?"

"Aye, it is that." The trees made a leafy avenue, shielding them from prying eyes. "No one has ventured back here for an hour or more."

"Hmm…" she said speculatively, the smile turning real.

"Hmm? What do you have in mind?"

"Only this." And she backed him against a poplar, shooting up on her toes to crush her mouth to his.

After a stunned moment, he gathered her into his arms, letting her kiss comfort him the way words never could. She'd rejected him for so long that he found himself wallowing in her sudden acceptance. Her soft fragrance surrounded him, more potent than any whisky. Her fingers trailing over him were like a balm, soothing the jagged edges of his feelings and leaving a blissful warmth in their wake.

When her hand raked one of his *draidgie* bruises, he sucked in a breath. Blinking himself awake, he wound one hand into her hair and let his lips drift over her soft cheek, then her ear. "You've never kissed me first before, *leannan*. What's got into you?"

Silent save for the uneven sound of her breathing, she pulled back and searched his eyes. The wind came up, sending the poplar's white-bottomed leaves into a silvery dance, and she leaned back in his arms. "It's this kilt, Trick. It drives me wild."

He threw back his head and laughed, startling several blackbirds from their perches above. "I will have to ask Niall if I can keep it."

She grinned. "The idea is not displeasing."

The blissful warmth returned. And spread. No girl had ever told him he drove her wild.

"But only if you kiss me again," he added, then did so himself before she had the chance.

He kissed her again and again, losing himself in her. She leaned into him, slipping her hands under the plaid, digging her fingers through the laces on his shirt to rest against his skin. Beneath her fingertips, the beat of his heart matched hers that he could feel through her gown. Frantic.

Breaking away, he pressed his forehead hard against hers. "Is this wrong?" he asked in a whisper. A strangled whisper, because he knew the answer.

Another gust of wind sent the brown shawl flying, but she let it go. "No, of course it's not wrong." A scant inch away, her eyes looked confused. "We're married, Trick."

"That's not what I meant." How on earth could he keep her at arm's length for the sake of respect, when after all these weeks she'd finally come around? He wanted her to understand. He wanted to understand himself. "I buried my mother today. And now I want...I want only to be with you. I'm thinking only of you. As though her death, her life, didn't matter."

"Of course she mattered." Her hands fell away and came up to grip his shoulders; her eyes cleared of the confusion and filled with concern instead. "It's natural, Trick. To want to reach out, reconnect. With people, with living. Like the *draidgie*, don't you see? Niall said it was to celebrate your mother's life, rather than dwelling on the death that ended it. It cannot be wrong."

She made a sort of sense, and he wanted to be convinced. When she touched her lips to his, his shoulders relaxed beneath her fingertips. The kiss turned from sweet to fervent, and for long, perfect minutes, all he thought of was Kendra.

The only person, it seemed, who had ever really cared.

"I don't deserve you," he whispered, wondering when this would end. Because everything good in his life always did.

A soft smile on her lips, she went on tiptoe to kiss him again.

"Patrick! Kendra!" Niall's voice slashed through the leaves overhead.

Trick tightened his hold around Kendra's waist. "What does he want?" he muttered against her mouth. When his brother appeared on the tree-lined path, he dropped his arms and groaned.

"Da is awake," Niall said. "And this seems to be one of his good days." Producing the escaped shawl, the lad offered it to Kendra. "He wants to talk to you both."

FORTY-THREE

"**E**LSPETH WASN'T dying." Though Hamish was still in bed, he was sitting up for the first time since Kendra had met him. "When she wrote that letter, she was in perfect health."

His voice was strong and sure, which Kendra hoped meant he was getting better. Seated at his bedside next to Trick, she reached to touch one of his hands. "Perhaps she was already ill but didn't want to tell you."

"Nay, lass. Elspeth and I kept no secrets."

A look of disbelief crossed Trick's face. "Why, then?" he demanded. "Why would she have written saying she was dying if she wasn't?"

"She wanted to see you," Hamish said simply. "She was hoping the thought of her death would bring you here to Duncraven, even though you'd never answered any of her other letters."

"I never received any of her other letters."

"So Mrs. Ross informed me quite tearfully this morning."

"But you didn't believe her."

Hamish blinked. "Of course I believed her. What makes you

imagine I'd think the worst of you, Patrick? If you say you never received the letters, I take you at your word."

A faint pink stained Trick's neck. "My father must have intercepted them."

Kendra took his hand and squeezed, feeling tension coursing through him. He didn't want to be here, talking about this. He wanted to be back in the garden. He'd grumbled as much to her three times on their long trek up the stairs.

"Your father..." Hamish's fingers tapped an irritated tattoo on the coverlet. "I wouldn't put destroying her letters past him, I can tell you that."

Trick set down the goblet of whisky he'd snatched in the great hall and brought along with him upstairs. "I assure you, sir, I didn't hold him in any higher esteem than you did."

Sitting on the bed beside his father, Niall sipped from his own cup of spirits. "Da, do you want to tell Patrick why Mam summoned him?"

Trick's gaze snapped to his brother's. "Did she not just want to see me, then? Had she another reason?"

"Aye," Hamish said, "and it's a long story I have to tell you. A story about the first King Charles and his ill-fated visit here to Scotland."

"What could that have to do with—"

"Just listen." Looking toward the closed door to ensure their privacy, Hamish settled back against his pillows for the telling. "Charles was born here, as you know, but left when he was yet a bairn, and we Scots heard tell he rather fancied himself an Englishman." He took a small sip of the green concoction Rhona had left him, then grimaced and held out a hand for Niall's drink. "Still and all, Charles was our king—a Scottish king. The nobles insisted on a second coronation, on Scottish soil with the Scottish crown jewels. Thirty-five years ago, in the eighth year of his reign, he finally assented to the visit."

Intrigued, Kendra leaned forward. "Had he not been home in all that time?"

"He didn't think of Scotland as home, as you will soon see." Hamish drank, closing his eyes for a long, contented moment as the whisky slipped down his throat. "Excitement was rampant," he said after smacking his lips. "Everyone threw themselves into the preparations. Roads were fixed and bridges were repaired. Thatched roofs were replaced with shingles, lest the king should think us poor. All in all, a great deal of money was paid out to improve and decorate the Royal route and show we were as good as the English. We hoped to appeal to his Scottishness, so he'd let up on us and allow us to live as we saw fit."

He paused for another sip. "But it soon became clear that he wanted to forget his origins. He arrived here for a month-long tour with a baggage train two miles long. Fifty wagons, two bishops, dozens of courtiers. Along the way, they stopped to lodge with our Scottish nobles, bankrupting them one by one with all of their costly demands. On a whim, Charles would change his itinerary, bypassing the places that had been so carefully prepared and making it clear he wasn't impressed with the preparations anyway. He treated us as inferiors when we hoped he'd relate to us as the Scot he was by birth."

Trick's thumb kept teasing the palm of Kendra's hand, and his lips quirked when she shivered in response. He didn't seem to be paying attention to the story at all.

"When the coronation finally took place, it wasn't the traditional Scots one that had been planned, but an elaborate religious ceremony instead. A Church of England ritual. The people were aghast to learn such Popishness and blasphemy had taken place in a Scottish kirk."

Apparently listening more than she'd guessed, Trick grimaced. "I expect they were angry."

The older man nodded. "His actions incited a rebellion that eventually led to his end. But I get ahead of myself." He wetted his papery lips. "After the coronation, his last scheduled stop was at nearby Falkland Palace. All the local nobles were invited, and your mother went, of course, along with her family. Every able-bodied commoner was drafted to help with the banquet, myself among them, although I wasn't even Niall's age yet."

"Did the banquet go badly?" Kendra asked, pulling her fingers from Trick's.

"Not at all. We all thought it a roaring success, the entertainment more impressive than any we'd ever seen. But by then Charles had tired of Scotland—no doubt as much as we had tired of him—and at three the next morning, he woke the household and announced that he'd decided to leave immediately. Everyone at Falkland scrambled to ready his belongings for travel."

"What sorts of belongings?" Kendra asked as Trick reached over and took her hand again, resting it on his lap and trapping it there with his own on top. Neither Niall nor Hamish seemed to notice, but, scandalized, she couldn't help thinking what was beneath the the folds of tartan on which her hand rested.

Nothing.

"You wouldn't have believed what he'd brought along," Hamish was saying, his gaze glazed with memory. "My eyes boggled, they did. Besides clothing and furnishings fit for a palace—he slept in his own Royal bed—King Charles traveled with his household goods, personal treasures, jewelry, and his entire kitchen including the Royal plate. Half a ton of silver and gold. Not for him to be eating off plain Scottish dishes or drinking from plain Scottish cups. It was this we were ordered to help pack for his return to London."

"Half a ton?" Kendra said. "It must have taken you all night."

"The smells of the banquet still hung in the air, and we had but a few hours to get it done. Charles couldn't wait to leave. At first light, he set out. On the journey up they had crossed the River Forth by the bridge at Stirling, but this day the king was too impatient to take the long way around. His men found three boats to cross the firth from Burntisland to Leith and loaded two of them with as much as they possibly could. When his goods wouldn't all fit, Charles insisted the rest be loaded anyway, till everything was aboard and the vessels rode low in the water."

Trick frowned and shifted, draping an arm around Kendra's shoulders. "Were you there to see it?"

"Nay, but I've heard stories. It was storming something awful, that I do remember. The wind blew fiercely, and the waves tossed the boats as they piled the treasure chests aboard. King Charles was rowed to the third vessel while his domestics and servants went with his goods. Twenty-five people on one of those boats…and only two lived to tell the tale."

"Oh, no," Kendra said. "What happened?"

"The rest of them ended up at the bottom of the Firth of Forth, along with the treasure. Safe aboard another boat, Charles could see the vessel founder and sink, but there was nothing he could do to stop it. Nothing anyone could do to save any of those lives."

A chilling vision. Kendra leaned against Trick's side, taking comfort from his warmth. "Charles must have been furious."

"Aye, that he was. Folk claimed the sinking was an act of God to avenge his religious misdeeds, but he decided that witches were responsible and rounded up people to punish. It was injustice of this sort that led to our siding with the Roundheads in the Civil War, wrong though we were to do so."

Trick's fingers traced lazy circles on Kendra's shoulder, and her free hand curled in her lap. The one on *his* lap felt hot against the wool. Keeping her face passive, she nodded at Hamish. "Were the chests ever recovered?"

"Nay, lass, for the Forth is cold and deep. They lie there to this day."

He briefly closed his eyes. Eyes that looked familiar, Kendra thought and wondered why.

"But the treasure," he said when he opened them, "is not in those chests."

Trick's hand stilled on her shoulder. "Pardon?"

"You must understand, the people were angry well before the

witch hunt. After the banquet, your mother stole from her chamber and met me in the storeroom along with Rhona and Gregor—the four of us were best of friends, even then. The Yeoman of the Buttery had been charged with packing the kitchen, which included the Royal plate. John Ferries was his name. Shorthanded, he was, and willing to accept whatever help he could find. So we helped."

He fell silent.

Trick reached for his goblet. Niall put a hand over his father's atop the coverlet. "Tell them how you helped, Da."

Hamish sighed. "First we helped get John Ferries drunk. Then we helped fill the chests, but not with gold and silver plate..." He drew a long breath, a dramatic pause. "With rocks."

Trick choked on a sip of his spirits. "Rocks?" he repeated incredulously.

"Aye." Shifting on the bed, Hamish looked less than proud of what he'd done. "The treasure we spirited away. Poor John Ferries's body washed up on shore shortly thereafter, so the secret remained between the four of us. The Royal plate remains hidden to this day."

"Where?" Kendra breathed.

"If you're willing, I'll send Niall to show you. First thing tomorrow."

Trick failed to see the point. Intriguing as the story might be, he was planning to leave for home tomorrow. He needed to complete the king's mission. And make a fresh start with Kendra.

He gave her hand in his lap an experimental squeeze, smiling to himself when the pulse at her wrist sped up. "It's an interesting tale, but what does this have to do with my mother's summons?"

"She hoped—we hoped—that you'd return the treasure to its rightful owner. King Charles II."

Disappointment scraped a raw place inside him. His mother

hadn't been wishing for a reconciliation. Like his father, she'd wanted only to use him for her own ends.

"They never sold even one piece," Niall put in, a transparent attempt to make light of his parents' wrongdoing. "It's all been locked away in twenty-three chests for thirty-five years."

Hamish nodded. "You must believe me, we didn't take it to enrich ourselves. It was a prank, an act of revenge. We were young enough—angry enough—to risk such folly. And although we were fortunate in that our rocks sank and were never discovered, the misdeed has preyed on our minds ever since."

It would, Trick supposed. But the fate of his mother's soul was in God's hands now, and he wasn't responsible for unburdening Hamish Munroe's conscience.

Without Hamish, perhaps Elspeth would have come to love her husband, or at least learned to live with him, and Trick would have had a family. He owed this old man nothing.

Hamish took a long, bracing sip from Niall's cup. "Charles was beheaded—he paid for his actions. His son is a better man, a better king. We don't want the treasure—we never did. But your mother feared that if we returned it, we'd face arrest. So she was hoping you'd do it for us. You have the king's ear, and he trusts you—"

"How would you know that?"

"Do you think your mother wouldn't keep watch on you the best she could? We—she hired people to report to her. If ever you'd really needed her, Patrick, she'd have been there."

He *had* really needed her. The times he'd been left alone in a horrid school in France, and the other times, the endless years he'd worked as little more than a slave for his father's shameful business.

But the past was done. He'd long ago accepted the hand he'd been dealt, and more pressing matters required his attention.

King Charles deserved the Royal treasure, and heaven knew he needed it. The poor man was reduced to selling titles to make expenses. Even now, his ambassadors roamed the country with blank forms for anyone wanting and willing to pay for a baronetcy. Regardless of whether this ill old man deserved Trick's loyalty, his monarch did.

Charles. His life these days seemed to be reduced to serving Charles, no matter the personal cost.

"I'll do it," he said with a resigned sigh. "Show me the chests tomorrow, and I'll find a way to get them home."

FORTY-FOUR

"IF I'M GOING to lug this treasure home," Trick muttered on the way down the stairs, "I need to make plans."

Behind him in the dark, narrow turret, Kendra sighed. All the special feelings between them seemed to have vanished into thin air. She a put a hand on his shoulder. "What is it you have to do? Maybe I can help."

"I must see these twenty-three chests and decide how many extra vehicles I'll need to transport them, how many additional guards I must hire. And what am I going to do with it all during overnight stops? We'll attract attention traveling through the country with an entourage worthy of royalty. The treasure will need to be protected around the clock."

"We'll work it out," she soothed. "Let's see the treasure first, then we'll deal with the logistics."

"My head aches just thinking about it."

"Perhaps it would be best to dispatch a messenger to Charles. He could send a contingent of soldiers to escort the goods."

"And wait here, twiddling my thumbs, for three weeks or more until the soldiers arrive? I think not."

They arrived downstairs to find that the dancing had ended

and the trestle tables were back in place. Torches had been lit on the walls to augment the light from the iron chandeliers, and women bustled about, setting out all the dishes they'd brought for the *draidgie* supper.

Trick handed Kendra a trencher from a stack on the end of a table, then took one for himself. The food smelled delicious, but he was in a foul mood, and the offerings he piled on his platter didn't seem to help any.

Odd, he was, for a fellow, she thought as she chose a piece of spice cake and a wedge of lemon tart. Her brothers had never failed to be cheered by a hearty plate of food.

Niall waved them over to join him at an empty table, filling two more goblets with ale from a pitcher. They'd no sooner settled themselves than Annag and Duncan dragged her young ones over to take the remaining seats.

"What did Da want with you?" Annag demanded, waving a girl onto the bench and plopping a runny-nosed toddler beside her.

Niall filled another goblet for her. "Nothing of your concern."

Duncan sat, lowering his trencher to the table with a thud. "Did he not tell you of a new will, then?" he asked in a voice pitched to sound casual.

"Nay," Trick said flatly. He cut a hunk of mutton with more vigor than was necessary.

"Here, Alastair." Annag shoved a dish of hoch-poch in front of another of her children. "Are you certain there was no mention of a will?"

"Aye." Niall reached for some bread. "And Da seems to be gaining strength. So whatever it is you're hoping to gain upon his death, you shouldn't be expecting it anytime soon."

Kendra found Annag's affronted look less than convincing. "I'm not wanting Da to die, you eejit."

"But now that *he's* shown up, a duke and all"—Duncan slanted a none-too-friendly glance at Trick before focusing back on Niall—"you won't be needing any of Da's paltry holdings. With a new brother to provide for you."

Niall's mouth opened and closed like a salmon out of water.

Kendra saw Trick's jaw set before he pointed his knife at Duncan. "What makes you so certain I'm willing to provide for Niall? I'd lay odds your father didn't jump to such a conclusion."

Duncan sipped from his ever-present whisky, glaring over the rim. "What do you know of our father?"

"Enough to suspect he wouldn't readily cut his youngest son out of his will." Trick met Duncan's glare with one of his own. "His *favorite* son."

Sensing violence about to erupt, Kendra bit the inside of her cheek. "Can we not all be civil?"

Annag turned in a huff, her gaze narrowing with disdain on Kendra's low neckline. "You stay out of this."

"You'll address my wife with respect," Trick said through gritted teeth. If Annag had been a man, he'd have been on her, Kendra thought, drawing the shawl tighter to cover the front of her gown. As it was, she sensed he was barely holding himself in check.

When Annag's son began crying, Duncan's face turned red to match. "Who needs this trouble?" he barked at Niall, half-rising to his feet. "Ever since *they* got here"—he waved an angry hand at Trick and Kendra—"I cannot have a word with you without them sticking their noses into it. Keep them out of our family business, or else—"

"Or else what?" Niall stood, his fists clenched at his sides. "I'm grown now, aye? You cannot beat me up anymore. I'll floor you in a minute."

It was no idle threat. Niall topped his brother by a good four inches, and his youthful frame was solid and honed, while Duncan's was softened by sloth and drink.

Apparently not as dim-witted as he was surly, Duncan sat back down. "Just keep them away," he growled. "Both of them."

"They're family as much as you," Niall shot back. "*My* family."

Annag aimed a pointed look at Duncan. "Blood will tell."

"Blood will *run* if you don't back off," Trick said darkly. His knife clattered to his trencher, and, as he stood, his hand went to the hilt of his sword.

Kendra rose quickly, reaching out a restraining arm. "Have we not seen enough violence here tonight?" Evidence still remained of the earlier brawl. "Come, Trick. I know where I'm not wanted."

She curtsied to Niall but ignored his siblings as she took Trick by his sword hand and led him away. He allowed himself to be dragged, although not before fixing Hamish's older children with a murderous glare.

Murderous…Kendra wondered for a second if she'd just narrowly prevented murder. Trick was a highwayman, after all, accustomed to violence, and she'd never seen him this incensed.

But then she shook her head, chiding herself. Her husband might be an enigma, but she felt certain he was no murderer.

Still, it couldn't hurt to get him as far from Annag and Duncan as possible. She led Trick out the door and around to the garden. The whole long way he didn't say a word, but as they stepped into his mother's wonderland of little model castles, she felt him begin to relax.

Night had nearly fallen, and the branches overhead were black silhouettes against the dark gray sky. Hand in hand, they walked in silence up the long avenue of trees and back, up then back again. The crunch of their footsteps on the gravel seemed lost within the sounds of rushing wind and rustling leaves. Trick's grip gentled on her hand, and his breathing settled; his gait became looser.

A light mist began to fall, and in mute agreement, they headed back inside.

The door shut behind them, blocking the rain and the noisy wind. In the tunnel that led through the thick stone wall, Trick stopped and put his hands on her shoulders. Illuminated by the torches that lit the entry, his eyes searched her face. Kendra gazed back, wondering what he was looking for.

"I don't like those two," she said quietly. "I wouldn't put anything past them. I don't know what Hamish has to bequeath to his children, but I suspect they'd go to any lengths necessary to see it ends up in their hands. All of it."

Trick shrugged, moving closer, backing her up until she felt the wall, hard against her spine. He ran a hand through his hair and sighed. "They're powerless, and they know it. They speak from desperation." He skimmed his knuckles across her cheek. "Don't worry your pretty head about them, *leannan*."

Leannan. It sounded different now that she knew what it meant. "My head is more than pretty," she retorted, not immune to his nearness or the sudden spark that lit his eyes.

He nodded slowly. "Aye, that it is." The wind had blown much of her hair loose from the bun, and he tucked it behind her ears, one side and then the other. He glanced into the great hall, sending a quelling glare to some poor soul who dared to look their way. Then, shielding her body from view with his larger one, he lowered his lips to hers.

The kiss was long and gentle, reawakening the feelings that had started in Hamish's chamber. Of their own accord, it seemed, her hands moved to touch the rough wool of the kilt where it stretched across his hips.

"Hmm." With a low laugh, he swept both her hands into one of his, then raised them above her head and pressed her against the chilly stone. In contrast, his body felt warm along the length of hers. And his lips this time moved faster, pressed harder. She felt strangely vulnerable with Trick restraining her arms, but it wasn't an unpleasant feeling. In fact, it was thrilling. Thrilling with an edge of…something else.

He pulled back and cocked a brow. "That'll teach you to take advantage of a man in a skirt."

"Will it?" she wondered, and a shiver ran through her.

She knew for sure it would happen tonight.

"Are you cold, lass?"

"Maybe a bit." Nervous and excited and backed against the cold stone wall. But the stones were more than cold. "There's something about this place…"

He put a palm to the wall and leaned his weight on it. "What?"

"I…well, I'm just not comfortable here." She tried to look away, but he captured her chin in his free hand, forcing her gaze to his. "Even as a child," she said, "exiled on the Continent, parentless with no home to call my own, I never felt as out of place as I do here in this castle."

One of his fingers traced a lazy line on her jaw. "Then you'll understand why I wasn't in a hurry to return."

Her skin tingling under his fingertips, she nodded. It wasn't only this place, these people, that contributed to her unease. It was also her husband. The enigma. The emotional distance between them. In many ways, he was still a stranger to her.

But he'd made a start today, confiding a bit more about his childhood. And she'd made a promise to herself, to trust in him fully, to stop holding back. And beyond all that…despite her lingering doubts…

Well, she just wanted him.

He drove her wild, and she wanted to see where that wildness took them.

And there was only one way to find out.

"Come upstairs," she whispered.

FORTY-FIVE

"**G**OOD EVENING, dearies." When Kendra and Trick stepped into their chamber, Mrs. Ross came forward, two goblets in her hands. "I thought you might be wanting a wee sack posset to help you sleep."

Sleep was the last thing on Kendra's mind, and she was fairly certain Trick felt the same. But she took one of the cups anyway, and sipped the warm, thick liquid, sweet and fragrant with the scents of cream and wine.

Gazing at Trick over the rim, she watched as he removed the roll of papers from the front of his kilt and tucked it into his trunk before turning to Mrs. Ross. "We thank you," he said with a nod and a smile. "And we wish you a good night," he added pointedly.

With a smile of her own, Mrs. Ross handed him the second cup as she left.

Kendra sagged against the door after Trick closed it. "How strange that she would be waiting here for us."

"She was my old nurse." He sipped from his cup before setting it on a bedside table, then unbuckled his sword belt and tossed it on the desk. "I reckon she saw us together earlier and figured it wouldn't be long until we were for bed." When she blushed, he pulled her close. "I don't want to be thinking about Mrs. Ross now."

His eyes burned into hers. She leaned away to sip some more posset, hoping the wine would bring her strength. And courage.

Trick gently pried the cup from her fingers and set it down beside his own. He slipped the shawl from her shoulders, balled it up, and tossed it on a chair. Running his fingertips over the skin revealed by the absence of the shawl—and her scooped neckline—he placed a shivery kiss just below her collarbone. "I much prefer these delightful English dresses," he murmured.

His lips tickled her skin. Until today, she'd never thought twice about the low necklines that had been in fashion since King Charles was restored to the throne. Trends were driven by Charles's love for everything French, which meant she'd worn gowns like this all her life, even as a little girl exiled on the Continent.

But, thanks to her exasperating, overprotective brothers, never before had anyone taken advantage of the sensitive skin such dresses revealed.

"I like this dress, too," she said breathlessly as he trailed kisses up her throat, all the way to her lips. Her hands went straight to the warmed wool of his kilt and hiked it up just the barest inch.

A chuckle rolled through his throat. "I think I like my skirt as well," he said against her mouth.

The heat in his tone made her whole body tremble, and she leaned into him, wrapping her arms around his middle to hold herself up. At a noise on the stairs, she froze, her heart beating double-time.

"Do you hear something?"

Trick's breath tickled her ear. "Something like what?"

"Like footsteps. In the stairwell—can't you hear it?"

"Nay." He raised his head. "Wait. Maybe I can." The sound was faint, muffled, so soft their heartbeats and breathing nearly drowned it out.

Nearly.

She bit her lip. "There are people in there, I'm sure."

"Don't worry about it." His lips grazed hers, sweet with the flavor of creamy sack posset. "It must be the ghosts of men going up to Prisoner's Leap," he murmured, and she couldn't tell if he was jesting or not. "They won't bother us in here."

"D-do you believe in ghosts?"

"Right now I believe in finishing what we've started."

She twisted away from his kiss. "What if it isn't ghosts on those stairs, but someone much more real and frightening?"

With an exasperated groan, he bodily picked her up. He walked to the bed and plopped down, sitting her on his lap. "Like who?"

Fear mingled with more pleasant sensations, turning her head. "Mrs. Ross, maybe? What if she only used the sack posset as an excuse, and she was really up here as part of a plot, but we surprised her—"

"A plot?" He shook his head decisively. "Mrs. Ross wouldn't hurt a midge." He reached to the bedside for his goblet of sack posset, taking a generous gulp as though to prove it wasn't poisoned. "She cared for me as a bairn. Why should she want to do me harm?"

"She cared for your mother more, and she's less than happy with the way you ignored her all those years."

"She was, true enough. But she knows now that it wasn't my fault. I cannot believe she still holds a grudge."

"How about Annag and Duncan? They surely do."

Trick's clever fingers pulled the pins from what remained of her bun. "I seriously doubt Annag and Duncan are hovering behind that door." The gray day had delivered on its promise, and rain slashed against the small window set deep into the wall. "It's the storm you're hearing, Kendra."

"Niall, then? He's been passed off as the duke's younger son. If something were to happen to you, he'd inherit it all. The duke-dom, Amberley, Duncraven…"

In the midst of combing his fingers through her loosened hair, Trick stopped and stared at her, his jaw slack with disbelief.

"No, I don't believe that, either," she admitted with a sigh.

A flash of lightning brightened the window. "Listen," he whispered. His gaze captured hers, and the backs of his fingers brushed over her jaw as the answering thunder rumbled. "It's naught but the storm. And another storm, brewing between us now." He held her steady with a gentle hand on each of her cheeks.

His tenderness should have calmed her, but instead it had the opposite effect. Her pulse doubled, her breathing ceased, and her body felt on fire, a fire that seemed to melt everything inside her all at once.

She was swept up into the storm.

The mysterious footsteps forgotten, she threw herself at her affectionate, golden, mysterious husband, sprawling with him on the bed, and kissed him with everything she had.

FORTY-SIX

T
HE STORM HAD diminished to naught but a light patter of rain.

"I cannot believe it," Kendra said.

"What?" Trick asked, his voice husky against her neck where he was kissing her.

"I just—" Shaking her dazed head, Kendra struggled to catch her breath. "Od's fish."

"What is it, *leannan*?"

She sighed, a sound of regret from the deepest place in her heart. "I cannot believe I deprived myself of five weeks of *that*."

His reply was a strangled laugh, but he held her close and found her lips once again.

She felt languid and tired and happy, and it was a long time before her heart slowed and her breathing quieted. Before the joyous reality sank in that she was now, finally, truly a wife.

Trick's wife.

There had been some pain—more than she'd expected, in truth. But it had passed, and what had come after…

She stifled a giggle.

What had come after had been nothing like she'd imagined. But good. Very, very good.

And if she didn't miss her guess, Trick had enjoyed himself to an equal degree. Though they still had a ways to go, tonight they had shared something special. She reached for him, pulling him down to her, enjoying his warm weight. It seemed they were the only two people in all the world for that moment.

Until she heard the phantom footsteps again.

"It's the rain," Trick reminded her. His voice sounded low and lazy. Perfectly content. She felt a little thrill knowing she had made him that way. "We're alone here at the top of the tower. It cannot be anything else."

"Annag and Duncan…"

Taking her with him, he turned over and nestled her against his chest. "Do you honestly think they've climbed up on the roof to come down these stairs and spy on us? On a stormy night like this?"

She shrugged. "I wouldn't put anything past those two. It's obvious enough they don't like you…or me."

"They're bitter. Odds are Niall has always been favored as the duke's son—Lord Niall while they were plain Duncan and Annag. Then their father left their childhood home to live here—although they were grown, that had to hurt."

"And now you've returned to claim that father—"

"A bit of his attention, maybe, but I've no claim on Hamish."

Rain thrummed on the roof above them, little needles of it striking the small window. She met Trick's eyes, remembering other eyes that had looked familiar. Beneath his shining hair, his brow furrowed in puzzlement. Suddenly she pictured Hamish, that same expression on his face.

And it all fell into place.

She reached a hand to graze his cheek, the faint stubble scratchy against her fingers. "Do you not see, Trick, how much you're like him?"

"Niall? Aye, I've said how uncanny—"

"Not Niall. Well, yes, Niall, but you must know there's a reason for that, for why you're so very alike." She hesitated, but much as she wished to linger together in a state of pure content-ment, she couldn't hide this knowledge from him, not even for a few hours. "It's because you share not only the same mother, but the same father as well."

"Do you think so?" Some of the puzzlement cleared, his amber eyes filling with a hesitant hope instead. "I suppose the timing makes it possible. Father was last here when I was nearly six, and Niall was born the next year....Maybe Niall *is* my full brother." He managed to sound bitter and elated at the same time. "Wouldn't that be something?" he added before he suddenly frowned. "But why, then, would he say he's Hamish's son?"

"Because he is," she said gently. "And so are you."

FORTY-SEVEN

THE BREATH LEFT Trick's body in a rush. "That cannot be."

"It is." Kendra's eyes searched his before she scooted up to sit against the headboard beside him, taking the coverlet with her. "No, I haven't asked Hamish about it, nor did he come to me. But I've eyes in my head, Trick, and I'm not as close to the situation as you are. You share his features and his manner, and then there's the way he looks at you."

"The way he looks at me? How is that?"

"With longing and pride. Were you the duke's son—his love's child fathered by another—wouldn't he view you with resentment, instead? He's your father, I'm sure of it."

He couldn't find the words to disagree, mostly because he wasn't sure whether he disagreed or not.

"Isn't it wonderful?" Kendra pressed. "I know you don't hold him in much affection, but that will come, don't you think? Deep down, I believe he's a good man."

"It's much to absorb," he admitted. "Finding a new brother, and now maybe a father."

It was *too* much to absorb with his mind still reeling over what he and Kendra had just experienced together. Tonight, everything had changed between them. He couldn't say what was different, exactly. Aye, they'd finally made love, and aye, it had been glorious—even better than he'd anticipated, after all those weeks of waiting and wanting. He would never forget this night.

But that wasn't all. He felt...

He knew not what he felt.

Except confused. About Kendra, about Hamish. About all of it.

"We found a new brother last year," said Kendra, a merciful distraction. He watched her move the amber bracelet back and forth on her wrist. "Jason had a run-in with a man who was revealed to be our half-brother, the son of our father before his marriage. But our brother turned out monstrous. A murderer, nothing like Niall." She glanced up. "It was a horrible thing to accept."

For a few moments he remained quiet, imagining. "That must have been very hard."

"It was. Although I don't expect accepting Niall and Hamish is easy, either." The amber stones glimmered in the firelight as she slid them with a finger. "An instant family."

"Niall felt like my brother right off. It's hard to explain." He focused on the bracelet, remembering when she first wore it on their wedding day. It had looked strange on her then, but tonight it seemed like it had belonged there all along. Just the way he felt with Niall. "But Hamish..." He met her gaze. "I feel nothing there. I hear what you're telling me, and it makes sense, but I'm not sure I believe it."

She took their goblets from the bedside table and handed him his. "Just think about it," she said and drained her remaining sack posset.

The drink was cold now, he was sure. The rain coming down sounded cold, too, but she felt warm wedged beside him. He wondered how she managed to smell like sunshine on a blustery night like this.

"There's no need to rush into acceptance," she said softly.

"He could be dying." Trick downed the last of his own drink. Cold, it was, but thick and bracing nonetheless.

"He could," she conceded. "But he seems to be getting better."

He took her cup and set them both on the table. "This may have just been a good day."

"Morning will tell." She yawned, then leaned over for a kiss, a kiss that tasted of the sweet, milky posset. With a soft smile, she lay down and curled tightly against him, like precious cargo carefully nestled in a ship's hold.

She felt good there, a perfect fit. "It's odd," he said quietly, his breath fluttering the downy hairs on the nape of her neck. "They don't know me, really, and yet they seemed to accept me from the first."

"They're family," she said simply. "They love you, Trick. Unconditionally."

And now she was family, too.

Unconditional love.

The idea was so alien to him that he thought about it far into the night as he watched her sleep.

FORTY-EIGHT

"**F**OR THE LAST time, you gaberlunzie, wake up!" Mrs. Ross poked Trick's shoulder, and he moaned and rolled over. "Lord Niall is downstairs, pacing and waiting to take the two of you off somewhere, aye? So get your bones out of that bed."

"I'll make sure he gets up this time," Kendra told her, sitting down to pull on a stocking. "If you're nearly finished in here, could you send Jane up to fix my hair?"

"Aye. That I can do." On her way out, the wiry woman gathered the empty goblets they'd left on the night table. "Did you enjoy this, then?" she asked with a kind smile.

"Very much." Kendra silently scolded herself for thinking the sack posset might have been poisoned. Trick was right; though she sometimes had a brusque manner about her, the old nurse wouldn't hurt a midge. "Do you know, Mrs. Ross, where that corner staircase leads?"

The woman swiped her dust cloth over the table—not that it helped very much. The dirt just flew up and settled right back down. "That turret comes from the dungeons, lass. And goes to the roof above."

"Oh." Just as Trick had said. Kendra glanced at her slumbering husband. He slept like the dead, like he'd spent another wakeful night before succumbing to exhaustion. She, on the other hand, had slept like a newborn babe, dreaming dreams that made her cheeks burn to remember them.

Mrs. Ross was watching her, a question in her faded blue eyes. Kendra put a cooling hand to her face. "Though Trick insisted it was surely the rain, I thought I heard footfalls on those steps last night."

The woman's gray head nodded sagely. "It's been said to happen."

"People go up on the roof?"

"Not people, lass."

"Ghosts, then?" Kendra's breath caught. "The ghosts of prisoners?"

"Not that I've heard."

Kendra blushed as the woman bent to retrieve yesterday's clothes from the floor. Cavanaugh and Jane ought to be doing that—not that she and Trick should have left their garments on the floor in the first place. What could Mrs. Ross be thinking?

But apparently she was still thinking about the stairwell. "Other ghosts," she clarified, shaking out Trick's discarded kilt. "One in particular, a young servant girl who was said to have borne an illegitimate Duncraven son in this room some two hundred years past. Potential threats to the title, they were, and both swiftly put to the sword by an anonymous knight."

Kendra swallowed. "Anonymous?"

"Well, you cannot very well tell who's in a suit of armor now, aye? But legend says it was Lord Duncraven himself. A heartless man, to hear the tales." She smoothed the folded tartan over one arm. "The girl still wanders the spiral staircase, searching for her bairn. Some say they've seen her in this room, watching at the foot of the bed where a cradle may have once rested." Mrs. Ross draped the red fabric right where Kendra imagined the poor murdered girl might gaze. "But don't you worry now, lass. She doesn't do any harm."

Was it the ill-fated servant girl she'd heard, then? Kendra wondered. Or had Mrs. Ross invented this story to cover her own wanderings? Or had Annag or Duncan been trodding the winding stone stairs?

Or had it only been the storm, mixed with her own imagination?

Her musings were interrupted when Mrs. Ross bustled over to Trick. "Wake up, lazybones." She thwacked him with her dust cloth. "Lord Niall awaits."

FORTY-NINE

HALFWAY DOWNSTAIRS, Trick's feet dragged to a halt on the second floor landing. "Bide a moment."

On the step below him, Kendra turned and looked up, tightening Mrs. Ross's shawl across the bodice of her lemon gown. "Niall is waiting to take us to the treasure chests."

"Then he'll wait." She looked so pretty this morning, all cheerful yellow against the dingy stone staircase, her mouth slightly swollen from his morning kisses. He bent down to give her another one, their lips clinging for a long, sweet moment before he straightened with a sigh and stepped from the turret, crossing the sitting room to knock on the master bedchamber door.

"Enter," came a muffled voice.

A voice not unlike his own? Trick hesitated, his hand on the latch.

"Did you not want to go inside?" Kendra asked.

He took a deep breath and pushed open the door. Beyond it, Hamish sat against the sturdy oak headboard, his long, skinny legs looking like stilts beneath the coverlet. Trick gazed at him, a question burning inside him—a question only Hamish could answer.

But he couldn't seem to make himself cross the threshold, nor could he force the question past his lips.

Kendra had no such compunctions. She pushed past him and hurried over to Hamish, grasping the old man's hand. "Goodness." With a flounce of her English skirts, she seated herself at his bedside, a bright ray of sunshine in the gloomy room. "Rhona's potion really worked magic, didn't it?"

Indeed, Hamish was munching on breakfast and looking much better. Younger. Trick was surprised to realize he wasn't such an old man, after all.

"Aye, I expect it did work magic," Hamish agreed. "But although she left a supply, I haven't been able to force myself to drink more of the vile stuff." He made a face. "She'll be at me like a screaming banshee when she sees how much remains. Maybe I can prevail upon you to tip it out the window?"

Kendra laughed. "Where is Rhona, anyway?"

Hamish shrugged. "I'm mending, aye, and she has her own life to attend to. There are people here to help me should I need it." His mouth curved in a smile very like Niall's—and his own, Trick grudgingly admitted. "To tell you the honest truth, it's been pleasant to spend a wee bit of time alone. A man gets cranky with people always fussing all over him."

"I'm sure he does," Kendra said, slanting a glance at Trick. She rose and went to open the shutters, letting morning light flood the room.

Hamish's gaze shifted to the open doorway, and his forehead creased in a frown. "Come in, lad, will you?"

Trick did so, slowly, still gazing at the man that Kendra insisted was his father.

"Have a seat," Hamish said.

Trick didn't. The question fought to get out.

The older man blinked. "It's uncanny how much you look like Niall. I used to catch your mother staring at him with a sad, faraway look in her eyes."

The same sad, faraway look that Hamish was giving him now. A look Trick suspected was on his own face.

At last, the words tumbled forth.

"Niall and I, we look so alike because…because we have the same father, don't we?"

Before Hamish even answered, Trick knew Kendra had been right.

"Why?" he asked. "Why was I never told? And why did my mother marry another man and then have a child with you?"

Hamish licked his lips, not so papery this morning. "It wasn't like that, Patrick. She was already carrying you when she agreed to the marriage. Her only other choice was to give birth to a bastard child." His light brown gaze met Trick's own. "Her father threatened to kill me if she refused to marry the duke."

Kendra gasped. "He cannot have meant that."

Hamish turned to her. "Can you blame Elspeth for not testing him, lass?"

"I don't know," she admitted. "I cannot even imagine…"

"Well, if you'd known the man, the threat wasn't so hard to imagine coming from him."

"Very well, then, maybe she had a reason." Trick ran a hand back through his hair. "But why keep the truth from me?"

"The duke never knew you weren't his child. We didn't mean to keep you in the dark forever, but you left here at five—too young to be told, to understand the importance of hiding your true parentage from the man you thought was your father. And when you returned…" Hamish's gaze flickered down to his lap, then back up. "I wanted to tell you the moment you arrived. But after all this time, I wasn't sure how you would react."

Trick wasn't sure how *to* react. Despite a wakeful night spent contemplating these matters—or perhaps because of it—he felt more muddled than ever. Surely anyone, even Hamish, had to be better than the duke, but the discovery of a new father left his head reeling.

"I'll have to get used to this," he admitted.

Hamish nodded, looking both solemn and pleased. "I've waited twenty-three years to acknowledge you as my son. I can wait a wee bit longer."

FIFTY

HE DAY WAS sunny, the ride toward the town of Falkland pleasant over rolling hills. It felt so good to be out of the depressing castle that Kendra found herself smiling at nothing more than the light breeze, the purple thistles dotting the hillsides, a pair of blackbirds flying by. She chattered to Niall about anything and everything, enjoying his easy company. Seeming as grateful as Kendra to be out and about, Pandora felt familiar and frisky beneath her.

Trick, however, was brooding.

Two miles into their journey, he finally turned to Niall. "Why didn't you tell me?"

"Pardon?" Niall cocked his head, gleaming blond in the sunshine. "Why didn't I tell you what?"

"That our mother's is not the only blood we share."

Niall reined in at that, turning sideways to block the road. His mount danced beneath him as he stared at Trick. "What are you trying to say?"

"Did you think I wouldn't want to know we're full brothers?" His jaw tight, Trick studied Niall a moment. "Did you think I wouldn't care to know that Hamish is my father as well as yours?"

The younger man's face went white. "I didn't know." His amber eyes wide, he swallowed hard. "Are you sure? I swear to you, Patrick, I didn't know. Mam and Da never breathed a word."

Kendra, for one, believed him. Nobody was that good an actor.

But her husband, evidently, was blind. "Why wouldn't they tell you?" he pressed furiously. "What possible reason could they have had?"

"Trick!" she exclaimed in irritation. Not unlike her own brothers, he could be thickheaded beyond bearing. "I expect they thought your parentage was none of Niall's business."

"Mam knew how to hold her tongue," Niall added, his amber eyes darkening to bronze. "And my Da is the most loyal man I've ever met. A loyalty I thought we'd share, now that we've found each other." With a jerk of his reins, he turned and trotted off down the road.

Kendra glared at her husband until his face turned red and he looked away. "All right," he shouted after his brother. "I believe you!"

There was no response, and looking at Niall's stiff back, she could sense his pain. Trick dug in his heels, motioning impatiently for Kendra to follow.

"You might also say you're sorry," she suggested under her breath as she drew alongside.

He gazed at her a moment, then looked back to Niall. "And I'm sorry!" he called. Maybe not as sincerely as she'd have liked, but the effort was there.

Yet his brother's back remained rigid.

She saw a muscle twitch in Trick's jaw. "Very well, then, I'm not sorry," he growled.

They caught up to Niall and rode three abreast, the men in an obstinate standoff on either side of Kendra. The blowing of the horses failed to drown out their alternating huffs. She felt like

Zeus in the Trojan War, stuck between the battling gods, wanting to stay neutral but suspecting she couldn't.

The gates of Falkland loomed ahead, and still neither of them softened. They were most definitely brothers, one as pigheaded as the other. As they entered the town, a few people waved to Niall, calling out greetings and condolences. He nodded his acknowledgments without uttering a word.

They rode past Falkland Palace, two long ranges of gray stone with a charming turreted gatehouse and slanting, moss-covered slate roofs. Kendra turned to her brother-in-law and forced a jaunty tone. "From how Hamish described the banquet, I expected the town of Falkland would be larger. Busier."

She'd known he wouldn't ignore her. "At one time it was more important," he told her, looking straight ahead. Heaven forbid he should inadvertently meet his brother's eyes. "But Falkland today is naught but a small market town, populated mostly by weavers who keep indoors practicing their craft. You can blame the Union of the Crowns for that."

"Why would that make a difference?" she asked brightly. "Trick, you know a lot of history."

"Not of Falkland." She'd never heard him sound quite so vexed, not even when he was fixing to murder Duncan. "For heaven's sake, I haven't lived here in eighteen years."

As her efforts at conversation ground to a halt, she heaved an internal sigh. The clip-clop of their horses' hooves on the cobblestones seemed loud as thunder against the men's willful silence. As they rounded the market cross, a dray cart coming from the other direction forced them to the side of the narrow street nearer the houses.

"The lintels are all carved," she remarked, prattling on like a featherbrained nincompoop. She pointed to the nearest door, the stone beam above it engraved with letters and numbers. "What do they mean?"

"They're marriage lintels—" Trick began.

"Look there," Niall interrupted. "Two lovers' initials, and

1610, the year they were wed—the year their household was established. And other markings indicate their occupations. See, the crossed mells of a stonemason. And there, a shoemaker's knife."

As they rode past a few more, Kendra started to make sense of the symbols. "I see a butcher's cleaver. But the big '4' with three little x's...what does that mean?"

Niall opened his mouth then clamped it shut when his brother rushed to answer before him. "A merchant—a burgess with trading privileges."

The carvings were lovely, she thought, determined not to let their attitudes affect her appreciation. Lasting memorials to marriages begun in hope rather than deception. She turned to her surly husband. "These lintels are so romantic."

Trick rolled his eyes, prompting Niall to nod—pleasantly, she would think, if she didn't know it was mainly to make his brother look bad. "Some go back a hundred years or more," Niall told her. "Watch for them as you ride."

She peeked down the wynds as they went, but soon they were passing through West Port, the gate that marked Falkland's boundary. Dense woodlands loomed ahead. "The trees are so near to the town," she remarked, sounding inane to her own ears.

"Why wouldn't they be?" Trick asked churlishly.

"Actually," Niall said with a smug smile, "though nearly all of Fife was once covered in forest, the only large tracts remaining are here by Falkland. One of the reasons the Stuarts of old so valued their palace, a place to escape from affairs of state and spend some time hawking and hunting the wild boar."

She half hoped to see a wild boar now—at least such a threat would put an end to this petty bickering. Here they had to ride single file, weaving through the trees, which looked much the same as trees in England. Finding nothing left to comment on, Kendra chewed the inside of her cheek, wondering why she'd bothered trying to get her husband and his brother to talk in the first place. Brothers would be brothers, that she knew—from entirely too much experience with her own.

They were both stubborn as mules, she decided, and they could hate each other for life for all she cared.

Suddenly Niall heaved a sigh and looked back, his gaze reaching past her to Trick. "Full brothers," he said, calm as anything. "Amazing, isn't it?"

"Aye." Aghast to hear Trick's agreement, she twisted in the saddle to see a smile teasing at the corners of his wide mouth. "Amazing."

And just like that, they were best of friends once more.

Men. She wanted to spit.

She was still muttering to herself when they came to higher ground, a sparser wooded area that must once have been a clearing. It was peppered with stone ruins so thick and old, they could be of nothing else but a long-ruined castle. Overgrown with clinging plant life, low broken walls seemed to tumble over the uneven land, and the foundations of a round tower stood open to the sky, a few worn steps leading up to nowhere.

"We're here," Niall said.

They dismounted and tethered their horses. Pulling a heavy key from his pocket, Niall stepped into the circle of stone and reached through a layer of dirt and dead branches that seemed stuck to the hard-packed forest floor.

Not by a quirk of nature, though—by design. His fingers found a concealed padlock and fitted the key inside. It opened with a rusty *click*, and he tugged it off, hefting a wooden trap door that lay hidden beneath.

"Go ahead," he said.

After staring for a moment, Kendra followed Trick down a steep stone staircase, pausing when the trap door thudded shut and plunged the space into blackness.

Holding her breath and her husband's hand, she felt her way to the bottom.

It was a dungeon, deep in the earth. The only light was a tiny shaft that came through the tall ceiling from behind an iron grille. As her eyes adjusted, the sparse illumination revealed gruesome instruments of torture. A musty smell seeped from the packed dirt floor, making her imagine the ground wet and red with the blood of prisoners.

Hugging herself, she shivered.

Near the center of the chamber a human cage swung, its door hanging drunkenly from ancient hinges. The wooden rack sitting in a corner would have been used to pull a man apart. Along the far wall, four sets of ankle manacles were anchored near the floor, with matching sets for wrists higher up.

She heard the scrape of steel on stone, then the soft hiss of a wick catching fire. "They're gone!" Niall burst out behind her, his voice laced with disbelief. She swung about to see him holding a candle high, his eyes wide in the flickering light. "The treasure chests are gone!"

FIFTY-ONE

TRICK LAID a calming hand on Niall's arm. "Where were they?"

"Here, I tell you. Here, and here, and here." He paced the dim chamber, indicating bare spots where Trick could see that heavy, rectangular objects had once sat. "I saw them but two days ago—the morning of the day you arrived. They were here, same as always. As they've been since before I was born. Before any of us were born."

The dungeon was damp and stuffy. While Trick found another candle and lit it from Niall's, Kendra slipped her cloak off and hung it from one of the manacles on the wall. "Whatever were you doing here two days ago?"

Niall hesitated but a moment. "This was Mam's secret retreat. I came…to feel closer to her. To escape the clamor of the wake for a wee while. How can all that treasure have gone missing since then?" He held out the padlock, staring at it. "How did the thieves get this open?"

Trick took it from his hands. "It wasn't forced or picked."

"How can you tell?"

"There'd be marks." Avoiding Niall's eyes, he handed the lock back. "Who else has a key?"

"Only Rhona and Gregor. So far as I know, nobody else is even aware this place exists. It makes no sense. Twenty-three enormous chests, all gone." Niall rubbed his brow, his face looking sallow in the light from the candle in his other hand. "Will you help me find them?"

Trick blinked. He'd planned to leave for England tomorrow —a search could take days. Weeks. "I must get home. This isn't my responsibility. But of course I will bring the news directly to the king."

"What if the thieves start selling the treasure, aye? Gold and silver platters and goblets? We're a poor country. Should anything so rich as that treasure show up, surely someone will figure out whence it came, and then an inquisition will be made, and Mam and Da could be implicated."

"She's dead," Trick said. "What does it matter now?"

"Hamish isn't," Kendra reminded him.

But he didn't want to be reminded. He still didn't know how he felt about his new father, and the last thing he wanted was a reason to stick around and find out while the rest of his life remained on hold.

"He could hang, Patrick." The flame wavered, ruffled by Niall's impassioned words. "Or worse. Stealing the Royal plate is treason."

"Treason," Kendra whispered. "Punishable by hanging, drawing, quartering—"

"I know the penalties for treason," Trick snapped. "But that doesn't change the fact that I must get home. And, heart's wounds, it's been thirty-five years since the crime."

Surely no evidence remained to tie the misdeed to his parents now. John Ferries, the only witness, was dead. These fears were groundless. Emotional rather than logical.

"Trick." She came close, capturing his gaze with hers. "Even should the crime continue undiscovered, King Charles would never regain what his father lost."

He hesitated but a moment, realizing his clever wife had

deciphered him already. Always it came down to what would be best for Charles Stuart. "Very well," he muttered. "I'll spare a day or two to help find it." That was the most he was willing to delay his return to England. "But let's not go off half-cocked. There may be some clue here of who took it or its whereabouts."

Niall's breath rushed out in relief. "Da may have ideas as well. Maybe someone else knew of the treasure or had a key to the lock. And in any case, he'll want to hear of this loss immediately."

"Go ahead, then, and speak with him. Kendra and I will remain behind to search for clues."

"You know the direction to Duncraven?"

"Aye. Back through the town, then southwest. Be on your way. We'll meet you later and formulate a plan. With any luck, one of us will discover something useful in the interim."

Niall gripped him by the shoulders. "I thank you."

"Think nothing of it," Trick mumbled. "We're brothers, aye?"

"Brothers." The younger man kissed him on both cheeks and pressed the lock and key into his hand. He gave Kendra his candle and was off, the trap door banging closed behind him.

Kendra released a long breath. "That was good of you, Trick."

"He didn't leave me much of a choice."

Hearing his voice hitch, she guessed it was the result of brotherly affection. "Why did you hesitate to agree?" she asked, stepping closer.

He trailed his fingers along her arm. "After last night, I'm suddenly wanting to get home and start anew with my lovely wife."

She sensed that wasn't the whole truth. But, very aware they were alone deep in the earth, his words caused her heart to race anyway. "After we help your family, there will still be time for that."

"You can be sure of it." He kissed the tip of her nose, then took the candlestick from her and set it atop the rack, where it bathed the stone chamber with a faint but welcome glow. He set the lock there as well, an unnerving *thunk* of metal on wood. "Shall we see what we can find?"

"I really don't like it down here."

"We won't be staying long." Another candle blazed to join the two already lit, and Trick set it into a holder and placed it across the chamber. "There now, it's not so eerie after all, is it? Rather cozy, don't you think?"

Was it her imagination, or had his voice taken on a suggestive tone? "Well, I don't expect it's haunted if it was your mother's secret place. But I cannot say I care for the decor, either."

"Early Torture isn't your style?" His easy grin helped calm her a bit, but his gaze on her had the opposite effect, making her suddenly feel shaky and overwarm. She put a hand against the rough stone wall for support.

The things I say are nothing compared to the things I do...

She shook away the images playing in her head. She had no business thinking of such things—and in a dungeon, for heaven's sake. It was wicked.

Had just one night with Trick turned her head?

"Kendra?" Her gaze snapped to his. She forced herself to stand up straight, thinking he looked entirely too pleased with himself as his eyes wandered down the length of her body. "We'd better start looking."

She shook herself again. "What are we looking for?"

"I wish I knew. A clue."

He slowly traversed one side of the room while she paced the other. Gingerly touching the cold instruments of torture gave her the shivers. The blackened metal felt evil beneath her fingers, the air thick and heavy with age, not to mention horrific tales.

When he let out a little hoot of discovery, she jumped.

"Footprints," he said.

She joined him, crouching down. "What do these tell us? They could be your mother's, or Hamish's, or even our own. No telling if they're hours old or years."

"But they're concentrated around where a chest once sat, see? As though people were recently here, trying to lift something heavy. And here, this deep line in the dirt. They used a board or something as a lever."

"One set of small prints and three larger ones. Yes, I see." She looked up. "But whose?"

He shrugged. "Just information to bring back to Hamish. Maybe it will jog an idea. Let's see what else we can find."

Half an hour's careful search revealed more footprints clustered around where other chests had sat, and little else. A scrap of dark fabric that Trick pocketed, a curved shard of cheap broken glass. It could have lain there for centuries, for all they knew.

He sighed. "Let's go up. We may find more clues outdoors."

It was a relief to ascend the stairs and see daylight once again.

"More of the same footprints." Breathing deep of the fresh air, Kendra followed the marks. "And wheel tracks," she called. "Here, leading out of the woods. How did we miss this before?"

"We weren't looking." He hurried over to see for himself. "Multiple tracks from the same vehicle. Many of them. I'm guessing the chests were carted away one at a time."

"Southeast," she agreed. "Around the town. And then where?"

Trick lifted a shoulder. "Shall we go find out?"

FIFTY-TWO

*T*HEY MOUNTED their horses and headed through the woods, following the ruts. Once clear of the ruins, the trees grew dense, providing reason for the chests to have been carted out singly. A larger cart wouldn't have made it through.

At the forest's edge, the tracks stopped.

"They loaded them on a wagon here," Kendra said.

"Two wagons. No, three, or maybe four. Look." Wider-set tracks turned south and continued. "Shall we see where they went?"

The tracks were easy enough to follow, leading Trick to believe they'd missed the thieves by not more than hours. Clouds were gathering again, and the trail would soon be washed away. But for now, the air was warm, the day bright as only a Scottish summer afternoon could be.

The colors seemed more brilliant here, slopes of blues and purples, the land's harsh contours brought out by shadow and sun. Rabbits scurried in the underbrush, and a flock of swallows soared overhead. Scotland was beautiful, and Trick had missed it in a way he hadn't realized till now, stuck in the confines of the dingy gray castle.

"What happened back there?" Kendra asked quietly.

"Hmm?"

"With Niall."

"Oh. That." Heat crept up his neck, his memories of the incident childish at best. "I'm not sure. But it won't happen again."

"It will."

"Nay, it won't. I'm not usually as volatile as you've seen me…" His voice trailed off, because he didn't know how to explain it. The longer he stayed at his crumbling childhood home, the more confused he seemed to get.

He'd learned his early years hadn't been as he remembered— or as the duke had later caused him to remember. His world had tilted on its axis. And though he'd found family, they were too new, too unfamiliar, to possibly lean on yet.

Which left him Kendra. He needed her more than he'd like to admit.

Thank heavens she was here. He gave her a wavery smile, and her lips curved in return. He wanted to kiss them. It seemed he *always* wanted to kiss them. "I just need to become accustomed to having family. It won't happen again."

"It will," she insisted. "He's your brother."

"Exactly, and so he deserves my best. I'll apologize for disbelieving him, and from now on I need to be more patient. He looks a man, but he's yet a lad, and I must remember that."

"No." Her laugh rang over the hillside, and her smile would lift the most morose man's mood. Losh, he was lucky to have her. "Don't be so hard on yourself, Trick. This is the way brothers are. Families are. We don't give each other our best, I'm afraid, but more often our worst. We slide into comfort and forget ourselves. It's the hugs after the battles that make it worthwhile."

A concept so unfamiliar it bordered on incomprehensible. It had been so very long since he could reliably expect a hug from anyone, let alone someone he'd wronged.

Lost in thought, he was caught by surprise when Chaucer

balked at the edge of a river. Kendra tugged on Pandora's reins. "Look, the tracks disappear. Shall we cross?"

There was no bridge in sight. The water didn't look too deep —waist high, he guessed, at most—but he eyed her long skirts and the sun overhead. "The day is getting away from us. Let's take what we've found back to Hamish and Niall. They may have an idea where the thieves were headed."

"I left my cloak in the dungeon."

"We also didn't lock up. We'll follow the tracks back. I'm not certain how to return from here, anyway."

FIFTY-THREE

KENDRA'S HEART felt light as they rode back. She'd heard a warmth in Trick's voice that made her feel perhaps he was finally opening up. When she smiled over at him, he smiled back. The glimmer in his eyes made her feel tingly all over.

How many more hours until they could steal up to their chamber at Duncraven tonight? She'd never thought she'd look forward to anything in that gloomy place, but they had five long weeks to make up for.

Back at the ruins, she tethered Pandora and followed Trick into the dungeon, shivering a bit as she descended the narrow, cold staircase in the slanting light of the open trap door.

He turned to her at the bottom. "You're not still frightened, are you?"

"Maybe. A little." The candles had all guttered out. She hurried to get her cloak from the manacle on the wall.

He blocked her path and snaked his arms around her middle, leaning in for a kiss.

As his mouth slanted over hers, a dizzying cloud of his sandalwood scent surrounded her, overwhelming the dungeon's mustiness. Her senses spun wildly, her fear evaporating in an instant. Before she knew what was happening, he'd lifted her by the waist.

"Oof! What are you doing?"

His only answer was a raised brow as he carried her across the dingy room, then set her in the open cage, letting her legs dangle out where the door hung loose. He gave the ugly black thing a push to start it swinging.

The metal felt cold beneath her skirts, and the swinging chain made an awful grating noise. Holding tight to the opening, she gave a shaky laugh.

He grinned. "See? It's not scary down here at all. Not with the sunlight and the company. And it must not have been scary to my mother, either, considering it was her special place."

Trying to be a good sport, Kendra reached her toes to push off again. The chain moaned a protest. "I can imagine her coming here to think," she told him, swaying to and fro. "The way you go to the cottage at Amberley."

He hesitated, then nodded his head. "Aye, just like that."

Pleased that he'd admitted as much, she pressed for more. "You write there, don't you?"

"Sometimes." He gave the cage another shove, sending the chain to its screeching song.

"I wonder if your mother wrote here?"

"I never saw her write anything other than letters. And if I were her..." He pushed her again, flashing a grin that was more like a leer. "I'd not squander this place on writing."

"What do you mean?" For some reason her voice came out squeaky.

"When we were together last night, you worried others might intrude on our privacy." He cocked a brow. "It's private enough here, is it not?"

"For *that?*" She was thankful the dimness covered her deep blush. "That's ridiculous. There's no bed."

"What makes you think we need a bed?"

She forced a laugh. "You're joking, of course. I cannot imagine—"

"Ah, lass, it's not really so hard to imagine."

Shocked as she was by his suggestion, she was even more astonished to realize it mirrored her earlier thoughts. A little thrill of excitement raced through her. But…

With his hands on the bars that flanked her head, he stilled the cage. She could feel the heat emanating from his body, chasing away the damp chill of the dungeon.

Her fingers clenched the rough iron while she mentally clung to her last shred of self-possession. "Wouldn't we be disrespectful? Making love in a place where others have suffered?"

He brought a hand to her cheek, his thumb moving over her lower lip. "Many people suffer in many places," he said softly. "Is that not good reason to take what joy we can find?"

He leaned in, and his kiss was the lightest, tenderest brush of lips.

"But if you don't want to…" he murmured against her mouth.

"It's not that. It's just—" Her hands slid around his waist, gripped his muscular back, drew him closer. She was already giving in. "It's just that it feels a bit, well…wicked."

He dropped kisses along her jaw, leaving a tingling trail in his wake. When he reached her earlobe, she felt a tiny nip, then his warm breath in her ear. "A bit of wickedness can be fun, aye?"

She shivered. "I still cannot imagine how we can—"

"Do you trust me?" He pulled away just enough to meet her gaze. His amber eyes burned into hers, the most fervent, forthright gaze she'd ever seen. "Do you trust me, *leannan*?"

"Oh, yes," she whispered.

And she did. No matter that he robbed Roundheads and told half-truths, he was patient and kind, and his presence made the most forbidding places feel inviting. In his own unique way he was the most honorable person she'd ever known. It seemed he always—always—wanted to do the right thing.

He smiled, drawing her attention to that tiny, enthralling chip on his tooth, and it was a moment before she realized she was fumbling with the laces on his breeches.

The smile turned wolfish. His hands moving to assist hers, he said, "This would have been easier in that kilt."

Which, in this heady, strange, and strangely meaningful moment, struck Kendra as exceedingly diverting. Laughter bubbled out of her, bouncing off the chamber's walls until her husband silenced her with another kiss.

FIFTY-FOUR

THE RIDE BACK to Duncraven was hardly short, but Kendra was still giddy when she and Trick walked through the tunnel and into the great hall. They were holding hands, and she couldn't help smiling down at their fingers clasped together. She'd spent a glorious afternoon with her husband.

Seated at a trestle table with a hearty meal before him, Hamish's gaze went to their joined hands as well. He also smiled, a sigh escaping his lips. "You two put me in mind of my Elspeth, you do. Happy newlyweds you are, and glad I am of it."

It was true they were happy. True for Kendra, and as she met Trick's gaze, she knew it was true for him, too. Perhaps he still carried the shadow of recent loss and upheaval, and perhaps she wasn't finished climbing the wall he'd built between them. But they'd turned a corner today—they had laid the foundation for trust. A foundation they could build on in the days and weeks to come.

"The first time Da's been downstairs in weeks," Niall told them with a grin. "Join us, will you? Da has been trying to puzzle out what happened. Did you find any clues?"

Trick handed him the key. "Not much," he admitted,

emptying his pockets. "Just this scrap of cloth"—he gave it to Hamish—"and this piece of glass." He set the shard on the table with an audible *clink*, then seated himself.

Kendra sat beside him, and plates were set before them. Seeing nothing sweet on the table, she took a wedge of spinach tart while Trick eyed a platter of meat slices swimming in onions and a savory-smelling sauce.

"What is this?" he asked.

"Mutton," Niall told him. "Scotch collops."

"Sounds good." He transferred a piece to his plate.

"Homespun." Hamish fingered the dark fabric. "It could have belonged to anyone, but most likely a common worker. Certainly not Elspeth or myself. As for this"—he picked up the curved piece of glass—"it looks to be part of an old bottle. Wine, I'm guessing. Elspeth and I broke our share of them down there over the years."

Feeling her face heat, Kendra exchanged a look with Trick. And a secret smile. He turned back to his father. "We also found many footprints—they looked to be of four different people, clustered around the chests as they lifted. Three larger sets of prints and one smaller." He polished off the mutton and reached for another serving. "So more folk than Niall supposed must have known about the treasure."

"More folk know about it now," Hamish corrected. His mouth straightened into a grim line. "After the original folk enlisted their help in this crime."

"The original folk?"

With a sigh, the older man ran a hand back through his thinning hair, a gesture that reminded Kendra of Trick. "Gregor and Rhona," he practically spat. "My *friends*. Or so I thought."

"Da!" Niall's eyes went wide. "You cannot really mean to accuse them?"

"No one else knew of the place. Or the treasure's existence." Hamish's voice sounded bitter, betrayed. "One small set of footprints—Rhona's. And three larger—Gregor and two men. One of them wearing homespun. Who else could it have been? The lock wasn't broken. The thieves had a key."

"Then they borrowed it or stole it—from you or Rhona and Gregor. Someone could have followed you there sometime. All those years…"

"No one followed. And as for all those years, there were things that happened in those years. Things you don't know."

Looking shaky, Niall took a long sip from his pewter goblet. "Such as?"

"Friends do not always get along. The four of us quarreled from time to time. Bitterly."

The spinach pie had turned out to be sweet after all, swimming in butter with cinnamon and sugar, but the last bite turned sour in Kendra's mouth. "What did you fight about?"

"For years now, Gregor and Rhona have wanted to sell off the treasure. The office of Town Clerk of Falkland doesn't pay so well, aye? At least not well enough for the two of them to live as they supposed they should, their best friend being a duchess. But Elspeth and I—we always argued with them, and we always won."

Niall ran his goblet back and forth on the pitted trestle table. "You were afraid if anything were sold, you'd be discovered."

"Aye, that was it in part, although Gregor always talked of carting the goods to London before selling them. Among the riches in that great city, he believed the treasure would go unnoticed, and in any case, not be connected to anyone back here in Scotland."

Kendra ran a finger around the rim of her own goblet. "But you didn't agree?"

"Royal plate is quite recognizable. But the truth is, we had other reasons for not wanting it sold. We only wanted it returned —off our hands."

Trick helped himself to a hunk of bread. "Could you not convince them?"

"We thought we had. Over and over. But always a few years

later they would bring it up again." Hamish cut a piece of mutton. "I can only assume, Patrick, that when you arrived, they saw their last chance slipping away. They knew Elspeth had been planning to ask you to return the treasure. So they took it upon themselves to enlist help and make off with it before it was too late."

"Gregor and Rhona." Reluctantly, Niall nodded. "I expect that's why they've been absent since shortly after the burial. I thought they needed rest, but come to think of it, it's odd they left you alone, Da. When they spent every day here since Mam fell ill."

Hamish returned the nod.

Trick pushed his plate away. "So you think they're bound for London?"

"I expect so, son."

If Trick noticed the endearment, he didn't react. "We found cart tracks outside the tower, heading southeast around Falkland, and then more tracks from four wagons that went due south. At the point where they crossed a wee river, we turned back. Where would they go from there?"

"Down and over to Stirling Bridge," Niall said. "It's the only way across the Forth."

"Unless they were in a hurry." Hamish dabbed at his lips with a napkin. "Then they'd head for Burntisland and the ferry over to Leith. Just as King Charles did all those years ago."

"They're in a hurry," Kendra said.

The three men turned to her. "How do you know?" Trick asked.

"They crossed the river instead of heading up or downstream to a bridge. Although it wasn't overly deep, there had to be some risk involved in traversing the water with such a heavy load."

A new appreciation lit Trick's eyes. "You're right. But still and all, even taking shortcuts they cannot have got far, not with a burden like that. The tracks were visible, which means they left today." His gaze went to one of the deep-set windows. A light mist had begun to fall as they'd headed back to Duncraven. "I imagine the trail is washed away now. And they're making even slower progress."

Niall nodded. "If we ride out immediately, we could make it to Burntisland before them. And wait."

Kendra could hear the excitement in his voice. Clearly he saw this as more than a mission for right. She imagined he envisioned an adventure—he and his new older brother, off to save the world.

He rose, looking eager. "I don't suppose it will be too difficult for the likes of we two to dissuade one old man and woman."

"Watch your tongue, lad," Hamish put in, a ghost of a smile transforming his grim face. "Who are you calling old?"

With a laugh, Trick stood. "I'll fetch my cloak." He started for the turret steps.

"Wait!" Kendra leapt up to go after him. But he was already far ahead of her, his boots disappearing around the tight curve as he took the steep staircase two steps at a time, while she could manage only one.

By the time she caught up, he was already inside their chamber, spreading his cloak on the bed. Breathless, she caught him by the arm. "I want to go with you."

He spun to face her. "No. We've been over this before."

"You're not going to play the highwayman this time, Trick. I'll worry—"

"And I'll worry more if you come." He touched her cheek with the backs of his long fingers, then moved away to root through the clothespress. "Stay with Hamish," he said, pulling out a black shirt and breeches. "He needs people around him."

"He has Duncan and Annag, and his grandchildren."

"Aye?" He tossed the garments on the open cloak. "Then where were they today?"

"At their own homes," Niall said behind them, "packing up their lives." They both turned to find him standing in the open doorway, holding a roll of parchment. "They'll return tonight. Seems they're moving here for good."

"Good?" Kendra asked incredulously.

"Bad choice of words." He half-grimaced, half-grinned. "But I don't want to upset Da by questioning this. Not until he's stronger."

"I understand." And she did. But that didn't mean she wanted to stay here with Niall's brother and sister. Left to deal with them alone, she could picture herself tearing her hair out. She'd be bald by the time Trick returned.

Suddenly she realized they were her husband's brother and sister as well. "They're yours, too, Trick," she blurted.

"Pardon?" He buckled on his sword belt.

"Duncan and Annag. They're your brother and sister."

In the act of shoving a pistol into his boot top, he stilled, the gun dangling from his fingers.

Niall leapt into the room to catch it. "*Half* brother and sister," he corrected.

Trick's face had gone pale. Kendra wished she could see the expression in his eyes, but his hair hung in the way.

"They're my half siblings, too, and I manage to survive," Niall joked weakly. "It's not all that awful."

"I just hadn't thought of it."

"Then have you thought about the fact that you're Scottish?" Niall handed over the gun.

Trick stared at it as if he'd never seen one before. "Scottish?" he repeated.

"One-hundred percent Scots," his brother said in an exaggerated burr. "Both your parents."

"I hadn't thought about that, either." Regaining his color, he shook his head as though to clear it, but the hair fell right back into his eyes. "I thought Mam was half Irish?"

Niall shrugged. "I suppose. But either way, you're not English, aye?"

A small smile tugged at Trick's lips. "I never did feel very English."

"Well, that's because you aren't." His brother returned his grin. "But you up and married a Sassenach, aye?"

"Guess I did, at that," Trick said, reaching an arm to pull Kendra close.

Seeing he was over the shock, she relaxed. He felt warm against her side, and she wished he wasn't leaving. She looked down, twisting the bracelet on her wrist.

Trick jammed the pistol into his boot top. "Are you ready?" he asked Niall.

"I brought a map." Walking to the desk, Niall unrolled the parchment. "I thought you'd like to see the way."

Trick helped him smooth it on the scarred oak surface. "We're here, are we?"

"Aye, and going here." Leaning over the map, Niall traced a finger southward. "Alongside the mountains and through the hills to the coast. Burntisland is directly opposite from Leith, do you see?"

"Across the Firth of Forth, aye." Trick's own finger followed the path. "How long should it take to Burntisland?"

"On horseback, not long. Two, three hours. With twenty-three chests of silver and gold, a whole day, maybe longer. Especially in the rain. The route is far from flat."

"That's in our favor." Trick rerolled the parchment and stuck it into his belt. "Shall we leave?

"I need just a minute to fetch my things. I'll meet you downstairs." Niall left, his footsteps hurrying through the garrison and then echoing as he descended the stairwell.

When the sound faded away, Kendra turned into Trick's arms. "Are you sure I cannot come with you?"

"I'm sure, *leannan*." He bent his head, his lips apologetic on hers. "This shouldn't take long. A few hours to get there, a day to get back with those chests." His lips brushed hers again, then lingered, exciting her pulse, making her want to beg him to stay.

But she wouldn't. Rhona and Gregor had to be stopped. And she wouldn't push any more to go along. She was determined to be better than in the past, the sort of supportive wife he deserved.

"Be safe," she said softly.

"I will." He gave her a final kiss. "I have a plan, so don't fash yourself."

"Don't worry, do you mean?" She squeezed him around the middle. "You're talking like a Scot already, you know that? Before much longer, Caithren will be the only one at home who can understand you."

With a laugh and a grin, he was gone.

FIFTY-FIVE

"**S**IT STILL, milady." Jane's hands curled and twisted. "You're restless this morning."

Feeling like little Susanna at the orphanage, Kendra sighed. Her gaze went to the bedchamber's window. It had rained all night, though it seemed to be letting up now. "I wonder how they're doing. All the night and into the morning."

"I'm sure they're fine, milady." Jane stole a cube of cheese from Kendra's untouched breakfast tray and popped it into her mouth. "They're probably on their way home already."

Kendra toyed with the amber around her wrist. Trick had said he had a plan. She hoped it was a good one. "I didn't say I was worried."

"Of course you're worried." Jane tied a purple ribbon and stepped back. "There you go. He'll be home soon. You're doing well here, are you not?"

Was Jason checking up on her here, too? Kendra wondered. The thought made her warm inside. Though she knew it was unlikely, Leslie Castle being far from here, she also knew that her brother would do so if he could. He cared—just like Jane cared enough to ask the question.

"How are *you* doing here, Jane?"

"Why, fine." Gathering combs, pins, and ribbons, the maid arranged them in her little traveling case. "I've a room to myself bigger than the one I share at Amberley—why shouldn't I be fine?"

"How is that?" Kendra frowned. "I would expect the servants' quarters to be crowded, what with Duncraven's staff and now Amberley's."

"Didn't you know, then, milady?"

"Know what?" She rose and wandered to the window. The rain had stopped, and she smiled at the scene below, watching a mama rabbit hop after her baby through Elspeth's garden.

"When his grace—not your husband, but his father—left all those many years ago, he stopped providing her grace's allowance. She had to survive on what Duncraven earns, which I gather isn't much. Most of the servants were dismissed."

"My heavens." Kendra swung from the window. That explained why a nurse companion was doing bedchamber duty. And why the castle was so run down. "His grace—my husband—doesn't know of this, Jane. That I can promise."

"Calm yourself, milady." Jane shut her wooden case. "No one here blames him, and besides, this all happened long ago. The remaining staff are happy to have employment. And since Mr. Munroe moved in, they're even getting paid." She took her curling iron from the hearth and blew on it to cool it off. "Shall I sit with you and play some cards? The day might pass more quickly."

"Maybe later. I think I may sit with Hamish a while."

Jane's round face split in a smile of approval. "Excellent idea. You know where to find me."

Kendra followed her maid out the door and down the winding, torchlit stairs, biting the inside of her cheek. She knew Trick wouldn't stand for his father and brother scrimping to the point they apparently were. Estate management was her strength, so she hoped to get to the bottom of Duncraven's problems before he returned. And find a solution that wouldn't involve him playing the highwayman any longer.

Coming into the sitting room, she headed for Hamish's door. Perhaps there were opportunities for income that they'd missed.

"Where did they go off to, Kendra?"

She whirled and, finding herself face-to-face with Annag, stifled a groan. "I told you, I don't know."

And told her and told her. At least a dozen times last night, before she'd escaped the great hall to toss and turn in her lonely bed.

She skirted past her sister-in-law, toward the master chamber's closed door. "Why are you so interested, anyway? Have you some stake in the outcome of today's work?"

Annag came around to block her way, fists raised. "Of what are you accusing me?"

"Go ahead, hit me. I've three brothers, and I can assure you they've schooled me well."

The woman's eyes narrowed, but she dropped her hands. "I'll get Duncan to find out, then." She flounced to Hamish's door, opened it, and slipped inside, slamming it behind her. "Dun-cannnn!" her voice came through the thick oak.

So much for consulting with Hamish—the last thing Kendra needed was another round with Duncan and his sister. So far she still had all her hair, and she preferred to keep it that way.

She headed downstairs and outside, hoping for some peace to appreciate the whimsical world that Elspeth had created. Once it had calmed Trick; perhaps the castle garden would work the same magic on her.

Though the rain had stopped, the day was blustery, the sky still gray and forbidding. She walked the paths, bending to touch a little castle here and there, smiling at Trick's mother's inventiveness. A blue one with little bits of metal to make it sparkle. A yellow one surrounded by miniature trees. She could almost picture Elspeth working on them, a small blond boy at her side. If he'd "helped" as well as the children at the orphanage did, she imagined it had taken the woman twice as long as necessary to build each one.

There was a fanciful one, painted pink, a green dragon guarding its entrance. It looked so pretty surrounded by bell-shaped purplish flowers.

She froze. Bell-shaped purplish flowers.

Black nightshade. Belladonna. Dwale.

She reached out, then snatched her hand back, hearing Caithren's voice in her head. *Don't touch. It's possible to fall ill without even eating it. Do you see these dark green leaves? They're lethal.*

She saw only a few of those dark green leaves…because most of them had been plucked off.

Like Cait, Rhona had knowledge of plants and herbs. And she'd been feeding a concoction to Hamish. Her "cure" with its dark green hue.

And Hamish's symptoms—likely Elspeth's symptoms as well—had been just what Caithren had described: shock, fever, slowed breathing, dilated eyes, stomach pain…

Rhona had been poisoning them both.

Dear heavens. She had to warn Trick and Niall. Her husband and his brother were all that stood between Rhona and Gregor and that treasure, and if the two of them had been willing to murder twice, they'd be willing to do it again.

Before she even puzzled it all out, she was running for the castle. Upstairs in her chamber, she ripped off her gown and threw a riding habit on instead. Grabbing her cloak, she lost no time heading for the stables and Pandora, praying that none of the family would see her before she could get on the road.

She'd hung over Trick's shoulder as he and Niall had pored over the map yesterday, and she was sure she knew the way.

Impatiently tapping a foot, she watched the stable boy lift the saddle to the mare's back. "Hurry, would you?"

The stable boy frowned. "You cannot go riding alone, your grace."

She forced a smile. "At home in England, I ride alone all the time."

"This is Duncraven, not England. Allow me to arrange for an escort."

"I thank you, but no." An escort would see where she was headed and ride right back. Then she'd be caught and kept from going altogether. Hamish would want to send someone else—a messenger or, heaven forbid, Duncan. And she wasn't going to sit here worrying while the men in her life were facing murderers. "I really prefer to ride alone. It clears my head."

The stable boy was backing through the doors, clearly going for help. Taking over where he'd left off, she cinched the saddle tight and swung herself up. "Tell Mr. Munroe I'll be back," she called as she rode off.

It was more miles than it had looked on the map, but Pandora was swift. The hours took her over rolling land nestled against a range of green mountains, then finally on a tree-lined road that wound through the hills shielding the coastline.

Cattle grazed in the meadows, and purple thistles sprouted everywhere. A fine mist fell from the sky, and the clouds were growing darker, promising heavier weather to come. When the twisting road crested and she could see the small village of Burntisland tucked into a bay in the distance, the Firth of Forth tossing fitfully beyond it, she began worrying about how she would locate her husband.

As luck would have it—bad luck—she barreled through a sea of cornflowers, rounded a bend, and nearly rode right over him.

FIFTY-SIX

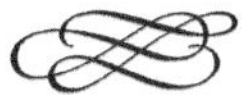

"**G**RAB HER!" Rhona yelled.

In the middle of tying up a man, Trick looked up to see Kendra yanked off Pandora. A heartbeat later, Gregor had a blade to her neck.

Where on earth had she come from?

Trick's heart leapt into his throat. Empty-saddled, Pandora reared and galloped up the embankment, his and Niall's mounts bolting after her.

Gregor glared at Trick. "Release my man, unless you want to see your pretty wife's head rolling down the road."

"Don't listen to him, Trick!" Tears swam in Kendra's eyes. "He'll only kill you. He's murdered once already, almost twice—"

"Now!" Gregor bellowed.

His gaze riveted to Kendra's, Trick dropped the rope and slowly stepped back, the blood pounding in his ears.

I'm sorry, she mouthed, her heart in her glistening eyes. She raised her clenched knuckles to her teeth while the tears slipped down her cheeks.

"Rhona, get the weapons."

Stalking over to retrieve the pistols Trick had made them

drop to the ground mere minutes earlier, Rhona smirked at Kendra. "Thank you, dearie." She handed a gun to one of their accomplices. "For a while there, your husband thought he had us fooled." The man Trick had been restraining struggled out of his half-tied bonds, and she handed over another pistol. "Imagine he and his brother thinking they could hold the four of us up."

Atop the rise overhead, Niall shakily stood, the lone real gunman among a dozen hats and pipes they'd arranged around him. He ripped the makeshift mask from his face. "We *did* fool you," he spat.

"Until your bonnie sister-in-law showed up and we put two and two together." Gregor tightened his hold around Kendra, and she flinched, making Trick nearly lunge. "Drop your gun, lad, lest you be the next to feel my knife."

"He'll kill you anyway, Niall! I'm telling you—"

Niall's pistol fell to the road with an ominous thud.

Seething—at Kendra, or Gregor and Rhona, or the world in general, he really wasn't sure which—Trick tore his own mask off and tugged the periwig from his head.

"Don't move!" Gregor growled. A tiny red nick appeared on Kendra's smooth skin, and her whimper was like a knife in Trick's gut. Gregor swung his gaze on one of the other two men, motioning toward Trick with his head. "Kill him first."

"I told you!" Kendra wailed.

"Kill?" Palms forward, his gun pointed to the sky, the man backed away. A Duncraven villager—Trick had slapped him at the *draidgie.*

Now he wished he'd pounded him into the floorboards.

"Nobody said anything about killing, aye? We were supposed to move some chests and go home with gold in our pockets. Nobody said anything about killing."

"I'm with you, Davie." The second man's pistol dropped to the dirt. "Good day to you people. I don't know what game you're playing, but I'll be heading back to Duncraven now—you may keep my horse with my compliments." Casting a wistful glance to the animal in question, which was hitched to one of the wagons, he started walking.

"Wait!" Rhona's eyes darted back and forth between the retreating men and her husband. "We don't have to kill." Her voice rose an octave. "Blast you, Gregor, I told you from the first that we didn't have to kill!"

The men halted and turned back around, apparently reserving judgment.

"Aye," Gregor barked. "And then you talked me into that milk-livered way of doing it, when we could've been done with the deed and clear to London weeks before *he* showed up." He aimed a deadly glance at Trick.

"A pox on you!" the first man said, pivoting away.

"Wait!" Rhona shot her pistol into the air.

Everyone froze. A choked sound came from Kendra's throat.

"We don't have to kill," Rhona repeated, her jaw tight with fury as she faced her husband. Visibly shaking, she gestured wildly at the four loaded wagons. "We cannot do this alone. We cannot let them walk."

Her gaze fell on the rope Trick had dropped to the ground. "We can tie the scoundrels up, like they were going to do us. We'll be long gone across the Forth before they can follow. The tide will turn, and they'll be stuck here till tomorrow."

Other than his labored breathing, Gregor remained silent. Resolute. The two other men exchanged looks and resumed walking.

A crack of lightning rent the air. "Come back," Gregor bellowed as thunder rumbled and rain began pelting the earth. "I'll hold this one until you tie up the others." His breath came in spasmodic jerks. "You!" he shouted to Niall. "Get down here unless you want to see the inside of your sister-in-law's gullet."

Niall didn't need to be told twice.

Using Trick's own ropes, they tied him and then his brother on the muddy ground, feet together, wrists crossed and bound behind their backs, then lashed to their bodies for good measure. Finally Gregor wrestled Kendra to the ground, and the two men gave her the same treatment.

"Ouch!" she yelled. "Ouch! Ouch! Ouch! *Ouch! OUCH!*"

Lying on his side, Trick winced with each tug of the rope, though frankly he couldn't imagine what she found so painful. The entire situation was aggravating as anything, but it didn't hurt so much as to warrant squealing like a pig.

His poor wife must have the lowest pain threshold in history, he decided, remembering her fear of the marriage bed. Should she ever give birth, he would do best to keep clear of the house. Or maybe the county.

He was jarred from those musings when Gregor came to stand over him, murder in his cold blue eyes. "You blasted smaik!" A swift kick to Trick's side knocked the breath from his lungs. Gregor's jaw clenched, and he kicked again, a blow so hard Trick heard the sharp crack of a rib. Pain knifed through him, exquisite agony that made the worst of his father's beatings seem insignificant.

He shut his eyes, gasping for air, hearing the wagons roll down the road as he waited for the pain to subside.

"Trick? Oh, dear heavens. Trick, are you all right?"

"I'll live." She was too far away to touch, but he opened his eyes and sent her a wan, forced smile. "Are *you* all right?"

"Yes." The tears welled up again, mixing with the rain. "Oh, hang it, I'm so sorry. I know you told me not to come, but she was poisoning them, Trick, they were—"

"We'll talk of it later." He was too confused right now, torn between fury that she'd shown up and relief that her throat was intact. The pain was becoming bearable, an insistent throb along his left side. "Niall? You all right, man?"

"Aye. I should have shot him."

"Don't be a horse's arse. It was four against two, and a knife at her throat." His eyes widened when he looked back to Kendra. "What on earth are you doing?"

"Getting out." She gyrated in the mud. "Angus and Davie, they're nice men at heart. I talked to them at the *draidgie*."

"What?"

"I thought if I could convince them they were hurting me, they'd leave the ropes loose." She wiggled a hand free. "It worked."

"Crivvens," Niall breathed. "She's brilliant."

And Trick was a deuced idiot.

Her arm was still tied to her body, and it took another few minutes to work it free. Then more long minutes to unravel the rest until only her ankles were bound. She made short work of those bonds and scrambled to her feet, shaking out the kinks, splattering mud to the ground.

"I never thought I'd say this, but thank goodness it's raining." She tilted her head back, letting the downpour run into her mouth and wash down her body.

A wry laugh shot from Trick's throat, shortened by the pain in his ribs. "Untie me, you brilliant wench."

Minutes later, he was free, hugging her like he never wanted to let go, never mind the ache in his side. He dropped kisses on her mouth, her cheeks, her eyes. "Sweet heaven, *leannan*." He pulled back, running his fingers over the tiny cut on her throat, convincing himself it was nothing. "I thought I was going to lose you." Then he kissed her all over again.

Laughing, she drew away. "Don't forget your brother."

He knelt, stifling a groan, and loosened Niall's bonds, grasping his hand to help him up. They embraced hard, then drew back and met each other's eyes. Niall raised a questioning brow.

Trick nodded. "Let's go get them."

FIFTY-SEVEN

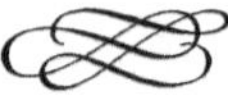

HE VILLAINS were already at the quay in the distance, unloading the wagons into a broad-beamed, single-masted boat. Or rather, the men were unloading. Rhona was wringing her hands. An agitated ferryman was alternately assisting and barking orders short-tempered enough to cut through the wind and the rain all the way to Trick's ears.

"No more, I tell you! She cannot hold it! And the tide has turned—we must leave, or we won't clear the harbor mouth—"

His words were cut off when Gregor turned a pistol on him. "Faster!" he shouted, shooting a shocked and then furious glance to where Trick and the others thundered closer on their horses. "Faster!"

"Enough!" the ferryman cried. "Take the last two off! She'll sink, I tell you!"

As the tide flooded out, the water level dropped between the two great stone piers that thrust east and west, the hundred-foot gap between them the only exit from Burntisland's harbor. In minutes, it would be too shallow and dangerous to navigate.

Trick reached the quay, his wife and brother arriving on Chaucer's heels. In unison they dropped to the dock, throwing their reins over a rail.

Ignoring the warnings, Gregor and the other two men thrust the last chest onboard and shoved off, the boat so laden there was barely room to stand. With a shouted oath, the ferryman jumped to the dock in the last instant, sputtering as the craft pulled away, already taking on water. In mute but panicked agreement, Gregor's helpers abandoned ship as well, leaping into the chilly harbor.

The boat's sails billowed, and it lurched forward, nearing the harbor mouth. Trick untied a smaller boat and scrambled aboard. "You, come!" he shouted to Niall. When Kendra made to follow, he waved her back. "You stay here!"

"A pox on you!" she screamed. With a running leap, she cleared the gap just as the boat pulled away.

Cursing under his breath, he shot a glance at the other boat floundering its way into open water. No time to argue, no time to turn back. He turned livid eyes on Kendra. "Have you learned *nothing* today?"

Niall grabbed two oars and began rowing. Before long, the ferryman looked like a tiny toy doll back on the quay, pacing and pounding his fists into the air. Another rumble of thunder ripped through the heavens.

"Look!" Kendra gasped.

From the west, a dense black cloud was sweeping down the firth.

"Rot it!" Trick had spent enough time aboard ships to know what that meant. Saying a quick prayer for the souls aboard the already-faltering boat, he snatched up the second set of oars to help row toward the laden ship, his ribs throbbing with every stroke. "If we transfer a chest or two aboard," he panted, planning as he went, "maybe we can lighten the load enough for the ferry to make it back. Niall, help me move them. Kendra, when I pull alongside, take the oars and try to keep her in place."

With the storm bearing down, he hadn't the luxury of being angry with her at the moment. He would use her now, and yell at her later for complicating everything.

Stubborn girl. Always doing exactly as she pleased. Riding out by herself and getting them trapped into marriage, showing up at a highwayman raid when he'd expressly told her not to, running after him to Scotland, following him to Burntisland. And now this.

A few minutes later, they bumped up against the bucking ferry. "Now!"

He leapt across, his landing painful but safe. Niall followed and dashed to the nearest chest. Blast, it was heavy—not easily moved by three men, and Trick was one injured man with a lad. But necessity bred strength, and together they wrestled it to the rail.

Frantically bailing water, Gregor and Rhona failed to notice them until they'd already half-shoved the chest onto their craft. A scrape and a *clunk*, and it was aboard—and Gregor rounded on Trick with a vengeance.

Trick took a punch to the gut that glanced off his tender ribs. He doubled over, wheezing in pain before he gathered force and returned the favor, smashing a fist into the older man's face. Niall added his own blow to the midsection, and Gregor stumbled backward, landing hard in a foot of water.

The ferry was pitching and yawing, slashing rain pounding its decks. As Gregor struggled to his feet, the vessel abruptly tilted. Thrown against the rail, Rhona screamed. One of the chests skidded past her, missing her by inches, and crashed over the side, taking a section of railing and Rhona along with it.

"Rhona!" Gregor scrambled after her, grabbing for her hand as she slid from the deck, their fingertips grazing but failing to grip. Trick leapt to keep Gregor from going overboard, his arms around the man's waist slamming him back into his abused body, while Niall jumped in to save Rhona.

Tossed on the roiling firth, Niall's head swung wildly in search, but she'd already slipped beneath the waves. He disappeared after her. Bracing between two chests, Trick grimaced and hung on to Gregor, holding his breath until his brother's blond head broke the surface, the woman draped limp on his back.

Niall fought his way to the vessel's outer ladder, shoving her aboard before clambering up himself, fighting the wind and the rain.

Gregor wrenched from Trick's grasp and threw himself on his wife while Niall lay on deck, panting, water washing over him and into his open mouth.

"We've got to move another one!" Trick yelled. "She's still taking water!"

Niall nodded and pushed himself up.

"Trick!" Kendra's panicked voice came thready through the storm. "It's slipping!"

He rushed to the other side of the ship. Tossing wildly, the smaller boat had drifted yards away. Though she strained against it with both hands and a shoulder, the chest he'd loaded was inching toward one end, threatening to overbalance the boat.

Threatening to drown Kendra.

Faster than the wind, Niall flew past him and into the water. Priming to follow, Trick found himself smashed to the deck by an enormous, roaring wave.

He gasped for air, the deck awash, the rush sucking him over the side.

Freezing black water covered his head.

He fought his way to the surface, only to be blindsided by a plunging chest.

Woozy, he flailed in the lashing surf, battered by waves and debris. Chunks of broken timber, lengths of rigging, thick hunks of rope. He took water into his lungs, and it burned like the fires of hell. His ribs screamed with pain, and he couldn't lift his arms, couldn't swim, couldn't keep his head above the pitching seas that seemed determined to send him to a watery grave.

His last thought was of Kendra, struggling against that chest.

Stubborn, willful, beautiful Kendra. Kendra, who put orphans above riches…Kendra, who'd accepted his own family before he did….Kendra, who could make his heart pound with a single glance…

By all the saints, he loved her.

$\mathcal{H}$E WAS FREEZING.

He wasn't dead, then. Hell was supposed to be hot. And heaven was supposed to be like floating on a warm, comfortable cloud. Yet he shivered with a bone-deep cold, so cold it felt as though he'd never be warm again. And he was far from comfortable.

A teeth-rattling jounce drove home that last point.

"He's coming around!" The voice, at least, was heavenly, the warm lips pressed to his face even more so. "Oh, Trick, I'm so sorry, I'm so sorry…"

"Cold," he murmured.

"Just a minute. I'm almost finished."

A tug against his side sent such pain spiraling through him, he decided death might not be far off. "Hurts," he grated out.

"I know. This bandage should help."

He forced his eyes open and lifted his head, which felt entirely too heavy—so heavy it dropped back with a skull-jarring bang. But he'd seen her. Kendra. Sweet Kendra. She hadn't drowned, after all.

His heart wanted to fly, but the rest of him insisted on staying earthbound. "Bandage?" he wondered.

"My chemise. Or part of it, anyway."

A bump sent his body into the air and back down with a wracking jolt. Not earthbound. Wagon-bound. He was in a wagon. And his precious wife was wrapping his ribs in a bandage ripped from her chemise.

His brain struggled to put the pieces together. How had he been hurt, but even more intriguing, how had she torn the bandage from the chemise? He pictured her lifting her skirts, her lovely, shapely legs revealed as she rent the ivory fabric.

Wishing he'd been able to watch that, he realized he must not be dying, after all. Parts of him were far from dead, although other parts made him long for that peace. Then she raised her gaze to his, and he was glad, oh so glad he was still alive.

"He's awake, Niall!" Her hair was a tangled mess, her face smeared with dirt, but her smile was enough to brighten the cloudy day. Then her expression fell. "Oh, heavens, Trick, I'm so sorry." Tears sprang to her eyes.

He wanted to tell her not to cry, but the words were stuck in his throat.

"Brother!" Elated, Niall's voice floated to Trick's ears from somewhere above his head. "How do you feel?"

"Throat hurts," he croaked, still gazing at his wife. Even red-rimmed, her eyes looked the most beautiful green.

"You tossed a heap of water," Niall explained. "Crivvens, was it disgusting." Something was passed over Trick's head. A flask. "Kendra, give him this."

She cradled Trick's head in one hand, lifting the flask to his lips with the other. He drank greedily at first, then choked when the liquor burned his raw throat.

"*Usquebagh*," Niall called. "Water of life. Whisky. Take more, it'll do you good."

He did, gingerly this time, feeling the spirits burn a path to his belly. "Warm," he murmured.

Drawing a shuddering breath, Kendra blinked back her tears. "I'll warm you in a moment."

She tied off the makeshift bandage, a blessed tightness that seemed to pull him back together, both his body and his mind. Memory rushed back, and with it some of the anger at her for interfering. But, too, he remembered his thoughts as he'd sunk beneath the water. Thoughts of love, that sentiment he'd felt certain was naught but meaningless tripe.

Later. He would think about all of this later.

As she struggled to tug down his shirt, he levered up and found himself surrounded by horses. Niall had roped the four dray animals together to pull the wagon, and their own three mounts trotted behind. With Niall driving, they were making good time.

Trick's feet were braced against a chest—the single chest they'd wrestled off the doomed ship. One chest saved out of twenty-three. He dropped his head to a makeshift pillow fashioned from his soggy surcoat. The rain had stopped, and the sun was struggling valiantly to peek between broken clouds.

"There." She drew up a blanket to cover him. It felt warm, then warmer still when she crawled beneath to nestle up to his good side, sharing her own heat.

Heavenly. He was in heaven, after all.

"The ferryman gave it to me," she said.

"Gave you what?"

"The blanket."

"After you puked all over his floor," Niall added from the driver's seat up front.

"Nice of him." Trick laced his fingers with Kendra's. "Especially considering he lost his boat."

Fresh tears wetted his nearly dry shirt where her head rested on his shoulder. "We lost them," she said, the words soft and regretful. "Gregor and Rhona and the treasure."

"But we didn't lose each other." He squeezed her hand. "We can thank God for that. And Niall."

"Nay," his brother called back. "Thank her. She's the one who pulled you from the water."

Stunned, he gasped. "How?" He was twice her weight, at least.

He sensed rather than saw Niall's shrug. "I managed to get to the boat, was dealing with the shifting chest. The next thing I knew she was leaping over my head."

"That wave." Kendra's voice shook with memory. "It was like a mountain. It came down, and you disappeared for a moment, then I saw you go over the side. It looked like you were riding a waterfall. I've never been more scared in my life."

"I know the feeling," he soothed, remembering the sight of her with a knife at her throat. "Rhona and Gregor? Did you see them, too?"

"No," she said. "We never saw them at all. They were there, they and the boat, and then they weren't. By the time I got you aboard, there was nothing where that ship had been but an eerie calm patch on the surface, along with some bits of debris."

Slowly he nodded, feeling an overwhelming weariness suddenly swamp him. Losh, she'd saved his life. Because she'd disobeyed him—because, in spite of his protests, she'd flown into that boat like an avenging angel—she'd stayed with him, and she'd saved his life....

"I'm so sorry," she whispered.

But Trick was already asleep.

FIFTY-NINE

IT WAS NEARING midnight by the time they arrived at Duncraven, cold, hungry, and—at least on Kendra's part—exhausted.

Trick's long sleep in the wagon bed seemed to have gone a good way toward restoring his strength, and Niall clearly found his second wind as they neared the castle, itching to tell his father all about the adventure of a lifetime. But she hadn't slept a wink on the bumpy ride, too caught up in wonder that they were all alive, tempered by a wrenching regret that her own part in the day's events had led to its tragic end.

While Trick and Niall went straight to fill Hamish in, she begged off and dragged herself upstairs, wanting nothing but a hot bath and a good night's sleep.

She'd almost accomplished the first when Trick came in, a platter in one hand and two goblets in the other. Quickly she slid deeper into the water, crossing her arms over her chest. No matter that he'd seen all of her before—no man had ever seen her bathe. It seemed different. Private somehow. And too intimate, considering what she'd put him through today.

He shouldn't want to see her at all.

"I can take over from here." He nodded a dismissal at Jane,

and she left, quietly closing the door behind her. "Hungry?" he asked matter-of-factly.

"Not really." Her eyes filled with tears. "I'm so sorry, Trick, for ruining your plan. If I hadn't arrived and tipped them off as to who you were, none of this would have happened."

"You cannot know that; we cannot know what would have happened." He set the food on the desk, his gaze filled with concern. "Maybe you ruined our plan, but you also saved my life. I thank you for that, sweet Kendra, from the bottom of my heart."

Her own heart hurt. Oh, if only she could forgive herself as easily as he seemed to forgive her. Then he ran a hand back through his hair, and she blinked, staring, so stunned her own guilt fled her mind.

"You cut it," she breathed. "Your hair."

A wry grin twitched at his lips. "Mrs. Ross cut it. There I was, telling Hamish all about what happened, her fussing over Niall and me both. Moving chairs near the fire so we could warm, pushing hot drinks into our hands. As we talked, she stripped off Niall's coat and ran a comb through his hair. And the next thing I knew she was standing over me with scissors."

"You didn't stop her."

His only answer was a shrug. But he was no longer hiding, not from her. The heart that he'd spoken of thanking her from was right there in his amber eyes.

He came close and knelt by the big wooden tub, setting the goblets on the floor beside him. "No more tears. I hold you blameless for anything that happened today. You must believe that."

When he drew her hands from her body, she forgot to be embarrassed. She squeezed his fingers, gazing into those unguarded eyes. "You blame yourself instead, don't you?"

"Aye," he admitted, toying with the amber on her wrist. "But Hamish—Da"—a fleeting smile curved his mouth—"did his best to set me straight."

"What did he have to say?"

He kissed her fingertips and sighed. "He thinks it's just as well that Niall and I didn't manage to keep his friends from drowning, since it saved him the trouble of having them hanged. As for the Royal plate, he believes it's fate…and only fitting that it ended up where it was thought to be all along."

She heard very little conviction in those words. "You don't agree."

"It's difficult to avoid feeling like a failure when you lose an immense fortune and two lives into the bargain. But I'm working on it."

She'd been working on trying to better herself, too. "I wanted to stay here like you told me to—truly I did—but then when I realized they were murderers, and thought of you out there not knowing that…your lives at risk…" Remembering, she felt her heart pounding all over again. "I tried to obey, but I'm not made that way, Trick."

"I know." He sighed theatrically, but the smile in his eyes told her it was only for show. "I expect I'll have to get used to that."

"I'm so glad you're willing to try." Though she still didn't hold herself blameless, relief flowed through her in heady waves. He was accepting her for who she was. More than anyone ever had in her life. "I was only trying to warn you of their wicked ways, but it all went wrong."

"Your heart was in the right place." His lips brushed her knuckles, and his breath on her hands warmed her somewhere deep inside. "I'm not used to anyone wanting to take care of me," he told her in a husky voice, "but I do appreciate it. And I'm hoping we can make a fresh start, and that some day I'll prove myself deserving of your special sort of loyalty."

Could they really begin anew and learn to trust each other? Her heart swelled at the thought. She sent him a tremulous smile, and he dropped her hands, reaching for a goblet.

She took it, sipping the fortifying wine while he walked over to the desk.

"Midnight supper." Carrying the platter, he dragged the chair over to sit by the tub. "Will you have some bread and cheese?"

She nodded, surprised to find herself suddenly ravenous. "I'm worried, Trick. About Hamish and Niall."

"Aye?" Balancing the platter on his knees, he cut a slice of pungent cheddar. "What makes you worry?" he asked, tearing a hunk of bread and handing them to her together.

"Things haven't gone well here since your father—the duke —took you away." She nibbled on the bread. "Jane told me he cut off your mother's allowance, and she had to dismiss most of the servants."

Taking a hearty bite of bread, he nodded as he chewed. "I guessed as much, noting the state of this place." He swallowed and washed it down with a gulp of wine. "I asked Niall about it on our long trek to Burntisland."

"And?"

"Hamish does well for himself in the cloth trade. But other than allowing him to make up back pay for the servants, Mam refused to take his money when he moved in." In three big bites, he polished off a slab of cheese. "Stubborn woman. She may not have been as bad as the duke had convinced me, but she was far from perfect."

"None of us are," Kendra reminded him. "Will they be all right here, then, do you think?"

"Aye, with Hamish's help. And Niall is planning to visit Amberley later this year and learn some more progressive farm- ing. Scotland is behindhand, it seems. I thought maybe you could help him with that."

His steady confidence did much to strengthen her belief in this fresh start of which he'd spoken. And Hamish and Niall would be fine. She sagged with relief, draining the rest of her wine.

"Feel better now?" he asked.

"Immensely." Everything was working out perfectly.

"Good." He rose and took the goblet from her hands. Was

that a gleam she saw in his eyes, she wondered, or was it only that she wasn't used to seeing them so clearly?

She got her answer when he began peeling off his clothes.

"Wh-what are you doing?"

"Joining you. I'm grubby as anything."

"B-but…together?" She half rose out of the tub.

With a hand on her shoulder, he pushed her back down. "Together."

"You're jesting," she said. "And you're hurt."

But the way he held her gaze made it clear he wasn't jesting at all. "Aye, I hurt a bit," he admitted. "I trust you'll treat me gently." Opposite her, he stepped into the water.

Though she was consciously looking elsewhere, a flash of white drew her eye to his body. "Your bandage!"

"Stop being such a worrywart, lass. I'm more comfortable with it on." As he lowered himself, he nodded toward her tattered chemise. "There's another where this one came from."

He emitted a small grunt of pain as he settled, but that didn't seem to signal any loss of enthusiasm. His lips went to hers immediately. Lulled by the taste of him, she moved closer. Smiling against her lips, he reached for the soap behind her head.

"I'm hurt. I think you need to wash me," he suggested, holding it out.

At the silky tone of his voice, heat flooded her cheeks, and when she took the soap, it slipped from her fingers and plunged to the bottom. His teasing smile only flustered her further while she fished in the water for the hard-milled ball. But when she brought it up and its scent wafted to her nose—her lavender fragrance, not his sandalwood—a rather wicked idea took hold in her mind.

Languidly, she passed the soap back and forth in her hands. "I'll wash you," she told him, "but only if you promise not to move. Not your arms, not your legs, not anything."

"Not even my head?" He lurched forward and stole a kiss.

Her lips tingled as she firmly pushed him back. "Not even. Not even one inch."

Contemplating that, he ran his tongue over the chip in his tooth. "Why?" he asked.

"You're injured. You mustn't strain yourself. And besides..." Her lips curved in a smile. "I wish to play Poseidon and rule these waters."

"Heart's wounds," he breathed, his mouth hanging open.

That made her smile grow wider. "Do you trust me, Trick?" she asked playfully, lathering her hands—though in truth she held her breath for his answer.

"More than anyone I've ever met."

The quiet sincerity in his voice made her eyes prickle with thankful tears. But she wasn't about to cry at a moment like this. Instead, she reached to close her husband's mouth for him, leaving a froth of soapsuds on his chin. He made to wipe it away.

"Uh-uh," she said, catching his hand. "No moving, remember?"

His lopsided grin made her heart flip over. "My deepest apologies. It won't happen again, *leannan*."

"Good." And with a happy sigh, she leaned forward to take his lips in a kiss.

SIXTY

*D*UNCRAVEN SEEMED lighter the next morning.

When Kendra woke, the chamber seemed brighter, and the walls seemed to hold fewer secrets. No ghosts lurked in the tower stairwell. She found herself almost sorry to leave.

But Trick was in a hurry.

"I want to deliver what's left of the king's treasure. Get it off my hands." He latched his trunk. "And I want to get back to Amberley. Although..."

He watched her look up from tying a garter. "Although what?"

"It shouldn't be mine." He'd been thinking about that ever since he'd had other obvious facts pointed out to him—that Annag and Duncan were his siblings, and that he wasn't really English at all. "Amberley, and the dukedom. By rights, by blood, they shouldn't belong to me."

And the shock of it was, he found that disturbing. Mere months ago he hadn't wanted Amberley at all, hadn't wanted anything that came from the man he'd thought was his father. His shipping concern had been more than enough to support him, the estate and title just another reminder of the life he'd wanted to forget, another responsibility he hadn't needed.

But he needed them now. He needed them for his wife and the family he'd begun envisioning. No sane man would reject something that so clearly benefitted the people close to him.

Loving Kendra had changed everything.

"Who would get Amberley if not you?" Always direct, his Kendra.

"I don't know. My fa—the man who raised me had no brothers...some distant cousin of his, I imagine. Someone I've never met."

"And do you imagine he'd use that dukedom for the same good that you do? Do you imagine he'd shelter orphans in the old manor house?" Always straight through to the heart.

"I don't know that, either."

She rose and walked close. "You know I didn't want to be a duchess any more than you wanted to be a duke. But you earned that dukedom, Trick."

"Did I?"

"Yes. With your sweat, and I suspect with your blood and your tears." She leaned up to press a soft kiss to his lips. "Legally, it's yours, and I see no reason on earth it shouldn't *stay* yours."

Maybe she was right, and there was no reason he shouldn't be able to keep it.

No reason except his monarch's threat hanging over his head if he failed to finish the job he'd started.

He kissed her back, a kiss filled with all the hope he had for their future. "Come, *leannan,* let's traipse down these endless stairs one last time. Let's go home and get started on our brand-new life."

SIXTY-ONE

KENDRA HELD Hamish's arm, thrilled that he was strong enough now to accompany them outdoors along with Niall.

They paused on the drive where the Amberley servants waited. "What will you tell King Charles?" Hamish asked Trick.

"I'll think of something." Trick looked up to the single chest he'd had lashed to the top of the ducal carriage. "At least nobody will suspect I'm carrying anything of special value."

He'd told Kendra that when they stopped for the night at an inn, they'd simply bring it with them into their room. They didn't need all the extra guards he'd been envisioning. Four Amberley outriders stood ready, and that should be enough. They planned to travel directly to London.

Her gaze followed his. "I want to see it," she said.

"See what?" Niall asked.

"The Royal plate that brought about all this treachery and heartache. It's beautiful, isn't it?"

"I wouldn't know." Her brother-in-law shrugged. "I've never seen it myself."

"In all those years?" She hadn't pegged him as being so uncurious. "I would have begged until my parents let me look."

"Oh, I did. But it was pointless. There's no key to the padlock."

Hamish gave her a hard hug. "I tossed all the keys into a loch years before Niall was born. After one of those bitter quarrels. To keep the pieces from disappearing one by one."

So he'd distrusted his friends even then. Unfortunate that he'd failed to take those feelings to heart—it might have saved Elspeth's life.

L'amitié ferme les yeux, Kendra thought with a pang of regret. Friendship closes its eyes.

Drawing her from her brooding, Niall stepped forward and planted kisses on both her cheeks. "God willing, I'll see you soon."

She was surprised to feel tears welling up. "I expect you at Amberley before too long."

He nodded. "After the harvest."

Trick embraced his brother. "I thank you for taking care of that for me."

"We—Da and I—thank you for allowing us to stay." Niall's gaze flickered over to the castle's open doorway, where Annag and Duncan stood glaring, her children behind them. "And allowing them to stay, too."

Trick shrugged. "They're harmless." And he was right. For all Kendra's wild imaginings, Duncan and Annag had never done anything to hurt either of them. "Besides, they're my siblings. I won't pretend to like them, but if it makes Da happy to give them a home, then I'm happy, too."

Tears welled in Hamish's eyes as he took Trick by both hands. "We don't deserve you, lad."

He shook his head. "It's I that don't deserve you—a father and a brother that would do any man proud. Family, after all these years." Blinking back his own tears, he wrapped the older man into his arms for a long moment. "We'd best be going."

"Aye, I suppose you must." Hamish forced a smile and watched them climb into the carriage.

Trick closed his eyes until they rode away, then opened them and pulled Kendra across the cabin for a gentle kiss. "When we get to London, I'm going to ask my solicitor to deed Duncraven over to Hamish, with Niall as his heir."

If she'd had any remaining doubts that her husband was a good man, they vanished then. "That's wonderful, Trick."

"Not wonderful, only decent." He kissed the tip of her nose. "Besides, the last thing I need is an estate in Scotland. My father —the duke," he corrected himself, "left me more than I can deal with as it is."

Maybe he could fool himself into thinking his actions were less than generous, but Kendra knew better.

IT FELT STRANGE to Kendra to be back in London but at Trick's town house instead of the one she'd always known in Lincoln's Inn Fields. And Caldwell House, a dark monstrosity built before the Civil War, was every bit as disgustingly opulent as he'd said. Standing in the master bedchamber, where she was dressing before attending court, she was reminded of an overdecorated cake.

A blue and orange one.

"Ghastly," she said, kicking off her shoes.

"I told you that you would hate it." Trick shrugged out of the surcoat he'd worn for travel. "Feel free to redecorate."

"I imagine I have better things to do that will keep me busy a while." Peeling off her garters and stockings, she frowned at the lavender gown that Jane had selected. Too insipid for her mood. They'd sent a messenger ahead to request Kendra's London clothing be moved from the Chases' town house, and she hurriedly flipped through the gowns that had been crammed into the master bedroom's wardrobe. "I wonder how all the children are getting along?"

"They're well, I'm sure," her husband said absently while pulling a fresh shirt over his head.

Cavanaugh had laid a blue velvet suit on the bed. Men had it so easy, Kendra thought with a touch of weariness-induced irritation. Brown or green, velvet or satin. Aside from varying quantities of braid, lace, and ribbon, everything looked the same. Their shirts and cravats were always white, their shoes—with the exception of some foppish court dandies—invariably black. High-heeled with fancy buckles for court, low-heeled and plain for every day. There was nothing much for them to decide.

She selected a cloth-of-gold gown and held it up. "What do you think?"

His back to her as he reached for his breeches, Trick answered, "It's fine." For a moment she stood there, aggravated, until he turned and favored her with one of his blinding white smiles.

He was right. Everything was fine, after all.

In a few short weeks, their relationship had come a long way —farther than she'd thought possible. The journey to London had been almost blissful. Trick had been attentive, but even more important, he'd answered most of her questions without resorting to evasion. The days on the road had gone a long way toward convincing her their marriage would be a happy one.

Bless her brothers for bringing them together, she thought, then silently laughed at her reversal of feelings.

"Come here," Trick said, and she did, letting the gown slip to the floor as she walked into his arms. His kiss was everything she hadn't known she needed before he'd come into her life.

They parted regretfully. "I'm sorry to rush you out of the house when we've barely arrived," he murmured. "but I want to complete my business with King Charles and take you home to Amberley."

With a sigh, she moved away and began detaching her stomacher. "I still wish I could see it."

"See what?" he asked, pulling up the blue velvet breeches.

"The treasure. Will we be bringing it along to court?"

Trick's gaze wandered to the massive chest sitting in a corner.

He wished he didn't have to deal with this. He wished he didn't have to deal with King Charles or his problems at all.

"I think I'll just meet with Charles tonight to explain, then arrange to send it along later."

She wiggled her gown down and off. "I cannot wait to see his reaction."

Losh, he couldn't let her be there. He had delicate matters to discuss with the king. Looking down as he tucked in his shirt, he made his voice as casual as possible. "I believe Charles will feel this is a matter best settled between men."

He raised his gaze to hers, expecting to see that look in her eyes. The defiant look she'd given him when he'd told her she couldn't come along to Scotland, again when he went off to Burntisland, and yet again when he'd ordered her not to get on the boat.

But instead he saw a different look. Hurt.

He wanted to hit something. Not an hour in London, and the accursed deceptions were coming between them already.

Characteristic of her, though, the hurt look was fleeting, and the one he'd expected came into her eyes, after all. He watched her draw breath, girding for battle. "Charles likes women," she said.

"In his bed, yes."

"No." She caught his gaze and blushed. "Well, yes, but that wasn't what I meant. He listens to women. Really listens, as if he cares what we say. Even about politics."

Lucky him, marrying one of probably three ladies in England who would think to discuss politics with their monarch. "If I let you see the treasure, will it make you feel better?"

"You cannot do that." She rolled her eyes. "There's no key, and Charles is going to wonder where the lock is if you hack it off."

"Then I won't."

"I knew you wouldn't."

"I mean I won't hack it off."

She glanced at the chest, then back to him, speculation narrowing her pretty green eyes. "Can you pick the lock?"

"You insult me." He swiped his knife off the dressing table, and she followed him to the chest, where he knelt and went to work, delicately probing the keyhole. "There isn't a good smuggler on earth who doesn't know how to pick a lock."

Wearing nothing but his amber bracelet and a chemise, she sat on the chest. When she crossed her legs right in front of his face, his knife slipped.

"Were you a good smuggler?"

Determinedly, he refocused. "Actually, I was a bad smuggler. My heart was never in it." A satisfying *click* reverberated in the room. "But I can pick a lock."

Removing it, he stood, and she jumped up to throw open the lid.

"Oh, my heavens, Trick. Look at this." She hefted a solid gold charger, running her fingers over the delicately engraved rim. "It's beautiful."

"He'll probably melt it down."

"No," she breathed, dropping to kneel before the chest. "He wouldn't." She set the charger on the floor and reached for a silver pitcher in the shape of a swan. "Oh, I just knew I wanted to see this." One by one, she removed pieces, each more impressive than the last. Plates, bowls, goblets, cutlery, serving utensils, platters. "Hamish was right. The first Charles truly did live like a king on his coronation journey."

He smiled as she delved deeper, her bottom rising as she leaned into the chest.

"Oh, what is this?" She drew out an ivory casket inlaid with scrolled gold wire.

He shrugged. "Small items?"

"In a beautiful box like this? And locked?"

Taking it from her, he made short work of that and put it back in her hands.

With a sigh of anticipation, she raised the lid. "Jewels!" She lifted an exquisite sapphire and diamond necklace. "My goodness, it looks like pirate's booty! How did jewels get in here?" Replacing the necklace, she slipped a gaudy emerald ring on her finger. "I don't understand this," she said, staring at it. Obviously made for a man, it dangled loose. "I thought Hamish and his friends only packed the kitchen."

"Supposedly." He ran a hand back through his hair, still surprised to find the front so short. "I guess somewhere along the way, someone filched this and slipped it inside."

"Rhona or Gregor, I'm guessing. I wonder if Hamish knows?" She dug around some more and drew out another necklace. "Od's fish, will you look at the size of these pearls?"

The largest round pearls Trick had ever seen, with one enormous teardrop-shaped pearl dangling from the center. "Fit for royalty, all right."

She dropped it back into the casket. "Oh, Trick, look at this." Her voice turned wistful. "Amber."

"When did you grow to like amber?" he teased.

She blushed and pulled the jewel out, only to find it was a clasp attached to a gleaming string of smaller, pure white pearls. "Oh, it's lovely," she sighed, dropping the strand over her head.

It was so long, he reached to double it, settling the second half around her neck. "Don't you own any pearls?"

"My father sold all the family jewels to help finance the Civil War." Her fingertips danced on the lustrous strand. "Of course, Jason has bought me things over the years. And Colin and Ford. They all know I love jewelry. But pearls are terribly expensive."

And immensely popular. All the court ladies wore pearls, and most of the men, come to that. "You look beautiful in pearls, *leannan*."

She blushed and took them off. "For the price this trinket could bring, I expect we could feed the orphans for a year."

"A decade, probably." He smiled.

She dropped them back into the box. "Help me put this all

away, will you? I still need Jane to do my hair, and if we don't get to Whitehall soon, we'll miss the presentations."

"**THE DUKE** and Duchess of Amberley!"

Trick shot the puffed-up court usher a sour look. "I abhor this sort of thing," he muttered to Kendra as they made their way down the aisle to where King Charles and Queen Catharine sat on the dais, dressed in crimson velvet with a swagged canopy overhead to match. "I really hate this."

"Oh, hush," Kendra chided. "A little pomp and circumstance never hurt anybody. And there will be dancing afterwards—"

"I cannot wait."

His tone was dry enough that under different circumstances she might be tempted to swat him with her fan. As it was, she flashed Queen Catharine a brilliant smile and dropped into a deep curtsy, pressing a kiss to the back of the woman's slim proffered hand. "Your Majesty."

"Lady Kendra," Catharine said in gracious Portuguese-accented syllables, "or have I heard it's the Duchess of Amberley now?"

"You've heard correctly," she said, then leaned closer to her husband. "As long as he behaves himself," she added for his ears only.

Coughing to cover a snort of laughter, he rose and traded

sides with her. King Charles smiled as she kissed his hand. "It's glad I was to hear that two of my favorite families are united."

She only just managed to conceal her surprise. "I'm happy to have pleased Your Majesty."

He nodded, then looked back to Trick. "We'll talk later, yes?"

"Aye. And I've something to give you."

"Do you, now?" The king was not above delighting in gifts. "Did you bring it along?"

"It's rather…large. And it's at my home, but I can have it delivered—"

"Amberley House, or your house here in London?"

"Here in London, but—"

"I have matters to discuss with you in any case." Charles raised a meaningful brow. "I shall sneak out of my bedchamber this evening and come to Caldwell House."

"Sneak?" Kendra burst out, then clapped a hand over her mouth.

Charles let loose a booming laugh. "My Master of the Backstairs is quite accustomed to making these arrangements, I assure you."

His eyes twinkled, and Kendra blushed. She knew he meant that he usually sneaked out for assignations with his mistresses, but she felt sorry for his long-suffering queen, who was studiously looking elsewhere.

She would never put up with that from her husband, not now that things were right between them in the bedroom. He'd promised her fidelity, and she expected him to give up his mistress. Just let him try to visit London alone again.

With another bow and curtsy, Kendra and Trick moved away so the next courtiers could be presented.

"Well, I expect we can leave now," Trick said as soon as they were out of earshot.

"I'm not leaving until after we've danced." Kendra flipped open her painted fan.

"Don't tell me you're going to titter behind that thing."

"Me? Titter?" She rapidly fanned her face. On this late summer night, the Presence Chamber was hot and close, lit by hundreds of candles in wall sconces and liveried yeomen holding flaming torches. "What did Charles mean, two of his favorite families?"

Trick tucked his tongue in his cheek. "Were you not aware the Chases are favored?"

For the second time this evening, she was tempted to swat him. "You know very well what I mean. I've never seen you at court—"

"I do my best to avoid it."

"And I don't remember you from the years in exile, either. So how is it you've come to know Charles so well?"

Trick leaned close to answer at a discreet volume. "My father —the duke—was a major supplier of kingly luxury items," he murmured. "All through the Commonwealth years, we had, uh…dealings."

Kendra stopped fanning. "You're jesting, aren't you? Charles was as poor as we were during those years."

"I'm not jesting. The duke was happy enough to supply him free of charge."

"Out of loyalty?"

He snorted aloud this time. "Out of greed. Charles promised him the dukedom restored upon his own restoration." He frowned across the chamber, then turned back to her, pulling at his cravat. "If you're not going to fan yourself, you may as well fan me."

"My wrist is tired. I've decided to sweat instead."

Chuckling, he leaned forward and gave her a kiss. "Ladies don't sweat. Ladies glow."

"I'm a duchess now, not a lady. I can do as I please." Suddenly she noticed him staring at a lady across the chamber. "Trick? Who is that?"

"Most people call her Lady Charlotte Waller."

She blew out a breath, her free hand curling into a fist. If this was his London mistress…

"Most people?" she asked carefully.

"Charlotte, Harlot—what's the difference?"

Despite her distress, she laughed, thinking there were very few women present who didn't deserve such a designation. "And what, pray tell, could this Lady Harlot have done to earn such a nickname at King Charles's court?"

"She slept with the Earl of Danforth."

"From what I understand, so have half the women here."

He raised a brow. "Not while they were betrothed to me."

"Oh." Dear heavens! Not a mistress, but the girl from Trick's poem. The one who had wounded him so deeply that Kendra despaired of ever putting him to rights—of ever hearing a declaration of love pass his lips.

If anyone deserved a good swatting, it was Lady Charlotte Waller.

Kendra glared at the simpering blonde across the room. Harlot. "I hate her."

"Aye. It should have been obvious she only wanted me for my title. And that despite her protestations of virtue, she was anything but virtuous." He looked mad enough to spit. "But I was too trusting. It took finding them in bed together to make me realize she was unworthy of my trust."

In which case Kendra wouldn't have had an uphill battle to prove herself worthy of her husband's trust. Though if Trick had married the harlot, he wouldn't be her husband. But that was beside the point.

No…that was the point entirely. He was *her* husband, not the harlot's. And although not long ago she'd never have believed it, she was very happy about that.

Courtiers were gathering around the dance floor, a rainbow of brilliant colors in the blazing light. Jewels glittered on ears, necks, wrists, and the hands of men and women alike.

Kendra couldn't help but notice that most everyone wore pearls. With a secret smile, she toyed with her amber bracelet. Who needed pearls, anyway? Looking down to her hands, she noticed the plain gold band around her finger. So very Trick. She should have realized from the first that he wouldn't be the type of duke she detested.

And she'd found she didn't so much mind being a duchess, either. Together in those roles, they could do much good. Whether it was fair or not, people listened to what dukes and duchesses had to say. With whispers in the right ears, they could raise enough money to open a hundred orphanages if they wanted.

And he wouldn't have to play the highwayman anymore. In fact, before they got to Amberley, she'd demand he stop. Now.

His attention still across the room, she stole a glance at her husband. His golden good looks set her heart to racing, and she knew that she couldn't stand to even think of the possibility that he might be hurt or—heaven forbid—arrested. She would find some way to keep the children fed and clothed until she could put her new plan into motion.

At the far end of the chamber, musicians were tuning up, and King Charles was leading Queen Catharine through the crowd to begin the dancing.

"Shall we dance?" Kendra asked Trick.

Tearing his gaze from the harlot, he looked down at her. "Am I not supposed to do the asking?" He smiled. "Oh dear, I nearly forgot. You're a duchess now and can do as you please."

Laughing, she turned into her husband's arms and let herself be led to the dance floor, where a minuet was playing.

He bowed to her, then did a small plié in a mirror of her own movement. "Do you realize we've never danced?" he said conversationally.

She stepped forward with her right foot, rising on her toes. "I danced with your brother, you know."

"Did you? When?" They both brought their feet together,

lowering their heels. "Should I be worried?" Trick asked with a mock-stern frown. "Remember what I told you about fidelity."

Though she was sure he didn't intend it, his gaze went to Lady Harlot, who seemed to be pointedly ignoring him.

She repeated the steps with her left foot, her own gaze going to King Charles. "Remember what *I* told *you* about fidelity."

His laugh made her feel a lot better. He dropped her hands so they could both turn. "Niall and I danced at the *draidgie*," she said coquettishly over her shoulder. "While you were outside writing." His hands felt warm when he reached for hers again. "It was a wild dance, I tell you—we weren't able to talk like this."

"Ah, yes, a Scottish country dance."

"Did someone mention Scottish?"

"Caithren!" Surprised, Kendra turned and threw her arms around her sister-in-law. "What are you doing here?"

"We've stopped in London for a few days before heading for Cainewood. Jase is insisting I see Dr. Willis."

Kendra frowned when a dancer had the nerve to bump into their happy little reunion. "The king's physician?"

"The very same." Cait sighed. "Just what I need—a man poking and prodding me. Wheesht!" she added as a broad-reared matron backed into her. "I've delivered a dozen or more bairns; I think I know what I'm doing."

"Shall we?" Trick asked, motioning them off the busy dance floor. "What's this all about?"

Kendra tried to look baffled. "Did I forget to tell you that Caithren is with child?"

"Aye, it seems you did." With a knowing smile, he turned to Cait. "Congratulations."

"Was Jason upset?" Kendra asked.

"Would you believe I convinced him I didn't know?" Concealed by a lovely rose-colored gown with a silver-embroidered stomacher, Cait's middle still looked flat. She grinned.

"The truth is he's not quite sure, and in any case, his main concern was getting back to England before the weather set in."

"So what *was* his reaction, then?"

"I'm thrilled." Appearing from out of nowhere, Jason bent to give Kendra a kiss. "How are you doing?" he asked in her ear.

Dressed in dark green and looking delightfully familiar, the sight of him made her wonder why she'd been so angry with him. "I'm happy," she admitted.

"I'm happy to hear it." He had the good grace not to look smug, although she knew full well he'd lord it over her in the future. He turned to his wife. "You didn't fool me for a minute, you know. I was too pleased to make a fuss…although now the excitement's worn off a bit, I've a mind to make you pay for that deception."

She raised a brow. "I cannot wait."

The stern look Kendra was more accustomed to settled on his features. "Your health could have been at risk. And the babe's as well."

"I've never felt healthier in my life." Cait slipped an arm around his waist, gazing up at him with a brilliant, calculated smile. "You're not really vexed with me, are you?"

His answer was an indulgent sigh. "So what are *you* doing here?" he asked Trick.

"I have something that belongs to Charles. Long story," he added when Cait went to ask. "I'm sure Kendra will enjoy the telling."

Kendra grinned. "He only says that hoping I'll make him out a hero."

"I cannot wait to hear," Caithren said, snagging her by the arm. "Shall we repair to the garden?"

The music stopped, and dancers began jostling past. His obligations over, King Charles caught Trick's gaze and sent him a significant nod.

"I'm afraid your talk will have to wait," he said. "I believe I've just been summoned home to Caldwell House."

"We'll talk tomorrow, then," Cait said, dropping Kendra's arm and threading her own through Jason's. "And my husband will dance with me instead."

"Nothing energetic," he warned. "You'll stick to the minuet."

"You see what I have to put up with?" she asked Kendra with a roll of her eyes. "Crivvens, you'd think I was an invalid."

SIXTY-FOUR

*A*T CALDWELL House later that night, Trick watched as Charles swirled Madeira in his glass and took an appreciative sip. "Amazing."

"The wine?"

The king's lips curved beneath his thin black mustache. "The wine's of admirable quality, to be sure. But then, your late father dealt only in the best."

Trick agreed with a curt nod. The best, aye. The best wine, the best fabrics, the best furnishings, the best books. His gaze wandered to the leather-bound tomes lining the walls in this, the most impressive study in all of London. He doubted the man had ever cracked open even one of them.

"However, it was your gift I was referring to." Charles set down the glass and reached into the chest, pulling out a solid gold dish and turning its heavy weight thoughtfully in his hands. "To think my own father's treasure has resurfaced after all these years."

"Only to end up where it was said to be in the first place." Pensively, Trick played with the lock in his hands—the one he'd hacked off in the king's presence.

"Od's fish—that was none of your doing. It's pleased I am

that you recovered what you did, and I'd be pleased as well to see you keep a part of it."

"I couldn't." He'd lost most of it already, no matter that Charles refused to place blame.

"I insist." He handed Trick the plate. "Here. As a memento, if nothing else."

"I appreciate the offer, but I really don't want to keep this." The dish had to be worth a small fortune, and Charles needed it far more than he did.

"There must be something here that strikes your fancy." The king set down the plate and raised a jeweled goblet. "This. Or something else."

"No, really, I—"

"What is this?" Metal servingware clanked as Charles reached into the bottom and brought out the small ivory casket. His black eyes glittering, he lifted the unlocked lid and extracted the short necklace of large pearls. Raising it with a hand, he flicked a finger to set the giant teardrop pearl swinging. "There's a painting of my mother wearing this," he murmured.

"Henrietta Maria will be happy to have it back. It will look lovely on her."

The king looked up. "Yes, it will," he said softly. "I thank you." He fished out the sapphire and diamond necklace that Kendra had held up earlier. "If you won't take something for yourself, then take this for your new wife."

Suddenly inspired, Trick reached for the box, setting it on his lap to extricate a long strand of pearls from the tangle.

"This," he said. "If you insist I take something, this is what I'd like."

Charles frowned at it. "Those pearls are ordinary. And the clasp only amber. I'd lay odds that's the least valuable item in the entire chest."

"It's the one I want." Trick's tone left no room for doubt.

"You shall have it then, with my thanks." The king shut the casket and set it atop the gold and silver that crowded the trunk.

He reached for his wineglass again, his long fingers worrying the stem. "How goes the mission?"

"Very well, but for the interruption." The pearls made soft clicking sounds as Trick shifted them in his hands, thinking about Kendra asleep in the late duke's gaudy bed upstairs. "I have some descriptions that I was preparing to give to Pendregast when I was called away to Scotland."

"Excellent." The king sipped. "I assume, being away, you missed hearing the latest news."

"News?" A tiny chill crept up Trick's spine. Or maybe the chamber was a bit cold.

"There's been a reward posted for the mysterious Black Highwayman."

"Blast it." He could only hope his leads would pan out and he'd have no need to pose as the highwayman again. "No one has connected him to me, so I don't expect I have anything to worry about."

"No one?"

"Just my wife. And her family." Unfortunately. "I haven't told them the purpose for the disguise—"

"Good. Let's keep it that way."

Broadsides were likely plastered all over the kingdom, advertising the reward. Kendra would see them and worry herself sick. "I'd like to tell only my wife—"

"If the mission is nearly complete, there's no sense involving anyone else."

"Just her—"

"I've never known a woman who could keep her mouth shut." Charles pinned him with his jet-black gaze. "Have you?"

Once Trick would have agreed, but now he knew he'd been wrong. His wife had kept Cait's secret, and she hadn't told her brothers about his supposed financial trouble or him continuing as a highwayman, either.

"Kendra's not like that."

"I'm happy your marriage agrees with you, Amberley. But I

trust no lady to stay quiet, not even your wife. And I'm trusting *you* to respect my wish for silence. Your loyalty will pay dividends. Your disloyalty…"

The unspoken words hung in the air. There it was, that veiled threat to withhold the pardon.

"I'm sorry," Charles added with a sympathy Trick knew was sincere. It was part of the charm that made the king so popular with the people. But under that genuine kindness lay a streak of ruthless determination that was every bit as integral to the man's personality. "I cannot afford to have it bandied about that the king is condoning robbery, no matter the reason or how deserving the victims. They're my subjects, nonetheless."

"But—"

"I'm asking you, as your monarch and your friend, to keep this wholly to yourself."

Trick mentally threw up his hands. Opposing the monarchy went against everything he stood for. And although he'd agreed to this mission out of patriotism for king and country, he needed to finish it for Kendra. For their promising, fragile relationship, and for the children he hoped they'd have. Even now, an heir might be growing inside her, and that son deserved Amberley.

He sighed. "Of course."

"Return to Sussex and arrange to meet with Pendregast. Fear not, for I've been thinking since I heard the news, and I've a plan to wrap this up. I owe you a debt for solving this little problem, and I won't see you or the Chases implicated in any way."

With a sinking heart, Trick listened to the plan. Despite his intentions otherwise, the deceptions would continue. For a man didn't put his wife before his sovereign.

Not a wise one, in any case.

SIXTY-FIVE

KENDRA WOKE to a husky whisper in her ear.

"I have a present for you, *leannan*."

Her head was lifted, and something cool and heavy slid down about her neck. Sleepily she reached for it, her fingers meeting a strand of smooth, hard orbs that could only be pearls.

Her eyes flew open. "Has it an amber clasp?"

"But of course." Standing over her, her husband smiled. Dear heavens, he looked gorgeous in the low light of the fire. "Charles tried to give me a solid gold platter as a reward, but I would have none of it."

She ran her tongue over her teeth, thinking of that tiny chip in his. "Well, are you going to come down here and let me thank you?"

She sighed as he joined her beneath the coverlet and settled his body beside hers, then laughed when he reached for the hem of her chemise to pull it off, needing to draw it through the necklace to accomplish his goal. With a grin, she grabbed the far end of the long strand and slipped it over his head, roping him close.

"I've got you," she said.

"You certainly have." His mouth met hers for a leisurely kiss, and she melted happily into his arms.

No matter how many times he kissed her, she still felt afire like it was the first. A flush heated her skin, warming the pearls that draped heavily on her neck. When the strand tangled, becoming an obstacle between them, she reached to pull it off.

"I'll take those." He held out his hand. And she gave them over, expecting him to drop them to the night table, as she had been about to do.

But instead, he just held the long rope in the air.

"They're beautiful," she said, watching them swing gently, firelight dancing off the gleaming round surfaces.

"Not half as beautiful as you."

She'd never thought of herself as especially beautiful, and she swallowed hard.

"Do you know how much I care for you?" he asked in a thick, velvet-edged whisper.

"How much?" she whispered back, breathlessly caught in his gaze.

"Enough to make me question my loyalties."

Loyalties? Though she didn't quite understand, she could tell the admission was wrenched from somewhere deep inside him, and it softened the pain of not hearing the words she'd so desperately hoped he would say.

I love you.

She should tell him first, she thought. She should tell him first.

But she couldn't. Because she still hadn't quite scaled his wall. Because part of him was still holding back.

Not here, though. Not now. He arranged the pearls on her body and leaned away. "Lovely," he murmured.

She mustered a weak smile. "I don't think that's the way they're meant to be worn. Rather scandalous, don't you think?"

"At King Charles's court? Not a soul would even take notice." But he drew them off and finally dropped them on the night table, meeting her lips for a tender kiss.

There was something about him tonight…something about

the way he was kissing her, the way he was holding her close. Something. Something that made her feel, for the first time since the night he'd learned of his mother's death, a vulnerability beneath his surface. That somewhere inside him lurked a lost little boy.

Waiting to get hurt.

So she was tender in return. Her arms held him to her, drawing him closer, closer, closer still.

If only she could climb the last of that wall and finally make them one.

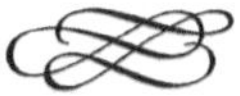

SIXTY-SIX

BEFORE LEAVING the next morning, Trick swept the strand of pearls off the night table. "Do you like these?

"I love them." Kendra's smile lifted his heart. "But Trick…"

"Aye?"

"I mostly love them because we can sell them."

His fingers tightened around them. "No, *leannan*. They're for you."

She grabbed them from his hands, cradling them against her. "They would feed the children for a decade, you said. No longer will you have to be a highwayman. I was going to beg you to stop anyway, Trick—I cannot stand the thought of you being hurt or caught in the act." If her smile had lifted his heart, her words sent it soaring. "It's bad of me, I know, but you're much more important than the children. To me. The most important thing in my life."

She looked pained at that guilty admission, but not as pained as he felt inside. That she could put him above everything else… if only he hadn't the obligations that kept him from doing the same.

If only.

"Do you see the gift that Charles has given us?" She held it up. "We no longer have to choose between your safety and the children's welfare." Looking half-wistful, half-thrilled, she brought the pearls to her lips. "I'll sell them on our way out of London. And I have other ideas as well, for how we can help more children. This—this gift—will get us started."

Her enthusiasm was more than he could bear. Soon he could bring her to the docks, show her whichever of his ships were in port, tell her that he could support all the orphanages she wanted. Soon this would be over, and he vowed to himself he'd be honest with his wife for the rest of his life. He would never make another promise that would be this hard to keep.

"You're not selling them," he told her, peeling her fingers from the pearls. He lifted the strand and slipped it over her head. "We're going home and taking them with us. And I promise you, the children won't starve."

❧

*B*ACK AT AMBERLEY later that day, Trick barely took time to see their luggage brought in before readying himself to leave.

Stunned, Kendra stood in their bedchamber watching him knot a fresh cravat. "We just got here."

"I have an errand I must see to," he told her, not quite meeting her eyes.

"An errand?" Although he was standing close, she felt as though he'd physically pulled away. "Are you going out to play the highwayman again? I told you—"

"Nay. I'm done with that."

And he wasn't wearing black—he'd dressed in a simple brown suit and white shirt. She should have noticed that. Her usually sharp powers of observation were dulled by disappointment.

Just last night, she'd felt so very close to him. She'd thought that with everything they'd shared in Scotland and since, things would be different now. But no matter that his hair had been cut and his eyes were unshielded—he was hiding from her again.

She backed away to sit on the gaudy red bed, her fingers going to the pearls around her neck. "If you won't sell these and you won't play the highwayman, where will we find the money for the children?"

"I told you this morning," he said, even more slowly than usual, "the children will have plenty to eat."

"How?" Her head swirled with confusion. "Did Charles give you more than the pearls, then?"

"You could say that," he said dryly and fell silent.

He gazed at her for a long moment without saying anything more. Without moving. Without even blinking.

Then determination lit his eyes and his jaw tensed with resolve. "It's time that I told you the truth," he said, moving closer. "I have plenty of money to fund the orphanage without resorting to robbery. You've no need to worry for the children, I promise. All right? Can you take my word for that?"

The truth, he'd said. "I don't understand."

He stepped yet closer. "When my father—the duke—died, I took the ships he'd used for smuggling and began importing with them instead. It's all legitimate. I have nine ships now and a London warehouse filled with goods from across the globe that are sold all over the country. I can well afford to support the children and anything else your heart desires."

As though she'd been physically hit, Kendra found it hard to draw breath. "Then why did you tell me you needed to rob in order to fund the orphanage?"

"I never said that, Kendra."

She thought back, frantically running through their conversations in her head. "But you didn't correct me when I assumed it, either. A lie of omission is a lie, nonetheless."

All the gains she'd thought they'd made seemed to be slipping away. She struggled to keep a hint of hysteria from her voice. "This makes no sense. Why is it, then, that you played the highwayman? Why keep doing it when you knew it worried me, and my brothers had asked you to stop? For your own amusement, as you once said?"

"Not for my amusement." Taking both her hands, he drew her to stand before him, his gaze filled with silent apology. "I had reasons, good reasons, but…I'm sorry, *leannan*. There are things I cannot tell you."

"Why?"

"I just cannot. You'll have to trust me." His knuckles skimmed her cheek. "Once you promised you'd trust me. Has that changed?"

Her memory flashed on that day in the dungeon, and her cheeks heated. But that had been in Scotland, where they'd spent every day, almost every minute, together. Where he hadn't kept secrets, so far as she could tell, and where they'd grown close and learned to be easy with each other.

Yet literally the moment they'd stepped foot in Amberley, everything had gone back to the way it had been before they left. She'd thought she'd got through to him—that his wall was nearly down—but that clearly wasn't the case. Not here.

She wished they'd never come home.

"I'm trying to trust you," she told him. "But it's very hard."

"It's hard for me, too. You must believe that. Just let me finish what I must do to put this all behind us."

And with one kiss, so heartfelt it left her reeling, he was out the door.

*I*T HADN'T QUITE been a lie. Charles *had* given him more than the pearls—he'd given him orders not to tell his own wife what he was doing.

Blasted obstinate man.

Though Trick never thought to hear himself curse his king, he did so all the way to the cottage to fetch his papers.

From there he traveled two villages over to meet the contact Charles had arranged for, a man going by the comical name of Zephaniah Pendregast and posing as a Roundhead. During the ride, Trick switched from railing at Charles to cursing himself.

What an idiot he'd been to tell Kendra about his shipping company. He'd thought it would help to come clean with as much of the truth as he could, to relieve her mind where the children were concerned, at least. But he'd gravely miscalculated. He'd seen the doubt and confusion come into her eyes, and it had made him sick inside.

He had no experience with being in love, and he was doing it all wrong.

The foundations they'd built in Scotland were crumbling out from under him. He could only hope this mission would come to an end before those foundations eroded entirely. Hope there would still be enough left upon which they could rebuild trust.

Hope his loyalty to the king wouldn't cost him his future.

Trick had sent a messenger before him, so Pendregast was waiting in back of the blacksmith's shop where Charles's men had arranged for his temporary employment. He suggested they walk in the fields behind the town's High Street shops.

"I hope it's good news you bring," Pendregast said, dropping his proper Puritan speech the moment they were out of earshot. He was tall and lean, dark haired with a long, hollowed-out face. The blows of hammer on anvil rang in the background as they paced together. "I'm stinking bored in this swiving establishment."

"It's sorry I am for the delay. I was called out of the country. In any case"—Trick pulled the roll of papers from his surcoat—"I have your descriptions."

They pored over the pages together, Pendregast asking questions and Trick answering as well as he could remember.

"So do you know these men?" Trick finally asked.

"I've attended enough secret meetings to last a lifetime, I'll warrant you that. This description here"—Pendregast stabbed a finger at one of Trick's pages—"seems familiar. And one other. I'll ask around, see what I can find. I'll be in touch."

Trick walked him back to the smithy, where they shook hands. "I'll be glad to have this behind me."

"No more than I," Pendregast grated out through the fake smile he put on his face as he reentered the shop.

SIXTY-EIGHT

KNOWING HE'D have to leave Kendra home alone soon, Trick spent a tense couple of days tiptoeing around her, avoiding her hurt gaze while wracking his brain for a plausible explanation that wouldn't cause even more pain and distrust. Mostly he kept out of the house, acquainting himself with his estate—which was a fair use of his time, since he now planned to be here more than he'd once thought.

Life near the docks in London had rather lost its charm. His new plan was to manage the company through correspondence along with occasional jaunts to the City to check up on matters, bringing Kendra along with him. Perhaps Niall might become involved as well. Having discovered a family, Trick found himself entertaining grand ideas. Expanding his company to include ships based in Scotland was just the start.

Both nights he delayed coming home until Kendra was in bed, when the darkness would save him from meeting her eyes. In those wee hours, he tried to tell her physically what he couldn't say with words. And if there was a new uncertainty in her response, if she seemed to be holding something back, he could only remind himself that things would be better soon.

Finally, a terse message arrived: *Meet me seven a.m. Saturday at the home of John Garrick. Z.P.*

John Garrick? Trick wondered. Was he working for Charles, too? Well, at least this would give him a solid excuse to spend the weekend away. Kendra shouldn't question a card party at Garrick's—a house party her own brothers regularly attended. With any luck, she'd happily send him off.

Evidently, however, luck wasn't on his side.

"So soon?" she asked when he found her going over menus in the kitchen. She turned to the cook. "Will you excuse me a moment, Mrs. Brown?"

Dejection dulled her eyes as she led Trick to the butler's pantry, then, finding it occupied by two maids polishing silver, all the way into the deserted two-story dining room. One foot tapping on the black-and-white checkered marble floor, she stared up at the plasterwork ceiling, studying the painted scenes there as though they might hold the answers to her problem.

Her problem being him, of course.

"We've been home less than a week," she said.

As she lowered her gaze to meet his, he shifted on his feet. "The card weekends have become tradition. It's been months since the last one, ever since our wedding. The men have been impatient for my return."

She ran a fingertip along the carved and gilded mantel. The old duke had really outdone himself gussying up this chamber. "Trick, I'm..." He watched her draw a deep breath. "I feel like I've lost you since we returned home."

"I'm right here." He forced a smile.

"You've been out and about doing heaven knows what. Why can't we spend some time together? Shouldn't our marriage come before a card game?"

"It's already planned," he said, wishing he could find a way to make her feel as loved and secure as she deserved. He wanted that more than he wanted to breathe.

But first he had to complete the mission. He was so close.

He'd already sent a message to King Charles saying the time had arrived to set their final plans into motion.

Soon he would be free.

The next morning found him leaving his lovely wife abed with a gentle kiss to her forehead. Wincing at her disappointed sigh, he tried to remember his duty.

These counterfeiters were undermining the economy, threatening the newly restored monarchy. He owed this to his country; he'd made promises to his king.

If a tinge of unease stayed lodged in his gut, he was determined to ignore it.

An hour later, he arrived at Garrick's estate to find Pendregast waiting along the road, he and his horse hidden behind a hedge that concealed them from the mansion.

"What gives?" Trick asked, reining in Chaucer. "Why aren't you inside?"

"We cannot just walk in and make an arrest. We need some incriminating evidence first. Have you any ideas regarding how to gain entry?"

"We might try knocking on the door." Trick peeked through the hedge. "Is Garrick in on this or not? How many men has Charles roped into this operation?"

"Just we two. Garrick is the suspect."

"John Garrick? A counterfeiter?" When Trick jerked upright at the thought, Chaucer danced beneath him. "Are you certain?"

"Not entirely. He could be just another link in the chain. But that description you gave me that sounded familiar? I asked around, found the man, and followed him for two-and-a-half days, until finally he led me here. Was in and out in five minutes. Then I hid for a while, and another man arrived. Didn't match any of your notes, but he was in and out in five minutes, too."

"So if Garrick isn't doing it himself…"

"I'm assuming he's involved in the distribution, at the very least. But we need proof."

Trick's mind reeled, remembering Garrick's preachiness, his

edginess, the way he always seemed to be snooping around. A closet Parliamentarian?

Blast it. That could very well be. These were unpredictable times. Perhaps Trick had been foolhardy to come into the county and indiscriminately welcome his new neighbors—strangers—into his social circle. He might have brought Garrick and the others to the cottage someday. They might have seen his props.

Blast it.

"We need an excuse to get in," Pendregast said. "He has too many servants to simply wait until he leaves. People are always around."

"I can gain us entry. I know him. And he owes me a meal."

"Pardon?"

Trick patted his stomach. "Breakfast."

SIXTY-NINE

"**M**RS. KENDRA?** Were you not going to tell us about Clytie?"

With a sigh, Kendra flipped the page in the wonderful book of lesser-known myths she'd discovered in Amberley's two-story library. At least she'd thought it was wonderful last month when she found it. Today, reading from it, it didn't seem so wonderful at all.

Once she'd thought that attaining her dream, the orphanage, would be enough. But she'd been wrong. Working with the children was fulfilling, but it didn't mend the hole in her heart that had opened when Trick left her this morning.

Dragging her attention back to the children, she smiled at their rapt expressions.

"Clytie loved the Sun God—"

"Apollo?" Andrew asked.

"Excellent memory," she said, trying not to sound annoyed at the interruption. Every little thing seemed to annoy her these past few days. "But for this story we think of him as the Sun God. You see, he found nothing to love in Clytie, and so she pined away, sitting on the ground out-of-doors where she could watch him. And she would turn her face, following him with her eyes as he journeyed over the sky. And so gazing, she found herself changed into the sunflower, which ever turns towards the sun."

"Did he ever love her?" a chestnut-haired girl asked.

Kendra met her big brown eyes. "I'm afraid not." She sighed. "Clytie loved him with all her heart, but he could never return her feelings."

Just like Trick. Her feelings for him had grown, but she feared his had not. The lies had started all over again, and so had the abrupt disappearances. How could any fellow love a girl and treat her this way?

Was she destined, like Clytie, to follow him with her eyes all her life? Never quite fulfilled, never truly possessing his love?

"Mrs. Kendra?"

She snapped the book shut. No use mooning about for these couple of days he'd be gone. He'd asked her to trust him, and she would do just that until she could confront him in person.

They'd come too far for her to let their marriage go without a fight.

Susanna wandered over to tug on her skirt. "Are we not going to finish the lesson?"

"Tomorrow, maybe." Feeling a shade more hopeful, she smiled. "For now, let's play blindman's buff."

"**L**ORD GARRICK is not yet awake," a stiff-necked butler told Trick.

"Well, then, rouse him." Without waiting to be invited, Trick stepped into the sprawling, dark manor house and motioned Pendregast to follow. "Tell him the Duke of Amberley is here to collect on a debt."

"With all due respect, your grace—"

"Aye, I *am* due respect. I believe I shall wait in the dining room until I receive it."

With a jerk of his head to Pendregast, he began wandering in the direction he figured a dining room might be located.

Sputtering, the butler marched up the stairs.

The third room Trick looked into had a dining table. He promptly dropped onto a dull-mustard upholstered chair. The rest of the chamber was no less drab. He'd seen no evidence of the remodeling Garrick had claimed was his reason not to host the house party, although the place was sorely in need of it.

Of course, the last thing a counterfeiter needed was construction workers roaming around his house.

"Forgot about this." Pendregast took a folded note from his

pocket. "It was sent by special messenger this morning, addressed to you."

Trick broke the red seal and unfolded it. A letter from King Charles—he'd have recognized his distinctive hand even without the "Your loving friend, Charles R." at the bottom.

The king wrote with good news that all was set, the plan to commence today and culminate sometime Monday evening.

Blast it. "A day or two," Charles had told him with his usual blithe indifference when describing the plan last week. Trick had fixed on the convenient card party excuse without considering the operation might prove too complicated to be carried out over a weekend.

Blast it, blast it, blast it.

He couldn't even go home and try to explain to Kendra. According to Charles's letter, the king's men would be waiting for him when he finished here.

"Is something amiss?" Pendregast asked.

"Aye. Nay." Trick shook his head to clear it. "I just need to get a note off to my wife. I saw a desk in the sitting room next door —I'll just fetch a quill and paper."

While he rummaged through the desk—finding the writing implements, but no evidence—he composed the note to Kendra in his head. Yet another half-truth. The web their relationship hung suspended on was becoming more and more tangled.

He had the note written by the time Garrick stomped into the room, bleary-eyed and hastily dressed.

"What's this about a debt, Amberley?"

"I seem to remember you showing up unexpectedly at my home, right in time for supper." Folding the paper, Trick plastered on a smile. "I just happened to be riding by this morning and noticed it was time for breakfast."

"What?"

"And you brought friends as well, did you not? This is my friend, um, Harold"—he slanted Pendregast a quick glance—"Gaunt. Sir Harold Gaunt."

"Pleased to meet you, Lord Garrick," Pendregast said.

Garrick gave him a curt nod before turning back to Trick. "The friends I brought were your friends, too."

"And so they were." Trick shrugged and held up the note. "Can I trouble you to have one of your staff run this to Amberley House? It's rather urgent." He licked his lips. "What are you serving this morning?"

SEVENTY-ONE

WHEN COMPTON met Kendra at Amberley House's door with his silver tray in hand, her stomach knotted.

Received an urgent message from my shipping company's manager, the note read. *Following the weekend, must go to London for a day. Be back Monday evening or Tuesday. Will explain later. My love, T.*

Her legs felt leaden as she trudged up the stairs. London. Without her again. Did he truly even own a shipping company? Or had he made that up as an excuse to run off to his mistress?

Arriving in her bedchamber, she leaned against the door and drew a calming breath. Surely her imagination was running wild. As usual, she was jumping to conclusions.

My love, T. She traced the words with a finger. He'd asked her to trust him. She had to believe him.

But three long, empty days yawned ahead, and she didn't have to stay at home pining for him, either. She was no Clytie. If he could spend his weekend in the "traditional" way, playing cards with the men, she could keep her tradition with her sisters-in-law.

In fact, Caithren was probably waiting for her, and no doubt

Amy and Jewel would be at Cainewood, too. While the men did whatever it was men did at house parties, they could have a party of their own.

Decision made, she packed a bag and headed for the stables. In no time at all she was barreling toward Cainewood, trying to enjoy the wind in her hair as she coaxed Pandora to go even faster. The miles sped by, the landscape becoming comfortingly familiar.

Amy and Cait would help her put everything into perspective. Surely their marriages had gone through precarious times as well, yet they were both happy.

She thundered over the wooden drawbridge, slid off Pandora, and ran toward Cainewood's double front doors.

A startled butler opened one of them. "Lady Kendra! I mean…welcome, your grace. What brings you here to Cainewood?"

"I wish to visit with Lady Cainewood. And—" Words failed her when she glimpsed her twin over the man's shoulder, pacing the upstairs landing with a contemplative look on his face and a beaker filled with bluish fluid in his hands. "Ford?" she called, stepping inside. "Why aren't you at the house party?"

"Kendra?" He blinked, looked down at her, then disappeared for a moment. Reappearing at the top of the stairs empty-handed, he ran down and caught her in a hug.

"What party?" he asked, pulling back. "Am I missing a party? Criminy. Are there pretty ladies there, too?"

She frowned. "The card weekend, or whatever it is you men call it. Why aren't you with the others?"

"We've had no card weekends since your wedding. They were always at Amberley—didn't you know that?" With a hand on her arm, he drew her down the corridor toward the drawing room. "What made you think there was a house party this weekend?"

Once in the chamber, she dropped onto a coral-colored chair.

Familiar, but not nearly as comforting as she'd hoped. "Trick. He told me he was leaving to play cards with the men, and he'd be back at the end of the weekend. Then he sent a note saying Monday or Tuesday." She bit the inside of her cheek. "Are you sure there's no party?"

"As sure as I can be. I'm sure Jason isn't playing cards, or Colin that I know of, either."

You'll have to trust me. Once you promised you'd trust me. Has that changed?

A lump rose in her throat as she hid her face in her hands. "I'm a fool then, aren't I? Over and over I believe what he tells me, but he always turns out to be hiding something."

"Perhaps he has a good reason." Ford sat in the adjacent chair and reached to pull her hands from her face, his brows knitted in sympathy. "I cannot imagine—"

"No." She leapt to her feet. Overwhelming sadness turned to bitter anger instead. "There's no good reason to deceive your spouse."

Trick had said there were things he couldn't tell her, and she'd accepted that, if rather reluctantly. But that wasn't the same as telling her an outright lie.

He'd lied to her from the beginning, before they were even married, starting by withholding the fact that he was a duke. Whatever had made her believe he'd change now? He'd implied that he needed to play the highwayman for the sake of the children, then claimed he owned a prosperous shipping firm. Which one of those facts was true?

My love, T. Another lie. Someone who loved his wife wouldn't treat her like this. Wouldn't say he was going one place and end up another.

"He's in London with his mistress." She gritted her teeth, pacing the patterned black-and-coral carpet. "That's why he was in such a hurry to return from Scotland. And after, to leave me at Amberley so he could go back to London alone."

And he'd made such a fuss out of telling her how he felt about infidelity. Over and over! The nerve of him, deliberately lulling her into false security with his trumped-up moral standards.

"Gentlemen talk, Kendra, and I've heard nothing of a mistress in London."

She looked away from the concern in Ford's deep blue eyes. "You're my brother. He wouldn't tell you about something like that."

"For heaven's sake, you've been wed only a couple of months." The concern was gone from his voice, replaced by an impatience that set her teeth on edge. "The last card party was before you even met the fellow, and I heard nothing of a mistress then. Yet there you go, as usual, leaping to conclusions. Wait to hear what Trick has to say for himself, will you? I cannot believe we misjudged him so keenly."

She crossed her arms. "Well, you did." She stared at a portrait of the first Marquess of Cainewood, some stern-looking, long-dead ancestor. Another controlling man, no doubt. Her brothers had misjudged Trick completely and pushed her into this marriage. It was their fault she was hurting now.

Their fault she had fallen in love.

Dear heavens. She turned away, bringing her hands to the wetness on her cheeks. In love—in love with a man who would never return it. Never trust her, never open up and share his life. She'd tried and tried to be the sort of wife he wanted, to no avail. She'd tried to listen, to trust him like he'd asked, only to be slapped with this bald-faced lie.

"Kendra." Ford drew her gaze. "You need to reconsider this in logical terms. I'm sure Trick has an explanation."

She'd come for her family's love and support, to find her own twin was siding with Trick. More tears threatened, but she wouldn't let them fall. Had Ford not heard a word she'd said?

Well, of course not—he was a man.

"This is your fault—yours and Jason's and Colin's. You stuck me with this lying adulterer of a husband. Where is Cait?"

"Upstairs, I think, probably napping. But Kendra—"

She was already out of the room.

SEVENTY-TWO

GARRICK'S KITCHEN had clearly been unprepared for breakfast guests. Engaging in desultory small talk with their reluctant host, Trick and Pendregast waited over an hour before an aging maid brought a tray of meat pottage and coffee. Two trips later, the table was also laden with spiced bread, caraway-seeded biscuits, fruited wheatmeal griddle cakes, and currant buns.

Sweets. Kendra would love this breakfast, Trick thought, wincing at the resulting stab of guilt.

The three of them ate until the butler arrived in the doorway. "A visitor, my lord."

Garrick blotted his flabby lips, then stood and patted his even more flabby belly. "Enjoy your breakfast, gentlemen. I shall return posthaste."

"Five minutes, I'm guessing," Pendregast said when the man had left.

"I'm going to follow him," Trick said. "If he returns before I do, tell him I was in need of a chamber pot."

He rose and peeked into the corridor. Thankfully, it was deserted. Slipping out, he flattened himself against the wall, moving along it until he nearly reached the front door.

Having already closed it, Garrick was leading a short man down the other wing of the house. Trick waited, watching, until he saw them enter a room. Then he hurried after them and listened through the door.

There was a scraping sound, something heavy sliding open and then shut. Hearing no voices, he cracked the door open and took a look.

A study. Empty, just as he'd thought. He ducked inside and hid himself in the kneehole of an aging oak desk. It wasn't long before the grating noise came again. He bent his head to see between the desk's claw-footed legs. A section of bookshelves disappeared, then slid back into place as he watched.

Garrick set something down on the desk above Trick's head. "Very well. But I don't want to see you for another month. Send someone else in the meantime—we cannot risk having the same men traveling the roads all the time. Not until that blackguard is caught."

"Yes, my lord."

"I'll see you out."

When the door closed behind them, Trick scooted from the cubby. A pewter candlestick now sat on the desk, and Garrick hadn't bothered to extinguish the taper. How convenient.

Trick felt around the bookcase for a handle, a button…ah, there it was. A latch. Throwing it, he was able to push the shelves behind the ones adjacent.

He took the candle and held it up to illuminate the window-less space beyond. A fair-sized room, if bare of luxuries. Atop a table sat three crucibles, a melting pan, dies, shears, and other equipment Trick didn't recognize. But the coins scattered over the surface were familiar indeed, as were the bars of base metal.

He'd seen all he needed to see.

Minutes later he strolled back into the dining room, adjusting his breeches conspicuously. "Nice place you have here, Garrick." He aimed a discreet nod at Pendregast.

Garrick grunted. "I'm due for renovations."

"So you've said."

Pendregast pulled out a pocket watch. "Lud, I've forgotten an appointment. Garrick, my thanks for the fine food and company. Amberley, I'll stop by to see you later."

More senseless chitchat that lasted an hour, then longer. Heart's wounds, Trick thought, would this never end? What on earth was taking Pendregast so long?

Garrick grew restless, pacing the chamber but unable to politely escape while Trick kept eating and engaging him in conversation. It got to the point where Trick wondered if he could cram in another morsel of food without vomiting, but he supposed the meal might hold him for the long ordeal ahead. Although this had been surprisingly easy, the next few days would be much more difficult.

But then this would be over. With any luck, by Monday night he'd be at home with Kendra. For the rest of his life, if he had any say in the matter. And no more secrets.

At last the butler announced another arrival.

Trick followed Garrick to the door. "Sir Harold," Garrick said, finding Pendregast on the other side. "Have you forgotten something?"

"I'm afraid so," Pendregast said as a balding man with a scar across his cheek stepped from around the corner. "The sheriff."

SEVENTY-THREE

"KENDRA! CAIT! Open up!"

Kendra scurried into the far corner of her old bedchamber while Caithren made her way to the door and opened it a crack. "Your sister doesn't want to talk to you," she told Jason. "Or Ford, either."

"Oh, for pity's sake. Tell her it's dinnertime, and we've strawberry tarts for dessert."

Trust a man to think food would solve his problems, Kendra thought. Most especially a Chase man. Well, he wasn't going to coax her by tempting her sweet tooth. "Tell him I'm not hungry," she called to Cait. "Tell him I'm not going to eat until the absurd marriage he arranged is annulled."

"She's not hungry," Cait started. "She's—"

"Forget it." Jason stuck his boot in the doorway when Caithren would have shut it. "Tell her I'll be here when she's ready to talk. Tell her that until then she can starve for all I care. Tell her Cook is baking cherry pie for supper." He paused for a breath. "Are you coming down for dinner, then?"

"Nay. I believe I'll stay here with Kendra."

"Women." Following the single terse word, Kendra heard his boots stomp down the corridor.

Cait closed the door. "Cherry pie later, Kendra."

"Oh, my. I suppose I'll have to save some room." She went back to her dressing table, where a veritable feast was laid out, smuggled in by Cait's loyal maid, Dulcie. Sitting down, she stabbed her spoon into her second strawberry tart. "I believe I'll skip the sallet and asparagus, then."

"You didn't mean that about an annulment, did you?"

"I'm not sure what I meant." She knew she and Trick had come too far to go back to their old lives, but she was too furious at his deceptions to think straight. "If I were you, Cait, I wouldn't believe a word I said right now."

Not about Trick and not about her brothers, either. After all she'd been through in Scotland, coming to love Trick and deciding her brothers had been right after all, her blaming them made no sense.

But then, her emotions rarely did.

Cait took a bite of roast beef. "Your anger certainly hasn't affected your appetite. For sweets, anyway."

"Nothing ever does." Kendra licked strawberry juice off her lips, looking at Trick's amber bracelet where it lay on the table's marble surface. Her wrist felt empty without it.

Her heart felt empty without him.

She turned to Cait. "Have you ever been this angry at Jason?"

"Don't ask. There have been times, especially when we first met, when I'd have been happy to see the back of him forever. But we always worked it out."

"But you never suspected he was unfaithful."

"Nay, never that. I know him well enough to feel certain that hasn't happened."

"I thought I was coming to know Trick, too."

No wonder Eros, the God of Love, was often portrayed wearing a blindfold. Love was truly blind.

"There could be another explanation, Kendra. Although I remember a time you wouldn't have cared if he cheated." Cait sipped from her cup of wine, regarding her over the rim. "Things have improved for you, then?"

"Things?"

"You know…in the bedchamber." Kendra felt her face heat, and Caithren laughed. "I can see that they have."

She couldn't stand to think about that now, let alone talk about it—not when she wondered if she'd ever feel that close to Trick again. "How was your visit home?" she asked Cait instead. "Is Cameron doing well? And Clarice and little Mary?"

Cait grinned. "Clarice is with child, too. And Cameron walks around all day with a smile on his face."

"I can imagine." Would she ever have children now? It was clear enough Trick would never be the sort of devoted husband she'd dreamed of all her life, but could she learn to live with less? Could she accept only that part of him he was capable of giving? "I'm so happy for them—"

A knock on the door interrupted, and Cait went to answer.

"Are you finished, my lady?" Soft-spoken, her maid entered and began gathering dishes. She refilled their cups with the dregs of a bottle of wine, then flashed a sunny smile full of small, even teeth. "Would you like another bottle now, milady? I can ask John to fetch one from the cellars." John Foster was one of Cainewood's footmen and Dulcie's latest *amour*.

"Thank you, that would be nice." Cait set a decimated tart on the tray. "How is Foster today, Dulcie?"

"Oh, fine, milady. He's had a half-day off and been into the village to visit with his mother. Would you know, he came back with interesting news."

Kendra drained her cup. She hoped this Foster fellow would fetch a new bottle soon. She needed more wine if she was going to decide whether to give up on the love of her life. "What news is that?"

"Word has it that the Black Highwayman has been caught and arrested at last. Hauled off to London this very day to be tried."

"Tried?" Kendra's cup clunked to the marble-topped dressing table. "When will he be tried?"

Dulcie's gray eyes filled with confusion. "Monday, your grace. Say…are you all right?"

SEVENTY-FOUR

KENDRA WOKE IN her old bed at Cainewood with two of her brothers hanging over her. She blinked at the mint-green canopy above their heads, wondering how she'd come to be here.

Had she fainted? She'd never fainted before in her life. Trick would pay for this.

Then she remembered, and an aching hollowness opened in her heart.

Trick wouldn't pay for this. Trick would be dead.

She struggled to sit, glancing around to make sure no one but family was in the chamber. "Did you hear?" she asked, her vow of silence forgotten.

Her brothers, after all, were not the villains in this tragedy, no matter how much she wanted to blame them. She needed them, and they were here for her, as they'd always been.

"Aye, they've heard," Cait said softly. "I told them."

Kendra's stomach felt leaden, and tears threatened to leak from her eyes. "How can this have happened now?" One tear did leak, running hot down her cheek. "He promised he was finished playing that game."

Though Jason's eyes were compassionate, his mouth was set in a grim line. "I warned him."

"He must have gone out and done it anyway. Stubborn fool." And more fool she, for believing him when he said he'd stop. She sat and swung her feet off the bed. "I must go to him."

Ford put a hand on her arm. "I thought you wanted to be rid of him?"

"I thought so, too," she said, her voice rising in a wail. Her earlier anger seemed to have vanished, replaced with a fear that clawed at her insides. "But I never wanted to see him dead!"

Jason sat beside her and wrapped an arm around her shoulders, patting her back as she sobbed against his shirtfront, wetting his shoulder. "Perhaps he'll be acquitted."

Accused outlaws were rarely acquitted, but she clung to that thin thread of hope. "I must go watch the trial. Take me to the trial."

"Think, Kendra." Ford crouched by the bed, looking up at her, his bright blue eyes filled with the calm reason that seemed to evade her but came so easily to him. "Why would the Chases attend the trial of a common criminal? What will you tell those who ask? Especially if you look…distraught."

Od's fish, he was right. As far as they'd heard, no one had connected the Duke of Amberley with the Black Highwayman, but if anyone discovered she'd been married to the notorious outlaw, her reputation would be in tatters—along with those of the rest of her family.

But this was Trick. No matter how badly he'd treated her, no matter what offenses he'd committed behind her back, she would go to him. Her heart left her no choice.

"I'll wear a disguise," she said. "But I'm going."

SEVENTY-FIVE

NEVER IN HER life had Kendra thought she'd find herself outside the Justice Hall at the Old Bailey. After nearly two days spent in a sleepless fog of wrenching misery, endless tears, anger, and self-doubt, she'd thought that actually getting here and seeing this trial through would be something of a relief.

But she knew now that nothing could be further from the truth.

The courtyard viewing gallery was mobbed with Londoners hoping to get a glimpse of the notorious accused, and even more people stood outside the spike-topped iron fence. Wearing Dulcie's gray skirt and plain blouse, with her telltale red hair stuffed under a mobcap, Kendra grasped Ford's hand and pulled him through the masses toward the front.

A light rain was falling, making the spectators—no polite crowd to begin with—even more surly. "Whyever do they make us stand outside?" she grumbled, dodging a sharp elbow as she made her way to the three-walled open courtroom.

Ford pushed back the straw hat he'd borrowed from a stable-man. "It reduces the risk of prisoners infecting the spectators with gaol fever," he explained in his usual matter-of-fact manner.

She returned a tradesman's dirty glare with one of her own, tugging her sleeve down to cover her amber bracelet as she pushed her way to the rail. "Dear heavens," she breathed, her heart clenching when she reached the front. She gripped the rail with both hands to keep her knees from buckling. "There he is."

Gazing at Trick, she slowly jockeyed herself over to the right, nearer to where he sat in the enclosed dock, chained to eleven other men.

He was wearing black velvet and the long brown periwig that she hoped would keep any spectators from recognizing him as the Duke of Amberley. But the wig was a tangled mess, the usually immaculate black suit all rumpled, and he looked more exhausted than she'd ever seen him. His head was bowed, and his hands hung limply between his spread knees.

A guard reached a pike through the bars to prod him to stand when the red-robed judge walked in, followed by jury members who shuffled to two long benches. The dock's door swung open with an ominous creak, and the prisoners began making their way to the bar, their chains clanking as they dragged on one another.

Watching Trick, Kendra felt as though her heart might burst. Literally pulled along by the others, he stumbled and had to be righted. Dark blood crusted his wrists beneath the iron cuffs. A sheen of sweat slicked his features, and he seemed to be having trouble simply drawing breath.

He was ill.

She pressed against the rail as though she could reach him. So close, maybe ten feet away, but oh, so far with the law between them.

So very, very far. And ill.

"Dear heavens," she whispered again, suddenly shivering though she wasn't particularly cold. "Can he have caught the gaol fever already?"

"Hush." Ford's hands gripped her shoulders, and she felt incredibly grateful for his familiar presence at her back. "It's starting."

The prisoner's names were called one by one, and they identified themselves by raising a hand. The charges were read in Latin before each of the accused pleaded either guilty or not guilty.

"But they cannot even understand the charges!" Kendra whispered in horrified protest.

With unbelievable swiftness, witnesses were brought forward and evidence was presented by the prosecution. Prisoners were not allowed counsel. Of the eleven men brought to trial before Trick, one was acquitted when no witnesses appeared. The other ten were all sentenced to death, for felonies ranging from stealing an orange, to setting fire to an outhouse, to murdering a neighbor.

By the time Trick's turn arrived, Kendra had lost all hope. Tears swam in her eyes, and her body felt like a single, heavy mass of dread.

"The Black Highwayman," the clerk read, and the crowd hissed gleeful disapproval. They had saved the best for last.

When Trick failed to raise his hand, the prisoner next to him did it for him.

"What be your name?" the clerk demanded.

Trick stared blindly ahead. A long silence stretched.

"What be your name?"

He hung his head, looking too weak to lift it. Too weak to answer.

A speculative murmur rose from the onlookers. The guard prodded Trick with his pike, and Trick stumbled to his knees, taking the prisoners on either side down with him. With a rattle of chains, they hoisted him back up.

"Black Highwayman, what be your name?"

Inside her, Kendra was screaming. He was too ill to defend himself; couldn't they see it? Couldn't they wait for another day?

"Black Highwayman, *what* be your name?"

"Can you not see he's ill?" she called out. A gasp of disapproval rose from the crowd, and the clerk glared in her direction.

Trick's gaze snapped to meet hers.

Recognition lit his eyes. But from where Kendra stood, they looked black, not golden. Dilated and dark, filled with regret and defeat.

She'd lost her amber highwayman already.

The clerk tried another tack. "Black Highwayman, what do you plead?"

Trick's gaze was still locked on hers. One hand reached into his pocket, and he slowly drew out a piece of paper, crumpling it in his fist. Something was written upon it in black ink, but much too far away to see.

"The press!" The crowd began to chant. "The press! The press!"

"What is that?" Kendra asked, afraid she didn't want to know.

"They call it *peine forte et dure*," Ford whispered. "Prisoners who refuse to plead are stripped and laid on their backs, a wooden plank placed upon them and piled with stones."

"Stones?" It was even worse than she'd imagined. Salty blood flowed into her mouth, and she realized she was chewing the inside of her cheek.

"Yes, stones." Ford's fingers tightened on her shoulders. "Three hundred pounds or more. And they add another fifty pounds every half-hour until the man agrees to plead."

"The press! The press! The press!"

They couldn't. They couldn't do that to an ill prisoner. How could this mob demand such a thing? What kind of barbarous riffraff were they?

"The press! The press! The press!"

"Silence!" The clerk's bellow rattled the very air, and the chant abruptly cut off.

Soft rain pattered in the sudden stillness as he looked to the man in red robes.

"Guilty," the judge declared, doubtless thinking his decision merciful since the prisoner was too weak to plead.

Ford squeezed Kendra's shoulders so tightly, it was a wonder her bones didn't snap. He succeeded in quelling her outcry. But inside, every fiber of her being was howling.

Though Trick had been spared the press, she had no doubt what the sentence would be for a highwayman when she'd just seen a man sent to the gallows for stealing a piece of fruit.

"Death by hanging." The judge banged his gavel. "Tomorrow at noon."

Trick's gaze remained on hers, his eyes imploring. His mouth moved, but no words came out. Her fingers worried the amber bracelet, and she could see on his face that he noticed. A single tear welled and rolled down his cheek, making her own tears flow faster.

Suddenly he looked away and began scraping with a finger-nail at one of the crusty scabs on his wrist.

Another queue of accused prisoners were brought clanking into the dock, and Trick's group began moving out. She watched in a haze of pain as he drew a red-tipped finger across the crumpled paper in his other hand.

"He's writing something," she whispered in horror to Ford. "He's trying to write something. *In blood.*"

His hand with the paper shaking, he reached it toward her as he was dragged by. She pressed against the rail, straining to get closer, their fingers nearly touching. She moaned when he was jerked back, the look in his eyes anguished but unreadable.

Seconds later, he was tugged through an archway and out of sight.

"He's ill." She sobbed, tears running freely down her face to mix with the miserable cold rain. "He was trying to tell me something, wasn't he?"

"He was too weak." Ford tried to enfold her in his arms, but she clung to the rail for all she was worth, her gaze trained on the archway. "Kendra, there's nothing you can do."

"He tried to give me a message in *blood*." Her eyes burned and her heart was cracking. Trick had only preyed on Round-heads—the real criminals in her eyes—and for the good of orphan children. No matter that he was a liar and an adulterer, he didn't deserve to die.

And she couldn't bear it.

She leaned far over the rail and shouted to the guard who was closing the gate. "Where are they being taken?"

"Newgate Prison," the man said as the iron bars banged shut.

SEVENTY-SIX

"KENDRA, YOU cannot go to Newgate." At the Chase town house in Lincoln's Inn Fields, Jason pushed her onto the drawing room's burgundy brocade couch and handed her a large goblet of Rhenish wine. "It's a nightmare. And you cannot help him anyway."

"I must see him." Perhaps she could smuggle him out. At least she could say good-bye. "I'm going." She set down the wine and rose.

He took her by the shoulders, his bright green gaze determined. "You cannot go."

Equally determined, she wrenched from his grasp. "You cannot stop me."

"We'll go to King Charles," Ford said.

She whirled to him. "What?"

"We'll go to Charles and ask for a pardon."

Hope fluttered in her chest. "Could...could that work?"

He shrugged. "It's certainly within his power. I saw him pardon Swift Nicks."

"Who?" Massaging her brow, she dropped back onto the couch.

"The infamous highwayman, Jack Nevison." Ford began

pacing. "Early one morn he robbed a fellow in Kent who recognized him and threatened to turn him in. To give himself an alibi, he rode for York, arriving the same evening—"

"Impossible," she burst out, never mind that she didn't care to hear this since it had nothing to do with Trick. The ride to York took at least four days, more likely a week.

"Apparently not impossible when his life was at risk. He had friends at the taverns all along the Great North Road who supplied him with a fresh horse every hour. When he arrived in the town that evening, he hurried to the bowling green, in time to play a game of bowls with the mayor and other city functionaries. When he was brought to trial later, no less than six dignitaries could honestly swear he'd been in York that day, not Kent."

"Then Charles had no need to pardon him."

"But he had past crimes. The tale made the London rounds, and when Charles heard it, he commanded Nevison to court to tell the story himself. The king laughed until tears came to his eyes and then dismissed him with a signed and sealed pardon for all his prior misdeeds. I'll never forget it. So you can see that Charles might be prevailed upon under the right circumstances."

"Perhaps he can be swayed by a bit of humor," Kendra said, "but how could that help Trick? There's nothing funny about his situation."

"True," Jason admitted. "But when Charles hears only Roundheads were robbed, it may soften his heart."

"Possible," Ford said. "And let's not forget that he knows and likes Trick as the Duke of Amberley."

"And Trick just brought him all that treasure." Kendra grasped at a wisp of hope. "But are you really willing to bring all of this up? Admit that my husband and the Black Highwayman are one and the same?"

"We'll do whatever it takes," Jason said. "Considering the alternative, I hardly think Trick will care if the Caldwell name is tarnished."

"And *our* name?" Trick's life took precedence for her—but he was her husband, not theirs.

Yet their expressions told her, unquestionably, they felt the same. Which chased away whatever resentment was left in her heart.

"Thank you," she said softly, knowing they were right. Not only about this, but about how she always jumped to conclusions without giving them the benefit of the doubt. "I know you married me to Trick with the best of intentions, and I shouldn't have blamed you for his lies." She drew a calming breath. "I'm sorry I got angry. It won't happen again, I promise."

Jason released a choked laugh. "Of course it will happen again. We're family."

Ford's blue eyes twinkled. "Besides, those times when you storm off not speaking to us are the only peace and quiet we get around here."

"We're your brothers," Jason said, "and we'll always be here for you to lean on."

"And abuse," Ford chimed in. "That's part of our being family, too."

Once she'd told Trick something similar. Her eyes flooded at the memory. "But I'm going to try to do better anyway. I love you both."

"We never doubted it," Jason told her. "Shall we go ask for that pardon?"

"It cannot hurt to ask," she said with a sigh.

No matter that the Chases and Trick were all intimates of Charles, she had little confidence they'd get him to pardon another infamous highwayman. One prank on that order made for a rollicking good story—Charles might feel that twice would make him look like a man with no care for his subjects' welfare. Appearances counted in politics.

Besides, the king might not even be at Whitehall for all they knew.

But they had to try. She began to rise. "Let's go ask now. I have my doubts this will work, but the sooner we find out, the better. Trick is ill."

"You're staying here." The gentle, forgiving smile on Jason's face disappeared as he pushed her down to the couch and shoved the wine back into her hands. "Ladies are rarely granted audiences, as you're surely aware, unless they take place in the Royal Bedchamber. Just sit tight, and we'll be back before you know it."

SEVENTY-SEVEN

*W*HEN HER BROTHERS left, Kendra was still wearing her disguise, and she was still determined to see Trick. Having heard that gaolers were fond of bribes, she pocketed some coins and slipped out into Lincoln's Inn Fields to hail a hackney cab.

On the bumpy ride to Newgate, she wondered what she could say to him. Though she was still furious at his lies and infidelity, this was not the time for hurling accusations.

Then the cab jolted and she heard his voice.

I'm sorry, leannan, but there are things I cannot tell you. You'll have to trust me. Once you promised you'd trust me...

A surge of panic overwhelmed her.

Could it be she'd misjudged her husband as badly as she had her brothers? Had she jumped to conclusions there, too?

Her heart raced as all the memories rushed back. The way he'd been slowly revealing himself; the hushed, earnest words; her conviction that he always wanted to do right.

Do you know how much I care for you? Enough to make me question my loyalties.

What had he meant by those words? What if he really did

have a explanation for all that had gone on? He'd been trying to tell her something at the trial and been cheated of his chance.

My love, T.

Heavens, she loved him, too.

She could have been wrong. As she'd been many times before, she could have been so, so wrong.

And now it might be too late.

Her brothers had to get that pardon. They just had to. And if they failed…

She would go to the king herself. The hanging wasn't scheduled until noon tomorrow, so she had all night. She didn't care if she had to go into the Royal Bedchamber. She would do whatever it took to save her husband from the noose.

But that was for later, after Jason and Ford returned. For now, she just wanted to get into that gaol. She just wanted to see Trick and wrap him in her arms and tell him she was sorry, so sorry…

When the cab rattled to a halt, she unclenched her fists and hurried to climb out.

Newgate Prison had burned in the Great Fire two years earlier and was only partially rebuilt. The new entrance was magnificently decorated. Four figures represented Liberty, Peace, Security, and Plenty, but behind the impressive facade, the gaol itself remained as miserable as Kendra had always heard.

After she paid a man at the gate, it creaked open to admit her to what seemed a dark pit of squalor. Her footsteps echoed in a stone corridor still blackened from the fire. Noxious odors of slops, rotten food, and unwashed bodies made her gag before she stepped into the relatively luxurious keeper's house.

"Walter Cowday," a hard, graying man introduced himself. "Who you here to see?"

"The Black Highwayman."

He raised a grizzled brow and held out a hand. Her heart pounding, she put a silver coin in it, and then another and another. When he remained silent, she added the one she had of gold. She clenched her hand around her few remaining coins; she'd never imagined it would cost this much.

"He went straight to the condemned hold. Lucky knave don't have to wait. Tyburn Fair day tomorrow."

When she failed to show the proper excitement for the public holiday that an execution meant, he pocketed the money and motioned for her to follow him back to the corridor.

He lifted a hatch door and pointed down. "There you go. If you've more silver, a guard will point the way."

Holding her cumbersome skirts in one hand, she descended a ladder and dropped to a damp stone floor.

Bleak gray cells lined both sides of another corridor, moisture trickling down their walls. Each looked about eight feet by six, furnished with a wooden bench and a Bible. The iron candlesticks, one per hold bolted to the stone, apparently were saved for night. The only light came filtered though a tiny window high in each cell, covered by heavy iron bars.

She swallowed hard and began searching down the corridor. It was cold and dark, and she stumbled more than once. Men hooted at her, and chains clanked as they stuck their arms through the bars and grabbed at her in the blackness. For what seemed the hundredth time today, tears pricked her eyes.

Trick was nowhere to be found.

"Who goes there?"

She couldn't remember ever being as relieved when a uniformed guard appeared in the corridor holding a burning torch. Blessed light.

"I'm looking for the Black Highwayman."

Wordlessly, he held out a hand, and she gladly filled it with the last of her silver. Yet he made no move to show her the way.

Through heartache and fear, indignation rose. "Well, where is he?" she demanded.

"Doctor took him."

Once again, hope fluttered in her breast. Maybe they'd noticed he was ill and brought him to an infirmary. Perhaps they'd let him recover and retry his case. It was possible the pardon would be unnecessary, after all.

"He's not here?" she asked.

The man shook his head.

It was like pulling teeth to get answers from the cur, and this after she'd paid. Impatience and worry combined to make her jaw tighten and her voice sound shrill. "Where did the doctor take him to, then?"

"The graveyard, mistress."

SEVENTY-EIGHT

"THE GRAVEYARD?" A wave of dread swamped her. Her breath abruptly ceased, and her chest felt as though it might burst. She couldn't have heard the guard right. "The graveyard? Are you sure? What happened?"

The uniformed man shrugged.

"Tell me what happened! I paid you, you blackguard!"

She rarely used such language, but it could be effective. He blinked and took a small step back. "He was ill when he came in, you see. A doctor went in to examine him, came out and said he was dead. Of the plague."

"The plague?" She knew it could kill swiftly, but she'd seen Trick only hours ago. Ill, but very much alive.

And he'd wanted to tell her something.

"Are you sure?"

"Well, I will own up I didn't go in there. One don't mess with the plague, mistress."

"Did you see him at all?"

"Aye, through the bars from a safe distance. He was dead, all right. Blue spots all over him, and he was stiff as a long-trapped rat. Within the hour he was put in a coffin and carried out. I imagine he was buried just as quick."

She sank to the sticky stones, not caring that she sat in filth shared with bugs and rats. Her lids slid closed against the tears that welled, poised to fall.

Trick was dead. Dead and buried. Along with his lies and his deceptions, his soft words and cherishing kisses.

And she was dead inside.

It was over, and she had no emotion left in her.

"Mistress?" The guard shook her shoulder. "Mistress, you cannot just sit here."

She opened her eyes and took a deep breath. No, she could not just sit here. The man reached down a hand, and she let him help her up.

Her brothers. She needed to get to her brothers. Hopefully they hadn't made fools of themselves already by asking the king for a highwayman's pardon.

And she needed to lean on them, too. To let them take her home. They would order up a bath, and she'd wash off the incredible stink of Newgate. Then she'd sleep and escape this horror her life had turned into.

She had no money left for a hackney, but when she tearfully asked a driver to take her to Whitehall Palace and promised to see he got paid, he agreed.

SEVENTY-NINE

THE GATEKEEPER at Whitehall was not about to let a servant girl in.

"I'm Kendra Chase, the Marquess of Cainewood's sister."

"Sure you are." Dressed in red livery, the man looked her over with patent disbelief. "And I'm King Charles himself."

"I mean..." Drawing a shuddering breath, she closed her eyes, opened them, and tried again. "I'm the Duchess of Amberley."

"Kendra!"

The voice, heavy and seductive, came from an open window overhead. She'd forgotten Lady Castlemaine's suite was over Holbein's Gate. Although both of them had spent the Commonwealth years with King Charles's exiled court, Barbara, the king's longtime mistress, had never been her favorite woman. But this wasn't the time to be choosy.

"Barbara!" she called up. "My brothers are here, and this gentleman refuses to let me in."

"Dolt," Barbara said. Her titian head disappeared from the window, and a minute later she was standing on the other side of the scrolled wrought iron gate.

Kendra felt like a guttersnipe beside Barbara's lush, fashionable form, but she couldn't dredge up enough energy to feel properly chagrined. She was so tired.

"Let her in, you clodpoll," Barbara said. She'd never been known for her tact. The gate swung open. "I know just where your brothers are." Before Kendra knew it, she was following Barbara down the maze of halls that traversed Whitehall's two thousand rooms. "And your husband along with them."

"What?" Kendra stopped in her tracks, her heart leaping with relief—until she realized Barbara had to be mistaken.

"You're married to Amberley, aren't you?" Barbara pouted as she took Kendra's arm and hurried her along. "And I wasn't invited to the wedding. You know how I like a good party."

"We didn't have much of a wedding," Kendra said woodenly. Trick wasn't here—he was dead in the ground in a graveyard near Newgate.

Coming to a stop, Barbara threw open a magnificent carved and gilded door. Beyond, Kendra saw a splendid sitting room in shades of gold and black. A fire blazed on a marble hearth. King Charles sat in a tufted velvet chair, his head thrown back in laughter. Jason sat in another, laughing along with him.

And reclining on a black satin daybed, a smile curving his lips and a cheroot in one hand, sat Patrick Iain Caldwell.

The scoundrel wasn't dead.

If she'd had a pistol at her disposal, she'd have rectified that.

SHE BOLTED past Barbara, retracing her steps through the palace and outside. The hackney was still waiting, and when a hysterical girl begged the driver to take her to a town house, he wasn't about to disagree.

She hadn't known it was possible to feel such deep hurt. No matter Trick's reasons, that he could let her go through all that, allow her to think he was *dead*…

It was the most unforgivable betrayal she could imagine.

He would never, ever measure up to even the lowest of her expectations. She couldn't live with such a man—couldn't live with herself if she accepted such a marriage. Such a lack of basic caring and decency.

Cold anger. It was the safest emotion to feel, the one—the only one—that would protect her from being ripped apart.

She was going to her house, not Trick's. Caldwell House had never felt like hers, and it never would, any more than Amberley or Duncraven had. When the hackney pulled up in front of the house in Lincoln's Inn Fields, she couldn't wait to get inside.

As always, Goodwin opened the door. "A bath, please, Goodwin. And pay the hackney driver, if you will."

Leaving him openmouthed, she barged past, heading for the wide, curving staircase and the comfort of her feminine chamber upstairs. A chamber no man had ever slept in.

Ford was waiting in the entry, seated on one of two matching brocade chairs. He leapt to seize her arm. "Kendra."

Not wanting to, she stopped and turned to him.

His blue gaze swept her costumed form. "When we arrived at Whitehall and learned from King Charles what had happened, Jason sent me back immediately to let you know your husband was well and would soon be free. But you weren't here."

His voice betokened more concern than vexation, but she didn't have it in her to express sorrow for causing him worry. Not now. She had no space left for any more emotions now.

"I sent six servants out looking—"

Pulling her arm free and turning away from his accusatory eyes, she climbed the graceful stairs, one foot in front of the other, just as she always had.

Her chamber was the same as always, too. A mint-green oasis of familiarity. Nothing in her life had been familiar lately—not her feelings and not her surroundings. Here, in her old room, she could flip back the calendar to last June, when she'd been an innocent girl living her placid, boring life.

Here, in her old room, she could call for a bath and wash away not only the foulness of Newgate, but all her confusing emotions. The first blush of love and the subsequent hurt. The incredible joy of fulfillment, the disappointment and disillusion. All of it—the ups and the downs, and the downs and the ups, and the final descent into that pit of despair.

She'd never appreciated how wonderful her old, predictable life had been.

When the bath was prepared, she peeled off Dulcie's clothes and sank into the steaming water right up to her chin, ready to recover that lovely, boring life. Who needed a husband? Especially one who felt so little for her that he would lie to escape her and then let her think he was dead and laugh it off like the world's best joke.

She knew when it was time to give up.

With shaking fingers, she unfastened the clasp on the amber bracelet and let it fall to the carpeted floor. Then she tugged off the plain gold band. When she dropped it, it rolled a few inches from the carpet onto polished wood before landing flat with a tiny *plop*. Until now, since that fateful day in Cainewood's little chapel, it had never left her hand.

She hardly noticed her tears dripping into the lavender-scented water. Just as she hardly noticed the knock at the door until it opened.

"Kendra."

The expression on Trick's face was achingly apologetic, but she'd been through that before. He wouldn't fool her ever again.

Sinking deeper into the water, she dashed the tears from her cheeks and narrowed her eyes. "Who let you in here?"

Still dressed in rumpled black velvet and looking more than a little unsteady, he quietly shut the door behind him. His gaze flicked to the amber bracelet, then back to her. "You didn't mind the last time I walked in on your bath."

Despite all the anger and hurt, she blushed to remember. "That was before I left you," she said. "That was a lifetime ago, when I was still blind and innocent."

He walked over, and, wordlessly, handed her a crumpled piece of paper.

Tearing her gaze from him, she unfolded it with wet, shaky hands. The five words were barely legible, thick swashes of rusty red-brown.

DON'T WORRY JUST AN ACT

Leaning close, he turned the paper over in her hands, and her heart turned over along with it. He straightened while she read the words in black ink—the writing she hadn't been able to make out at the trial.

When love on my sweet wife's wings
Comes to hover within my walls
If I turn it away with untruths and deceit
'Tis myself I must blame for the fall

Trust must be earned then earned again
Ere forgiveness can overcome sorrows
Yesterday's errors wiped from the slate
May leave room for joyful tomorrows

Stone walls do not a prison make
Nor iron bars well-turned
While I bear hope, mayhap forlorn
My love will be returned

Poetry written in prison.

Reassurance written in blood.

Tears flooded her eyes, blurring her vision. Instead of her mint-green chamber, what she saw was the damp, crowded courtyard outside the open courtroom of the Old Bailey. Instead of the soft swish of water, what she heard was the jeering crowd. And she remembered Trick's stricken face as he tried to reach her, first with words and then with this very same note—and the expression in his eyes when he failed to succeed.

"Why?" she asked, finally ready to listen. "Why all the lies?"

He stayed riveted in place. "Before I ever met you," he said slowly, "I made a promise to King Charles. I thought that promise, to my sovereign, was more important than my wife. I was wrong. And if I've lost you because of that mistake, I'll never forgive myself."

Dear heavens, he was getting to her. Could she allow herself to feel this again? "What was this promise?"

"I was never really a highwayman. That was naught but a ruse to find some counterfeiters who were bedeviling the country's economy, emptying the king's purse and undermining his credibility. I was part of his scheme to uncover it."

"Just as I guessed, only I never completed the connection."

He nodded. "And I'd sworn not to tell a soul. I never considered that the Black Highwayman might become a wanted man. When that happened, Charles devised a plan to get rid of him, so I could live my life as the duke without anyone ever suspecting that the highwayman and I were one and the same. He arranged for the arrest and the public trial. And he had a doctor drug me to make me look ill, and that same doctor visit later and paint blue spots on my body, then declare me dead and carry me away. I suggested we use black nightshade."

"Dwale." The fever, the slowed breathing, the weakness, the dilated eyes. She should have realized. "It killed your mother, Trick. It could have killed you."

"Weeks of it killed Mam, and Da recovered, after all. It was one dose. A calculated risk, and at least I knew what I was getting into."

"It was a perfect plan," she admitted. "Brilliant."

"Not perfect. Because Charles still refused to let me tell you. And I was foolish enough to believe we could pull this off over a couple of days when I could give you another excuse to be gone, and you'd never find out."

"But I did."

"Aye." He took a step closer, then swayed. "I was wrong, *leannan*. I trusted you even if Charles didn't, and I should have told you everything, no matter that he ordered me not to. I was wrong to think you wouldn't figure it out, and I was wrong to lie to you about what I was doing. But most of all, I was wrong to think any promise to a king, or the king himself, was more important than you. Nothing is more important than you."

Disregarding Royal orders was considered much worse than highway robbery. *Punishable by hanging*, she heard herself whisper deep in a dungeon in Scotland. *Punishable by hanging, drawing, quartering…*

"Nothing is more important? Not even treason?"

"Nothing. I knew it—I knew it while I sat in that prison awaiting trial, wondering where you were and whether rumors had reached your ears to cause you torment. And then, when I saw you standing at that rail…"

His eyes mirrored the anguish she'd seen in them that moment.

"But by then," he continued, "it was too late. I was too weak, too drugged." He swayed again. "I still am, it seems. They told me I wasn't recovered enough to come to you yet, but, like you, I didn't listen. Like you, I *couldn't* listen, not when my love was at stake." He risked a tiny, tentative smile, that chipped tooth peeking through.

It cracked her heart.

She'd been wrong, too. He'd asked her to trust him, said there were things he couldn't tell her. But she hadn't listened. She wanted to say she understood, but her throat closed with emotion.

She looked down to the paper in her hand, the precious words blurring through fresh tears. In his own blood, he'd tried to tell her not to worry. And he'd written a poem for her, admitting his love, promising to earn her trust, asking for forgiveness.

Poetry. He'd shared that most secret side of himself with her, just as she'd always hoped. His wall had finally come down.

Or maybe she'd managed to scale it.

He came forward and took the paper from her trembling hands, setting it aside.

Then he stepped right into the water.

"Your boots!" she gasped.

In the big tub, he knelt at her feet. "I own a fleet and a warehouse stacked with imported goods from all over the world. I can buy a hundred pairs of boots."

His voice was thick and unsteady, his amber eyes so intense they seemed to spear her to her very soul.

He reached beneath the water to take her hands in his. "Don't you understand? I can buy almost anything—anything, sweet Kendra, except your love."

"You have it," she whispered.

EPILOGUE

Six years later

KENDRA RAN DOWN Amberley's marble front steps, then, waiting for Trick, paused and looked back at the house. She smiled at the incongruous stone lintel over the elegant double front doors—a long, decidedly inelegant rock with symbols chiseled into it: the letters KC and PC, a ship, a heart, and a date. 1668.

"What's that?" she'd asked Trick the day she first came home from the orphanage to see it.

He'd blinked. "Do you not remember Falkland? And the marriage lintels?"

"Well, yes. But this isn't a weaver's cottage in Scotland—it's a mansion in Sussex. And this house wasn't built in 1668."

"Maybe it wasn't," he'd told her, lacing his fingers with hers. "But that was the year it became a home."

Remembering now, the same joy filled her heart that had filled it then. She touched the stones on her amber bracelet, knowing with a certainty that she'd never take it off again.

Trick finally sauntered out, displaying none of her own impatience.

"Hurry, Trick, or Cait's babe will be born before we get there."

"Slow down, or *our* babe will be born too early." Walking her over to the caleche, he smiled and ran a possessive hand over the slight bulge of her middle. "Besides, we were there already. It was you who insisted we leave everyone and return home for the gift you forgot."

"It was *you* who insisted on the hour we just spent in our chamber." Grinning as he climbed up beside her, she leaned in for a quick kiss.

With a hand on the back of her neck, he held her close, his lips meeting hers in a much longer, warmer embrace, sending a swirl of excitement spiraling through her. The soft, paper-wrapped package in her hands slipped to the caleche's boards.

He broke off and, with a chuckle, reached to collect it and set it back on her lap. "Do you want to go back upstairs, *leannan*?"

"Oh, yes," she whispered on a sigh. "But no."

"Women." He shook his head, bright gold in the sun, and lifted the caleche's reins.

"Drive fast," she urged, and then, "Faster," until they were racing toward Cainewood at an alarming speed, considering her delicate state. "I want to be there with Cait when the babe greets the world."

But as she was hurrying up Cainewood's carved stone staircase, the thready cry of a newborn split the air. She paused with her hand on the gray marble rail.

Trick squeezed her around the shoulders. "Sorry we're late, lass, but do you not think our little interlude was worth it? We so rarely have time to ourselves these days."

"I suppose." She gave him a mock pout. "Let's go meet the child."

The door to Jason and Caithren's chamber was wide open, the room crammed with cooing Chases. Cait reclined like a queen in the cobalt-curtained bed, a squalling infant in her arms.

"For me?" she asked with a smile, indicating the gift in Kendra's hands. "Or the babe?"

"Both." Kendra handed it to her. "Though really it's from your cousin Cameron. I wrote asking him to send it. Then he wouldn't accept my money." Looking around the noisy chamber while Caithren opened the package, she spotted Jason and Colin, but not her twin. "Is Ford not here yet?"

Jason sat beside Cait. "He sent a message from Lakefield House that they'd be a bit late," he said, helping his wife unfold a green and blue tartan blanket. "Seems to think he's on the verge of some discovery."

"Turning iron into gold? He always did want to be Midas." Kendra laughed, moving closer as a grinning Cait wrapped her child in the Leslie plaid.

Like magic, the babe quieted.

Swathed in its maternal homeland's colors, the baby looked so precious and content. Feeling her heart melt with tenderness, Kendra ran a fingertip along its downy cheek. "Everything went well?" she asked Cait while smiling down at the newborn. "You're both healthy?"

"Aye. Everything went perfectly."

The baby grasped her finger with tiny fingers of its own. Such a miracle. Beneath the new blanket, it was swaddled in plain white. Kendra looked up. "Well, what is it?"

Cait gave a happy sigh. "A lad."

"*Another* boy?"

That made three. The Chase family had multiplied in the six years since Kendra and Trick were wed.

Cait's two older sons were bouncing on the canopied bed. Thankfully the infant didn't seem to mind the wild ride.

The rest of the chamber was no more calm. Amy and Colin's two boys were racing around the room, chasing Kendra and Trick's two giggling daughters and gleefully careening off the tapestried walls. The oldest of the cousins at seven, Jewel was a bit more sedate. Of course that was because she was busy at the moment, serenading the new arrival with a lullaby—at the top of her lungs.

One of Kendra's young daughters rammed into her knees, the result of a hopeless attempt to escape her pursuing cousins. As she lifted the girl into her arms, Trick moved close. "Chaos, as always," he whispered.

"Yes," she said, turning to him. "But a happy chaos, don't you think?"

He grinned and took her lips in a soft kiss, right there in front of her brothers and everyone, like their first kiss in Cainewood's chapel so many years before.

And this kiss left her every bit as breathless.

A glorious thing, true love was, she thought as she pulled back with a smile, their daughter wriggling between them. Once, long ago, she'd promised Trick he'd find true love, and she'd followed through, hadn't she?

A Chase promise was never given lightly.

~

DEAR READER,

King Charles I's baggage ferry really did go down in the Firth of Forth that fateful summer of 1633, although—so far as I know!—nobody had substituted rocks for the treasure. Interestingly, the sinking wasn't common knowledge until the early 1990s. Apparently embarrassed by the loss, Charles did his best to keep it quiet, and it was centuries before a historian noticed a footnote and began to look into it. Since then, three accounts have been found that make mention of the sinking. But although all the writers were contemporary to the incident, none of them were actually present, and therefore little is known about what actually lies at the bottom of the Firth of Forth.

We know that one of two wooden ferries went down, carrying a portion of the king's household property, but which possessions were aboard remains to be seen. It is assumed to be mostly kitchen goods—a Royal "kitchen" consisting mainly of solid silver and gold serving pieces—but this is only a guess based on accountings of replacement items that were ordered in the months afterward.

The search for the shipwreck began soon after the discovery of its existence, but progress has been slow, because conditions in the Forth—frigid choppy water, strong tides, poor visibility—severely limit diving opportunities. Early on, an American team searched for several summers, but their efforts proved unsuccessful. Following two years of inactivity, the project resumed, this time under a nonprofit group formed for the purpose, Burntisland Heritage Trust. The search is being carried out in acceptance with strict archaeological guidelines, and Historic Scotland is responsible for assuring that those standards are met and maintained. The world waits with bated breath to see what will rise from the Firth of Forth...here's hoping they don't find chests filled with rocks!

As for the highwayman Jack Nevison (nicknamed Swift Nicks by King Charles II himself), the story Ford told of his ride from London to York was true, as well as the tale of his court visit and pardon from Charles. But alas, not one to learn from his mistakes, the notorious robber continued his life of crime. His escapes from prison were legendary, including the stunt I borrowed where a doctor friend painted him with blue spots and declared him dead. In 1685, he was caught for the last time in York. Brought to a hasty trial before he could devise an escape, he pleaded the king's most gracious pardon, which he claimed covered subsequent as well as prior misdeeds. Not surprisingly, the court dismissed his defense, and at the ripe old age of forty-six, Swift Nicks found himself hanged.

The homes in my stories are usually inspired by real-life places, and this book is no exception. Although I put it in a different geographic location, Amberley House and its beautiful gardens were loosely modeled on Hatfield House in Hertfordshire, England. The original palace, built in 1497 by the Bishop of Ely, was the childhood and young-adult home of the first Queen Elizabeth. Two portraits of her can be viewed in the home today, along with some of her clothing and letters.

Elizabeth's successor, James I, didn't care for Hatfield as a home, preferring Theobalds, the residence of Robert Cecil, first Earl of Salisbury. He proposed an exchange, and the Cecils agreed. In 1608, the earl tore down most of the palace and began building the present house in what was then a modern style, at a cost of over £38,000, a staggering amount of money in those times. Though first designed by Robert Lyminge, the plans were modified by others, including, it is thought, young Inigo Jones. This is the house that you can visit today, and the one Kendra saw when she first rode up that long drive.

From the seventeenth century until present day, Hatfield House has served as both a social and political center, hosting luminaries from royalty on down. Well worth a visit, the magnificent house is open for tours from March through October, and most of the gardens are open year-round.

Duncraven Castle was invented when I stayed at Borthwick Castle, twin towers located just south of Edinburgh in Scotland (although, once again, I took the liberty of moving it). Built in 1430 by the first Lord Borthwick, whose sepulchre can still be seen with that of his Lady in the old village church, its virtually impregnable stone walls sheltered Mary Queen of Scots in her last days of freedom. When a force of some thousand men surrounded the castle, her husband, Bothwell, escaped, leaving Mary behind under the protection of the Borthwicks. Disguised as a page boy, Mary then climbed through a window in the great hall, lowered herself by rope to the ground below, and set off through the gate and across the glen in search of her husband. The stuff of romance novels, isn't it? But sadly, their reunion was a short one, and the tragic queen never again knew true freedom.

Nearly a century later, Borthwick Castle was besieged by the forces of Oliver Cromwell, whose letter demanding surrender— the same one read by Trick in my story—hangs framed in today's great hall. Weathered and nobly scarred, Borthwick still stands hundreds of years later. Sir Walter Scott described Borthwick as by far the finest example of the Scottish castles which consist of a single "donjon," or keep. So it was, and so it still is, now run as a bed and breakfast. Do treat yourself with a stay there if ever you get a chance. After a delicious gourmet dinner, you may sit before the immense fireplace, sipping spirits while the caretakers regale you with stories of ghosts and legends. And when you climb the winding staircase to your chamber, don't be surprised if you find yourself looking over your shoulder...

I hope you enjoyed *The Duke's Reluctant Bride*! Next up is Ford's story in *The Viscount's Wallflower Bride*. Please read on for an excerpt!

Always,

Lauren Royal

Read on for an excerpt from

The Viscount's Wallflower Bride

Book 5 of the
Sweet Chase Brides series
by Lauren & Devon Royal

Lady Violet Ashcroft isn't planning to marry—she'd rather spend her time reading books than finding love. That is, until a handsome viscount named Ford Chase moves into the neighborhood...

~

England, 1673

"GOOD AFTERNOON, my lord."

A warm, melodic voice. Ford Chase turned and frowned at the owner, who stood at the edge of his embarrassingly overgrown garden. Although he had a feeling the pleasant-looking matron wasn't quite a stranger, he couldn't for the life of him place her.

She plucked two stray twigs off her bright yellow skirts, then raised a groomed brow. "So nice to have you in residence, Lord Lakefield. Trentingham Manor can seem lonely when all our neighbors are away in the City."

Mystery solved. Trentingham. As in *Earl of.* The neighboring estate.

Still holding his five-year-old niece, Ford executed an awkward bow. "Pleased to be here, Lady Trentingham."

When her wide mouth curved up, her brown eyes smiled to match. Plainly curious, her gaze flicked to little Jewel before focusing again on him. "Will you be staying long?"

"Just while I finish a project." And until he felt up to showing his face in London. He pushed his way back through the hedge and set Jewel on her feet, grimacing as he brushed leaves from his breeches.

The countess shot a glance down the side of the house—he noticed the paint was peeling—to where her carriage waited, a coachman sitting up top. The door was open, and someone waited inside as well, enjoying the sunny day. A lady's maid, if he could judge by the woman's starched white cap.

"Pretty lady," Jewel said, staring up at his neighbor.

"Why, thank you, Miss..."

"Jewel," the girl supplied.

"Lady Jewel," Ford clarified. "My brother's daughter. I'm looking after her while her family recovers from measles."

"Ah," Lady Trentingham murmured. Some of the confusion cleared from her face. "I'm glad of your acquaintance," she said with a graceful curtsy, for all the world like they were meeting in Whitehall Palace.

Jewel mimicked the motion. "I'm glad of your ac-ac—"

"Acquaintance," Ford said helpfully.

But apparently Jewel didn't take it that way. She fixed him with a malevolent green glare. "I can say it."

"Of course you can." Palms forward, he took a small step back. "Forgive me."

"All right." She turned to the woman, focusing on something in her hand. "What's that?"

"Don't point, baby," Ford said. Though his twin sister forever accused him of being oblivious, he did know his manners.

Lady Trentingham knelt by Jewel's side. "It's a bottle of perfume. I brought it for the lady of the house. And I suppose"—she looked to Ford for confirmation—"that's you?"

He nodded his agreement as Jewel squealed. "For me?"

"For you, sweetheart. Would you like to smell it?"

"Oh, yes," his niece breathed. She waited, dancing from foot to foot while the woman removed the stopper and handed her the bottle.

Jewel waved it under her nose. "It's lovely, my lady!" Tipping the bottle, she wet her fingers and dabbed the potion on her neck, wetting some of the overgrown greenery in the process.

"You must use only a little," Lady Trentingham warned her, "or you'll smell like a field of flowers."

"I like flowers."

"Then you must come and visit Trentingham Manor." She rose to her feet, smiling at Ford. "My husband enjoys gardening."

"I've heard that of the earl." Everyone had heard that of the earl. And standing in his own shambles of a garden, knowing what Lady Trentingham and her husband must think every time they saw it, made Ford want to squirm.

"Who is caring for Lady Jewel?" the countess asked.

"I am, now. Her nursemaid fell ill, so I sent her home."

"Alone?"

"No, with my coachman and two outriders."

Amusement flickered on her face. "I meant, are you caring for Lady Jewel on your own?"

"Oh." Feeling thickheaded, he cleared his throat. "I suppose I am."

"And how are you getting along?"

His neighbor had a straightforward way about her that Ford found refreshing.

"Well, I've had Jewel for…" He twisted around to peer at the sundial. "…it's going on eighteen hours. And no disaster has befallen her yet, so although I haven't managed to find time for anything else, I reckon I'm doing all right."

Lady Trentingham's laughter tinkled through the tangled vegetation. Her gaze turned contemplative. "I have a son."

"Do you?" he prompted, feeling more thickheaded still.

"Rowan. He's six years of age, and his favorite playmate is away from home for the month—perhaps I'll bring him over to play. That might give you a bit of a respite."

"A *boy*?" Jewel interjected.

"A kind one," the woman assured her. "He doesn't have maggots."

Jewel looked dubious. But she also looked lonely. And as far as Ford was concerned, Lady Trentingham could be his savior.

An angel sent from heaven. A fairy come to wave her wand and sprinkle magic dust.

"I shall bring Rowan tomorrow," she decided. "He has lessons in the morning, but perhaps after dinner."

"He's welcome for dinner," Ford offered. Breakfast and supper, too. Anything to keep his niece occupied so he could work. He was so close to finishing his design…

He must have looked as desperate as he felt, because his neighbor released a tiny, unladylike snort.

"After dinner," she confirmed, hiding a smile as she turned to make her way back to her carriage.

"HOW DID IT GO, milady?" Anne asked Chrystabel as the coach set off for Trentingham.

"Fine," she assured her maid.

Perfect, she added silently.

Now she just had to make plans to keep both her younger daughters busy tomorrow. As well as herself. Violet—her wonderful, willful, bookish daughter Violet—would be the one to take Rowan to visit Lady Jewel.

Picking dead vegetation off her skirts, Chrystabel smiled. She'd met young Ford Chase before, but this visit had confirmed it. If ever a perfect husband existed for Violet, it was the charming, slightly preoccupied but ambitious Lord Lakefield. These two needed each other.

Her daughters were dead set against her arranging their marriages, and well Chrystabel knew it.

But a resourceful mother could always find a way.

"PLEASE WAIT, Margaret," Violet told her lady's maid the next afternoon. "If all goes well, I'm going to leave Rowan here and come back for him later."

She stepped down from the carriage and grumbled all the way to the front door of the large, if shabby, Lakefield House. She couldn't fathom how she'd ended up here, escorting her reluctant young brother to play with a strange little girl.

Her mother's convoluted explanation had made sense at the time, but how was it that suddenly Rose and Lily both needed to be measured for gowns, and she didn't? True, she hadn't been clamoring for new clothes like they had—she'd never really cared about such things—but Mum had always been careful to treat her three girls evenly.

At the bottom of the chipped stone stairs that led to the entry, she pulled Rowan out of the bushes where he was hiding. He promptly scurried to hide behind *her* instead. With a sigh, she mounted the steps and raised the knocker.

Before she had a chance to bang it down, the door swung open, and she stumbled forward and nearly fell into the house. She was saved from that indignity by someone's hands clasping her shoulders. Warm hands, keeping her upright. They belonged to a young man—a footman?—and when she looked up, his face was only inches from hers. She nearly gasped.

In all her life, she'd seen relatively few men up close—close enough to *see* with her poor vision. And this one was quite literally the most beautiful man she'd ever seen.

A distant part of her recalled that she ought to speak, but the rest was busy sinking into brilliant blue eyes. "I—I'm—" Backing away a little, she cleared her throat and tried again. "I'm here to see Lord Lakefield—"

"At your service." The stranger bowed. "Ford Chase," he added with a wide, winning smile that made her stomach feel odd. "And you are...?"

This was the viscount?

He couldn't be. "You're not wearing a periwig," she said nonsensically.

"Pardon?" He blinked. "I never wear wigs. I don't care for them."

She supposed her father often went wigless out here in the countryside, but—never? She squinted at the stranger, realizing he wasn't wearing a footman's livery, either. She'd been but twelve or thirteen the last time she'd met Lord Lakefield, and all she really remembered of the encounter was long, untidy dark hair and a distracted manner.

This fellow *did* seem rather distracted. He raked impatient fingers through his hair—still dark, but no longer untidy.

And those eyes. She'd never noticed Lord Lakefield's eyes... well, she'd probably never been close enough to properly see them. Aristotle had said that beauty was the gift of God. She wondered what this man could have done to be so deserving of the Lord's favor.

"And you are...?" he repeated.

She shook her head to clear it. "Violet Ashcroft."

"The Earl of Trentingham's daughter?" He looked somewhat perplexed. "I expected your mother."

"Well, you have *me*." She was regaining her equilibrium. She was, after all, a very levelheaded young woman. "And this is my brother, Rowan, who has come to claim the pleasure of meeting young Lady Jewel."

The pleasure of meeting young Lady Jewel? Why, she was babbling like a featherbrained courtier. Drawing a deep breath, she pulled her brother from behind her skirts.

The viscount gave him a proper, grave nod. "Pleased to meet you, Lord...?"

"Tremayne," Violet supplied, since Rowan seemed unlikely to say anything. "He's Viscount Tremayne. But you can just call him Rowan."

Much more stoically than normal, Rowan bowed.

"Uncle Ford!" A little girl came bounding up to the door,

recognize an empty compliment, "Jean de La Fontaine has written that all flatterers live at the expense of those who listen to them."

Lady Jewel blinked. "Huh?" She shook her head, then knelt on the floor next to Rowan. "Do you think I'm pretty?" she asked.

~

FORD HURRIED to the kitchen, not least because he had a feeling Violet Ashcroft was poised to bolt. And he couldn't allow that to happen.

Philosophy. Truth be told, he loathed the discipline—if one could even call the study of unprovable and oft indecipherable prattle *a discipline*. But at least this Violet seemed to have a keen brain in her head, which was uncommon, in his experience. Not that the ladies he knew were simpleminded, but he tended to gravitate toward girls of the fun and frilly variety. To be perfectly honest, after a long day at his studies or in his laboratory, he was seeking a diversion, not a fellow academic.

Tabitha, for instance, had been a lovely diversion. But a diversion was the last thing Ford needed just now, and as he'd come to realize he couldn't avoid all of womankind entirely, he'd decided to limit his female contacts to those who proved practical. Hilda, for example—his housekeeper—was a useful woman to have around.

And as for Lady Violet…

With her thick, chocolate-brown plait and eyes the color of his favorite brandy, Violet was nice-looking, although not the sort of beauty who would turn heads. Which was fine with him, since he wanted his head right where it was, thank you: square on his shoulders, where he could use it to concentrate on his work.

If he could convince Lady Violet to stay a while and maybe even come back with Rowan tomorrow, perhaps he could finally sneak away to his laboratory. In which case he'd have to admit that his twin, Kendra, was right—ladies *were* good for more than just flirting and adorning one's arm.

Though not to her face, of course.

As he barged into the kitchen, his housekeeper looked up from polishing the silver, one gray eyebrow raised in query. "Yes, my lord?"

"Are the refreshments ready?"

Hilda never answered a question—she always had one of her own. "Is Lady Trentingham here?"

"No," he said, wondering where Harry, Hilda's husband, had gone off to this time. The two of them might be servants, but their marriage mimicked most of the aristocracy's—which was to say they stayed as far from each other as possible.

"Lady Trentingham is at home," he told her. "The countess's daughter came instead. Lady Violet."

"The sensible one?"

"Come again?" Spotting a tray of biscuits on the kitchen's scarred wooden worktable, he inched his way over.

"The oldest, yes? Lady Trentingham calls her 'the sensible one.' The middle girl—Rose, I believe—is 'the wild one,' and the youngest, Lily, is 'the sweet one.'"

"She has three daughters? All named for flowers?" How absurd.

"Are you not aware that her husband enjoys gardening?"

"Yes. I am." He slid one of the small, round biscuits off the tray and popped it into his mouth. Mmm, cinnamon. Dusting crumbs off his fingers, he clasped his hands behind his back and began to pace. "How do you come to know all this?"

Hilda frowned. "Why shouldn't I know my neighbors?" She shoved at a gray hair that had escaped her cap, then went back to polishing the silver. "Lady Trentingham, she's a perfumer, you know. Every once in a while, she drops by with a new bottle. Spiced Rosewater, I prefer."

"Spiced Rosewater?" He paused to reach for another biscuit.

She slapped at his hand. "Leave it, will you? I laid them out in a pattern."

He scrutinized the tray, but his mathematical mind could discern no regular design.

"Do you not like Spiced Rosewater?" she asked.

He leaned close to a wrinkled cheek and sniffed. "It's lovely." In truth, she smelled like one of her cinnamon biscuits. But whatever made her happy.

"When Lady Trentingham brings the perfume, she likes to sit a spell and chat. I've heard all the stories of her girls as they've grown."

"Lady Trentingham sits and talks to the household help?"

"And why not? We're people too, you know."

Of course they were—he just didn't think about it much. And he was woefully ill informed about his neighbors. It seemed Lady Trentingham was well-nigh as eccentric as the earl.

"Here comes Harry," Hilda said, watching out the window. "Don't you think it's time to serve these refreshments?" She shoved a steaming pitcher into Ford's hands and, taking the tray of biscuits, hurried out of the kitchen before her husband could make his way in.

Hilda came up to Ford's shoulder and seemed as wide as she was tall. Obediently carrying the hot beverage she'd prepared, he followed her ample behind down the corridor to the drawing room. They stepped inside to see Violet Ashcroft on her hands and knees, her bottom jutting into the air beneath its layers of petticoats and sturdy, serviceable skirts. Which weren't frilly in the least. A fitting gown for The Sensible One.

Even through all that fabric, Ford could tell she had a rather nice bottom. Especially compared to his housekeeper's.

He frowned, mentally clamping down on his thoughts. He wasn't supposed to be noticing *any* female's bottom. He was supposed to be appreciating women for their practical uses only.

Lady Violet's brother was under the low, square table that sat before the couch. "Rowan," she said. "You come out here this minute."

"No." The boy crossed his arms, not a simple feat given he was lying on his belly. "Not until *she* leaves."

"C'mon, Rowan," Jewel cooed, getting down on her knees herself. "Come out and play. I've always wanted to play with a boy."

Knowing Jewel had two brothers at home, Ford choked back laughter. And she wasn't pronouncing *boy* at all the same way she had yesterday in the garden.

His niece was clearly in love.

And Rowan was having none of it.

"We've brought biscuits," Ford declared, announcing his presence. Lady Violet gave a little embarrassed squeal and jumped to her feet. Her pinkened cheeks matched his faded upholstery.

"Biscuits?" Rowan asked. "What kind?"

Ford grinned. Little boys were so much easier than girls. "Cinnamon," he said.

"I'm still not coming out," Rowan said.

"Would you like a drink of chocolate?" Hilda coaxed, taking the warm pitcher from Ford's hands.

"Chocolate?" The boy inched forward. "Real chocolate?"

"He cannot have it," his sister said firmly. "Chocolate gives him hives."

Rowan crawled closer and bumped his head on the apron of the table. "Ah, Violet..."

She reached to grab him by the wrist. "Got you, you little monster." She dragged him out. "Now, I cannot blame you for being intimidated, but you must mind your manners. Guests don't hide under tables."

"I want to go home."

"Guests don't say things like that, either. It's very rude."

Jewel rose, brushing off the mint green skirts that Ford had spent half an hour struggling her into. "Here." She offered

Rowan a biscuit, and he reluctantly climbed to his feet. "Eat this, and then I'll show you Uncle Ford's laboratory."

"No you won't," Ford said. Not again. He'd taken her to his laboratory yesterday afternoon, hoping she'd sit quietly while he worked. Ten minutes later he'd hauled her out—just before she'd managed to destroy the place.

"Please, Uncle Ford?"

"No."

"Puleeeeeze?" The look in Jewel's green eyes bordered on pathetic. Chase eyes, like Kendra's. Just what he needed… another Chase lady who could wrap him around her little finger.

She must have realized her feminine wiles were working, because she turned her lavish charm on Rowan. "You must stay," she told him. "Uncle Ford has magnets, and bottles of smelly stuff, and a pen-pen—"

"Pendulum," Ford supplied, remembering too late that she didn't like to be helped.

But she was so intent on convincing Rowan, she failed to take notice. "Yes, a pen-du-lum. And lots of clocks and a telescope. That's a thing to see the stars."

"Is it?" Lady Violet asked, interest lighting her eyes. "I've never really seen the stars."

~

AVAILABLE NOW!

Learn more about *The Viscount's Wallflower Bride* at www.DevonAndLaurenRoyal.com

ENTER FOR A CHANCE TO WIN
the long strand of pearls Trick gives Kendra in this book!*

Visit the Contest page on Lauren & Devon's website
at www.LaurenandDevonRoyal.com
and answer a question to be
entered in the monthly drawing.

No purchase necessary. See complete rules on the site.

*Please note: Depending on when you enter, the prize may be another piece of jewelry associated with one of Lauren & Devon's books. The authors reserve the right to discontinue this promotion at any time.

~

LAUREN ROYAL decided to become a writer in the third grade, after winning a "Why My Mother is the Greatest" essay contest. Now she's a *New York Times* and *USA Today* bestselling author of humorous historical romance novels. Lauren lives in Southern California with her family and their constantly shedding cat. She still thinks her mother is the greatest.

DEVON ROYAL is the daughter of romance novelist Lauren Royal. After attending film school, she wrote an award-winning TV comedy pilot and worked in digital video production before turning her focus to fiction writing. Devon lives in Southern California with her husband and son. She also thinks her mother is the greatest.

ACKNOWLEDGMENTS

~

OUR HEARTFELT THANKS:

To Ian Archibald, Project Manager for the Burntisland Heritage Trust, for information regarding the search for the Charles I shipwreck.

To seventeenth-century poets George Herbert, Robert Herrick, Richard Lovelace, and Samuel Rowley, for inspiring Trick's poetry (and generously—if unwittingly—allowing him to borrow a line or two for period flavor).

To all the honorary Chase cousins in our Chase Family Readers Group, for their enthusiastic support.

And, as always, to all the readers who have taken their time to write and tell us how you feel about our stories, for being our inspiration.

Thanks to each and every one of you!